Toby Jones

HAT TRICK!

MICHAEL PANCKRIDGE

WITH BRETT LEE

Toby Jones

HAT TRICK!

Toby Jones and the Magic Cricket Almanack
Toby Jones and the Secret of the Missing Scorecard
Toby Jones and the Mystery of the Time-travel Tour

Angus&Robertson
An imprint of HarperCollins*Publishers*

All references to *Wisden Cricketers' Almanack* are by kind permission of
John Wisden & Co. Ltd.

Angus&Robertson

An imprint of HarperCollins*Publishers*, Australia

Hat Trick! was originally published in Australia by HarperCollins as three separate books
(books one to three in the Toby Jones series):
Toby Jones and the Magic Cricket Almanack in 2003
Toby Jones and the Secret of the Missing Scorecard in 2004
Toby Jones and the Mystery of the Time-travel Tour in 2005
This combined edition was first published in Australia in 2008
by HarperCollins*Publishers* Australia Pty Limited
ABN 36 009 913 517
www.harpercollins.com.au

Story copyright © Michael Panckridge 2003, 2004, 2005
Additional cricket material © Binga Pty Ltd 2003, 2004, 2005

HarperCollins*Publishers*

25 Ryde Road, Pymble, Sydney NSW 2073, Australia
31 View Road, Glenfield, Auckland 10, New Zealand

National Library of Australia Cataloguing-in-Publication data:

Panckridge, Michael, 1962– .
Hat trick / Michael Panckridge with Brett Lee.
ISBN 978 0 7322 8837 2 (pbk.).
For primary school age.
Cricket–Juvenile fiction.
Panckridge, Michael, 1962– Toby Jones and the magic cricket almanack
Panckridge, Michael, 1962– Toby Jones and the secret of the missing scorecard
Panckridge, Michael, 1962– Toby Jones and the mystery of the time-travel tour
Lee, Brett.
A823.4

Cover images: ball and wicket by Rosemary Weller/Getty Images; boy by Tomas
Rodriquez/Photolibrary.com
Cover design by Darren Holt, HarperCollins Design Studio
Typeset in 10/15pt Stone Serif by Helen Beard, ECJ Australia Pty Limited
Printed and bound in Australia by Griffin Press
60gsm Bulky Paperback used by HarperCollins*Publishers* is a natural, recyclable product
made from wood grown in a combination of sustainable plantation and regrowth forests.
It also contains up to a 20% portion of recycled fibre. The manufacturing processes
conform to the environmental regulations in Tasmania, the place of manufacture.

6 5 4 3 2 1   08 09 10 11

In cricket, when one bowler takes three wickets with three balls, one after the other, we call this a **hat trick**. The taking of the hat trick may be spread out, eg another bowler might deliver from the other end of the pitch or the opposing team might have an innings. Hat tricks are rare.

It is thought that the term dates from the late 1800s in England, when the club would mark the achievement by awarding the bowler a new hat. Nowadays, the term is used in almost any sport to describe a run of three impressive feats by an individual, eg a soccer or hockey player scoring three goals in a game, a pitcher in baseball striking out three consecutive batters or in horse racing, when a jockey wins an annual race three years in a row.

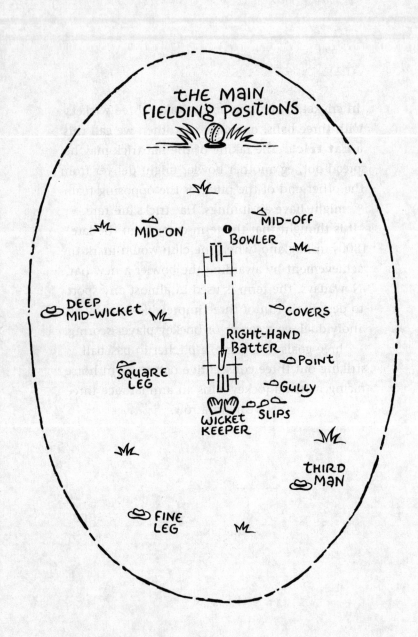

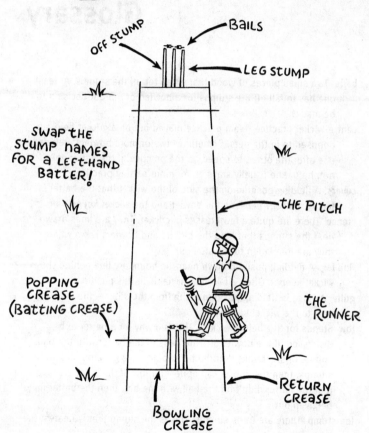

CLOSE UP OF THE CENTRE WICKET

OFF STUMP

BAILS

LEG STUMP

SWAP THE STUMP NAMES FOR A LEFT-HAND BATTER!

THE PITCH

POPPING CREASE (BATTING CREASE)

THE RUNNER

RETURN CREASE

BOWLING CREASE

Glossary

bails Two small pieces of wood that sit on top of the stumps. At least one has to fall off the stumps for a bowled or run-out decision to be made.

centre-wicket practice Team practice played out on a cricket field, as opposed to in the nets. Sometimes two or more bowlers are used, one after the other, to speed up the practice. If the batter goes out, he or she usually stays on for more batting practice.

covers A fielding position on the side of the wicket that the batter is facing, halfway between the bowler and the wicket keeper.

crease There are quite a few creases in cricket. They are lines drawn near the stumps that help the batters and bowlers know where they are in relation to the stumps.

fine leg A fielding position down near the boundary line behind the wicket keeper. Often a fast bowler fields in this position.

gully A close-in fielding position along from the slips — the fielders next to the wicket keeper.

lbw Stands for 'leg before wicket'. This is a way for a batter to be dismissed. If the bowler hits the pads of the batter with the ball, and he or she thinks that the ball would have gone on and hit the stumps, then the bowler can appeal for lbw. If the umpire is sure that the batter didn't hit the ball with the bat, then the batter may be given out.

leg-stump There are three stumps. This is the stump that is nearest the legs of the batter.

maiden If a bowler bowls an over and no runs are scored from it, then it is called a maiden.

mid-off A fielding position next to the bowler. It is on the off, or bat, side of the pitch as the batter looks down the wicket.

mid-on A fielding position next to the bowler. It is on the on, or leg, side of the pitch as the batter looks down the wicket.

no ball If a bowler puts his or her foot entirely over the return crease (the marked line) then it is a no ball and the batter can't be given out — unless it is a run-out.

off-stump The stump that is on the batting side of the batter.

third man A fielding position down behind the wicket keeper but on the other side of the fine leg fielder. The third man fielder is behind the slips fielders.

yorker The name for a delivery, usually bowled by a medium or fast bowler, that is pitched right up near the batter's feet. It is full pitched and fast.

Contents

Foreword

JUST like Toby Jones, I was obsessed by the game of cricket when I was a kid. I was always looking for ways to improve my game. I learned so much from my elder brother, Shane, and from seeking the advice of coaches. I read every cricket book I could get my hands on and I watched and learned from my idol: Dennis Lillee. Dennis was my inspiration, someone who I looked up to. I wanted to be just like him. (As it turned out, he has had a lot to do with my cricket career.)

I am sure you will find that this book is not only an excellent read, but also a very useful guide to the game of cricket. It contains lots of great hints and information that I hope you will be able to use to improve your own game.

When I first became involved in cricket, I had no idea where the game would take me. The opportunities and possibilities it has created for me are endless. Cricket has taught me many valuable lessons. Most of all it has shown me that if I always play hard and *enjoy* the opportunity of representing my country, I will be successful.

Every time I get asked to offer cricket advice to kids, my answer is always the same: enjoyment is the most important part of the game. When I am on the field, you will nearly always find me with a huge smile on my face. After suffering several injuries in my younger years, I have learned to make the most of every moment I get to play cricket.

This book reminds me of my own childhood days spent in the backyard with my brothers, always battling hard on the pitch to see who would be the champion player at the end of the day.

Toby Jones and the Magic Cricket Almanack, *Toby Jones and the Secret of the Missing Scorecard* and *Toby Jones and the Mystery of the Time-travel Tour* all bring back truly great memories for me. I hope you enjoy reading *Hat Trick!*

Brett Lee

Prologue

What wonders abound, dear boy, don't fear
These shimmering pages, never clear.
Choose your year, the Wisden *name,*
Find the page, your destined game,
Then find yourself a quiet place
Where shadows lurk, to hide your trace.

Whisper clear date, place or score
While staring, smitten; then before
(You hope) the close of play,
Be careful now, you've found the way.
So hide your home, your age, your soul
To roam this place and seek your goal.

Be aware that time moves on —
Your time, this time; none short, or long.
So say aloud two lines from here
Just loud enough for you to hear.
From a quiet spot, alone, unknown,
Back through time, now come — alone.

And never speak and never boast,
And never taunt, nor ever toast
This knowledge from your time you bring.
To woo the rest, their praises sing:
They wonder, and your star shines bright...
Just this once, this one short night?

But every word that boasts ahead
Means lives unhinged, broken, dead.
Don't meddle, talk, nor interfere
With the lives of those you venture near.
Respect this gift. Stay calm, stay clever,
And let the years live on forever.

BOOK 1

Toby Jones

——AND THE——
MAGIC CRICKET
ALMANACK

IT'S NOT JUST A GAME – IT'S TIME TRAVEL!

1 The Equation

Thursday — afternoon

'OKAY. Here's the equation. Listen up. Six balls to go. Nine runs to win. Can they do it? Jono, check your field. Toby, are you ready?' he said to me.

Mr Pasquali was excited. Boy, does he love his cricket. He is our cricket coach, and our class teacher too. Everyone wanted Mr Pasquali as their class teacher. Even the Year 3s were talking about him and hoping that they'd get put in his class when they got to Year 6. And if you were mad about cricket — like I was — then his class was the place to be. Mr Pasquali had a way of bringing cricket into most of the subjects we did.

It was the end of centre-wicket practice. We were tired, but Mr Pasquali always managed to keep us interested. Better still, I was batting. The only downer in the situation was the bowler, Scott Craven. He was fast, mean and ugly. Jono, our captain when we play against other schools, was going on the attack. He had two slips, a gully, third man, fine leg, then a ring of fielders around me. If I could go over the top and score a two or maybe even a four (you hardly ever ran three on our small school cricket oval) then Jimbo and I just might score the nine runs we needed to win. Win what? Nothing, but still, getting one over Scott was something.

The first ball thumped into my pads. Scott yelled his appeal. Mr Pasquali had a good long look at me, then at my pads, and said firmly, 'Not out!'

Five balls left, still nine runs to get. Jimbo Temple strolled down the pitch.

'Toby, I'm running this ball, no matter what.'

You didn't argue with Jimbo. He was an awesome cricketer, but there was something about him that made you think twice before you spoke to him. He liked to keep to himself, and even Scott Craven kept pretty well clear of him.

I didn't see the next ball. It whacked me on the body. Jimbo was screaming at me to run. He was halfway down the pitch before I'd got my balance and set off. I felt clumsy and slow. My pads were flopping everywhere and my bat was heavy. And I had a throbbing pain in my ribs.

I hobbled up the pitch. WHACK! The ball smashed into my back. I groaned and stumbled on, finally making the crease at the other end. I really needed to work on my batting.

Once again Jimbo strolled up the wicket.

'Smart running, Toby. You saved your wicket. You okay?'

This was just about the most Jimbo had ever said

to me in one go. I was in pain, but Jimbo was on strike. What had I been imagining — putting Scott away for a four?

'You're history, loser,' Scott sneered at Jimbo as he walked past us.

Jimbo didn't seem to notice. 'Back up, and listen for the call, okay?'

I nodded.

Jimbo strolled back, took a look at the field, which hadn't changed, then settled down to wait for Scott. The boys in the field were clapping and urging the bowler on.

Scott raced in and sent down a thunderbolt. It was a beamer. A massive full toss heading straight for Jimbo's head. He ducked out of the way, just, as the ball flew past him. It was too hot for Martian — Ivan (Ivo) Marshall, the keeper. The ball bobbled down towards fine leg. Jimbo looked at me. I can't have looked too keen. He held up a hand and shouted, 'No!'

'You're a wimp, Toby Jones. Gutless wonder,' Scott sneered at me as he walked past.

'Okay. It's going to be tough,' yelled Mr Pasquali. 'Four balls to go, seven runs to win.'

'Hang on. What do you mean four balls? I've bowled three already.'

Scott Craven was looking mean. He knew the answer.

'That last ball was a no ball, Scott. Extra delivery and a run to the batting team. If you're good enough you should win it from here. Look alive, everyone!'

5

o tapped his bat on the crease and waited. He looked as calm as ever. Scott started his run-up. He was actually a very good bowler.

Suddenly there was a mighty THWACK. I almost missed it. One minute Jimbo was tapping his bat in the crease, the next he was leaning back, bat high in the air, watching the ball sail over covers and out towards some sheds near the school fence.

'Hey, Jay. Did that clear the line?' Mr Pasquali called.

Tough call for Jay, but he was in the best position to judge. He nodded.

'I think so,' he shouted, then jogged off to get the ball from up against an old hockey goal.

Scott Craven was fuming. In one shot, Jimbo had reduced the equation to three balls and one run. We were level.

'Control and focus,' Mr Pasquali was saying to everyone. 'Each of you, think of your role here.'

Jono was bringing all the fielders in close to the wicket.

'Good thinking, Jono. No good having anyone out now. You've got to stop the single,' Mr Pasquali said.

I looked at Jimbo. His expression hadn't changed. There was no excitement on account of his six. We hadn't won yet.

I turned round to look at Scott Craven. He was waiting at the top of his run-up, looking down at the ball. He was changing his grip. Being a bowler helped me know about these things. He was going to bowl a 'slow' ball. You know, when everything looks the same: run in just as fast, and then out it comes — slow — either through the back of the hand, or with a finger tucked behind so it doesn't come out with all the power it should.

Jimbo played all round it. He completely missed the ball. It made him look clumsy, but luckily the ball was wide of the stumps.

'Two balls, one run,' bellowed Mr Pasquali. He didn't need to. Everyone knew.

Scott's next ball was probably his best of the over. A fast yorker. Jimbo just managed to get a bit of bottom edge onto it, which was just as well: otherwise he would have been lbw.

Now everyone was tense. Scott Craven was talking with Jono Reilly at mid-off, nodding his head. I looked at Jimbo and started walking towards him.

'I can tell if it's a slow ball. I'll raise my bat if he's going to bowl it.'

Jimbo looked at me. 'Good idea, Toby. Then get ready to run.'

I had a job to do, but I didn't want to make it too obvious. I turned away from Jimbo and looked out past Mr Pasquali to where Scott was standing.

'Okay everyone. This is it. I want a winner here,' called Mr Pasquali.

Scott hadn't looked down at his hands. He started to move in. I stared at his bowling hand, desperately trying to see his grip. He was halfway in now, almost at full speed. Suddenly his other hand shot down to the ball. He was changing his grip. I pushed my bat up into the air as Scott approached the bowling crease. I just hoped like anything that this was going to work.

Scott swung his arm over and let go. Jimbo waited. The ball seemed to take ages to get to him. Jimbo stepped back, but the ball was bang on line, heading for middle stump. He pushed at it with all his force, looking for the gap between bowler and mid-off.

'Yep!' he shouted, as Scott dived towards the ball. I took off. A moment later I heard a yell from behind. Scott had grabbed the ball and flicked it at the stumps. Everyone looked at Mr Pasquali, who was staring at the broken wicket.

He pointed both his hands up to the sky and drew a box in the air. He was asking for the third umpire, the way they do in cricket matches on TV. Jimbo had kept on going, not even interested in the result.

'Too close to call that one, boys. Great finish though.'

'I thought you wanted a winner,' said Scott Craven. He looked tired.

'You're all winners today,' Mr Pasquali beamed. 'Now let's get this gear packed up. And don't forget that tomorrow some of you are coming on the excursion to top all excursions: the MCG visit.'

As if any of us could forget that. I couldn't wait!

Thursday — evening

At the dinner table, I told Mum and Dad about cricket practice. They were always interested to hear how practice went — I reckoned Dad was sometimes more interested in cricket than he was in any of my school subjects. Even Natalie, my eight-year-old younger sister, was tuning in.

'Anyway, you can bowl faster than Scott Craven can't you, Toby?'

'Of course I can, Nat. I can bowl faster than Brett Lee!'

'And I've climbed Mount Everest in a kilt,' Dad said, ruffling my hair.

'Well, I might bowl as fast as him one day.'

Mum looked across at me. 'Yes, Toby, one day you just might.'

The best bowling figures in a World Cup match are held by Glenn McGrath of Australia. He achieved 7/15 against Namibia during the 2003 World Cup. Two other bowlers have taken seven wickets in a World Cup game. They are Australia's Andy Bichel (7/20) and the West Indies' Winston Davis (7/51).

2 The Library

Friday — morning

THE next morning I was up early. It was the day of the excursion to the MCG — *the* Melbourne Cricket Ground! You could choose to go to other places, but any chance to get to the MCG — and with Mr Pasquali as well — was something you didn't knock back. My best friend, Jay Bromley, felt the same. He'd never been there, but he'd heard me talking about it often enough.

There were 10 of us going from my year — all boys, except for Georgie — plus Mr Pasquali and Jono's dad, Mr Reilly. Georgie loves sport, and it didn't bother her that she was the only girl taking the MCG tour.

Georgie was great. She lived with her mum at the other end of our street, and we'd played together since we could walk. Our house was like a second home for her. Often Georgie's mum would call round and end up staying for dinner. Georgie and I, and

11

sometimes Nat, would play cricket outside, or down the hallway if it was dark.

Most of the cricket team were going on the tour except for Jimbo, who was doing the Old Melbourne Gaol. Jimbo was different, somehow. He was friendly if you spoke to him, but he didn't seem to be too interested in being with other kids. Georgie said that the opposite was actually the truth, that he really wanted people around him. I wasn't so sure. There was something about him that I liked all the same.

Anyway, Mr Pasquali, Jono and his dad, Jay, Rahul, Martian, Cameron, Minh, Georgie and I, as well as Scott Craven and his best mate Gavin Bourke, were taking the tour from heaven.

When we arrived at the MCG we passed through a modern front section with lots of glass and then went through an older-looking gate. This was the back of one of the big stands, which we walked around underneath.

Jay was looking pretty impressed, but he really wanted to get out to the actual ground, which we kept getting little glimpses of. He wasn't really listening to the stuff we were being told about the dressing rooms and other places.

They took us upstairs past some fantastic pictures of old players; they were massive. I kept thinking how much Dad would have loved this. It was sort of like a museum.

Then we came to a little library, stacked with books — all on cricket. The floor creaked as we moved quietly into the room. It was cluttered and busy. There were piles of books on tables and on the floor. The place was messy, but you got the feeling that this was how it was meant to be. There was a heap of brown and yellow books in a bookshelf just on the right.

'*Wisden Cricketers' Almanacks*,' said a small voice behind me. I jumped. An old man with a wrinkled face and a kind smile was looking at me. 'Would you like to see one?' he asked.

I looked across at Jay. He shrugged.

'Um, yeah, okay. Thanks,' I replied.

The old man unlocked a glass door and pulled down one of the brown books. It had '1949' in gold letters on its thick spine.

'Have you heard of the Invincibles?' the man asked me. His eyes were sparkling.

'Wasn't that Sir Donald Bradman's team?'

'He was part of the team, yes, and other great players too. Go on, open it.'

I must have been holding the book as if it was some kind of treasure, too afraid to open it and turn the old, musty-smelling pages. The rest of the group were leaving the library, but I couldn't put the book down. It felt so warm and comfortable in my hand.

The nice old guy was smiling. 'My name is Jim Oldfield — and do call me Jim, boys,' he said. 'I was wondering, would you mind opening the book and telling me what you see?'

'C'mon, Toby,' called Jono's dad from the library door.

It was as if a spell had been broken.

'Coming, Mr Reilly,' I said reluctantly. 'Mr Oldfield — er, Jim — was just showing me these old books.'

'You want to stay on a bit? We're just heading out onto the ground,' Mr Reilly said.

'Yeah, okay. I'll catch up with you soon. See ya, Jay.'

I looked over at Jim's friendly face then back down at the book I was holding in my hands. Jim was nodding at me, urging me to open the book.

My first reaction was that there must be something wrong with my eyes. Maybe they had dust in them. There was probably plenty of that floating around an old room like a library. Everything on the page — the words and numbers — was blurry and shimmery, as if it was in water. The words kept dissolving, then reappearing. I closed my eyes and shook my head. Then I looked back at the open book in my hands. It was the same again.

'See if you can find page 221,' Jim suggested.

It was so weird. 'What's going on?' I stammered. 'I can't read this.'

There was a pile of different cricket books on the oval table where Jim was sitting. He pushed one towards me.

'You open it,' I said.

He smiled and did so.

We both stared at the open page. Everything looked normal. There were no swimming words. I grabbed another book and flung it open. It was the same. I squeezed my eyes shut again.

There was something about the old brown book. I turned it over in my hands, peering at the sides and the spine, trying to work out how the blurry effect was achieved.

'Toby,' said the old man, 'page 221. Go on.'

'Are you coming, Toby?' It was Jay, standing at the door of the library. He must have come back to find out what had happened to me.

'Jay ... come over here and look at this wisdom book.'

'*Wisden* book, Toby. *Wisden*.'

Jay was looking a bit surprised. He glanced over at me with a questioning sort of look. I was glad I hadn't told him what I'd seen. I was wondering whether the book would have the same effect on him.

Jim passed Jay the book.

'Is there a famous cricket match in here or something?' asked Jay, sitting down and opening the book at its first page.

'Try page 221,' I suggested.

Jim sat there, nodding his head.

Jay flicked through the pages fast, then stopped turning, presumably at page 221. I sat down next to him.

Jim was staring at me, almost sadly. Then his eyes went to the book. 'Read it, Jay,' he said.

'He probably won't be able to,' I offered, my eyes finding their way back to the page.

'What do you mean, "won't be able to"?' scoffed Jay, and he started to read.

'"Essex v Australians. At Southend, May 15, 17. Australians won by an innings and 151 runs. In light-hearted vein, they made history by putting together the highest total ..."'

Jim was chuckling, the wrinkles on his face crinkling like cracks in dry mud. His chuckles turned to coughs.

Jay looked up from his reading. 'What's the joke, then?'

'Tell him, Toby. Tell Jay here what you see when you open the *Wisden*.' Jim was speaking softly, his voice a bit raspy.

I picked up the book yet again and opened it. The letters were a blur. Now and again vague shadows would appear, then just as quickly they would vanish into the white mist of the page. I pushed the book towards Jay, who was looking at me oddly.

'Jay,' I said, 'can you really see the stuff on this page here?' I pointed at the page. I even touched it. It felt warm and alive, like the book had when I'd held it.

By now, I knew that Jay sensed something was up. 'Is it your eyes or something?' he asked me.

'Close the book and look at me. Both of you.' Jim was speaking softly but firmly. 'There is nothing wrong with you, Toby. On the contrary, we have discovered that there is something quite special about you. If you give me five minutes, I can explain exactly what I mean.'

Jay and I looked at each other. He shrugged and

said, 'You tell me later, Toby. I'm heading back to the group.'

Jim stood up and made his way over to the glass bookcase where all the heavy brown and yellow books stood. He reached in and took down another *Wisden*. It looked even older than the one lying on the table in front of us.

'You see, Toby, you and I share a special gift. These pages are the doors to cricket matches from the past. It's a funny thing, but I knew that you would eventually arrive here in the library. That's the thing about time travel — you learn all sorts of things about the future that you normally wouldn't know.

'Let me explain. In 1930 I was nine years old and living in Leeds, in England. Don Bradman was touring with the Australians. My father had bought tickets for both of us to go to the first day's play. But the night before the match, I became very ill; I'm afraid I deteriorated so badly that by the time Don Bradman walked out to bat on that second day, I was lying in a hospital bed.

'I missed one of the most remarkable innings ever played in the history of Test cricket. Instead of marvelling at the greatest batsman anyone will ever see, I lay on a hospital bed fighting for my life.

'Well, as you can see, I survived the illness. But six months before the Second World War started, my father died quite suddenly. My mother and I came out to Australia and she let me bring my father's collection of *Wisden*s, all 11 of them.'

I had a thousand questions flying through my brain, but Jim raised a finger to his lips as I was about to speak.

'Now that I'm an old man my powers have weakened and I can't travel, without the help of someone else who has the gift,' he explained. 'And even with you here now, Toby, and even if you were willing to help an old man like me, I fear that my time for travels of this kind are well behind me. Alas, that match of 1930 will remain a dream. As it always has been. You see, I have a memory of six words that I have played and repeated in my head all these years. "Don't ever come back here alone." I took it to mean don't come back to the time of 1930 alone. I don't remember who said the words to me. My father? Perhaps my grandfather. Anyway, I have obeyed the instruction.' Jim looked away for a moment. 'But you, Toby, with my help, have the opportunity to, to ...'

I swallowed.

'To travel back through time. To watch any game you choose. To ...'

There was a noise behind me. The wall opened and a lady walked in with a plate of food. I jumped.

Jim chuckled and said, 'This library is full of surprises.'

'Jim's spinning his stories to you, is he?' the lady asked cheerfully, setting a plate of sandwiches down in front of him. She headed out again, but left the door open. I bounced up and looked at it, checking

18

both sides. From the inside it looked like a solid wall, but there was a handle on the other side.

'Alas, I fear the spell has been broken,' Jim said quietly.

I went back to my chair and stood behind it.

'Here, Toby. Take this.' Jim had pulled a small sheet of paper out of his shirt pocket and passed it over to me.

'That's my father's handwriting. He copied it from a letter that his father wrote to him.'

I took the sheet from him, and without looking at what was written on it, slid it into my shirt pocket.

'Come back will you? Sometime?'

I walked over to the door. 'Thanks for the story and all that, Jim.' I turned towards him but was afraid to make eye contact.

Jim didn't reply.

The first catch taken by a substitute in Test cricket was an odd affair. In 1884, the Australian captain, Billy Murdoch, came on to field for England as a substitute. He caught his own team-mate, who had top scored with 75. The injured English player was W.G. Grace.

3 The Chase

FOR the rest of the excursion I was in a daze.

'You're quiet, Toby,' someone was saying to me.

'Huh?'

It was Georgie. 'I said ...'

'Yeah, I know.'

'He's been freaked out by an old guy in that library,' said Jay.

'Well?' she was looking at me, expectantly. Georgie never missed out on anything.

'I'll tell you later,' I said.

'Before he dies. Promise?' she chuckled.

I must have looked a bit shocked.

'Just joking!'

The sheets of paper on my clipboard stayed blank. It wasn't till I was on the bus, sitting next to Jay, who had three or four pages of notes and sketches, that I reached into my pocket and pulled out the piece of paper that Jim had given me.

20

When Jay looked over and asked me what I was reading, I filled him in.

'Why don't you just chuck it away and forget about it?' he said, watching me scan the words in front of me.

I didn't answer. It was as if the words were talking to me. There was no washy effect with these words. They were clear and still on the paper.

> What wonders abound, dear boy, don't fear
> These shimmering pages, never clear.
> Choose your year, the Wisden name,
> Find the page, your destined game,
> Then find yourself a quiet place
> Where shadows lurk, to hide your trace.
>
> Whisper clear date, place or score
> While staring, smitten; then before
> (You hope) the close of play,
> Be careful now, you've found the way.
> So hide your home, your age, your soul
> To roam this place and seek your goal.
>
> Be aware that time moves on —
> Your time, this time; none short, or long.
> So say aloud two lines from here
> Just loud enough for you to hear.
> From a quiet spot, alone, unknown,
> Back through time, now come — alone.

And never speak and never boast,
And never taunt, nor ever toast
This knowledge from your time you bring.
To woo the rest, their praises sing:
They wonder, and your star shines bright ...
Just this once, this one short night?

But every word that boasts ahead
Means lives unhinged, broken, dead.
Don't meddle, talk, nor interfere
With the lives of those you venture near.
Respect this gift. Stay calm, stay clever,
And let the years live on forever.

Dear Jim,
'Tis all, perhaps, for another time ...
Your loving father,
Ernest James Oldfield

For a few minutes I stared at the words, trying to work out their meaning. I was a bit spooked by the unhinged, broken, dead part. I thought of showing Jay, but he was talking to Martian across the aisle. Somehow, these old words from another time didn't seem right. I was also afraid that Jay would convince me that all this time travel stuff was stupid. I didn't want that. There was something exciting happening here. I wanted to explore it further. Maybe I'd show Georgie. She was really smart. She'd know what it all meant.

The most exciting thing about the last two days of the school week was the announcement of the cricket team for our first match of the season.

Jimbo hadn't been selected. None of us could work out why, because he was probably the best batsman in the school.

'There's a reason for everything,' Georgie said, shaking her head as she looked at the team sheet outside the gym. 'But I sure would like to know the reason for Jimbo not playing tomorrow.'

'He's lazy, that's why.' Scott Craven had come over to add his thoughts to the conversation. 'He's not a team player. I reckon Mr Pasquali's giving him an ultimatum. Play for the team or you're not gonna be a part of it.'

I wasn't about to start arguing with Scott — even if his reasons were wrong. That's what he was waiting for. Scott Craven was forever looking for a reason to start an argument.

I looked again at the team sheet. All the familiar names were there. Cameron and Jono, our openers. Rahul, Jay, Scott, myself and Gavin and Georgie. Then Martian, our keeper, and finally Minh and Ahmazru. I didn't think it was the batting order, but it wouldn't be a bad one if it were.

Saturday — morning

I pulled my hands out of my pockets, rubbed them together, then turned to watch Scott Craven run in to bowl the first ball of our first game of the season.

We were playing Motherwell State School. There were six teams in our competition for this season. Our team was Riverwall. The other teams were St Mary's, TCC, Benchley Park and the Scorpions. Everyone was talking about the Scorpions and their players. They were new to the competition and not much was known about them. But their name was different, and the rumours were that they were a tough, strong and talented group of cricketers.

The ball thudded into the batsman's pads. The batter buckled over, and amid the shouts looked up at the umpire. Slowly the umpire raised his finger.

'Yeah!' shouted Scott, and he pumped both fists in the air.

The cricket season had started.

Scott Craven was awesome. In many ways it wasn't fair that he was playing school cricket. He was so good he probably should have been playing with older kids. We had two amazing cricketers — Scott Craven, our fast bowler, and Jono Reilly, one of the opening batsmen. Without them, we would have been an average team, winning only some of our games. With them, I reckon we were pretty well unbeatable. There was a third great player — Jimbo. I just hoped that I'd get to see him play in a real game.

It was lucky for the opposition that you could only bowl five overs and had to retire at 40 runs.

None of us really liked Scott Craven or, for that matter, Gavin Bourke, his best friend. But we were glad to have him on our team. Scott was loud, confident and extremely short-tempered. He could be quite mean with his comments to us, and we usually got a spray from him if one of us dropped a catch from his bowling.

Scott took another wicket in his next over, clean-bowling the batsman and sending the off-stump cartwheeling back towards Martian, our wicket keeper.

I was used as a first-change bowler. Sometimes I opened, but I think Mr Pasquali liked to give the opposition a break from having to face two fast bowlers first up.

I wasn't as quick as Scott, though I didn't try for flat-out pace. I was working on swinging the ball through the air and trying to perfect a slower delivery.

My first ball was a full-length delivery outside off-stump. The batsman took a swing at it and missed. I repeated the delivery with my next ball, but this time put it out a fraction wider. Again the batter went for the ball, and this time it caught the edge of his bat and flew through to Martian. He took a neat catch in front of Jono at first slip.

My other wicket came in my third over. It was an attempted slower ball that would have been called a wide. But the batter reached out for it and flat-batted it out to cover. Scott Craven took the catch.

Scott picked up another two wickets himself to add to his earlier two.

Cameron, Georgie and Jono each got one wicket. The last wicket was a run-out. We ended up having to score 109 runs to win. Mr Pasquali must have been confident because he changed the batting line-up. Martian was pushed down to number seven, my normal spot, and I went up to number four.

Jono and Cameron put on 47 runs before Cameron was bowled. I got my first bat of the season after Rahul was run out for only five. He had lost his glasses halfway up the pitch and for a moment it looked as if he was going to stop and pick them up.

Jono and I put on another 30 runs before Jono was caught on the boundary for 33. By then we had scored 88 and the game was as good as over. Jay strode out to the wicket. He normally batted further down the order too.

Mr Pasquali retired me on 25 not out. Gavin came in and left almost as quickly, clean-bowled for a duck. Then Scott Craven blasted two sixes to win the game for us.

We batted on until we'd faced the same number of overs we had bowled. You got bonus points for batting and for bowling — a point for every 30 runs and for every two wickets. We ended up making 164. I couldn't wait to check the paper to see how the other teams had gone.

It was a good first-up win. Nothing spectacular, as Mr Pasquali said, just a solid all-round team performance.

After the game I asked Georgie what she was doing that afternoon, and when she said nothing, I said I'd get online at about four o'clock, as I had some news for her. I wanted to tell her about my conversation with Jim at the Melbourne Cricket Club library, and I particularly wanted to show her the poem that Jim had given me. She'd take that seriously, even if she didn't believe anything else I said.

We liked to chat online and had made a chatroom for ourselves last year, when we'd first started playing together in the same team. We called it CROC — Cricketer's Room of Chat. It was a bit like a secret club, I suppose, but cricket was the general theme. I suppose we could have just used the phone, but somehow it was more fun chatting over the Internet. The other bonus was that suddenly Jay or Rahul or Martian could jump in and join the conversation.

I logged on just before four o'clock. Georgie was the only other person logged into the room.

Georgie: so, what's news?

Toby: maybe i sh have told you earlier ... you rem. the old guy in the lib at the mcg?

Georgie: yeah.

Toby: well, this'll sound v stupid but i think i have this gift that makes me able to travel in time. georgie, you there?

Toby: hey! georgie ...

Georgie: yeah, i'm here. toby?

Toby: yeah.

Georgie: you're an idiot!

Toby: i know. but it's true.

Georgie:	are we going to keep on with this, cos i've got better things to do
Toby:	wait. i've got a poem for you.
Georgie:	that sounds better. when did you write it?
Toby:	i didn't. but you'll like it. scanning now.

I pulled the piece of paper out of my desk drawer, and, keeping it in its plastic pocket, placed it on the scanner. A moment later I was waiting for Georgie to accept the file I was about to send.

Toby:	what do you think? georgie?

But that was the last I heard from her. She was either totally sick of the whole idea of time travel, or else of reading the poem and trying to work out just what the heck it meant. I guessed I'd find out. Eventually.

I caught up with Georgie at recess the following Monday.

'Interesting poem, Toby. Where'd you get it?'

I explained everything to her, not leaving out any details. It was actually good to say it all out loud. She listened carefully, without interrupting.

'That's it?' she said, when I had finished.

'So far, yes.'

She looked at me for a moment. Slowly a smile spread across her face.

'Like I said, great poem. Can I keep it?'

'Of course. But what about the rest? You know, the *Wisden* cricket book stuff? The wishy-washy writing?'

'Well, go back to the MCG and do it. That's the only way to prove anything.'

'You don't believe me, do you?' I asked her.

'I believe *you*, Toby, but I sure don't believe anything else.'

'Meaning?'

'Meaning that I don't think you would make up all this to trick me, but I think someone else has made it all up to trick you.'

Georgie sure had good logic. You could never argue with her. About anything.

'Okay, maybe you're right,' I said. 'Will you come with me next time I go?'

'What, to the library?'

'Yeah. You can meet Jim yourself.'

'Okay, but I won't hold my breath or anything.'

'Cool. Hey, did you book the gym for lunchtime tomorrow?'

'Yep. And I'm bringing a friend too.'

'Who?' I asked.

'You'll see,' she said mysteriously, and then turned and headed off towards a group of kids near the playground.

Monday — afternoon

The great thing about having Mr Pasquali as our teacher was that he let you do a sport project of your choice. For this one we could just concentrate on cricket. Later in the year we could do another cricket project, but that one would have to have a history and culture theme.

After school that day, Rahul and Jay came around so we could work on our projects together.

Rahul was doing the Tied Test that happened way back in 1986 between India and Australia. Being Indian himself, Rahul was pumped to be working on something so close to his heart. It was close to his family too. They came from Madras (now called Chennai), the place where the match was played, and migrated to Australia not long after it took place.

I was doing my assignment on the 1999 cricket World Cup. Jay had finally decided to study Don Bradman. He had changed his mind about four times.

Even Craven was putting in a huge effort. He was doing the Bodyline series, and was using a computer program to put together a whole lot of pictures, and even some film (so he said). I didn't tell him, but I was actually looking forward to when we would all present our assignments. He'd chosen an awesome topic.

Dad came in at one stage and asked whether we had other homework to do. 'Yeah, sure, Dad,' I replied. 'I'll get on with it after the others leave.'

As Dad was rummaging through some of my books, a little card fell out. I hadn't even noticed it myself.

'Hey, this sounds good,' he said. 'You never told me about the MCG excursion. How was it?'

'Bit weird,' Jay said before I had a chance to speak.

'Nah, it was okay, Dad. There was this nice old guy ...'

'Strange, more like it.'

I glared at Jay.

'This nice old guy who was looking after the library there. He must have slipped that card into one of my books when they were on the table.'

'Well,' said Dad, 'it sounds interesting enough. "Slip through the ages of time. A journey of discovery for all your cricket research. Get lost in another world." Well, well. Rather a full-on advertisement for a library of old books, eh, boys?'

Dad loved his cricket as much as anyone.

'Let's all go down sometime soon, hey? I'd love to see this place. Maybe Georgie would like to come, as well? You could all do some more work on your projects.'

Dad liked Georgie. Being a bit of a writer himself, he was forever talking poems and stuff with her when she came round. And Georgie, of course, loved the attention.

'Yeah, that would be great, Dad,' I said as he flipped the card over to me.

'Sounds good to me, Mr Jones,' added Rahul.

'Great. How about Wednesday? Cricket training's on Tuesday and Thursday, isn't it?'

'Wednesday'd be great, Dad,' I said, not sure if I was ready to go back to the library just yet.

Between March 1979 and March 1994 Allan Border (Australia) did not miss a Test match. This amounted to 153 consecutive Test match appearances. This put Border 47 Test matches ahead of his nearest rival, Sunil Gavaskar, from India.

4 The Gym

Tuesday — afternoon

THE gym was booked; Georgie hadn't forgotten. I often met up with friends there at the start of lunchtime and usually other kids would call by and end up joining in. Even Jimbo had stopped in for a look one lunchtime a few weeks back. He sat on one of the long benches at the back of the gym and watched. He was eating a salad roll. I remember this because you are not allowed to eat in the gym. But no one was going to mention this little rule to Jimbo.

We played with three pieces of equipment: a stump for a bat, a set of kanga wickets and a tennis ball that was half-covered with black tape. It swung like crazy.

We picked a couple of teams.

'Where's your secret friend?' I asked Georgie as I took my place behind the stumps to be keeper. Martian, the regular keeper, said he had a bit of a headache and was sitting out this game.

'She'll be here soon. And when she gets here, I want her to have a go at keeper, okay?'

'Yeah, sure,' I said.

Rahul whacked the first ball back past Jay and into the back wall for four. He had a great eye — even if he did wear glasses — and it always looked as if he was playing with a real bat.

'Hey, Georgie, I'm here.'

A tall girl with long hair was standing at the door. I had seen her before, though she wasn't in any of my classes.

'Hey, Ally,' Georgie called out. 'Get in here. Toby, get out in the field, would you? Ally, go behind the stumps and just grab the ball if it comes your way, okay?'

'Watch out, Marshall, looks like a girl's gonna take your keeping job,' said Scott Craven, who had just arrived with Gavin Bourke. I wondered if they had come with Ally.

I looked over at Martian to see if he would react to this teasing from Craven. But amazingly, he had his eyes closed and his head tilted up towards the roof.

I walked over to him.

'Hey, Martian, you okay?'

He didn't open his eyes but smiled slightly and put one thumb up in the air. 'Sort of. Bit of a headache, but I'll be okay.'

Meanwhile, Ally had got herself behind the stumps and was waiting for Jay to bowl. It was a wide one. Ally took it easily and flicked it back, low and hard, to Jay.

'Okay? Now can I go?'

'Ally! C'mon,' said Georgie. 'You said you'd stay for at least 10 minutes.'

'Okay, 10 minutes. Nine now. Let's do it!'

She was amazing. She didn't miss a ball. And most of the deliveries went to her as most of us still couldn't hit the ball with a stump. Her throws were neat and strong too. True to her word, though, she waved goodbye to Georgie about 10 minutes later and headed out the door.

'Hey, Ally, did you enjoy it?' Georgie called.

'Yeah. Actually it was good. I'd like to stay, but I've got some stuff to catch up on.'

'Ally's a good keeper, huh?' Georgie said, as we headed off to afternoon class.

'Awesome,' I replied.

'She plays representative softball. She's the catcher. I just thought it would be interesting to see if she could handle being a keeper.'

'No problems there. Does she want to play?' I asked.

'Not sure.'

'You want to add to that answer?' Jay asked.

Georgie thought for a moment.

'No.'

'Pity,' Jay responded.

We all turned. Martian had joined us, obviously having heard our conversation. Suddenly he stopped and headed for the library.

'Hey, Martian,' Georgie called out, 'I don't mean for her to take your place.'

But Martian didn't turn around. He kept on walking.

'Bummer! Toby, will you see him in class this arvo?' Georgie asked.

'Yeah, I'll talk to him.'

'Thanks. I really didn't mean it like that. It's just that it'd be nice to have another girl in the team, you know.'

'Yeah, I know,' I said.

As it turned out, I didn't catch up with Martian during the afternoon. He didn't show up at all. Instead, I spent a lot of the lesson thinking about how weird the MCG excursion had been. Jay didn't seem to want anything to do with it and Georgie didn't believe me. At least she didn't believe the time travel bit. I needed to talk to someone smart, someone straight. Someone who'd call it as he saw it. I thought of Jimbo.

Jimbo always took a bus home from school, but it didn't leave until 10 to four. I seized my moment.

'Hiya, Jimbo.'

He looked at me and nodded. Not mean, or angry. Almost a bit surprised.

'Can I ask you something?'

Again Jimbo nodded, without speaking.

'Well, you know how we had that excursion last week, and I went to the MCG? Well, there was this guy, an old guy ... like, a really old guy actually ...'

'Yeah?'

'His name's Jim. Jim Oldfield.'

Jimbo was looking at me politely, waiting for me to finish.

'Well, he told me some really weird stuff —'

'Like what?'

It was hard to know where to start, as I knew the whole thing was going to sound stupid. A bus pulled up. Jimbo turned to look at it, then turned back to me.

'So?'

'Nah, it's okay, Jimbo. Doesn't matter. Is that your bus?'

'Nope. Tell me, Toby. What did he say? You said it was weird. I want to know.'

It took a few minutes, but I told him everything. I even dragged the poem out of my pocket and showed it to him. Jimbo didn't say anything. He just shook his head and whistled softly.

Another bus had pulled up.

'This one's mine. See ya, and thanks for telling me all that.'

He picked up his bag and climbed onto the bus.

And then I realised that I hadn't asked him the one question I really wanted to know the answer to: why he wouldn't, or couldn't, play cricket for us. Maybe one day I would go and visit Jimbo and try to find out.

In an 1884 Test match between Australia and England, all 11 players, including the keeper, got to bowl for England. Guess who got the most wickets? Yes! The keeper! His figures were 12 overs, 5 maidens, 4/19. The first 200 scored in a Test match occurred in this game: Billy Murdoch made 211 out of Australia's 551.

5 The Cricketer

Wednesday — afternoon

WHEN school finished I walked over to the car park behind the gym and met up with Jay and Rahul. Georgie arrived a few minutes later. She was coming to the MCG too and then staying at my house for dinner.

'Did you speak to Martian, Toby?' Georgie asked.

'I didn't see him all day. He told me in the gym at lunchtime yesterday that he was feeling sick, so maybe he went home.'

'Georgie, get real. Your friend Ally won't play cricket. She's too pretty to play cricket.'

Oh, boy. Jay had just put his foot in it. Big time.

'What?' Georgie said to him, in a hissing tone.

'Well, I mean, she doesn't look the type, that's all,' Jay stammered.

'Georgie, tell Ally what Jay said and then maybe she'll play cricket,' said Rahul.

We all looked at him, a bit perplexed.

39

'You lot coming to the MCG?' a voice yelled at us from an open car window a moment later.

Dad had arrived.

We piled our bags into the boot and jumped in.

'Crikey, you kids don't know how lucky you are. Getting to do projects on cricket! Can you believe it? In my day it was the Battle of Hastings and the Peasants' Revolt.'

Dad chatted most of the way, and each of us was left to our own thoughts. I could imagine what some of those thoughts were.

Georgie would be wondering about how to get Ally playing cricket without hurting Martian's feelings. Jay would be angry with himself for saying the first thing that came into his head, and he'd be thinking of a way to get back into Georgie's good books.

'Hey, Georgie, you want me to try to hunt out that book of cricket poems my uncle gave me for Christmas last year?'

(See, what did I tell you?)

And Rahul? Actually, I wouldn't have a clue what Rahul would be thinking. I turned to look at him. He was staring out the window and smiling as we turned into the MCG car park. Probably smiling at Jay's comment. Then again, it's just as likely that he was thinking about something else.

As for me, I was getting a bit nervous about seeing Jim again, especially having Dad and the others with me.

* * *

But as it happened, I was in for a big disappointment. Or maybe it was relief. After we'd shown the little card to the lady at the desk, we were taken up to the old part of the stand. On the walls of the passageways were the old photographs and massive paintings. Cricket bats stood in a glass cabinet. Some of the old ones looked like paddles for a little rowing boat. When we walked into the library, there was no one sitting at the oval table. There was no pile of books lying scattered across it. The glass doors of the bookshelves were shut. They looked as if they hadn't been opened in years.

The only person in the room was a man sitting in a green chair over to the left of the room. His glasses were pushed up on his forehead and a closed book lay in his lap. He appeared to be asleep.

Jay looked at me and smiled.

'Just as well he's not here, I reckon. Let's forget it ever happened, eh?'

For a moment I was about to agree. But then I noticed the rows of brown and yellow *Wisden Almanacks* lined up across the top shelves. I walked over to them, reached up and tried to open the cabinet door. It was locked.

'Found something interesting, mate?' Dad asked me.

'*Wisden*s, Dad. There's one for every year since way back, with all the scores and stuff from every game played in that year.' Dad was nodding his head and sighing.

'Well, not quite every game, my boy, but all the important ones.'

My heart stopped. I wheeled around and found myself staring at a smiling Jim. I smiled too. The secret door in the wall had opened and closed. Dad was looking confused, though I felt safe with him standing next to me.

Dad held out his hand and introduced himself.

'Good to meet you, Peter,' Jim said, nodding his head as Dad introduced the others to him.

'The kids are all doing cricket projects at school. They probably told you.' Dad was prattling on. 'That was a very kind invitation of yours, Jim. And what a treasury of old books.'

'And some not so old either, Peter.'

Dad was nodding enthusiastically.

'Right then, everyone. What are you all studying again?' asked Dad. There was something tense and unsure about the moment, and I think Dad was picking up the vibes.

'Well, I'm doing women in cricket. I'm really interested in what I've read about women inventing over-arm bowling.'

Georgie had spoken up, of course, and Jim moved over to a small table, grabbed a set of keys from a drawer and limped off to a distant bookcase.

'Excellent, excellent!' Dad was excited. He led us over to the table and we took out our folders to get stuck into a bit of serious research. It looked as if time travel was off the agenda — for that day, at least.

When everyone had settled down to a bit of study,

I sneaked a look at Jim. He was smiling at me. It was a gentle smile.

'Peter, did you ever play cricket?' Jim was still looking at me.

Dad looked up from where he was sitting on the floor with a huge book open on his knees.

'Yes, I played a bit.'

Dad had never spoken much about his cricket-playing days. Well, to me he had, but the others didn't really know that he used to play at a pretty high level. 'At school,' he added.

'And what about after school?' said Jim.

Dad looked at me. He shrugged.

'Yes, and after school.'

'Where, Mr Jones?' Rahul asked. 'Who for?'

'You don't want to hear ...'

'Toby's dad here played for Victoria,' Jim chimed in, his eyebrows raised.

I sensed the others looking up from their books.

'They don't want to know about that,' said Dad, staring at Jim.

There was an uneasy silence.

'Wow, Mr Jones, that is so cool! Did you play here, at the "G"?' Georgie asked

Dad closed the book he was holding and said, 'Well, Jim, I fear a little cat has been let out of a bag. You say those brown and yellow books up there have all the games played? Well, let's pull down a few from the '80s and see if we can find a Jones among a few others more famous.'

'No!' I jumped up from my seat.

'It's all right, Toby,' said Jim.

Dad was looking at me strangely.

Jim had pulled down a *Wisden*. It had a hard yellow cover. I didn't see the year. The others had gathered around. Jim was flicking through the pages. I couldn't bear to look.

'Here we are. Victoria versus South Australia. At the MCG.'

Slowly I looked up from the table in front of me to the open pages of the book. The letters and numbers swirled and blended, spinning round and round in a sea of black and white. I closed my eyes.

'Here, let's have a look,' Dad said, reaching out for the book.

'No!' I yelled again.

But before I had a chance to stop him, Jim had passed the book over to Dad. I looked at Dad's face. He was smiling.

'It's all right, Toby. They don't bite. I think I've got a few of them stashed away somewhere. Ah, here we are! P. Jones, bowled, for 23. That was my highest score for Victoria. Jim, you've found the best page about me!'

'Dad, you can read it?'

'Yeeeees,' he said slowly, 'I picked up that handy skill about 35 years ago. Hadn't I told you that?'

'Did you get a bowl, Mr Jones? Or take a catch?' Rahul asked.

'Nope. Nothing. We won the game, though.'

Dad closed the book and handed it back to Jim.

'Do you know, I can remember that game quite well,' Jim said, nodding thoughtfully. 'I was here in the library and I had a visitor. Quite a young visitor. Though unfortunately we never met. A most curious thing it was.' It sounded as if Jim was rambling.

'Well, I think we've probably taken up enough of your time, Jim.'

'Oh, yes, by all means, yes indeed,' Jim replied, though a bit hazily.

As Dad helped the others put their books away, Jim quietly called my name, then spoke softly.

'Have you ever heard of talents skipping a generation? They say it of music and musicians. When my father read *Wisden*s, he read *Wisden*s. When I read *Wisden*s, I travel through time. Just as my grandfather did. I think it's the same with you, Toby. Of course I can read the words now too. That takes time to learn, as you will discover.'

'Okay then, people, ready to go?' called Dad.

'Can you all come again? It's wonderful to see young people here learning about cricket.'

'I'm sure they'd love to. What do you think, kids?'

Rahul and Georgie nodded. Jay was looking down at his shoes. I mumbled something that meant nothing.

'Well, I think I can persuade them, Jim. As long as you don't reveal any more secrets about me.'

They both laughed as we headed out.

On 15 March 1877 a player gained a record
that may never be broken. He represented England
in the first official Test match played against Australia.
He holds the record for being the oldest player to ever
represent his or her country on debut. His name was
J. Southerton — he was an off-spin bowler
and he was 49 years and 119 days old.

6 The Past

Wednesday — evening

WE dropped off Rahul and Jay. Georgie had picked up on my weird behaviour — unlike Dad, who was sometimes a bit vague about things around him.

This time Georgie's approach was different. She got all efficient. She knew me as well as anyone, and sensed that something had been going on in the MCC library that afternoon.

We headed for the computer. Georgie opened up a new document and started to type up a summary of all the important facts.

1. *Old Jim works in the library at the MCG*   *(fact)*
2. *There are heaps of* Wisdens *in the library*   *(fact)*
3. *When Toby looks at a* Wisden, *the words go swirly (?)*
4. *Jim says you can travel back in time*   *(???)*
5. *No one else seems to see the swirly writing*   *(fact)*

We figured the only solution was for us to head down to the MCG on Friday after school and, once and for all, get to the bottom of the whole thing with Jim.

'And what? We just walk through the gate and straight up to the library?' Georgie asked.

I pulled out the little card that Dad had read aloud on Monday.

'I think taking this means that you're allowed to go up and do cricket research,' I said.

'Okay, bring it. And bring the poem too,' she added.

Thursday — morning

At recess I headed for the gym hoping to catch Jimbo there. I still wanted to ask him why he hadn't played in the game on Saturday.

Once again he looked at me without saying anything. For a moment I thought he wouldn't reply. Finally he said, 'Too busy.'

'Geez, it's a pity. You're such a good bat.'

'Thanks, Toby. You're a great bowler. No, my dad's trying to teach me that there's more to life than just cricket. I do other things on a Saturday.'

'More to life than cricket?' I shook my head.

Jimbo smiled. 'We have weekend projects. At the moment we're clearing out the garage.' I must have been looking a bit sorry for Jimbo. Not being able to play cricket on a Saturday sounded pretty disastrous to me. Cleaning out a garage just made it worse.

'It's okay, Toby. One day I'll play in real games.'

'Well I hope we're on the same side when you do.'

'Yeah, me too.'

'You want to come over to the nets with the others then?' I asked him.

48

Jimbo looked at his watch.

'The bell's going pretty soon. Another time, maybe?'

I was halfway over to the nets when the bell did go. I turned back to look at Jimbo.

'See you at training,' he called.

Thursday — afternoon

We were in the nets. Mr Pasquali took one of the nets himself and threw ball after ball at a couple of batters who he said were sluggish with their feet. Mr Pasquali was a great coach. He took the time to talk to you about your batting and bowling. And fielding too. As I padded up for my turn, I watched him working on Jono's front foot, on-side attacking shots. He made you feel like a real cricketer.

We hung around after practice, waiting for the team to get put up on the notice board, but Mr Pasquali, who had been on the phone, came out of the gym and said we'd have to wait till tomorrow. He looked worried.

Martian wasn't at training, and I wondered if that had anything to do with Mr Pasquali's behaviour. Whatever it was, it didn't look like good news.

That night I lay in bed for a long time thinking about Jimbo cleaning out the garage, about Mr Pasquali looking worried, and about Jim in the library. Perhaps this was my chance to see some other cricket matches. Maybe some famous ones. Maybe the World Cup. My mind drifted to stories that Dad told me about amazing cricket games. Like the time he lay on his mum's and dad's bed listening to the radio, not daring to move as Allan Border and Jeff Thomson got closer and closer to achieving an incredible victory. It was in the early '80s. Dad said that he lay totally still on the bed. He thought that if he moved, the spell would be broken and one of the batters would be dismissed, leaving England as the winners.

They were the last pair. I can remember the scores easily. Thomson came in on the fourth day, when the score was 218. Australia needed 292 to win — 74 runs. England only needed one wicket. And they had a whole day and a bit to get it. But by the end of that day Australia had knocked off 37 of the runs. Which was exactly half the runs they needed to make.

The next morning, according to Dad, radios were on everywhere. Cars had pulled over. Maybe the drivers were getting stressed out with the tension. People were hanging around in shops listening to the game. Dad said that they let people in for free on that final morning. They were expecting a couple of thousand people. Eighteen thousand turned out to watch the game. I reckon I would have too.

Border and Thomson (he was a fast bowler and the number 11 batsman) batted on and on. They refused to take singles. They got to 288 — only four runs from victory — when Thomson edged a ball into the slips. The first guy got his hands to it, and managed to bump it up so that the second slip fielder caught the ball just before it hit the ground.

Dad said he cried.

And then there was Hobart. The Test match against Pakistan when Adam Gilchrist and Justin Langer put on an amazing partnership to first rescue Australia, who were 5 for 126 in their second innings, and then take them on to victory. They had a partnership of over 340 runs!

Dad also talked about a fast bowler from New Zealand called Richard Hadlee. He's a knight now. I sure would like to see him bowl. Dad said that in one Test match he totally cleaned up Australia, taking eight wickets in an innings.

Actually, Dad's a bit like Mr Pasquali. He's a guy who loves his cricket. I wonder if Dad's all-time dream was to play for his country. This got me wondering about all the cricketers who had played for Australia. Did Don Bradman have the dream? What about all the players now? Did they lie in bed at night staring at their bedroom walls thinking of 60,000 people roaring and cheering as they walked out to play?

My last thought before falling asleep was that there was no way I was going to miss out on what Jim and the *Wisden* books were possibly offering. Didn't Jim say that this was a once in a lifetime opportunity?

Friday — afternoon

Georgie and I had no trouble getting permission to visit the library at the MCG. We caught the tram and were going to be picked up later. I was beginning to feel at home there. This was only my third visit, but the quiet and the calm in the little library gave it an almost magical feel. It almost seemed wrong to speak in there.

The man with glasses was there again, this time reading a book. He looked up as we entered, smiled briefly, then went back to his reading.

A moment later Jim appeared, hobbling slowly towards us from behind a table.

'Hello, Toby, Georgie.'

'Hello, Jim.'

I thought back to last night. To the cricket matches I'd recalled Dad talking about. And to the many more I'd dreamed about.

'I'm ready,' I told him, firmly.

'Yes, I know you are.' Jim walked over to the glass cabinet and pulled down a *Wisden* from the shelf. It was the 2000 edition.

'The 1999 World Cup, Toby. That's what you're studying, isn't it?'

I nodded, keeping my eyes on the book Jim was thumbing through.

Georgie hadn't said a word, which was surprising for her. But now she was reaching into her pocket, and yanking out a creased copy of the poem I had emailed to her.

'Great poem, Mr Oldfield,' she said to him.

Jim paused from his browsing and looked at Georgie.

'My father wrote that many years ago. Actually, they are the words of my grandfather.'

'Yes, well I was just wondering about the word "dead".'

Jim winced.

'Whose lives are dead?' she asked.

'I wonder, my dear, would you mind hopping along to the kitchen and getting me a glass of water? It's just down the hall to your right.'

Georgie and I stared at him.

'Excuse me?' Georgie said.

'I just wondered . . .'

With a sigh, Georgie walked to the door.

'Toby,' said Jim firmly when she had gone. 'It's now or never. Come on.'

Jim passed Georgie's copy of the poem to me. He gestured for me to follow him. We moved to a place behind the shelves, slightly around the corner from the main part of the library, and hidden from the front section where the big oval table stood.

The man in the chair hadn't moved.

'Toby, look at me. If this should work, and you find yourself in a strange place, read aloud two lines from the poem. Straight away. Do you understand? Straight away. You only ever have two hours, anyway — the time it takes to complete a session of cricket. Toby, how long?'

'Two hours,' I breathed, startled at Jim's urgency and energy. He nodded.

'Now, I want you to focus hard on the page here and try to stop the words and numbers moving.'

He passed the book across to me. Everything was happening in a rush. Georgie would be back in a moment, but for some reason I didn't want her to return. Not yet, anyway. I looked down at the open book that Jim was holding. The swirl of black and white was no different from last time.

'The top of the page, Toby. Concentrate. Try to make the words settle. Force the letters to stop moving. Then say the word that appears.'

I shook my head and lifted my eyes to the top of the page. There was less black here, but still the swirly effect continued. I wasn't sure what I was supposed to be doing, but as I thought of asking Jim, I sensed the page settling. I hadn't looked at a *Wisden* page yet for as long as this. For a moment, I thought I could make out a word. Then it went washy again.

'Keep at it, Toby. Keep going,' Jim urged.

Another word drifted in, then away, but this time I could read the word. 'South.' I didn't dare look down the page, where I still sensed a flurry of black marks swishing and surging like ants in cream.

'What can you see, Toby? Can you read to me?'

'S-S-South Africa,' I stammered, peering into the mess. 'Oh, hang on. It's a date, June, I think, and there's a ...'

Someone was speaking.

Something about a glass of water ...

I looked up. A roar surrounded me. I stood, transfixed.

Utterly confused.

I thumped myself, to feel my own body, and swung around. I was surrounded by people, but no one was paying me the slightest attention. There was no carpet beneath me. Just grey concrete.

The bright light was glaring. There was a gasp from the crowd and then applause. I couldn't help myself. I looked out towards the players. Someone had just belted a four.

I took another glance around me. There was a lot of noise and chatter. I noticed some empty seats about 10 metres away. Nervously I walked to them and sat down. I felt as if everyone should be looking at me, but when I turned to check, people were just concentrating on the cricket.

I checked the scoreboard. Australia were batting. South Africa were in the field. I was in England, in the year 1999, watching the World Cup semi-final! Steve Waugh and Michael Bevan were in. The score was 4 for 86. Bevan was on six and Steve Waugh was on 13. I suddenly realised that no one here knew what was going to happen. They didn't know that they were going to see one of the most exciting finishes to a cricket game ever — well, that's what Dad and I thought.

I opened my mouth to speak, then quickly closed it again. Maybe now wasn't the right time to be showing off my knowledge.

I looked around at the people beside me.

'They're struggling, aren't they?' A lady was speaking to me from two seats away. She was the first person who appeared to have noticed me.

I opened my mouth but nothing came out.

'You alright then, love?' she asked. She had an English accent.

I nodded.

'Where are you from then?'

'Australia.' The word came out a bit garbled, but she'd heard me.

'Oooh, really? Well, you'd better hope that Bevan and Waugh put on a partnership, otherwise you're done for.'

Someone started talking to her and she turned away. I turned back to the cricket. I felt calmer when I was watching it. I took a few deep breaths then closed and opened my eyes a few times. Nothing changed.

A surge of excitement and exhilaration charged through me. Jim was right. I had travelled in time. I really was here at the World Cup! It was the most awesome and spectacular thing imaginable.

But then a thought occurred to me. How long had I been away? Was the time I was spending here the same as the time that Jim and Georgie were spending at the library?

I decided to give it one more over. That couldn't hurt. Allan Donald was bowling and Bevan was facing. He didn't look in any hurry to score. But that was okay. He actually let the third ball go through to the keeper, but he scored a run off the second-last ball and then Steve Waugh scored a single off the last.

'Not your seat, I don't think, lad.'

I turned around. A couple of men were standing over me. The first guy was holding three plastic cups.

I stood up and scuttled past them and back to the spot where I'd arrived. I took out the scrap of paper with the poem on it and read out the first two lines I saw:

Now, hide your home, your age, your soul
To roam this place and seek your goal.

'What?' someone was saying loudly, close by me.

'Georgie?' I gasped.

'What are you doing?' She looked at me queerly. 'You look as if you've seen a ghost.' I looked down, this time at red and blue carpet.

'Where's Jim?' I whispered.

'Over there, sipping his water.'

In a daze, I walked past Georgie and over to Jim. He looked up from his book, his eyes shining.

I stared at him. I swallowed. I was totally speechless. 'What?'

Georgie had followed me and was looking at both of us in turn.

'You said you liked the poem, young lady?' said Jim, still looking at me. He had a habit of doing that.

'Yes,' she replied. 'So?'

'I think Toby here thinks it's quite a special poem too, eh, Toby?'

'Yes.' It came as a croak. 'Yes,' I repeated. 'How long was I there, Jim?'

'What? Where?' Georgie was getting exasperated.

'Or would you like to know how long you were away?' Jim was smiling. 'How long did it feel like?' he asked.

'About five minutes,' I replied, 'but it must have been longer.'

'Remember the words of the poem, Toby.

Your time, this time; none short, or long

'The time matches up quite closely, you know, though it can distort if you travel quite a way back,' Jim said. 'But don't forget, two hours is your limit.'

I had a hundred questions to ask Jim. I was still in shock, and I suppose if I'd stopped a moment and thought about what had just happened I would have run out of the room, never to return. Ever! But I didn't move.

Even though I'd told Georgie about the time travelling she didn't seem to realise where I'd been, although she knew that something weird had happened. I grabbed her hand and the 2000 *Wisden* that was lying on the table in front of Jim.

'Toby, not yet!'

Jim had risen, his hands stretched out towards me, for the book. I looked at him. His face seemed concerned.

'Please, Toby, don't be foolish. You're not ready to carry. To take others with you,' he added when he saw my questioning look.

Georgie flung my hand out of hers and jolted me round.

'What are you doing, Toby?' she yelled.

'Georgie, you'll never believe me otherwise. Never. I've got to take you there. Please?'

'Take me where, you idiot? Behind the shelves for a quick kiss? Is that what you mean?'

I couldn't believe what she was saying.

Slowly I walked back to the table and sat down. I placed the *Wisden Almanack* down in front of Jim, who was sitting down again too. He pushed his half-empty glass of water across the table to me. I reached out, took a gulp and sighed.

'Okay. Good. All is calm, all is bright. All is splendid on Friday night.'

'Thanks for that, Georgie,' I said to her.

'My pleasure. What now?'

'Georgie, you're a breath of fresh air,' said Jim with a smile.

'Probably more like hot air, Mr Oldfield,' she replied, almost breaking into a smile herself.

'Well, enough adventures for one afternoon, don't you think?' Jim said.

'Yeah, I guess. Getting that water was just non-stop action and excitement for me. I couldn't go through that again.'

At least Georgie had recovered her sense of humour.

The lowest number of runs scored in a day of Test cricket was 95. This happened in Karachi, Pakistan on 11 October 1956. On that day Australia were dismissed for 80, and Pakistan, at stumps, were 2/15 in reply.

7 The Run-out

Saturday — morning

IT was a classic summer's day. By 8.30 the temperature had already gone past 25°C. Today was our first two-day game, but I was glad the games would be over by lunchtime.

I wolfed down some toast and checked my cricket kit for the seventh time that morning. Mum headed out early — she was taking Nat to her tennis game.

'Good luck, Toby. Hope all goes well,' she called from the door.

'Thanks, Mum. Hey, good luck to you too, Nat!' I called.

I was ready and sitting in the car. Dad finally arrived with all his gear: camera, deckchair, binoculars, mobile phone, wallet and sunglasses. After a stop at the local milk bar he'd have even more stuff — newspapers and some drinks and snacks. It was Dad's favourite time of the week, I'm sure of it.

* * *

Jono won the toss and we batted. We would bat for three and a half hours, and then the following Saturday, St Mary's, the team we were playing, would bat for the same number of overs as they bowled to us today. I'd checked out their form in the paper. They had lost to TCC by about 20 runs, and TCC weren't supposed to be very strong either.

It was a good day not to be standing out in the field. And it was good to empty my brain of time travel, Jim, poems, kissing Georgie and all that had been happening this week. I loved playing cricket. I loved getting involved in the game I was playing. It was like going to the movies. You lost your sense of anything that was going on elsewhere, and what time it was.

Again there was no Jimbo, and no Martian either. Mr Pasquali told us that Martian had been involved in a car accident and would be missing a bit of school. Rahul would have been wicket keeper if we'd been bowling.

'Maybe Martian will be right to keep next week, Mr Pasquali?' asked Cameron, putting on his pads. He was our other opener, a neat, left-handed batter with a rock-solid defence.

'Yes, Cam, maybe.'

Mr Pasquali didn't sound very hopeful. But he looked as if he didn't want to say any more. Maybe that was the phone call he got at training last Thursday.

'Is he okay?' Georgie asked.

The whole team had gone quiet. Mr Pasquali looked around at us.

'Ivo's going to be fine, everyone. He's been quite shaken up and is going to need some time in hospital to recover.' Mr Pasquali nodded. The matter was over.

'Okay, plenty of time, people,' Mr Pasquali said. 'Let's knock up a few 40s today. It's a fast outfield and we've got some short boundaries square of the wicket. Respect the good balls, and belt the wide ones, but keep them along the ground.'

'Unless you reckon you can go over the top,' added Scott Craven, staring out at the witches' hats and licking his lips with anticipation.

'Each ball on its merit, Scott,' Mr Pasquali said, shaking his head.

Scott Craven could tear a bowling attack apart with his tremendous hitting. I'd picked his bat up once, a few weeks back, at practice. He'd seen me almost straight away. For a moment I thought he was going to belt me with it. But instead, he'd strolled over, smiling.

'It weighs a tonne!' I'd told him.

'It's a 16-kilo slugging machine,' he'd said, taking it from me and twisting it in the air. Then he'd aimed a cut shot at my head.

'And it would knock your head off, Tobias.'

He had a nasty habit of using my full name. No one else ever did.

I'd nodded slowly. 'Guess it would, Scott.'

I'd mumbled a few more not-so-choice words under my breath as I headed out to the nets.

St Mary's had an accurate attack and we were scoring at about three an over. Georgie was doing her usual routine. She was already padded up, even though she wasn't due to go in until five wickets had fallen. I had the pads on too, but I was batting fourth. One in front of Scott.

By the time I walked out to bat, the sun was beating down and the bowlers were looking tired. They'd been out there for an hour and a half, and had only taken one wicket: Cameron caught at mid-off for 27. We were 1 for 95. Scott Craven came in after Rahul retired on 42. The first ball he faced he padded back down the wicket. The second, he smashed way over mid-wicket for six.

He strolled down at the end of the over and told me to feed him the strike because he was feeling 'like a good hit-out'. But disaster struck soon after. Scott was getting impatient watching me block the first few balls I faced. Mr Pasquali had said we had plenty of time, and I was just getting my eye in, but Scott was becoming annoyed.

'C'mon, Toby, look for the gaps,' he called out to me.

Finally, I nudged the last ball of the over out between cover and point. There was an easy single. I called Scott through. He wasn't moving.

'Yes!' I shouted. I couldn't believe he wasn't

running. By now I was halfway up the pitch. The fielder had run back to where the ball had stopped and was picking it up. I don't know why, especially as it was Scott standing at the other end, but I kept on running. Scott had moved a few metres out of his crease, not aware that I had now passed him and made it across the line.

The ball was tossed to the keeper, who gently knocked one bail off the stumps.

'You idiot, Jones. You've just gone and run yourself out!'

But the umpire had different ideas. 'You're out, son,' he said, looking at Scott.

Then I did a really weak thing. I knew who was out too. Perhaps I was after a bit of respect from Scott.

'It's okay, I'll go,' I said to the umpire.

'No, you actually crossed, so you're not out. This feller is.'

Scott was going white with anger. Not red. The umpire obviously didn't know him. 'Off you go, son,' he said cheerfully, then raised his finger to confirm, publicly, that a run-out had just occurred. Amid the cheers of the fielders now running in towards the pitch, Scott glared at me, then shook his head. I knew I was going to hear more about this.

Gavin Bourke, Scott's best mate, strode out to the wicket. I saw Scott hurl his bat onto the grass, then throw down his gloves. He turned around again and glared across the oval at me.

65

'You're in deep, mate,' Gavin said cheerfully. 'Which end am I at?'

I pointed down to the other end, where the umpire had moved into position for the next over. My mouth was dry.

Both Jono and Rahul came back and made their 50s. This probably made Scott even madder. If he'd batted through to his 40, he would have got another bat too. I reckon there could have been 100 out there for him today, given the tired bowling and the short boundaries. We made 271.

'Don't forget, it wasn't your fault,' Georgie told me at the end of the innings. 'Scott's just so greedy that he didn't want you to take a single off the last ball of the over.'

'It was my call. I called, and he didn't respond.'

'Yep,' she agreed. 'There was an easy single there. It looked as if you were about to walk yourself.'

'I was.' I wasn't looking at Georgie. 'I just thought it'd be easier if I went. You know how he gets.'

'Toby, he gets his way so often. He doesn't need favours from you as well.'

'You're right.'

'Toby?'

'Yeah.'

'You don't need his respect either. C'mon. I've got some jobs to do for Mum, then she said I could come round to your place and watch the cricket on TV. What do you say?'

'Brilliant.'

We packed up our gear and headed over to Dad's car.

In 1890, in a game in Victoria between Portland and Port Fairy, a square-leg umpire, Umpire Threlfall, fielded the ball then hurled it back, hitting the stumps, before he realised that he wasn't actually a fielder. Amid howls of laughter, one of the fielders appealed.
The umpire had to say, 'Not out!'

8 The Mistake

Monday — morning

FOR a couple of classes that morning, we went to the library to work on our cricket projects. I was sitting next to Rahul, who was struggling with his Madras Test match. He had plenty of books on India but not much on the actual game itself.

'Hey, Rahul, why don't you interview one of the players from the game?' I suggested.

He looked at me and smiled.

'Right, so I just go and ring up Dean Jones or Greg Matthews or Allan Border and ask them if I can interview them?' he joked.

'Well, yeah. Who else played in the game?' I asked. 'Any other Victorians?'

'There was Ray Bright. He took seven wickets in the game. Five in the second innings,' Rahul answered.

'It can't be too hard. We could ask Mr Pasquali. Or look up, say, Dean Jones on the Internet or in the telephone book. We could find him. Do it!'

'Do what?'

'Ring him! Go visit! Do an interview. It'd be awesome!'

'Oh, right. I just go and look up Dean Jones in the phone book and tell him I want an interview. How many Joneses are there in the phone book? You reckon his name will have "Test cricketer" beside it? And even if I do get to speak to him, do you think he'd waste his time talking to a kid? Like he's got nothing better to do.'

'Well, you might need to get Mr Pasquali or your dad to make the first call. You know, set it up for you,' I said.

Rahul thought for a moment. 'I guess it's worth a try. It'd be brilliant if it came off. I suppose it'd be almost as good as being at the game. Okay, Toby, yes. Great thinking. Hey, Toby?'

I was staring at Rahul, my mind a thousand miles away.

'Toby?' Rahul was looking at me. 'What's got into you?'

'What did you just say, Rahul?' I asked, a grin spreading across my face.

'I don't know,' he replied. 'Something about it being almost as good as being there.'

Suddenly I was aware of Jay, Scott and a few others listening in to our conversation.

'Then let's go there,' I laughed at him. 'I'll take you to Madras.'

'I think the game might have finished by the time you get there, Toby,' Scott said to me.

I kept smiling. 'Trust me, Rahul. It can be done. I'll bring you back a memento, Scott,' I said, without being quite sure why I was saying it.

'Toby, are you okay?' Rahul asked me, puzzled.

'Come round after school, Wednesday night. Okay?'

'Sure. Maybe we can plan that interview, yes?'

Excitement was bubbling up inside me, but I didn't carry on with the conversation. It was enough to know that I had this power, this knowledge, this extraordinary gift that none of the other kids in the library had any idea about.

And the more I tried to explain it or tried to make them believe it, the more stupid it would seem. I had the best secret in the world and I would reveal it in my own time.

Tuesday — afternoon

The next night at training, Mr Pasquali chatted to us at the start of the session. But it wasn't about last Saturday's game or about how he wanted the practice to go that evening. Instead, he explained that Martian would not be playing with us for a while and that the keeping duties would be taken over by Ally McCabe. We wondered how bad Ivo's injuries were, but Mr Pasquali told us to concentrate on our practice.

Mr Pasquali worked us through another centre-wicket practice during the session. We all had plenty of bowling and fielding to do. Ally stayed behind the stumps all the time we were out there. She was good too. She was very quick to pick up the direction of the ball and was clean with her glove work — hardly ever dropping the ball. The only problem she seemed to have was if the batter got in the way when the ball came down the leg side. She was willing to listen to suggestions from Mr Pasquali — and from some of the players too. Best of all, she seemed to be really enjoying it.

Luckily, I was able to avoid Scott for most of the session, though he put me away for a couple of big fours near the end. I hoped that might have got the anger out of his system. Time would tell.

At the end of practice Mr Pasquali brought us all back into a close group.

He must have heard all of us talking about Martian. 'As I told you, Ivo is going to be okay but he won't be with us for quite some time.'

Everyone started asking questions, but Mr Pasquali held up a hand.

'I know you are all concerned. But Ivo's mum has told me that everything is going to be fine.'

The mood of the afternoon had changed as we gathered up our gear and packed it away. I noticed Mr Pasquali talking with Ally. A moment later she approached me.

'Hey, Toby, can we do a bit of work together? Your bowling was a bit hard to read, you know?'

'It was?'

'Yeah, sometimes it swung one way, sometimes the other.'

'Cool. That's good to hear. Okay, Ally, sure. You want to meet in the gym sometime, then?'

'Yep. I'll see if I can book it for sometime next week. I'll let you know.'

We all hung around for a bit, chatting about Ivo.

'You reckon we should just go in and see him?' Jay asked.

'Better ring up first,' I suggested.

'Poor Ivo. He always seems to be the one who gets knocked about. Remember last year he broke his arm and he had those pins inserted in it?' Georgie shook her head.

'My dad often talks about fate and luck.'

We all looked at Rahul.

'That's a bit deep, Rahul,' Ally said.

'Yeah, well I'll ring him soon,' I told them.

Wednesday — afternoon

Mum took Rahul and me into the MCC library again after school the following day. She dropped us off outside the front and told us that she would collect us in exactly an hour. We waved goodbye and raced off to the entrance.

I was excited, that was for sure, but I was also working hard to keep a lid on it. So far, only Georgie had an inkling of what was going on. It was a secret, and I wanted to share it. But I wanted to protect the secret from people I didn't trust. Rahul, I thought, was someone I could trust.

It was spooky to think that maybe the next time I hopped in Mum's car, I could have been to India and back. And what was even more spooky, travelled through time to get there!

When we arrived at the library there was a man working at a computer on the far side, obviously the librarian, and another man with glasses, sitting at the big oval table reading. It was the same guy we had seen last time. Maybe he worked here too. If he did, it sure wasn't too tough a job.

There was no sign of Jim, and no one looked up when we walked in.

'Rahul, come with me. I want to show you something.'

I found the 1987 *Wisden* on the shelf and walked over to the secret door in the wall. I pushed the door open and we went out into the corridor.

Rahul was a few metres behind me and looking doubtful. 'Toby, where are you going?'

'You'll find out in a minute, okay?' I turned to the contents pages at the start. For some reason I could read these. But I couldn't find the right section. 'When did you say that tied Test was again?'

'1986.'

'That's weird. How come it's not in the 1987 *Wisden*?'

'Probably because it was later in the year, September. You need the next year's book, I think. Can we go back inside now?'

Maybe this wasn't meant to happen after all, I thought. But when we got back into the library I got a big shock. There, on the oval table, was a copy of the 1988 *Wisden*. I looked around, but no one seemed to be paying us the slightest bit of attention. Maybe it had been left by the guy with the glasses. He'd closed his book and his head had slumped forwards onto his chest.

I picked up the 1988 *Wisden* and headed over to the far side of the library. Rahul followed.

'Okay, Rahul, hold on.'

Maybe I should have thought a bit more about what I was about to do. Maybe I should have thought about the fact that Jim had expressly forbidden me to take anyone. Carrying, as Jim called it. But in the excitement of trying to impress Rahul, who always seemed so much in control, none of these thoughts entered my mind.

I grabbed Rahul's arm, and dragged him closer. I was holding the precious book in my other hand and trying to scan down the contents page.

There it was, clear as day: 'The Australians in India, 1986–87'. I flipped chunks of pages till I got close to the correct page. The numbers in the top corner of each page were becoming clearer.

I knew I had to be quick or Rahul would drag me back.

'Toby!' he hissed at me. 'What are you doing? Why can't we look at the book at the big table over there, like normal people?'

I got to page 920 then flicked on a few more pages, trying to focus on the headings at the top. I didn't know exactly what page the Test would be on. 'Rahul, was the tie in the first Test match?'

'Yes. Can I see?'

I had a thought. 'Good idea. You find the correct page, then give it to me.'

Everything was racing. I didn't have time to think about what I was doing. Maybe it wouldn't work. Maybe I needed Jim here, with his magical powers. My heart was thumping. I would just give Rahul a taste. Just prove to him that we could go there. Go anywhere! It would be so exciting to show someone else. Especially Rahul. He would be amazed.

He passed the book back to me. I stared with total concentration at the top of the page. I could just make out the word India in a swirly mix of white and black. Rahul was close by.

'India,' I said quietly, staring at the word as it materialised into letters.

There was a gentle knocking, thudding noise going on somewhere in my head. I grabbed Rahul's wrist. The thudding turned to a roar; to a great, whooshing rush of what sounded like air and water surging through my head. I could hear Rahul talking about how useful the match report would be for his project, when suddenly he seemed to stop in mid-sentence.

I opened my eyes. It was as if we were standing in an oven. The heat was amazing. It wasn't just heat; it was sticky, dense heat that squeezed at you from all sides. And there was a terrible smell of really gross toilets. For a moment I thought I was going to be sick.

Beside me Rahul gasped and fell to his knees.

'Rahul,' I cried. 'Get up!'

Slowly he struggled to his feet.

'Wh — what?' he stammered.

We had arrived a little behind the crowd. We were inside the ground but couldn't see the oval. It was like last time. I knew, without knowing exactly why, that we had arrived without anyone knowing. Somehow that seemed important.

Taking him by the shoulders, I forced Rahul to look at me. He wasn't looking too good.

'Rahul, as soon as you've got over being totally freaked out by what's happened, the sooner we can get a look at the game. Okay?'

I was giving it to him straight up. He stared back at me, his eyes not blinking.

'We are in India,' Rahul whispered.

It was more a statement than a question, but I answered anyway.

'Correct.'

'In the year —,' Rahul looked at me.

'1986.'

'I'm not even born yet.'

'Well, that's debatable. I can see you.'

'My mother is alive in this city somewhere. My father too,' Rahul said.

'Yeah, well, let's take a quick look at the cricket. Then we'll head back, okay? Rahul?'

But Rahul looked as if he had other things on his mind.

The noise and the heat closed in around us. Men wearing really long shirts streamed past us, kicking up dust that stung my eyes. There was a dull roar coming from near the oval and an amazing mixture of smells. Half the crowd seemed to be behind the stand here, with us. Everyone was babbling, shouting, pushing and hurrying.

'It's time to go, Rahul. C'mon. Let's move away from here.'

I grabbed him by the arm and dragged him in the opposite direction to the people rushing at us till we were near a fence. Rahul was resisting. At this rate we weren't even going to see any cricket.

'Listen!' I yelled. 'I'm not supposed to do this with someone else.'

I was beginning to worry about having Rahul here with me, especially with Jim's warning about not taking anyone else with me. And Rahul was not looking himself.

'We have to go back. *Now!*'

But Rahul was in another world. He was looking at me as though I wasn't there. Maybe he was thinking of his family. Then I realised that I didn't have the poem on me. I looked around, in absolute panic.

I checked all my pockets, but all I could feel was the little card old Jim had given me for getting into the library.

A large man in what looked like a police uniform was striding towards us.

I closed my eyes and tried to picture the poem. But the only word I could remember was 'dead'.

The man was getting closer. He had a long stick dangling down the side of one leg.

Something about lives being broken, and respecting the gift.

The man stopped in front of us and spoke to Rahul. I couldn't understand what he was saying but Rahul replied, presumably in the same language.

Now there was a horrible stench in the air that had overpowered all the other smells. The heat was beginning to get to me. I was sweating like anything and finding it hard to breathe. My jeans were sticking to me. Desperately, I dipped into my front pocket and pulled out the card.

The man was nodding at me and waving an arm at Rahul.

I turned the card over. Relief flooded through me as I saw two neat lines of handwriting across the back that I hadn't known were there. I had never turned the card over before.

I turned to see the policeman shaking his head, pointing at me and then at the ground.

He made a final comment and walked away. Rahul was starting to sit down.

Again, I grabbed him by the arm, and without even asking him what they'd been talking about, I read aloud the two lines on the card.

Now, hide your home, your age, your soul
To roam this place and seek your goal.

The last word had hardly left my lips when the roaring inside my head started again, though not quite as loudly as before. I was aware of us leaving the heat and the smell behind. I tried to keep my eyes open, but it was impossible — like when you sneeze. It only took a moment, but I knew that we had gone. And that the going and the arriving were split by a second, no more.

The first Test match played over five days took place in Sydney, during February 1892. This was also the first time six balls were bowled in each over. In all the Tests before 1892, overs were just four balls long.

9 The Heat

'WHAT the heck do you two think you're playing at?'

I looked up at the librarian. 'You won't find anything down there on the floor. Now hop it back to the table. Don't kids nowadays use tables to do their work on? Eh?' He was shaking his head as he headed back inside and over to his computer.

Luckily he hadn't seen the *Wisden*, which was lying on the floor, half underneath me. I watched him walk off, grabbed the *Wisden*, and hauled Rahul to his feet. We walked back to the oval table as calmly as we could. The man with the glasses had gone.

Rahul hadn't said a word. I looked at him. He looked pale and worn out.

'Rahul? Speak to me.'

He turned to me slowly, a smile beginning to take shape.

'We have to go back again, you know. When can we go? I'll get some things together then you can take me back, okay?'

80

It was as if something or someone had taken over Rahul's thinking. He wasn't sounding like his normal, controlled self.

'Not yet. Not until I talk to Jim,' I whispered and told him all about Jim and our shared gift.

'Right. Okay. Sorry. Where is he, then?'

'I'm not sure. Leave it with me though, okay?'

Rahul looked at me closely.

'Toby? What on earth just happened?' A drop of sweat fell from my forehead and landed on the table next to the *Wisden* book. 'We've just been to India. It was hot, wasn't it?'

We looked at the tiny splash of sweat on the table. Wonderingly, Rahul touched it with a finger.

'Sweat from India,' he said.

We stayed for another 20 minutes or so. Rahul jotted down notes from the books in front of him, while I sat in a daze. I couldn't believe he could have suddenly become so calm, sitting there quietly, going from book to notepad as if nothing had happened.

Just before we left, the librarian came over to see how we were getting on.

'Where's Jim today?' I asked him.

'Jim's not very well at the moment, I'm afraid.'

'Could you tell me where he is? I'd like to send him a get well card.'

The librarian seemed a bit surprised. 'Well, that's a nice thought. If you send it care of the Simpson Hospital I'm sure he'll get it.'

'Okay, thanks,' I said, getting up.

'You boys come back any time.'

'Sure. Thanks.'

I headed across to the secret door.

'But maybe using the normal door,' he added, smiling at us. We paused. 'No, no, go on. It's our secret, okay?' He chuckled.

Thursday — afternoon

Scott Craven was his usual self at practice the following day. Rahul was quiet, though I didn't think he'd go rushing about, telling everyone of his encounter with an Indian policeman nearly 20 years ago!

'Here, I'm sure Toby would have forgotten your memento of Madras, but I didn't,' he told Scott.

Before I could say anything, Rahul had reached into his pocket and pulled out a couple of pebbles. I stared at them, then held out a hand to take a close look.

'You sure you didn't take them out of your brain?' Scott reached over, grabbed the small stones and hurled them onto the dirt road by the nets.

'You're weird,' Scott said to us.

He scowled. A moment later he wandered off, cursing and muttering under his breath.

At practice I got Mr Pasquali to toss ball after ball at me as he watched me play down the line. He called it a 'V'. I really didn't need a helmet or gloves, because he was throwing them pitched up and making me play forward defensive shots. But he insisted that we should duplicate real batting conditions as often as we could.

Later, a few of us went to the centre-wicket and bowled to Ally. There was no batter, just a set of stumps for us to aim at. After a while, Ally didn't bother replacing the bails on the stumps.

She moved quickly into position and took each ball neatly. I showed her how I held the ball to get it to swing the way I wanted to.

'So that's why you guys work so hard at keeping one side of the ball shiny?' she asked me.

'Yep. We also try to keep it off the ground when it's being thrown back to the bowler.'

Ally looked at me questioningly.

'The more the ball stays off the ground, the longer you can keep the shine on it.'

'Okay, so don't roll it up to, what do you call them, middle-off or something?'

'Mid-off and mid-on. No. Well, of course it doesn't matter when Scott's bowling.'

Ally laughed.

'I guess you don't have that problem to worry about in a softball game?' I asked.

'Nope — I'm sort of missing its simpleness, though, compared with cricket.'

'But are you enjoying wicket-keeping? Oh, yeah, until Martian comes back, that is.' I added quickly.

We worked on a little leg-side trap, where I sent a slightly quicker ball, after a few slower ones, down outside the leg stump. After a few goes, we both had it working well. Ally called it our 'TLT' — Toby's leg trap. I told her that if I pointed to the covers, there would be a TLT on, next ball.

'Okay, so if you see me point to covers, come up and stand behind the stumps. I'll bowl two slower ones outside the off-stump, then the third one will be a bit quicker down outside his pads. If the batter is out of his crease, you whip the bails off after you've caught the ball. Actually, whip them off anyway, it's good practice.'

We practised the TLT a few times and it wasn't long before Ally was taking the ball cleanly and in one easy movement swiping the bails off the stumps.

'All we need is a batter,' I called to her.

'Bring him on!'

I noticed Scott Craven wander off in the last few minutes of practice. Jay had also gone, and he wasn't looking happy when he returned a few minutes later.

Georgie noticed that Jay wasn't his usual cheerful self too. Maybe she'd seen them head off together.

'Did Scott do anything?' Georgie asked him, as we were packing up the gear.

'Nah, didn't even see him.'

'Oh, it's just that I saw the two of you heading off together and I wondered.'

Jay didn't look up from the pads that he was putting into pairs. I wasn't convinced about his answer. Georgie and I exchanged glances.

'By the way,' she said, 'I asked Mr Pasquali about Ivo. He said that Mrs Marshall hadn't wanted him to make a fuss, but if anyone asked, he could tell them Ivo was at the Simpson, and we could see him. But we've gotta ring first.'

'The Simpson!' I wheeled round.

'Yeah. Why, what's the matter? You had some bad experience there or something?'

'Georgie, that's where Jim Oldfield is. You know, the guy at the library.'

'Great. Maybe I can fetch him another glass of water.'

The highest partnership in a one-day international was made by Rahul Dravid (153) and Sachin Tendulkar (186) against New Zealand on 8 November 1999. The two added 331 runs for the second wicket. India's score for the game was 2/376.

10 The Warning

Thursday — evening

I logged into the CROC room, expecting a few others to be there.

Georgie: hey, who's here
Toby: just got on, you still here, georgie?
Rahul: thought you'd never get here, toby
Toby: hi rahul
Rahul: evening all, toby, are we on for fri?
Jay: i'm here to
Georgie: jay — thought you were out tonight?
Jay: i'm aloud to change my mind, are'nt i

Suddenly I knew it wasn't Jay. He was the best speller in the class, by a mile. My mind jumped back to when Georgie had seen Scott following Jay near the end of practice.

Georgie: hey toby, i've told rahul all about jim and
           everything, hope that's okay

Rahul:	I can't wait to meet him myself, toby
Toby:	maybe now's not the best time
Jay:	no, tell
Georgie:	go on toby, you're dying to
Rahul:	careful everyone, this is major deep, how much do you know, georgie?
Georgie:	only that there's this nice (I think) old guy at the library at the mcg who has given toby an awesome poem and is telling him weird stories about travelling through time and stuff. it's cool
Rahul:	what do you know, jay?
Toby:	yeah, tell us what you think, jay. tell us what happened in the library when we first met jim
Georgie:	jay — you there?
Rahul:	he's gone
Toby:	no he hasn't, he's watching us and reading it all
Jay:	your a pack of sicko loosers
Toby:	get out of the room everyone, now

There was no more conversation. I rang up Georgie, then Rahul, explaining my suspicion. They both agreed that there was only one solution. We would have to dump that room and create another. The problem was, would we include Jay? Was it his fault? Or did Scott bully the information out of him?

Sometimes Georgie wrote by just putting down on paper the first things that came into her head. I tried it myself. I took out a pen and some paper, sat down at my desk, and started writing

- ○ *I have travelled to different parts of the world, and to different times, and only Jim knows.*
- ○ *Except for Rahul, who went all freaky when it happened to him.*
- ○ *And Georgie, who sort of knows something weird is going on.*
- ○ *And I should tell Jay — after all, he is one of my best friends.*
- ○ *Ivo is in hospital, obviously pretty sick.*
- ○ *Jim is there too.*
- ○ *Jimbo isn't allowed to play cricket.*
- ○ *Georgie, and the kiss comment.*
- ○ *Scott is out to get me, for running him out.*
- ○ *Scott has got to Jay, and logged into CROC and now must surely know there is something big happening that he isn't a part of.*

The answer never did come to me. Maybe I just needed to share this whole thing with someone — an adult. But something was holding me back.

There was a tap at the door. Mum came in.

'Hey, kiddo, do you want a snack? Dad's making pancakes. He needs some eaters!'

'Sure, Mum, coming,' I said.

I wasn't that hungry, but I went to the kitchen anyway. Mum had got out the family videos, and there were Nat, my younger sister, and me, prancing about, opening presents and looking cute and cuddly. It was good to forget about things for a while.

Then, suddenly I thought — if there was a game of cricket happening at the MCG that day, the day my sister and I were messing about in our little backyard pool all those years ago, I could travel back in time with the correct *Wisden* book, walk from the cricket ground, sneak up to the back fence, lean over, and watch myself, aged three, playing in the pool with my sister.

Could I?

Would I?

I knew there was no way I could answer that right now.

In 1884 the captain of an English team forced the touring Australians to show their bats.
He wanted to make sure they were not too wide!

11 The Simpson Hospital

Friday — afternoon

DAD had been fine about visiting Ivo.

'Of course I'll take you,' he said. 'Poor kid. He deserves a change of luck, doesn't he?'

On the way there in the car he shared old cricket stories. 'Did I ever tell you about the time a spectator ran out onto the ground and got tackled?'

'No. Who did the tackling?'

'Terry Alderman, a great fast bowler from Western Australia. Actually, Toby, not unlike you in terms of style. He could swing the ball both ways. There was a great bit of graffiti up during the Ashes tour, '89 I think: "Thatcher out". Then someone had scrawled next to that, "lbw Alderman".'

We both had a chuckle. I had no idea who Thatcher was, but Dad thought it was funny.

'Anyway, this guy got tackled by Terry Alderman and he ended up dislocating his shoulder.'

'Who?'

'Terry Alderman. Absolute disaster. He was out of the game for ages.'

'Dad?'

'Yes, Toby?' Dad looked at me. 'What's up?'

It was the closest I'd got, so far, to telling him about the *Wisden*s and the time travel. Dad, of all people, wouldn't freak out. But there was something holding me back.

'Tell me about that Test match between New Zealand and the West Indies. You know, the one when the West Indies were none for 276 and —'

'Ah, yes. Amazing game. Probably one of the greatest escapes of all time.'

I decided I would tell him my secret later, and we would go on journey after journey, visiting all the famous games that have been played. We would make a list of them.

Maybe the biggest thing stopping me was the thought of Jim, lying somewhere in a hospital bed. Did he have a family? Was he someone's grandad? I wanted to know a bit more about him. And then, maybe with him, decide what I would do with this magical power I had.

I owed Jim that.

While we were all visiting Martian, I would duck out and try to find him, just to let him know that I

91

hadn't forgotten him. But mainly I just wanted to see him again and make sure he was okay.

Hospitals are quiet and lonely. Well, the parts that most people see are. There's probably plenty more action in the operating theatres, and more noise down in the emergency section, but I didn't want to go and test out that theory.

I was meeting the rest of the guys in the foyer, where Dad said he would wait for me. We made our way up to Ivo's room on the first floor. His parents were with him. Ivo lay propped up on a heap of pillows and there was a drip next to him.

'Does it hurt?' I asked him, looking at the place where the needle must have been passing some solution into his body. His mum smiled at us, and left with Mr Marshall, saying that she was going to buy some fruit.

Ivo looked at the drip, smiled, and shook his head.

'Thanks for coming, guys,' he said, tears brimming.

'Oh, God, I knew this would happen,' Georgie burst out, starting to cry herself. 'What is it, Ivo?' she asked, between sobs. 'Why are you here?'

Ivo looked at our worried faces.

'Nothing,' he replied, shaking his head. There was a silence. Rahul picked up a clipboard at the end of his bed.

'You going to tell us, Ivo, or am I going to have to find out for myself?' he asked, adjusting his glasses.

'Well, they're doing a few tests and stuff and they did a bit of surgery too. I've just got to stay here a few days till things settle down.'

Georgie recovered, blew her nose, perched herself on the end of the bed and said, 'Ivo, I want to tell you that you're the number one keeper in our team, and that as soon as you're back you're going straight to the keeper's spot. Okay?'

'Sure, George. You bet.'

'Yep. If that doesn't happen, this team is going to lose both its female players.'

'Both?' I asked, looking at her.

'Yep,' she said. 'Absadoodle.'

'Well, I don't think I'll be pushing for selection for a few weeks yet,' said Ivo.

We told him about the game against St Mary's and me running Craven out.

I caught Georgie's eye and nodded to the door. She shook her head.

'I'm just going to duck out for a moment, okay, guys?'

I didn't wait for a reply. I walked over to the nurses' area and asked the man there where Jim Oldfield was. He clicked his mouse and looked at his screen.

'Room 225. Up another floor. Are you a relative?'

'I'm sort of his godson. My dad's just gone to buy some fruit,' I added, as an afterthought.

He shrugged, and went back to his work.

* * *

I tapped on the door. There was no reply. I eased it open and poked my head around the corner. There were two beds. Two old men lay asleep. Jim was by the window. There was a cricket book on his bedside table.

I walked over and looked down at him. He lay very still. For a panic-stricken moment I thought he was dead.

Then he opened his eyes.

'It's all right, Toby. I'm a light sleeper,' he whispered, smiling. 'It was good of you to come.' He sounded as though he was expecting me.

'That's okay, Mr Oldfield.'

He turned his head towards me. 'Jim,' he said. 'Remember?'

'Yes. Jim. Of course. I've travelled again,' I blurted out. 'I know I shouldn't have, but I did. And I took Rahul with me to India. It was scary. It was —'

'Ssh,' Jim whispered, looking over at the other person. 'I know you did, Toby. And I hope you have learned a valuable lesson. Those you carry are prone to go against your will. Against the will of the poem. Did this boy want to stay? Did he make it hard for you?'

'Yes,' I whispered back, 'he did. It was like he was destined to be there or something.'

'What did you say his name was?'

'Rahul.'

'Of Indian descent?'

'Yes,' I replied.

'Then he had other ties that are very hard to work

94

against. He is one who perhaps should not travel with you, Toby.'

I had heaps of questions to ask Jim, but now that I was here they stuck in my throat.

'Why are you here, Jim? Are you okay?'

'My heart is not what it used to be, and it's playing up just at the time when a certain special boy has come into my life,' he replied.

'Do you mean me?' I asked. 'I should never have walked into that library.'

'Ah, but you had to. Don't you see?'

I didn't. Not one bit.

'Jim, are you in danger?' I asked, fearing his answer.

'Not while I'm here, Toby. No, not at all,' he added, sensing my anxiety.

'But, why did I —'

A nurse walked in and started shooing me off as if I were a dog or something.

'Please,' Jim protested, rising slightly from his pillows. 'He is my only family.' He slumped back down again.

'And where's your mother?' the nurse asked me as she straightened Jim's bedclothes.

'Dad's just out buying some fruit,' I told her. I might as well have just announced the fact over the loudspeaker system. I seemed to be telling everyone what Ivo's dad was doing.

'Right, then. Visiting time's over. You can come back tomorrow.'

Jim reached out a hand. It was dry and lumpy, with veins and other marks. I reached over and took it. He clasped my hands in his.

'Re-read the poem tonight, Toby. Promise me you will do that?'

'I'll read it, Jim. I promise,' I said quietly.

He lay back and sighed. He looked content. Then he mumbled something. I didn't quite catch what he said.

'Pardon? What was that?'

But he just smiled, and shook his head.

I stayed a moment longer, looking at his wrinkled, gentle face. Then I turned around and left.

Jack Gregory, playing for Australia, holds the record for the most catches (by a non-wicket keeper) taken in a series. He took 15 catches during the five matches Australia played against England in 1921.

12 The Visit

I was running late for the game and this time it was Dad who was sitting in the car waiting for me. I couldn't find my gloves. Nat had been belting some forehands at me and I'd put them on to protect my fingers. I eventually found them outside, under the trampoline. There were a few teeth marks in the soft, padded bits that go over the fingers but they were okay.

I grabbed the gloves and raced out to the car.

'You going to use anything else to bat with?' Dad asked, as I slammed the door and started to buckle up.

'What?' I said, looking at him blankly.

'Your cricket bag!'

'Oh yeah!'

Dad just chuckled to himself and turned the radio up as I raced back inside.

97

As expected, Scott Craven denied being online the night before last.

'Why would I want to do that stupid chat stuff? With you?' he scoffed, spinning his bat through his hands. Jay wasn't talking to anyone.

It was much cooler this Saturday. We jogged out for a warm-up, with Mr Pasquali hitting us some short, and then longer catches. No one was really too concerned about defending such a huge total. The highest score we'd made was 271, and with Scott measuring out his long run, I didn't think there was any way St Mary's would get near it.

Once again Scott was in the action, taking three wickets himself and a catch at point. I stood next to Ally in first slip, answering all her questions and giving her hints about what to do after the ball had been played. She certainly seemed to be picking it up quickly.

I was brought on to bowl when they were 5 for 72. My first two overs were maidens. Scott Craven was itching to get back on and clean up the rest of the batting.

'One more over,' Jono said to me, 'or two, if you get a wicket.' I nodded. I bowled the first three balls a bit slower, pitching them just outside off-stump, trying to entice the batter to come out of his crease. Ally had moved forwards and was standing just behind the stumps — as she would for a spin bowler. The batter pushed forwards again on the third ball, but only managed to pad it back down the pitch. I looked at Ally, then pointed out to the covers.

'You want me to move or what?' Scott yelled. 'Whaddya pointing at me for?' I waved for him to come in a few metres. He walked in about five, looking at Jono, our captain, as he did so. Jono nodded.

I got to the end of my run-up, looked up, and nodded at Ally. She nodded back. I noticed her move, just slightly, towards the leg side.

But the ball, which was meant to race down the leg side, ended up more on middle and leg-stump. Again the batter pushed forwards, but in trying to turn the ball to the leg side, it spooned out to short cover, having caught a leading edge. Scott raced in a couple of metres and dived forwards to take the catch.

I clapped my hands, shrugged my shoulders at Ally and walked over to Scott.

'Nice work, Toby,' Jono said to me. 'You can take over all fielding positions!'

'Great catch,' I said to Scott. He tossed the ball back to me with a look that was almost friendly. I think he was impressed with my decision to move him in.

'We won't tell anyone about TLT yet, eh, Toby?' Ally laughed at the end of the over.

'No, maybe not,' I replied.

I got my extra over, and was whacked for two fours and two singles. Still, the wicket was worth it.

We won by 111 runs. Before we left, Mr Pasquali reminded us that next week's game, a one-dayer against the Scorpions, the top team on the ladder, was the big one.

I caught up with Jay as he was walking across to his family's car.

'Hello, Jay!'

'Hi,' he said, in a flat voice.

I got straight to the point.

'Jay, you shouldn't have given Scott your ID for CROC. I reckon —'

'I couldn't help it. He threatened me. He said he was going to hurt you big time because of the run-out if I didn't tell him what was going on, you know, with all the stuff happening.'

'So you gave him your ID and told him to find out for himself?' I said.

'I was protecting you, okay!' he said, sounding annoyed.

'Okay. Fair enough. I would've probably done the same thing too.'

'I know there's something weird going on, that's all.'

'Yeah, but do you want to know about it?' I asked.

Jay didn't reply.

'Were you in CROC last night?' I asked him, my voice quieter.

'Nope. I couldn't get on. Craven must have been waiting for you guys for ages. What happened?'

'He can't spell like you can.'

Jay looked up at last and smiled.

'I was kind of hoping something like that might happen,' he said. 'Are you going to tell me what this is all about?'

I felt a bit bad that Jay didn't know, like Rahul or Georgie and even Jimbo, and I at least owed him an explanation. After all, he was the one that I'd dragged back to the library during the excursion.

'Of course. Come round this arvo and I'll tell you then. I've also been thinking for a while about going to visit Jimbo, you want to do that?'

'Jimbo?' He looked surprised. 'You sure?'

'Yeah, why?'

'I dunno. It's just, well, I don't reckon Jimbo would have many visitors.' Jay looked anxious.

'Well, maybe we'll be the first. Okay?'

'Yeah, okay.'

But he didn't sound convinced.

We got there about mid-afternoon. I was hoping they'd be watching the one-dayer on TV. But then I remembered that Jimbo's Saturdays were reserved for garage cleaning.

Jimbo's dad met us at the door.

'Yes?' he asked. He was holding a pair of glasses in his hands and rubbing his eyes.

'Um, is Jimbo in?' I asked.

'He's busy right now. Sorry.' He started to close the door.

'Well could we come back later?' I tried to sound cheerful. I didn't feel it.

Another voice, maybe his mum's, was calling out somewhere inside the house.

'Who is it?'

'We were just wondering whether we could see Jimbo,' I called into the darkness.

We stood there for a moment, a bit confused.

'Here to see Jimbo, did you say?' Jimbo's mum stood at the door wearing a pair of jeans and a shirt way too big for her. She looked sort of neat and trendy. She had a mobile phone in one hand, and it was pressed to her stomach. She was obviously on a call. She was smiling.

Boy, this was like major security.

'We're not armed,' Jay whispered under his breath. I nudged him.

Jimbo's mum came out onto the porch and looked at us closely, as if she'd never seen kids before.

'Well you'd better come in,' she said finally.

'He's not busy?' Jay asked, with a trace of sarcasm.

'Jimbo? He's always busy. Jimbo! There are some friends here to see you. Jimbo!' she called.

The first thing I noticed, lying in the hallway, was a cricket kit, an old-looking one, along with a whole range of other stuff, lined up along the walls.

Jimbo's dad saw me looking at the stuff and said, 'Garage sale. We're getting rid of a whole pile of junk.' He kicked the kit. Jimbo had also appeared. He looked surprised to see us.

'Toby. Jay. Hi there.'

'Hi, Jimbo.'

'You can't be interested in that old stuff,' his dad said, seeing me still staring at the old off-white cricket bag. The initials R.T. could just be made out on the front.

'Come through,' said Jimbo. We walked up a wide flight of stairs and into his bedroom. It was massive. It was like his own living room with a huge bed, a desk, computer with all the attachments, bookcases stacked with books and a couple of big, wooden chests. Probably filled with interesting stuff. He noticed me looking around.

'I guess being an only child has its benefits,' he smiled. 'So, what brings you two here?'

'Well, actually, I suppose I, well ... we, really want to know why you can't play in the cricket team.'

'Even though you can make it to training,' Jay added.

Jimbo didn't speak.

'Well, most nights you can make it to training,' I said.

'Yeah, except for Thursday night,' said Jay. We were blabbering.

Jimbo sat on the bed, picked up a cricket ball and started spinning it in the air. He looked at the door, raised his eyes and nodded in that direction. I went over and closed it.

'And, if I tell you, then you'll go?' he asked us.

'Sure,' I said. 'You really don't want us here, do you?'

'Do you want to be here?'

'Yes. We came to see you,' I replied.

He paused for a moment, then caught the ball and held it.

'Well, the reason I don't play is that my father won't let me. I'm allowed to train three nights a fortnight, but I'm not allowed to play in any games.'

I was shocked.

'Why?' Jay asked.

Jimbo shrugged and shook his head. 'Dad had a bad experience playing the game himself. It turned him off. He vowed on that day that he would never play again. It looks like his vow has extended to me.'

'But can't you tell him that his problems are nothing to do with you? This is your life. What the —'

Jimbo was looking at me impatiently.

'It's not your problem, Toby, but thanks for your concern.' He was about to say something else, then stopped.

'What?' Jay asked.

'Well, since you're both so interested, there is one other factor. I won't mention any names, but someone you know is also involved, indirectly.'

Jimbo wasn't making sense.

'Come again?' I said.

'Dad played against one of the fathers of the current team,' he told us.

'And that was his bad experience?' I asked.

'You'd better go, guys. I've got heaps to do.'

'But it's Saturday, Jimbo!' exclaimed Jay, struggling to stay calm.

'Unless it's your cricket project,' I offered.

'No such luck. Can't do that at home, either.'

'Sounds like cricket doesn't get much of a look in at your house,' I said.

'So how come you've got a cricket ball in your hand?' Jay asked.

'Mr Pasquali lent it to me one night after practice. Dad doesn't know I've got it.'

'C'mon, let's go,' Jay said, walking towards the door.

'Well, see you round, Jimbo,' I called.

'You will. See ya, guys.'

'Weird,' Jay muttered. I was inclined to agree with him, and wondered what it was all about.

'There's something sort of different about Jimbo, isn't there?' Jay said to me as we grabbed our bikes.

'I like him, but I know what you mean. I wish there was something we could do, you know, to get him to play cricket with us.'

'What, like talk to his dad?'

'Dunno. Maybe. I wonder if his dad knows just how awesome a cricketer Jimbo is.'

'My dad would be over the moon if I was even half as good,' Jay said, racing off ahead of me.

I clipped my helmet on and pedalled after him.

13 The Garage

Sunday — morning

GEORGIE came round the next day. She found me out in the garage, earning a bit of pocket money by cleaning the place up. I had stumbled across a box full of Dad's books, and when she walked in I had just pulled out the find of the century — a couple of old *Wisden*s.

I looked up sharply as her shadow loomed over me. It was a spooky moment, especially as I was about to open one of the *Wisden*s.

'You can't keep your hands off those old books,' she said, striding into the dimness.

'Look!' I said, holding up another three books.

'Great! Let's spend the rest of the afternoon sitting here in the dust reading them.'

'Really? You mean it?' Then I saw her face. She didn't mean it.

'Anyway,' she went on, 'your dad said I'm not to

distract you from the cleaning, and since I'm not too keen on helping, I'm going inside to write.'

'Okay. We'll make a new CROC site when I come in. Won't be long.'

'Cool,' she called as she slipped away.

I settled myself comfortably on the box of books, and opened the *Wisden* at the contents page. I knew what I was searching for. I had noticed the year when Jim had pulled down the *Wisden* to search for Dad's game. It was the obvious choice and a fantastic chance to try another time travel trip.

Would it work from the garage? Could I use *Wisden*s that weren't from the MCC library?

I searched down until I came to a line that said Overseas Domestic Cricket. It was getting easier for me to navigate my way through the sections, trying to focus on the team names when they appeared.

Soon I sensed the rushing, swirling noises in my head as the names of the teams became clear. I had to turn away quickly, because the game turned out to be a Victoria–Western Australia match. A few pages on, though, it happened. The words Victoria and South Australia dissolved, then became clearer. I glanced down the page. There was a paragraph of writing and then the scorecard itself. It was impossible to focus on. The writing was small and the blur was making my eyes sore.

I dragged my eyes back to the top of the page. I was getting better at it. The whooshing in my head suddenly went quiet. I opened my eyes. There was a shout from somewhere to my left.

I was sitting in an empty part of one of the huge stands at the MCG. For a moment I just sat, hardly daring to breathe. The shout I'd heard was from a man who, along with a sprinkling of spectators around the ground, was applauding the fact that someone had just taken a wicket.

I looked up at the scoreboard. It wasn't the electronic one I was used to. It was an enormous black box with all the players' names. My eyes raced across it looking for Jones. And there it was: P. Jones. There were no numbers next to his name, as there were with some of the others. Dad hadn't had a bowl yet.

Then the realisation of where I was and who I was looking at hit me like a train. I wanted to jump and scream 'Dad!' and run out and say, 'Hi!'. It was the weirdest feeling to be looking at my dad, and yet he wasn't my dad. Not yet, anyway.

I walked down to the fence. It was hard to tell who Dad was. I could rule out the bowler and keeper. I should have asked him what position he fielded in. Maybe he would have forgotten. Maybe I'd be able to jog his memory when I saw him next.

I wasn't nervous any more. As long as I travelled alone, it seemed easy enough to return. So I thought I would spend a bit longer here, exploring, and at least getting a good look at Dad, the cricketer.

And then I had another thought. Why not go and look at the old library while I was here?

I settled down to watch the match. I noticed that a little light went on next to the player's name when he fielded the ball. It took a few overs, and I had eliminated most of the players by their build and looks anyway, but finally, out at mid-on, Dad stopped a full-blooded on-drive. He didn't field it cleanly, and he spent the next few minutes shaking and looking at his hand. He got a good clap from his team-mates. I clapped pretty hard too.

'Way to go, Dad!' I yelled, before I'd had time to think about how stupid I was for saying it. A couple of heads turned to look at me.

A short time later the players left the field for a break. It was the perfect opportunity for me to visit the library. I had to leave the stand and walk around outside the ground itself, to get to the other side.

I used the little ticket I was given to get back into the ground, but a man wearing a blue coat stopped me from going into the Members' section.

He was staring at me. Or, more exactly, at my shorts.

'You'll be pulling them up then, young feller?' he said, frowning slightly.

I gave them a tug, but they slipped straight back down again. I took my baseball cap off before he made a comment about that too.

'Hand-me-downs, eh?' he chuckled. 'You need a belt, lad.'

'My dad's playing,' I explained to him, trying to change the subject.

'Oh, is he? And who might that be?'

'Peter Jones,' I told him. 'He asked me to take a message to Jim Oldfield — in the library,' I added, as an afterthought.

'Well, be quick about it,' he said. The mention of Jim's name seemed to work like magic, even back in this time.

I raced off before he had time to do some quick mental sums and realise that Dad would have to have been about 12 when I was born. Maybe the guy wasn't a keen cricket fan.

The place was only half the size it was the last time I was here. It still felt the same, though. The secret door was still there, and the floorboards creaked as I made my way up the stairs and over to the oval table. I thought there was a whole row of *Wisden*s missing — until I realised that they hadn't been published yet!

I got that shivery, goose-bumpy feeling again as I thought of just where, and when, I was. I wanted to tell someone that P. Jones would make 23 and not take a wicket, and that the Vics would win.

But the lines of the poem, some of them now locked in my memory, reminded me of the dangers of doing that.

> *And never speak and never boast,*
> *And never taunt, nor ever toast ...*

So I walked quietly across the room and spoke to a man standing by a large desk near the card file.

'Is Jim Oldfield around?'

'He's gone to lunch, young feller. Are you his grandson?'

'No.'

'I think he said that he wasn't coming back in this afternoon, too,' the man added. 'Can I give him a message?'

'No, it's okay. Just say that Toby called.'

'Toby. All right then.'

I took a last look at the *Wisden*s and headed back out.

I spent another 15 minutes soaking up the atmosphere of a sunny afternoon, watching the cricket. This time I found a seat a bit further back from the oval itself. I couldn't take my eyes off Dad. He wasn't getting to do much, but every time he fielded the ball I clapped loudly. One time he misfielded. The ball bounced from his shin and the batters stole a run. I felt awful.

I wanted to shout, 'Head up, Dad!', the way he sometimes shouted to me while I was playing sport. Now he was rubbing his shin. No one else was paying him any attention, but I couldn't focus on anyone else.

I watched a couple more overs, then suddenly realised that I had other things I should be doing. I was supposed to be in our garage cleaning it out!

I found a quiet spot — away from the few spectators sprinkled around where I had been sitting — and reeled off a couple of lines of the poem.

Suddenly I was back home. The *Wisden* book I had used was closed and back in its box. For a moment I was worried that somehow time itself had done something weird, and I had returned a day later, or even a week. I glanced at my watch. It was five past five. I raced inside, belted through the kitchen and into the living room. Georgie was watching TV and Dad was reading.

My first thought when I saw Dad was to ask him if his shin still hurt, but I stopped myself just in time. Instead I just stared at him. He wasn't just any old dad — he had just been playing cricket at the MCG!

'Dad!' I called.

He looked up, a bit surprised by the excitement in my voice.

'Hi!' Now Dad and Georgie were both looking at me. 'Sorry I've been so long!' I blurted.

They seemed baffled.

'We've missed you terribly, haven't we Georgie?'

'Oh, terribly,' she said.

'I hear you found some cricket books out there,' Dad remarked. 'They're not very interesting, you know.'

'Oh, I wouldn't say that,' I replied.

The highest number of catches taken by a wicket keeper in a Test match happened in November 1995, when Jack Russell, playing for England against South Africa, took 11 catches. Bob Taylor (England) and Adam Gilchrist (Australia) have each taken 10 catches in a Test match.

14 The Agreement

RAHUL was fired up about doing the Madras Test for his cricket assignment and, amazingly, had arranged a couple of interviews, as we'd discussed. The teachers were impressed too. They said that it would 'add another dimension to his assignment', whatever that meant.

'I guess that should give you all you need, Rahul,' I said to him, hoping that he had lost interest in getting back to India. No such luck.

'Toby, I have an opportunity to see cricket in my own country. You cannot possibly not take me back. Just once more, I say. Please?'

I shook my head. 'I can't. Jim said something about how tricky it is to take someone with you. How they can make it hard by getting too involved.'

But Rahul wouldn't give up. After he had interviewed Dean Jones, he became even more insistent.

113

'Toby, you wouldn't believe how Dean Jones suffered. I talked to him on the phone.'

'Yeah? What'd he say?'

'That he lost seven kilos from the heat and humidity and that it took him two months to put it back on.'

'Phew, must have been hot.'

'Hot! It was over 40°C, with the humidity at 90 per cent. He couldn't keep any fluid down, but he kept on batting and batting. All through the day. When he was on 170, he told Allan Border, who was batting with him, that he'd had enough. That he was really sick.'

Rahul paused, shaking his head.

'And?'

'Do you know what Border said to him?'

'Course I don't. What did he say?'

'He said, "Okay, I'll get someone tougher to come in."'

'But didn't Dean Jones make over 200?'

'That's just it. He got the message. He stayed out there.'

Rahul was waving around a wad of notes he'd obviously scrawled during his phone conversation with Dean Jones.

'I need to get my notes in order, Toby. I'll tell you more tomorrow.'

Rahul caught up with me the next day, during lunchtime. He was out of control with excitement.

'Toby, I've been thinking carefully about what you

said. And it's true. When we went to Chennai I was just a bit overcome by the whole thing. But I know what to expect now. And I want to give you this.' Rahul pulled a piece of paper out of his pocket and unfolded it. It was a list of points. 'Go on, read it!' he said excitedly.

- Toby is to decide when to do the travel, both to and from Chennai.
- I will not question his decisions.
- Toby is to carry this piece of paper with him while we are in Chennai.
- I will never ask to go again.
- I will tell Scott Craven everything I know about the time travel if I do not go once more.

Signed _____ (Rahul) _____ (Toby)

He looked at me expectantly.

'You wouldn't tell Scott Craven, Rahul?' It was more a statement than a question, but it didn't come out that way.

'Yes, I would. I'm very sorry but I would. This is the opportunity of a lifetime for me. And for you, of course. You can't go to India on your own.'

'Why can't I?'

'Well, for one, you would get lost. You would need someone to help you with the language. With dealing with all the weird situations that can arise in a place like India.'

'Maybe I don't want to go to India.'

'You know what? Dean Jones made 210 for the Aussies. He was throwing up on the field. He was totally exhausted. He was cramping. But he kept on going and going and going. When they finally got him out, he was taken to hospital. Or so they say. But was he? Or is it just a big myth? We can be the first to find out. As soon as I see Dean Jones lying in a hospital bed, then we can come straight home.'

'But didn't you ask him?'

Rahul looked up.

'He has very little memory of what happened after he was out.'

'Anyway, you didn't write that bit about coming straight home on your little piece of paper here,' I said, waving it in his face.

He grabbed the paper from me, pulled a pen from his shirt pocket, and squeezed in another sentence.

As soon as I have seen Dean Jones in hospital,
we can leave.

'No.' As soon as I said it I knew I didn't really mean it. I think Rahul did too.

'What did you say?' he asked, flabbergasted.

'Oh, well, okay,' I said, shaking my head. I thought for a moment that he was about to hug me. Instead he stuck out his hand. I took it.

'You won't regret this. I promise.'

We decided that I would stay the night at Rahul's

on Sunday. Dad would drive me over to his place late in the afternoon. We would say that we wanted to put in a good couple of hours on our cricket projects as Mr Pasquali would be checking on our progress on Monday morning. We felt sure there wouldn't be a problem.

'You're lucky, Rahul. I found some old *Wisden*s in Dad's garage last weekend. I'm pretty sure he had the 1988 one.'

'Fantastic. You won't forget it, will you?'

'I'll try not to.'

Monday — afternoon

Nat had set the hallway up for a monster game of indoor cricket. She had bundled together 25 pairs of socks, all different shapes, sizes and colours. The game was simple, but heaps of fun. She would throw the socks at me as hard as she could. The wicket was an open door behind me. I had to belt the socks with the bat. The scoring was simple.

○ *Side wall*   *1 run*
○ *Side wall on the full*   *2 runs*
○ *Back wall*   *4 runs*
○ *Back wall on the full*   *6 runs*
○ *Caught out by Nat, or bowled*   *lose 10 runs*

Having 25 pairs of socks was great — 25 deliveries. It meant she had raided all available drawers in the house and that I was a good chance to make my 50 —

as long as Mum didn't catch us first. If I got my 50 I would definitely be giving Nat a bat.

'Nat, you want a hit?' I asked her. I'd made 67, but had been bowled once and caught once. I was happy with 47.

'Only if you bowl under-arm.'

'No probs.' We gathered up the socks and I thought of Ally, the catcher in softball, as I pinged the socks at Nat, who was swinging the bat like a softballer.

After dinner I put through a call to Ivo at the hospital. He sounded pretty flat.

'How are you feeling, Ivo?'

'I've been better. But Mum says I'm over the worst.'

'So will you be in there long?'

'Probably another couple of days. I've got some internal bleeding, which they want to monitor or something. They had to operate too.'

I didn't want to ask about the actual crash. I was assuming that no one else was hurt.

'Watch out for driveways, Toby.' Ivo's voice was quiet.

'You were on your bike?'

'Yup. Remember that day in the gym when I had that headache?'

I nodded.

'I was riding home and could hardly see, my headache was so bad, then this car rammed into me.'

'Geez. They probably weren't even looking.'

'I think we both weren't.' There was a pause.

'The cricket's going well. We've got a one-dayer coming up this weekend.'

'Oh, cool. They're the best, aren't they? When you can go home with a result. Hang on.' I heard Ivo talking to someone. 'I'd better go, Toby. Thanks for ringing.'

I liked Ivo. And I felt sorry for him, stuck in a hospital bed. Still, it sounded as if it wouldn't be too long before he was back with us playing cricket. I wondered if Ally would be willing to give up her wicket keeping to him.

I rang the hospital again and this time asked for Jim, but he wasn't available to talk.

'Is he okay?' I asked.

'Who's calling?' said a bossy voice.

'His grandson,' I lied.

'Well, you ask your mum or dad to ring.'

Maybe it was time to try a new one. A new fib, that is.

Wednesday — afternoon

We had our library session on Wednesday. Rahul told us all, including Mr Pasquali, more about his interviews. The one with Dean Jones had been by phone. Even Scott Craven was listening, though he pretended to be working. Gavin Bourke was so interested that he started asking a question — before Scott gave him a not-so-gentle whack in the ribs.

'Go on, Gavin. That sounded like a good question,' said Mr Pasquali, giving Scott a bit of a warning look.

'Well, he said that you'd actually have to be there to get a feel for the heat.' Rahul was looking at me, pointedly. 'He said it was just shocking. And smelly too. There must have been some sort of sewerage place, nearby.' Everyone was saying 'yuk' and 'gross' and wrinkling their noses.

'It was gross!' I said, without thinking. 'I mean, it would have been,' I stammered. 'Rahul was telling me about it earlier.' I felt my face going red.

I had brought Dad's copy of the 1988 *Wisden* to school. At the end of the library session I ducked over to the photocopier and copied the page describing the tied Test match. The scorecard for the game was on the second page.

I didn't know what to expect when the sheets came out, but I was relieved to find that I could read them without a problem. The writing and numbers were clear and still. It must be the *Wisden* book itself that was the trigger for the time travel.

I folded the pages and put them in my pocket. I would practise with those, training my eyes to go straight to the correct spot. Hadn't Jim said that, with practice, you could go to any specific part of a game by looking at the relevant section of the scorecard?

Rahul's interview with Mr Bright, as he called him, was great too.

'Poor Ray Bright,' said Rahul. 'You know, he was very, very sick too, just like Dean Jones. He almost didn't play. He was so relieved when Australia won the toss and batted. It meant he didn't have to go out into the field.'

'So he just watched from the comfort of the dressing room?' I asked.

'Comfort? Oh, no. He lay on a table all day with wet towels on him. He doesn't remember anything about that first day until the captain, Allan Border, came up to him with about half an hour to go and said, "You're night watchy."'

'Night what?' someone asked. Everyone was leaning forwards, listening to Rahul.

'Night watchy. Night watchman. You come out if a wicket falls close to the end of play to protect the batters up the order.'

'Sounds stupid to me,' said Scott.

Rahul looked at him. 'Well that's what they did. And sure enough, a wicket fell and poor Ray Bright had to struggle off his sick bed — having eaten nothing all day — and walk out into 40°C heat to face the Indian bowlers.'

There was a pause.

'Well?' I asked.

'It will all be revealed in my talk,' Rahul said, smiling.

'Yeah, but what happened to Bright?' Gavin asked.

'You'll hear it all when I present my assignment,' said Rahul with a cheeky grin. There were a few groans of disappointment. 'It'll be just as if I was really there,' he added.

I gave him a look. He just shrugged and smiled.

In a 1903 game between Victoria and Queensland, Victoria used only two bowlers in each innings. In the first, Saunders 6/57 and Collins 4/55 took all the Queensland wickets. In the second, two different bowlers grabbed all 10 wickets (Armstrong 4/13 and Laver 6/17).

15 The Proof

Thursday — morning

BEFORE school started the next day, Jimbo approached me when I was talking to Ally, Jay and Georgie.

'Hey, Jimbo,' I said.

'Toby, can I ask you something?'

I moved away from the others and Jimbo followed.

'I've been thinking a bit about our chat the other day. I want to find out some more about what happened the day my father decided to walk away from cricket, and I thought you might be able to help me.'

'Oh,' I was a bit shocked. Jimbo was the sort of guy who never asked for anything. 'How could I do that?' I asked.

'All I know is that it happened on his birthday, which is the same day as the Boxing Day Test match. And I've also been hearing some pretty amazing things about some *Wisden* books and your ability to time travel from a library.'

'You have?' I asked, surprised.

'Yes, from Rahul, and he isn't the sort of guy to make up stuff like that.'

'Rahul told you?' I was stunned.

'Not as such. But like I said, I've heard things. You know how you do.'

I wasn't exactly sure what he meant, but somehow, if there was anyone who would know what was going on without appearing to — or even seeming interested — it was probably Jimbo.

'Anyway, I rang up my grandfather and found out that Dad's game wasn't far from the MCG itself. It was in a big park where there are heaps of ovals and grounds.'

'Hmm. So we go back to the Test match, then try and get to the ground where your dad is playing. And then what?' Two lines from the poem ran through my mind.

> *Don't meddle, don't talk, nor interfere*
> *With the lives of people you venture near.*

'Nothing. I just want to see and understand for myself why my father has made this decision. Then maybe I can accept it and we can get on better.'

I thought of Rahul and his reaction to the Madras Test.

'Jimbo, strange things happen when you travel through time. You sort of lose control. You might do something stupid. If you interfere with the past it can change things and stuff up the present.'

Jimbo looked at me hard. 'I can be trusted, Toby.'

Jimbo rang his mum during lunchtime. He'd said she was a safer bet for getting permission for him to come round to my place.

'Yeah?' I asked as he put the phone down.

He nodded.

'Yeah. I think she was actually pretty pleased. Dad's going to pick me up at nine o'clock. He's working late. I think that helped. Should you ring up your parents?'

'Nah, it'll be fine. I'm always bringing home friends. They're used to it.'

I introduced Jimbo to Mum and Nat after school when they collected me. Mum seemed pleased that I was bringing home a new friend. She celebrated by stopping off for ice-creams on the way home.

Nat had taken a fancy to Jimbo right from the outset, and I had to wait till she had given him the full tour of the house before we could get upstairs and onto the computer.

'Can we do corridor cricket?' Nat whispered to me at my bedroom door. 'I'm gonna get every pair of socks in the house — you'll see.'

'Okay, Nat, but later, okay?'

We logged into the best site on cricket that I knew. I had it bookmarked and often went there myself to check up on various games, especially the ones that Dad spoke about.

Every game — Test match, World Cup, one-day international and any other official first-class game — was listed. Most of them had full scorecards and match reports and some of the later ones even had a commentary so you could read what happened, ball by ball.

'Jimbo, what year did your grandpa say for that game with your dad?'

'Not sure, but it was early '80s and the Boxing Day Test was an Ashes one, which means —'

'Yep. Australia–England,' I said, excitedly. I scrolled down, searching for the December Tests played in Australia. I knew that 1982 was an Ashes series; since England only came out every four years, it would have to be that year.

'Oh, my God, Jimbo.'

'What?'

'It's the 1982 Boxing Test match. The one that Border and Thomson had their huge last-wicket partnership and nearly won the game for Australia. Better still, Dad's got the *Wisden* down there in the garage.'

'What do you mean?'

'The *Wisden*. It's what we need to get there. And the exact game is down there, in the 1984 *Wisden*!'

We spent the next 10 minutes looking over the scorecard. I told Jimbo the story about the match that I still loved having Dad tell me.

I was just up to the final morning when Dad called us down for dinner.

'No worries. I'll get him to finish the story. He won't mind.'

We raced downstairs and into the kitchen. Dad told the story during dinner. He went a bit overboard when he got to the part about everyone stopping what they were doing to listen and watch the game. This time he had parliament stopping and trains and buses coming to a complete standstill as the whole country tuned into those fateful last minutes.

After dinner — and a quick game of corridor cricket — we raced back upstairs.

'Okay, here's the plan. We're going to head out to play some cricket in the nets. On the way we grab the street directory from the car —'

'And the *Wisden* book from the garage?' Jimbo added.

'And the *Wisden* book from the garage. No! We'll go to the garage. Let's go from there.'

Jimbo nodded excitedly. In fact, it was the most excited I'd ever seen him.

'You are so going to like this,' I told him.

'It'll be the best nets session I've ever had!'

I gathered up some loose change from my desk and we headed out, saying we were going for a hit in the nets at the oval across the road.

'You expecting that someone has left all the gear there for you, too?' Dad asked as we headed out the front door.

But Jimbo was a quick thinker. 'I left my kit down in your garage, Mr Jones, we're going to take that.'

'Fair enough. You want an extra bowler?'

We stood there shuffling our feet.

'Then again, maybe I'll clean up the kitchen first.'

'Okay, Dad.' I felt a bit bad. Dad loved a hit. I'd make it up to him. We'd have a massive hit over the weekend.

A few minutes later the two of us were standing in the garage. Jimbo was holding the street directory, and I was holding the *Wisden*.

'Here Jimbo. You find the Boxing Day Test match. Check the contents page.' I passed him the *Wisden* and took the directory from him. I found the MCG and looked around for some green patches — ovals where his dad might have played.

'Did your grandfather have a name for these ovals, Jimbo?'

'Not that I recall. He just said that there were stacks of ovals, for rugby and hockey and soccer. Footy, and of course, cricket. Oh, and they were next to a hospital. A hospital that had — probably still has — a helicopter service. You know, for emergencies.'

'Yep, I know.' Jimbo heard the excitement in my voice. 'I know exactly, I think.'

I flicked to the next page.

'Got it. I reckon we'll just take this with us,' I said to Jimbo, holding the open page to him.

'Here we go, England in Australia and New Zealand. Page 879.' Jimbo flicked through the book.

'Toby, you can get to any of these games? And this is just one *Wisden*!'

'Yep. I think so. As long as there's a scorecard for me to look at.'

Jimbo was shaking his head.

'This is just crazy.' He was searching for the right page. 'What Test match was it?'

'The fourth.'

'Here we go. Pages 898 and 899. This is it.'

'Okay, let's swap again.' We passed the books back.

'What happens to the *Wisden*? Does it come with us?'

'No, it sort of just falls to the ground.' For the first time, Jimbo began to look a bit nervous.

'You okay?'

'Yep — let's do it.'

'Here, grab my hand.' Jimbo took it. We sat down on the floor of the garage, next to the open kit.

I looked at the page of the *Wisden*. I must have been getting better at it, because almost straight away the shifting swirl of names and numbers had settled. Soon I saw a Cook, then a Fowler.

'Cook, Cook,' I said, slowly and clearly.

'Now, Jimbo,' I whispered as the familiar sound of rushing air and pressure surged through me.

A second later we were standing outside the MCG. I'm not quite sure how we managed to be outside the ground, but it was a good place to be. I had focused hard on the names of the first few English players on the *Wisden* page, and as I sensed the movement, kept my eyes away from the numbers. Even then, we had no idea how long it would take to get to the ground and then how long before whatever happened to Jimbo's father actually happened.

Jimbo looked totally stunned.

'Don't ask,' I said. 'Just trust me. It works. We've just got to blend in.' I looked at him. He was wearing runners that looked three sizes too big, the laces were undone, his cap was on back to front and his shorts went down below his knees.

'Blend in as best we can,' I added, spinning my cap the correct way. Jimbo's mouth hadn't closed.

We must have been the only two people walking away from the game. It was a beautiful sunny day and hordes of people with cheerful faces and huge Eskies were streaming towards the ground. Tight T-shirts, tight shorts, small white towelling hats, moustaches and thongs were everywhere. I felt as if I was from another planet, especially as I was walking away from the start of a Boxing Day Test match.

I spotted a line of taxis dropping people off.

'C'mon, Jimbo.'

'Yep. Just don't leave my sight, Toby. You hear?'

'I won't.'

It proved easier than we thought and we didn't

need the directory. We climbed into the back seat of a taxi, gave the driver the name of the park and took off.

The cab driver's radio was blaring out a song I'd heard on one of those radio stations that play 'Golden Oldies' music.

'I know this song,' I said to the driver.

'"Eye of the Tiger"? Of course you do — it's on the radio all the time.' He smiled.

I reached into my pocket and pulled out some coins.

'Seven dollars will do you,' said the driver. I handed over the coins. The driver grunted.

'Well you can keep your foreign coin. That's no good to me.' He tossed a two-dollar coin back.

I opened my mouth, then closed it again quickly. He passed me back a few more coins.

We jumped out of the taxi and headed across the grass towards the first of the cricket games being played.

'Hope none of those coins you have were made in the 1990s,' Jimbo whispered to me. I hadn't thought of checking. But it was unlikely the taxi driver would check himself. Still, it was a mistake. To have a coin floating around for 10 years before it had actually been made was something Jim would not be impressed with.

Jimbo had recovered well during the car trip, pointing out a few landmarks on the way that hadn't changed. I think he was trying to convince himself that he wasn't actually 20 years back in time.

There were a number of games going on, but it didn't take us long to find the correct game just by asking for Jimbo's father's team. I could sense that Jimbo was getting nervous, what with the time travel and now the thought of seeing his father. He had been pretty calm during the travelling part, saying little. But now he was edgy.

'Remember, don't get involved,' I warned him. 'We're just here to watch, from the outside.'

Jimbo licked his lips, and nodded. 'Yep. I know.'

We sat down by a tree and watched the game. A few wickets fell but nothing much seemed to be happening.

'I reckon that's him coming in to bat now,' Jimbo said, as we watched a guy wearing glasses stride out to the pitch.

The first ball was a lifter and Jimbo's dad just managed to fend it off his chest. The fielders were urging on the fast bowler, who we hadn't seen bowl before.

'C'mon, Cravo, give it to him!' a fieldsman yelled.

'Oh, my God,' I whispered. 'It's Scott Craven's dad!'

I stared at the bowler. He was big and strong, mean and fast, just like his son was going to be.

'Like father, like son,' I whispered.

But Jimbo wasn't listening. The next delivery reared up and struck Jimbo's dad a glancing blow on the side of the head. The next ball thudded into his chest. Jimbo winced and jumped to his feet.

'Hey!' he shouted. 'He's a tail-ender.'

A few of the fielders turned to look. Scott's dad, who was bowling, didn't. I grabbed Jimbo by the arm and pulled him down.

'Jimbo, no!' I said to him. 'You can't interfere. Remember?'

The last ball of the over was another bouncer and it caught Jimbo's dad right above the eye. Jimbo gasped as his dad crumpled to the ground. His bat fell from his hand and toppled against the stumps. There was a shout of 'Howzat?' from the bowler. The umpire nodded, then raised his finger.

'Yeah!' shouted Craven and he pumped his fists in the air just the way I'd seen Scott do it so many times before.

I looked at Jimbo. There were tears streaming down his face and his fists were clenched. He wasn't moving, though, which must have taken a lot of self-control.

A few of the fielders had run in to help Jimbo's dad. There was blood streaming down his face. For a moment I felt sick, not only because of the injury but because of the rule that allowed a bowler to intimidate a player in that way, and even get him out just because he had lost control of the bat after being smacked in the face.

It just didn't seem fair and I could sort of understand Jimbo's dad's decision never to play again.

The highest score made on debut (someone's first match) in women's cricket was by Michelle Goszko. She scored 204 in the First Test against England in 2001.
She was playing for Australia.

16 The Enemy

'C'MON, Jimbo. We've seen enough. Your dad'll pull through. Otherwise you wouldn't be here, watching this.'

He wiped the tears from his face.

'Jimbo, wait here. I'm just going to check the scorecard, and make sure it was Craven. Okay?'

He nodded and watched forlornly as his father was helped from the field. I raced over to a group of players, standing and waiting for their batters to arrive. The fielding team had headed off in a different direction.

I wondered whether it mattered if Jimbo's dad actually saw me. Would he remember my face? Would anyone else? Surely not. But I certainly wouldn't be doing anything stupid or freaky that someone might remember. Just in case.

'Can you hear me?'

I froze.

A harsh, gravelly voice had whispered in my ear. I spun around.

A tall man wearing a hooded cloak was walking

away from me. Had he been talking to me? Everyone else was looking at Jimbo's dad, who was sitting on a chair, with ice and a blood-soaked towel wrapped around his face.

I turned away quickly. No one else seemed to have noticed him. And yet how could they miss him? When I turned back again he had disappeared.

I raced over to Jimbo. My heart was thumping.

'Jimbo!' I yelled. He turned.

Then suddenly there was the creepy man again — between the two of us. Again he seemed to have come from nowhere. He had his back to me and was walking towards Jimbo. He looked so out of place in the park here, but still no one saw him. The few people scattered around the ground kept on with their picnics or their walking. The man was tall, but the weird cloak he was wearing made him look bigger than he was. He definitely looked sinister. He kept his head down and his back to me.

I stopped. Jimbo wasn't moving either. He raised his eyebrows slightly, as though he was asking me if everything was okay.

No, Jimbo! Everything's not okay! I tried to will my thoughts across the space between us.

'What do you want?' I asked the man, my lips trembling.

'You're going to help me, you hear?' he said, but without turning his head. His voice hissed and spat. He was only a few metres away. A horrible stench came from him.

'Y-y-yes,' I stammered.

The figure stopped and turned slowly.

I seized my moment. I yelled at Jimbo, then started reciting the first line of the poem. I wanted a glimpse at the man's face, but the need to escape was more urgent.

I kept on with the poem, dashing towards Jimbo and grabbing his hand as the final words of the second line came out.

My head crashed into the side of the garage and Jimbo piled on top of me a moment later. He looked at me incredulously as he gathered himself up.

For a moment neither of us spoke. Jimbo was breathing hard and staring at me.

'Jimbo,' I stammered. 'Did you see that man? Who was he?'

'I dunno.'

We both turned at a noise from further back in the garage. Without another thought we scrambled up and out of there. Then we stopped, hearts pumping.

'My kit,' Jimbo said, looking at the garage door swinging to and fro.

'Yep. The directory too. C'mon, let's get it.'

'Then straight back into the house?'

'Yep.'

We snuck in, eyes down, avoiding the darkness near the back, heading for the kit and the directory. I found the *Wisden*, closed it and shoved it back into its box. We were out again within moments.

'Toby?'

I turned and looked at Jimbo.

'I'm sorry —' I began.

'No. Thanks. That was incredible.'

I nodded. 'I know.'

I raced up the path to the front door and nearly crashed into a man standing on the first step. I almost fainted in fright.

'Hello Dad,' I heard Jimbo say.

I looked up. How long had he been watching us for?

'You boys been playing cricket?'

I didn't like the way he said the word playing.

'Actually, we've been watching cricket, Dad,' Jimbo replied.

Well, it was an honest answer.

The front door opened. It was Mum. She was nodding and smiling and welcoming Jimbo's dad into the house. As we followed them in I wondered if things could really change between Jimbo and his dad.

What a shocker. Sometimes, in the early days of cricket, teams got caught on stickies. These were rain-soaked wickets that were drying out. Wickets back then were never covered. On this particular day, Victoria, playing against the MCC, were knocked over for 15. They lost their first four wickets without a run being scored. And it would have been 5/0, but the next guy was dropped.

17 The Advice

Saturday — morning

'SO, you guys went on the prowl instead of to the nets the other night?' Dad said to me first thing on Saturday morning. I'd slept in on Friday morning and Dad had got home too late to catch up with me on Friday night.

'Yeah,' I grinned, trying to look relaxed. I sat down, hoping that I didn't look as tired as I felt.

'Gee, you look whacked,' Mum said to me, one hand on my shoulder, the other setting down a bowl of cereal.

So much for that hope, I thought to myself.

'Big game today,' I explained. 'Kept on going over it. Couldn't get to sleep.'

'Well, if it hadn't been raining for the last six hours, I would have to agree with you, Toby. John Pasquali phoned through about an hour ago. We thought we'd let you sleep on a bit.'

I was in such a daze that I hadn't even noticed the grey day outside, the water on the window and that cosy feeling when you wake up and it's raining on a non-school day.

'It's going to be this Thursday, after school,' Dad said.

'Which means we'll all be able to watch, honey,' Mum said.

Nat had tennis on Saturday mornings, which kept her and Mum away. Then again, as Mum often pointed out, my cricket kept Dad and me away from Nat's tennis too.

'So, we can all go to tennis this morning,' Mum said.

'Sure,' I replied. I was glad to tag along. It might take my mind off the creepy man Jimbo and I had met the previous night. Nat was a great tennis player, too. She played against girls way older than her — and usually won.

After tennis I asked Mum if I could go and visit Ivo at the hospital.

But when I got there, a nurse told me that he wasn't allowed to have any visitors. I took the lift up one floor, but this time skulked around a bit, making sure I wasn't seen by any of the nurses.

The door to Jim's room was slightly open. I pushed it and walked in. Jim looked pale and weary, lying there alone on the far side of the room.

'Jim, it's me. Toby.'

He smiled but didn't open his eyes.

'Ah, dear boy. So good of you to come. Tell me of your adventures.'

And I did. I told him everything. I told him about India and Dad's *Wisden*s in the garage. I told him how I had taken Jimbo back to see his dad. Jim winced on hearing that, but he didn't look angry. He didn't look strong enough to be angry. And I told him about the man I'd seen.

Suddenly Jim's eyes were open, his body tense.

'Describe him, Toby.'

'He was tall — and looked really weird. He had on a long hooded cape, so I couldn't see his face. I sure could smell him, though!'

Jim sighed, but he looked worried.

'He said something about helping him.'

Jim closed his eyes, and settled back on his pillows.

'You must not carry, Toby. You must not take others with you. You are exposed and vulnerable when others are with you. I'm sure that's how he found you. Do you understand me, Toby?'

'Yes,' I croaked, for a moment almost forgetting to breathe.

'Which means that my one selfish hope of getting back to 1930 may never come to pass.'

'But why don't you just go?' I asked.

'No, Toby. I have respected that warning all this time. And now, I'm too old to travel. Especially those distances. No, I would need someone young, like yourself, to get me there.'

'I'll carry you,' I said.

For a moment, as I looked down at his sad face and tired body, I felt as though there was nothing I wanted more than to get Jim back to see that 1930 game when Don Bradman made his big score.

'Are you okay, Jim?'

He opened his eyes again, and this time turned his head slightly to look at me directly.

'No, Toby. I'm very tired.' He kept on staring at me. He smiled. 'If everyone's life has a limited number of innings, then perhaps I have seen my Don Bradman innings anyway.'

The door of the ward opened. A nurse bustled in. She carried a clipboard.

'Come along,' she said to me.

'I must think more about this man, Toby.' Jim had grabbed my hand and was holding it tightly.

'Off you go now, mister. That's enough chatting. You'll wear poor Jim out,' the nurse said. She pointed to the door.

'Please!' The nurse and I stopped, surprised by the rifle-crack of Jim's voice.

'Please,' he repeated, less sharply. The nurse looked puzzled. She looked at her watch and busied herself with Jim's chart.

'What does he want?' I asked. I still couldn't believe the world I was entering and talking about with Jim.

'That, I don't know, Toby. But I can tell you that —'

'Well, I know what I want,' the nurse interrupted, writing something on a chart. 'Some peace and quiet in here.'

'We will talk again, Toby and I shall tell you more of what I know.' He turned his weary body slightly to face me. 'It's time to go, Toby.'

'It most certainly is,' said the nurse.

I stared at Jim's worn face. His bottom lip was twitching.

'Have you learned the poem off by heart?' he whispered.

Ignoring the nurse, I remained by the bed and recited the poem for him. I got to the end without missing a line. By then it looked as though Jim had fallen asleep. I turned to go.

But Jim wasn't asleep.

'It's one thing to say the words of the poem. It's another thing altogether to understand and honour them, Toby.'

'I'm doing my best. I could just walk away from it all,' I said.

'You most certainly could.'

I left Jim's room wondering for a moment whether I should just stay in my normal world. My year. My time. Forever.

In 1915, J.C. Sharp, a schoolboy batting for Melbourne Grammar, scored an amazing 506 not out against Geelong College. A team-mate, R.W. Herring, scored 238. The total score was 961 and the game was won by an innings and 647 runs.

18 The Return

Sunday — afternoon

DAD dropped me off at Rahul's at five o'clock on Sunday afternoon. Rahul greeted me at his gate, looking very excited.

'Look! I've got some rupees, notepaper, a camera —'

'No camera, Rahul. No way,' I told him.

'Oh, well. It was a long shot.' He grinned.

I was so keyed up I didn't eat much at dinner time. Rahul's family were always very polite and pleasant. Rahul had a sister and another brother, both younger than him. They asked me heaps of questions, and made me very much the centre of attention.

When we went to bed Rahul and I chatted quietly for about half an hour after his mum had come up and said goodnight. The rest of the house was quiet.

'Are you sure there's nothing else you're going to do, Rahul?' I asked for the hundredth time.

'No, Toby. I just want to get a quick look at the game, then see Dean Jones in the hospital.'

'Okay. A quick look and then we're back. You hear me?'

'I hear you,' he grinned at me.

'And if we're nowhere near the hospital, then —'

'Then we maybe get a quick look at the game, and come home,' Rahul finished.

'And have you thought about the fact that we might not be anywhere near the hospital, or have no way of getting there?' I asked him.

'Of course. I have worked hard on this.'

I was less confident.

'It's my call, Rahul.'

'It's your call, Toby.'

'Right. Let's do it.'

We walked over to the lamp and I opened the *Wisden* up to the correct page. The words swirled and spun, round and round.

'Rahul,' I whispered. 'Point at the bit about Dean Jones' big innings.'

'Here,' Rahul said, pointing to a spot halfway down. I grabbed his hand, trying to bring to focus the swarming letters.

Rahul was reading the words. All I saw was a swirly mess.

'"On the second day, Jones ..."' Rahul spoke the words that I was trying to decipher. He read on, and the swirl became letters, and the letters became words ...

'Come on, Toby!'

I looked about. The smell and the noise were

like last time. Again, we seemed to have arrived in a quieter spot, behind one of the stands. This time we walked towards the noise — the ground itself.

The crowd was chanting and the noise was huge. It was a constant roar, occasionally rising to a crescendo when something happened out on the field.

The first thing we both did was turn our heads to the scoreboard. Australia was batting. Dean Jones was on 209.

'It's okay, they'll get him soon,' Rahul called out. He was excited with the knowledge he had and that the other 25,000 people at the ground didn't.

'Rahul!' I exploded. 'No!'

'No one is listening,' he said.

I looked back out across the brown oval. The stench in the air was making me cough and gag. Dean Jones looked exhausted. The other batter — that must have been the captain, Allan Border — was talking to him. Dean was looking at the pitch. A moment later he moved away. His body shook as he tried to vomit.

He hit a ball way out into the deep and walked the single. Walked the whole way. But that was the last run he made.

Rahul had moved a few metres away and was talking to someone — another kid. I moved across to him, worrying about what he might be saying.

Just as I got to him there was a tremendous roar from the crowd.

I looked up. Dean Jones had just been bowled. Everyone was jumping up and down, screaming their lungs out.

'Come on,' Rahul shouted to me, 'this is our chance. Let's go.'

He dragged me away, down the way we had come. We walked around behind a big stand, where we waited for a few moments.

'How do you know we're in the right spot?' I asked him. 'And what do we do when he comes out? Hop in the ambulance with him and tell them we're doctors?'

'It's okay, Toby. Like I told you, I've been doing research. It's all worked out.'

We waited and waited.

'So maybe he doesn't go to hospital,' I said.

'Don't worry. He'll be having his iced bath —'

'Listen!' I called.

Above the noise of the crowd, away to our right, was the sound of a siren. It was getting closer.

'Dean Jones has just collapsed onto the floor,' said Rahul. 'He is cramping severely. The ambulance will be here in a moment.'

We stepped back as the siren got closer. People were coming from everywhere. It seemed as if we weren't the only ones who knew what was about to happen.

A stretcher was taken from the ambulance and wheeled through a door. A few minutes later the door opened again and a few men appeared. Dean lay on

146

the stretcher. His eyes were open but he looked as if he wasn't really noticing anything. I took another step back. Rahul didn't.

We followed the group, about 10 metres behind them, through a gate and out into a car park, where the ambulance waited. The crowd was getting bigger. Everyone was talking excitedly.

'What now?' I asked, feeling frustrated. 'We steal a car and chase them?'

'No, silly. Come on.'

Rahul seemed to know exactly where he was going. We came to a line of taxis. Rahul leaned down to the open window of the first cab and spoke to the driver. A moment later he motioned me to get inside the taxi. If anything, it was hotter inside the car than out.

'What did you say?' I asked.

'Can you take us to the hospital, please?' He smiled. There was something more happening here, I sensed. But I couldn't for the life of me work out what.

'Are you really so interested in seeing Dean Jones lying in a hospital bed?' I asked him.

'Oh, yes, terribly,' he replied. Even Rahul was sweating in the heat. 'You see my whole assignment is based around Dean Jones' innings. Did you know that some of the Australian staff wanted him to come off at tea, when he was about 200? Did you know that he walked his last 20 runs? And it was a tie, Toby. The game was a tie!'

'Rahul!' I hissed.

'Oh yeah. Okay.' He was obviously very excited by the whole Dean Jones story. And it looked as if we weren't the only ones who had followed the ambulance in. Cars were parked everywhere, and people were running in all directions, shouting and giving advice. Inside the hospital was no different.

And I had thought the cricket ground was packed! The hospital was swarming. Doctors, nurses, patients, old people, children, visitors — they were everywhere, choking the rooms and corridors.

'Rahul, we'd better stick close.' People were jostling and pushing us from behind.

'Rahul?' I turned right, then left. He had vanished.

'Rahul!' I screamed. But my cry was lost in the noise and bustle.

'Rahul!' Now I was running — pushing and bumping into people. Then I stopped. There was no way I was going to find him like this. I needed to go back to the front and put out a call for him.

'Rahul Prahibar. Please report to the front desk on ground level, immediately,' came the message over the loudspeaker system a few minutes later.

I sat down to wait. It was then that I started to panic. Suddenly the whole idea of sitting here, alone, in a busy hospital in a city in India nearly 20 years ago was too much. I put my head down in my hands, my shoulders starting to shake.

'Not a happy chappy?'

I froze.

Slowly I peeled my hands from my face and looked up. A man wearing a white coat, his arms crossed, looked down at me. He was obviously a doctor come to see what was wrong.

At that moment, a screaming, wailing noise erupted from the sliding doors to our left. A woman rushed in, carrying a small child. The piercing noise from the mother drowned out everything else.

Without thinking, I jumped to my feet, charged past the doctor, raced around a corner and was soon swallowed up in the mass of people. I half-walked, was half-pushed into a lift. I didn't care what floor I went to. I got out on the eighth. It was quieter. The noises here were only of crying babies.

I ran over to a nurses' station.

'Please, I'm looking for Dean Jones.' I panted.

The nurse on duty looked at me blankly.

'Emergency?' I asked.

'Ah,' she nodded. 'Ground floor.'

Great. I walked back towards the elevator. The sound of clapping and laughing made me stop. I looked around a corner and down a long corridor.

Rahul was standing halfway down, staring into a large window.

'Rahul!' I screamed in delight, rushing towards him. He didn't move.

'Rahul, come on. We've gotta go. Now!' I stopped. There were tears streaming down his face. He made no noise.

'What is it?' I looked in through the window. A young Indian man was standing by a bed. A lady lay in the bed, a tiny baby in her arms. Other people stood around the bed. The man picked up the baby and kissed it. Everyone clapped and cheered again.

'That's my brother,' Rahul whispered, through sobs.

'Rahul, we shouldn't be here,' I told him. It only needs someone to turn around, and —'

'Toby, I can't remember my brother,' he continued. Behind us the lift clanked and shuddered to a stop. 'I just have to see his face. He's my brother, Toby!'

'Rahul, you've got the rest of your life to see his face. Come on, let's get out of here.'

Finally, Rahul tore his eyes from the scene in front of him.

'My elder brother,' he said. 'The brother who scooped me out of a river of rushing water and threw me into my father's arms. He saved my life. I was just a baby. He was swept away. That's him there. Being kissed and loved.'

A rush of footsteps made me turn. Two men appeared to be bearing down on us. Rahul made a dash for the half-open door, a few metres to his right. I started reciting a line from the poem, reaching out for him as I did so. He shrugged my arm away and reached for the door handle.

'Rahul!' I cried, frightened beyond belief. 'You

can't go in there!' We were lying entangled, at the foot of the door. It started to open wider and we tumbled forwards. Grabbing Rahul's ankle, I managed to fire off two lines of the poem.

I never turned to see who had been running along the corridor towards us.

We arrived in a heap on Rahul's bedroom floor. A moment later, the door was flung open. Light streamed into the bedroom.

'Rahul! What is it?' Mr Prahibar stood at the entrance. Rahul wiped his face with the back of his hand, struggled up, and fell into his father's arms.

'I think he's had a bad dream,' I said.

'I heard a thump on the floor,' said Mr Prahibar.

'And fell out of bed too,' I added, lamely.

His dad looked at him kindly.

'What was your dream, son?'

'Dad,' Rahul started sobbing again. 'I dreamed that I w-was at the hospital where my older brother was b-b-born, and you and Mum and all our family were there. And ... you were h-h-holding, w-w-were holding —'

Rahul's dad hushed him, and Rahul fell silent, except for the sobs that were racking his body.

'Rahul and I will go downstairs, Toby. I'm sorry that you've been involved in all this. Come on, Rahul,' Mr Prahibar was saying as they left. 'Let's talk about this dream you had.'

I crawled back into bed. What had I done? Jim was right. The gift of time travel was not meant for others. All sorts of worries and problems swirled round in my head. The light coming through from the partly open door lit up the *Wisden* on the floor. I got out of bed, kicked the door shut then shoved the *Wisden* under the bed. It thudded into the wall.

Nowadays, cricket pitches are covered, prepared, and looked after with great care. But 100 years ago, things were quite different. In a 1910 game between Victoria and South Australia, with a particularly wet wicket, the match was delayed when a frog appeared from a crack in the pitch.

19 The Letter

Monday — morning

AT breakfast the following morning it was as though nothing had happened. Rahul greeted me with a formal handshake. His eyes met mine.

'Thank you, Toby. It was a gift from heaven. I shall not ask you again. Ever. I promise.' He smiled.

'How'd it go with your dad last night?'

'Very good. I sort of knew bits and pieces about what happened, but Dad had never fully explained everything. He said the time would come. I think it was good for him too. He found it difficult. He was crying too. But it is the best thing to have happened.'

'Does he know about — you know, the time —'

'No. The dream was an excellent idea.'

'It just came into my head,' I said. 'You tell me about it — one day. Okay?'

Rahul looked down at his shoes, then back to me. 'Yes. I will. But not yet. And we'll take Dean Jones' word for it that he went to hospital, eh, Toby?'

153

After school I headed up to my room. I flicked on my desk light, hit 'play' on the CD player and started thinking.

I'd had an idea ticking over in my head. If I could somehow convince Jimbo's dad to change his mind about not letting Jimbo play cricket, then maybe I could get Jimbo onto the team. Surely Jimbo'd want that. But how would I do it? How can you change someone's mind?

I lay on the bed staring at my cricket posters, thinking about Jimbo and his dad. My mind wandered to his house. The hall ...

Then suddenly it came to me. I shot up off the bed, my heart racing. The hall! The cricket kit! The kit that Mr Temple was putting in the garage sale. If I could get back to the game when Mr Temple was hit, and sneak a letter into his kit — a letter that would convince him to change his mind about his attitude to cricket — then maybe, just maybe, he wouldn't notice the letter for all those years that he didn't play cricket. Until, one day ...

I shoved things off my desk and grabbed a piece of paper. I would have to type it. But I'd write a draft first.

Fifteen minutes later I had written a rough copy. I put it aside and headed downstairs for a snack. On the way a thought struck. What if the cricket kit had already been sold? Weren't garage sales usually on a

Saturday morning? I hoped it was next weekend. I already had a plan to get Jimbo's dad looking in the kit.

Monday — evening

This time I would be travelling alone. I was going to head back to the same park that Jimbo and I had visited. With any luck the creepy guy in the long cloak with the scary voice and the nasty smell wouldn't be there. Jim had said that solo travel was safer.

I told Dad I was going to do a bit more cleaning up in the garage.

'And don't come in until I tell you, Dad. I want it to be a surprise.'

'Sounds good to me,' he called from the kitchen. 'You've got as long as you like!'

I managed to arrive a lot earlier this time, and walked to the park. I kept out of the way too, shielded by a clump of trees on the far side of the oval.

I waited patiently. Life here felt gentle. There were birds and dogs and empty spaces. The picnic rugs were out, and people were pouring drinks and opening up containers of sandwiches. As I sat there, enjoying the peace, it occurred to me that there was cricket happening all around the world, and every game, every situation, was different.

As the moment drew near, I started to focus more on the game. I looked at the envelope. I took out the sheet of paper and read it one more time.

You made a decision. And given what happened
to you, it was perfectly understandable. But now
it is time to give someone you love the
opportunity to play the game he loves. And
display the skills that, being your son, he surely
must possess.

I folded the sheet back into the envelope and sealed
it. I made my way down to where the players were
mingling. Some had left. I hunted around for the
cricket bag with the initials R.T. on it. It was right in
among the players, who were moving around.

Don't meddle, talk, nor interfere
With the lives of those you venture near.

I stopped in my tracks. The words had suddenly come
into my head. I looked about, half-expecting someone
close by to be telling me the poem. But no one was
paying any attention to me. As quickly as the words
had come, they were gone.

Without another thought I moved over to the bag. I
bent down. A Gray Nicholls bat lay across the top of it.

'You looking for something?' A voice called
behind me. I turned. One of the players had noticed
me down near the kit.

'Um, no. I saw this fall out when the bat was
thrown onto the kit,' I said, showing him the
envelope. 'I was just going to put it back.' He stared at
me then shrugged.

156

'Hang on. I'll grab Richard's stuff and you can pack it all in properly.'

He came back a moment later with pads, gloves, a thigh pad, protector and a cap. There was blood on it.

'Good man,' he said. Carefully, I placed the gear into the bag. I slipped the letter down, resting it between the bat and the side of the bag.

I did up the straps.

It could be opened that night. Or maybe, not for years. I got up and walked away, not looking back. When I had reached a tree about 20 metres away, I turned. No one seemed to be paying any attention to the kitbag, or to me.

But for every word that boasts ahead
Means lives unhinged, broken, dead.

Seven batters have recorded over 10,000 Test runs in their careers. Sachin Tendulkar (11,821), Rahul Dravid (10,122) and Ricky Ponting (10,099) are still playing. Brian Lara (11,953), Allan Border (11,174), Steve Waugh (10,927) and Sunil Gavaskar (10,122) are the other players

20 The *Wisden*

Wednesday — afternoon

I knew Mr Pasquali collected old cricket stuff, so I gave him a call and told him I'd seen a complete cricket kit including a Gray Nicholls bat, maybe 25 years old. I gave him Jimbo's address and told him to check it out.

After that I made the decision — no more time travelling. I would go and see Jim in hospital and tell him it was over. I had tried a few times to get through on the phone. Then finally, on the Wednesday, they told me that he had gone.

'What do you mean — gone?' I asked.

'Who am I speaking to?' the lady at the hospital asked.

I covered the mouthpiece, and tried to explain to Dad as quickly as I could what was going on. Dad took the phone.

'I'm a friend of Jim's, and we're wondering how he is, that's all.'

158

Dad listened for a moment, said a few 'I sees', then hung up.

'Strange,' he said. 'They're not exactly certain what's happened. Seems he's just taken himself off. Evidently he's done this once or twice before. They're working on it.'

I must have been looking worried.

'Hey, Toby, I know how you feel, but it's not really our problem.'

'Dad, if it's not our problem, and if it's not anyone else's problem, then there's an old sick man alone somewhere, maybe in trouble.'

'Hmm. So what would you have us do?'

'I want to just check out one thing.' I hit redial and passed Dad the phone. 'Ask them if there's a fat book lying open next to his bed. A *Wisden Cricketers' Almanack*.'

'What? You do it!' Dad said, thrusting the phone back at me. 'I'm not going to ring just to ask a question like that.'

I asked for Jim's room number. A few moments later the same sharp voice came on the line. I shoved the phone back at Dad. At least she would listen to him.

'Hello, Peter Jones here. We spoke before. Um, look, it might seem a silly question really, but I was just wondering whether, ah, there was a book, a fat book, next to Jim's bed?'

'Open!' I said, loudly.

'An open, fat book,' Dad added, giving me a pained look. He made a face at me. I smiled, giving him a little punch on the shoulder.

'There is? Really? Right, well, thank you —'

I grabbed the phone. 'Excuse me. This is really important. Please,' I begged. 'Can you tell me the year of the book and the page number that it's open to? Please! Maybe there was a bookmark —'

The phone clicked.

I love my dad so much — 20 minutes later we were striding through the entrance to the Simpson Hospital. We raced up the stairs to Jim's room.

'We've just come to collect that book. It's important to Mr Oldfield,' Dad added.

'Suit yourself. You can take his bag of belongings too. I put the book back on the bedside table,' she added.

Both beds had been made, and the room was empty.

'1931,' I whispered.

'What's that?' Dad asked.

'Maybe we could check the library at the MCG. Jim could be there.'

'Okay, but if he's not there, we'd better let someone else do the searching.'

'Like the police?'

He nodded. 'Like the police.'

* * *

While we were in the hospital we paid a quick visit to Martian too. He'd been given the all-clear and was coming out of hospital the next day.

'When will you be able to play cricket again?' I asked.

He looked across at his dad, who was sitting on the bed next to him.

'Not sure. But it won't be too long, I hope,' Ivo replied.

'That's great,' I said.

We didn't talk much about the accident, but I told him more about the team and how everyone had been going. He was interested in knowing all the scores and stats.

The floorboards creaked and the musty smell of old books hit me as I entered the library, a few paces ahead of Dad. Jim was sitting at the oval table, a glass of water and a plate of sandwiches in front of him.

'Jim!' I cried, rushing over to him. A few heads looked up.

'My dear boy,' Jim looked pleased to see me. Dad stood behind.

'Hello, Jim,' he said.

'Peter, a pleasure. Excuse me for not standing.'

'We've, um, brought your things from the hospital,' I said, putting the *Wisden* and a bag on the table.

'Thank you. My thanks to the pair of you.' Dad was eyeing the *Wisden*s in the bookshelf. 'Do have a look, Peter. The bookcase is open.'

'Did you get there?' I whispered to Jim.

He looked down at the old *Wisden* in front of him and shook his head. 'I tried, Toby, I tried. But instead, I got back here. The place of my last departure. Which was some time ago now. Still, it's good to be back.'

'Are you okay?' I asked.

'Better for being back here, Toby,' he replied. 'What have you got there?' he asked me. I had reached into my pocket and was fiddling with a dice.

Dad turned round. 'Watch out, Jim,' he said, seeing the dice. 'He's going to nab you for a game of dice cricket!'

'Splendid. I shall send for more sandwiches. Come along, let's clear the table here. I'll choose a team from the 1930s.' Jim started to reel off a list of names.

We ended up spending the rest of the afternoon eating sandwiches and playing the best game of dice cricket. Dad was the roller. Jim insisted on giving Don Bradman seven chances because he was so far ahead of everyone else. I managed to make sure Adam Gilchrist and Ricky Ponting got plenty too. During the game, Jim would suddenly start talking about a player from his team. His memory was amazing. He told his stories as if he'd just returned from the game. A couple of times I noticed Dad looking at me.

'Great stories,' I whispered to Dad at one stage, when Jim had gone off to find a book to check a score.

He nodded. 'Amazing. You two seem to get on very well,' he added.

'Yeah.'

'Something bothering you, Toby?'

'He's very old, Dad,' I said.

'Well, we all have a journey to make. Some are longer than others. I think Jim has had a pretty decent one, don't you?'

'I guess.'

Jim came back, a book in his hand, his eyes shining.

And even though Ricky Ponting scored 143, it wasn't enough to trouble Jim's 'Invincibles'.

I must have been looking a bit down about the result. Dad said to me, 'Head up, Toby.'

I smiled a secret smile.

Then we said goodbye. I think Jim knew that my goodbye was sort of final. When Dad was putting away the *Wisden*s he had pulled out, I leaned over and told Jim that I didn't think I would be time travelling again.

He nodded his head, and said nothing.

'Jim, *will* I time travel again?' I whispered, not really wanting to hear an answer.

'Perhaps only to help an old man fulfil a lifelong dream,' he said quietly.

I didn't say anything.

'Come along, Toby.' Dad's hand rested on my shoulder. We shook hands with Jim.

'Toby, I want you to have this,' Jim said, handing me the 1931 *Wisden*.

'Jim, no —' Dad interrupted.

'Please, Peter. Toby deserves this. Please.' Jim's voice was insistent.

I didn't know what to say. I held the precious book in my hands.

'Off you go,' Jim said.

'Well, I hope we catch up again, Jim, and thank you very much for that generous gift. He'll look after it, I promise,' Dad said, shaking Jim's hand.

'Yes, I know he will,' Jim smiled.

I was quiet for a while on the way home.

Dad picked up on my thoughts, as always, and said, 'You okay, son?'

'Dad, I don't have a grandfather, do I?'

Dad flicked his head round, then turned back to the road. 'No.'

'I sort of feel like I do, now.'

'Jim's someone else's grandfather, Toby.'

'Maybe not in this time,' I mumbled. Luckily, Dad didn't seem to hear. 'I wonder where he lives. I wonder who looks after him.'

'Maybe Jim looks after himself.'

'Dad, he's just come out of hospital. He didn't get any visitors.'

'We don't know that, Toby. You can't just enter someone's life and assume he needs your help and guidance.'

We didn't speak for a while until Dad said, 'We'll invite Jim over for a barbecue. How's that?'

'That'd be great, Dad. I reckon he'd love it.'

We were silent once more. I started thinking about my decision to give up time travel. Had I made the right choice? Then I remembered the evil hooded man again and became convinced that I had.

Three Test players have taken four wickets in five balls. M.J.C. Allom achieved this in his first-ever Test match for England, against New Zealand in the 1929/1930 season. When another Englishman, Chris Old, managed the feat, in 1978 against Pakistan, he took two wickets, then bowled a no ball, then took another two wickets. Wasim Akram, for Pakistan, took his four wickets against India in the 1990/1991 series.

21 The Game

Thursday — afternoon

I still couldn't get the thought of the mystery man out of my head as we drove to the ground after school the next day. I had dreamed of him again the previous night. I couldn't work out why he'd been after me. *Was* he after me? Maybe I'd just happened to be in the wrong place at the wrong time.

Still, I didn't have to worry about it any more. And right now, there was a game of cricket to be played. Maybe my nerves were because of the game, and not the time travel stuff.

After all, it was the Scorpions we were up against. I thought we were going to be able to handle the other four teams — Motherwell, TCC, Benchley Park and St Mary's. But the Scorpions were an unknown.

Jono won the toss and decided to bat. Mr Pasquali told us that we were totally on our own today. We would be responsible for the batting and bowling order, the fielding positions and all other decisions. It was a 30-over game, batters retiring at 30, and with a maximum of four overs per bowler.

Of course Scott Craven opened the batting, along with Jono. Five balls and two fours later, Scott was walking back to us, caught behind, for eight. The very next ball, Cameron was bowled. We were 2 for 8.

Rahul had only just managed to get his gear on. Normally he had a routine of tapping the ball up on the edge of his bat to get his eye in. There were some tense moments as Georgie, Jay and I scrambled to get our pads on.

The other opening bowler was even quicker, but maybe not as accurate. His first two balls were wides, but his third smashed into Jono's pads. There was a loud appeal from every player on the ground, and even some of the dads standing in a group away to our left.

The umpire looked hard, then raised his finger.

'Oh, no,' groaned Jay. 'Hey, I'm not ready. Georgie, you go in, can you?'

'Get out there, you wimp!' roared Scott.

'But I can't find my box!' he wailed.

'I'll go,' I said. I gathered up my helmet and gloves, adjusted my thigh pad, and strode out to the wicket, trying to look confident. Rahul met me halfway.

'Toby, we've got to stay in until these two fast bowlers have finished their spell. Don't worry about the runs. Okay?'

That was easy for him to say. He was a regular top-order batter, and he wasn't on strike. I took guard, had a look around the field, then settled over my bat and waited.

A split second later the ball was flying past my head and through to the keeper. I danced on the spot, trying to get some spark into my body. Five minutes ago the openers were walking out to bat and already I was in the firing line. I could see Dad, the newspaper dropped to the ground beside him, leaning forwards in his deck chair, concentrating on the game.

I managed to survive the rest of the over, only having to play at one delivery. Rahul scored a single off the first ball of the next over and I was back on strike. I wasn't as nervous now, having played a few deliveries already.

The next ball changed all that. It rose from just short of a length and crashed into the top half of my bat. There was a huge cracking noise as leather struck wood. The ball sailed away over slips and down to the boundary for four. The bat — all except the handle — fell onto the pitch.

There were hoots of laughter from the kids around me. Even the bowler was smiling. A moment later, Craven rushed out, offering me his bat.

'Are you sure?' I asked.

'Course. Just don't snick any or I'll make you lick off the cherry. You hear?'

The bat weighed a tonne. It was all I could do to lift it just as the bowler delivered the ball. But when

168

I connected, which I did twice more in the over, with a nicer cracking sound, the ball raced away for four.

It's amazing what a few fours can do for your confidence. I swung and missed a few times, and Rahul and I kept on reminding ourselves that it would get easier once the two opening bowlers had finished their spells, but I still managed to find a few gaps, and after eight overs we had pushed the score along to 3 for 31.

Mr Pasquali was nodding in approval from square leg as we started to pile on the runs. Craven's bat was incredible. Between balls, I let it rest against me, not picking it up until I absolutely had to.

We had got the score to 72 before a guy bowled a quicker, more pitched-up delivery — a yorker. I couldn't jam the bat down quickly enough and the ball slammed into the base of my leg stump. I was out for 29.

I got plenty of cheers and applause as I trudged off.

'Bloody lucky I gave you the bat. You wouldn't have got past 10 without it,' Scott chuckled. He seemed to be in a good frame of mind, considering he'd had two failures in a row with the bat.

'Guess not,' I said. 'Thanks.'

We went on to score 174, with some good hitting from everyone else — including Jason Vo, playing his first game for us. Georgie and Ally belted the bowlers around a bit and made 32 between them.

Our opponents had made the mistake of using up their two best bowlers too early. I wondered if Jono would do the same. I was in for a surprise.

He threw the new ball to me.

'You're up, Toby. Hit the spot.'

I was fired up after my batting. We set an attacking field. My first ball dropped a bit short and in a flash the batter was in behind it, belting it over mid-wicket for four. Jono clapped his hands, yelling encouragement. Craven groaned.

I bowled flatter and faster for the rest of the over but they took seven off me. Craven bowled a maiden from the other end, the batters not really looking troubled by his pace. Maybe they were used to it, with the practice they got facing their own opening bowlers.

I was on again. Probably for only one more over if it went like the first. My first ball was whacked out over mid-on for four. It was a bit of a slog, but it was four. Jono kept the fielders in, though, which was good. I liked it when the batter was having a go.

I sent the next ball (pitched a bit shorter) down much quicker. It fizzed past the bat and Ally took it neatly. One to the bowler. I pitched the third delivery slightly wider outside off-stump. The batter's eyes lit up. He danced out of his crease, took a huge swing, but this time it caught the edge of his bat and Ally completed the catch.

Things settled down after that. I completed my four overs, not taking another wicket, but not giving away too many runs either.

Jono kept Craven back for the final overs, and when he came on to bowl his last, they needed four runs to win. They had lost nine wickets. It was a tough field to set. You could sense the tension around the ground. Players, umpires and parents were all on edge.

'It's Madras!' Rahul called to me from mid-off. 'This is exactly the same as Madras: one over left, one wicket left and four runs to get.'

I clapped my hands together, urging everyone on.

I walked in from my position in the covers as Craven charged in to the wicket. It was a good-length ball, a bit slower, and the batter blocked it. He slashed at the next delivery and carved it out to my left. I dived full stretch and got a hand on it. The batters had assumed it would get through. It had 'four' written all over it. I fumbled around, picked up the ball and hurled it to Ally, who had run up to the stumps.

She whipped the bails off. Appeals were screamed from everywhere, even from the other side of the boundary. The umpire stared for a moment at the broken stumps, then shook his head.

Three runs needed for the Scorpions to win the game.

The batter chopped the next ball away between the slip and gully fielders for two more runs. I looked across at Rahul. But it was the two figures behind him that caught my attention. I stared in amazement.

I turned back only when Craven was about to bowl his fourth ball of the over. It thudded into the batter's pads. Craven was on his knees, appealing for lbw. Mr Pasquali shook his head.

'This next one, Scott,' Rahul called across from mid-on.

The scores were level. You could feel the tension. No one was moving. I looked again at the two figures, still and silent, watching from a spot away from the other spectators.

Jono brought everyone in. A single run would win it for them, so we might as well try to prevent that.

It was the second-last delivery of the over. Scott bowled a slower ball. It was bang on target. It caught the batter right back on his crease and smacked into his pads. Craven didn't even appeal. He just kept on running towards the batter, his arms in the air.

The batters were running a leg bye. There were screams and shouts from everywhere.

Finally Rahul, out at mid-off, yelled an appeal. By then, the runners had completed a run, and were scampering away, waving their bats and shouting and cheering. We all raced over to Mr Pasquali. Even Scott had turned around. Mr Pasquali shook his head and headed across to the other umpire. They met at mid-pitch, chatted for a moment, then shook hands and walked off together.

'Looks like everyone's a winner today, Mr Pasquali!' I said to him, picking up the ball. He smiled.

There were two other figures walking away from the ground.

'Jimbo!' I called. He stopped, and turned. His father had an arm around his shoulders. Jimbo nodded a few times, gave me the thumbs up, then turned and walked away.

I turned to Mr Pasquali and said, 'What happened about the cricket kit? Was the bat really a Gray Nicholls?'

'It was, Toby, and the kit was in fantastic condition. But when I went over to check it out, Richard opened up the bag and decided at the last moment to keep it for Jimbo, which I thought was a great idea.'

'That's excellent news!' I exclaimed. I could hardly believe my plan had worked. Maybe time travel could be useful, after all.

'We just need that little extra something in the team to get us over the line,' Mr Pasquali told us a few minutes later. He looked over at a car that was backing away from the oval. 'And I think we might just have the ingredient we're looking for.'

'But who won?' Gavin asked.

'I think Rahul can give us the answer. He seems to know what happened.'

Everyone looked at Rahul.

'It was a tie,' he said. 'Just like the Madras game.'

Monday — afternoon

The moment had finally arrived for the presentations. I couldn't wait to hear what the others had done, as we had all put plenty of effort into our cricket projects.

I sat there listening to all the others, feeling a bit nervous, but enjoying the talks all the same. Mr Pasquali had put me last.

When my moment came. I walked out to the front and opened up the file on the computer that Mr Pasquali had set up.

The first slide appeared on the big screen and I began my talk.

I looked across at the sea of faces in front of me. No one said a word.

'Really, I felt as if I was there,' I said to them.

'Well, it certainly came across that way, Toby. Well done.' Mr Pasquali was nodding and started to clap. The rest of the class joined in enthusiastically.

'Tell me,' asked Mr Pasquali, after the clapping had stopped. 'Where did you get all that detailed information, Toby?'

I bent down and took out a *Wisden* from my bag beneath the table. I held it up to the class.

'Toby!' cried Jimbo, Georgie and Rahul, almost in unison.

Mr Pasquali turned to look at them. 'Is there a problem?' he asked.

'No, no,' they all said at once. Mr Pasquali turned back to me.

'Toby, you were saying?'

'Well, these *Wisden* books, Mr Pasquali, are filled

with all the information you could ever wish for. They have reports on all the games played for the year just passed. They choose the five cricketers of the year. Plus, they have this amazing section where all the records are listed.' I could have kept on going for ages.

'I know. There's always one beside my bed! I'll see if the library can buy some.'

Rahul and Jimbo were staring at me. I looked across at Mr Pasquali. He was jotting down a note in his book. Maybe it was my score for the talk I'd just presented.

'Great,' I said, looking over at Georgie. She smiled.

Mr Pasquali looked up. 'So these *Wisden* books inspired you, Toby?'

Yes, you could say that, I thought to myself as I smiled at him.

There have been 23 tied one-day internationals played since 1984. In only one of these games were the actual scores different. This happened in the 2003 World Cup game when Sri Lanka, chasing South Africa's score of 9/268, got to 6/229 after 45 overs before having to leave the field because of heavy rain. Their innings couldn't be resumed, and the game was declared a tie under the Duckworth-Lewis method.

See page 603 for more details about Toby's Under-13 competition.

BOOK 2

Toby Jones

— AND THE —
SECRET OF THE
MISSING SCORECARD

IT'S NOT JUST A GAME – IT'S TIME TRAVEL!

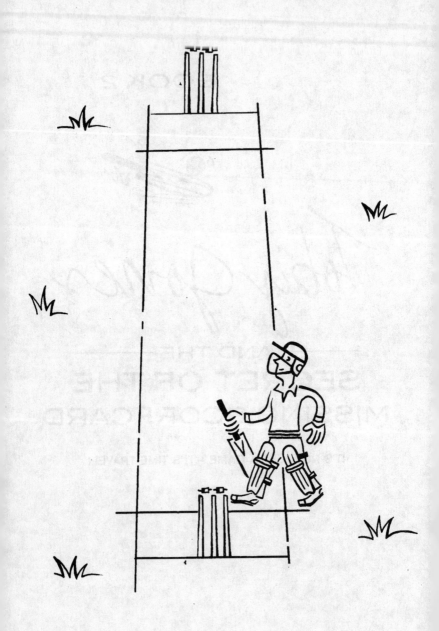

1 Imagination

Monday — afternoon

IT was raining. But our cricket coach, Mr Pasquali, who was also our teacher, wasn't going to let that get in the way of cricket practice.

'I'll meet you outside the gym at a quarter to four,' he said to Jay and me as we left the classroom at lunchtime. 'See if you can find Ally and the others too,' he added.

'That shouldn't be difficult for you, Toby,' Jay laughed. Mr Pasquali had gone but I knew my face was turning red. Jay was always matching me up with some girl.

Only Martian was missing when Mr Pasquali led us into the gym. He had been our wicket keeper until he'd had an accident on his bike. But he was out of hospital now and getting better. His wicket-keeping had been taken over by Ally after the accident. I think Mr Pasquali, our coach, was going to have a tricky time when Martian was ready to return.

Mr Pasquali explained some rules for the indoor cricket game then quickly divided us into two teams.

'Jono, Georgie, Rahul, Martian, Minh, Gavin, Jason and you Toby. Go over to that corner there and work out your batting order.'

'Can I open?' Georgie asked almost straight away.

'Scott'll be bowling,' someone said.

'I know,' she replied, firmly.

Scott Craven was our number one strike bowler and all-round mean guy. I was glad we were on the same team, though even being team-mates hadn't stopped Scott and me from crossing each other a couple of times already this season.

No one else seemed to be jumping up and down to take Georgie's spot.

'Okay, who wants to open with Georgie?' I said. No one spoke. 'Rahul?' I asked.

Rahul sighed, but nodded.

I watched Georgie as she strode out to open the batting.

'Have I gotta bowl slow to the girls?' Scott asked.

'Bowl as fast as you like,' Georgie called out to him before Mr Pasquali had time to reply.

'A tennis ball can't hurt too much,' I muttered to Jono, our captain for the Saturday games.

He smiled. 'Depends where it gets you,' he said, trying on a pair of batting gloves. 'I'll go in next, then you, Tobes, then Jason.'

We settled down on the benches along the far wall as the fielders took up their positions. There was a sense of excitement in the air as Scott yelled out his instructions.

'Not that far!' he shouted to Jay, who was now standing against the back wall. Jay smirked and moved in half a step.

'Right then, everyone ready? Play!' Mr Pasquali called.

Scott ambled in off a few paces then hurled the ball down to Georgie. She took a step back and swung at it. The ball raced towards the back wall, bisecting two fielders on the way. Georgie and Rahul walked through for the bonus run.

'Whoa! Way to go, George!' Ally called from behind the stumps. Ally was awesome. She played softball for a State league team and had amazing reflexes. She'd fitted into the team really well.

'You *don't* encourage people in the other team,' Scott sneered, snatching at the ball that Jimbo tossed back to him.

'Oh, lighten up, Scott,' Ally muttered, crouching down to wait for the next delivery.

'That's enough!' Mr Pasquali barked, clapping his hands. 'Focus on your job, all of you.'

After that the game settled down. Scott brought himself back on to bowl when it was my turn to bat. That didn't surprise me. Neither did the fact that Mr Pasquali no-balled three of his six deliveries for being too high. He was aiming for my head. I hooked the third of his no-balls and was neatly caught off the wall by Jimbo. Scott's yell of triumph was shortlived, though, when he noticed Mr Pasquali's arm outstretched to indicate another no ball.

Maybe the only assignment tougher than facing Scott Craven at full speed was bowling to Jimbo. His dad hadn't let him play for the first three games of the season, but after last week's game, when we'd seen Jimbo watching with his father, it looked like that might change.

Jimbo was a natural. He never seemed to rush. His timing and placement were perfect. During his four overs at the crease, he scored a massive 27 runs; and he hadn't hogged the strike. Unlike Scott, Jimbo would be the last person to do that. We finished up with a score of 75 and won the game by 12 runs.

During the last part of the session, we did some short fielding drills. Mr Pasquali yelled out instructions and encouragement to everyone. He made you want to try again, even if you made a mistake. As usual, I felt tired but excited when the training session was over.

* * *

I stood behind the grandstand and looked left then right for the nearest drink stand. A deafening roar filled my ears. A six? Or maybe a wicket? But the thought vanished as the noise of the crowd dulled. I took a quick glance behind me. A terrifying figure was closing in on me, its long dark cloak billowing.

Where was everyone? Where were all the people who a moment ago were jostling and bumping me?

On the other side of the stand thousands of people sat transfixed, watching a game of cricket. But on this side, there was only the hooded figure and me. I edged away, my hands feeling behind me for the brick wall I was about to bump into. The figure advanced. I turned and ran, speeding off to my right, tearing around the outer perimeter of the grandstand. I plunged into a set of stairs, but immediately fell back, blocked by some invisible force. I struggled to my feet. The creature got closer.

My breath was coming in gasps as I focused on the path ahead. My strength was fading. I screamed in terror, realising I couldn't outrun the figure.

Hot, foul breath steamed over my left shoulder. I gagged, gasped again for breath, then collapsed.

For a moment there was silence. Even the crowd had calmed.

Then I felt his bony hand on my shoulder, trying to turn me over.

'Nooooooooooo!' I screamed. 'Heeeeeeeeeeelp!'

'Look at me,' the creature hissed. I gagged again as another blast of putrid breath spread over me.

I was shaking uncontrollably. But I obeyed. I turned my head slightly and opened my eyes.

'Aaaaaaaaaaaggggggggggghhhhhhhhh!'

The scaly remains of a face glared down at me, blotched and red, with parts of bone protruding, scabby flesh dripping and hollow eye sockets.

With a burst of energy I jumped to my feet and tore off in the opposite direction, desperately searching for an opening to escape.

Suddenly the scene changed. Ghostly people slowly materialised before my eyes. For a few moments I charged straight through them, until I was bumped off course by a big guy with a beard and tattoos.

'Oi! Look out, feller! Bloody idiot!'

I had just run straight into him and the four drinks he was carrying. We were both splashed.

'S-s-sorry,' I panted, easing up.

There were people everywhere now, talking, laughing. Kids were playing cricket on the grass down near the fence and there was a delicious smell of hot dogs, pies and chips. I bounded up the steps and looked out across the oval. Then I took one last fearful look behind me. It was as if I'd stepped into another world.

'Toby!' came a familiar voice. 'C'mon, boy. Let's have some lunch. I've got some great sandwiches up there, but I thought we'd do a bucket of chips each too. What do you say?'

'Great idea, Dad.' Tears welled in my eyes.

'You okay, lad?'

'Yep. I'm fine ... now.'

'C'mon. It used to get to me too when we lost a wicket last ball before lunch. But I'll take three for 261 any day.' Dad smiled and put a hand on my shoulder.

The hand felt bony. I jumped back and looked up into his face. Dad's skin was cracking and shedding layer after layer, I saw the bones beginning to break through and ...

'Noooooooooo!'

I woke with a start. The familiarity of my bedroom washed over me: the Brett Lee poster, the collection of bats, racquets and other sporting things behind the door, the cricket ball on my desk. My nerves settled. Then I glanced at the old brown *Wisden* that Jim Oldfield had given me and my heart started to race again. Gently I pulled it down from the shelf. The feel of the book calmed me. It was heavy and strong. It was like a reliable friend. My thumb brushed its dull brown cover. I could open it now and be transported anywhere. These *Wisden*s were a free ticket to any game of cricket from the past. It was the most unbelievable gift. But it was also dangerous. I'd vowed never to travel again. I knew life would be safer, and a whole lot simpler if I just left these *Wisden*s alone. Then again . . . Shutting my eyes, I opened the book.

'Toby?'

With relief, I closed the pages. 'Dad?' my voice croaked.

He opened the door. 'You look like you've seen a ghost. Or dreamed about one. C'mon, you bludger, you promised me half an hour in the garage before school, remember? You said you wanted a go at soldering something too, didn't you?'

I hopped in the shower quickly, threw my school clothes on and joined Dad in the garage.

'So, did you have a bad dream?' Dad asked, putting the soldering iron down and walking over to

185

the boxes of books. I looked at his face. There wasn't any crackling or peeling happening. But I held back all the same.

'It was spooky — batting collapse. And I was a part of it.'

'Ooh. Nasty. They're the worst sort of dreams.' Dad paused. 'But *spooky*?'

'Yeah, well, these strange creatures were bowling. They were wearing black clothes and had six arms and you couldn't tell which hand had the ball.'

I was making it up as I went but luckily Dad was distracted by the *Wisden*s in the boxes. He flicked one of them open to the contents page, mumbled a few words, then thumbed through to the back.

'He took nine wickets, you know. Not eight.'

'Who?'

'Richard Hadlee. *Sir* Richard Hadlee. And the 10th wicket?'

'Run out?'

'Nope,' Dad said. 'Caught Hadlee, bowled Brown.'

Dad had often talked about this game — the First Test match between Australia and New Zealand in Brisbane in 1985.

'Here we are. Australia were 2 for 72. Struggling a bit, but not a *bad* position to be in at lunch.'

'And?'

'Well, even at 4 for 146 the Aussies would have been thinking 300, which in the conditions would have been a good, solid score. But Mr Hadlee had other ideas. We lost our last six wickets for 31 runs.

Hadlee's bowling analysis? Here you go, Toby, you read it out.'

I reached out to grab the book, then realised what would happen if I started to read the numbers.

'Nah, you read it, Dad. You make it sound like you're a commentator.'

'I do?'

Dad looked a bit confused, but turned the book around and started reading.

'23.4 overs, four maidens, 9 for 52.'

'Is that the best Test bowling effort ever, Dad?'

He was just about to launch into a long spiel when Natalie, my younger sister, appeared at the door to tell him he had a phone call. Dad dropped the *Wisden* into my lap, picked up the box with all the other *Wisden*s in it and headed out.

'Why don't you see if you can find out,' he called. 'Then we'll compare stories.'

Which was all very well except that I found it hard to read *Wisden*s. When I opened a *Wisden* I didn't see a neat page of words and numbers; I saw a sea of blur. A spinning swirl of dairy-whip ice-cream; the words and numbers like little bits of chocolate chip, spinning in front of my eyes. I had 'the gift'.

Jim, the old guy I met at the Melbourne Cricket Club library on our school excursion to the Melbourne Cricket Ground, the MCG, also had the gift. It was Jim who had guided me and helped me understand how to time travel. And who'd made me learn by heart the poem I needed to quote from to bring me back. He'd also warned me about the dangers involved. Like only being able to stay out of your own time for two hours before you had to return. And the danger of 'carrying': taking someone along with you. Jim had said that carrying could make you vulnerable to other presences and forces. I thought of the hooded figure in my dreams, and the one Jimbo and I had encountered when I took him back to see his father playing cricket as a young man. But I wouldn't be carrying if I took a quick trip now.

'Toby?'

I looked at my sister standing in the doorway. I knew what she was going to ask.

'You want a game of corridor cricket? You can bat first.'

Natalie is nine years old and already a good tennis player with a mean double-handed backhand. She also loved playing cricket.

'I still haven't had breakfast,' I said. 'Maybe if we've got time later, okay?'

It would be the quickest trip I'd ever taken. What harm could it do? Five minutes, then back inside for breakfast and corridor cricket.

I waited for the door to close behind Natalie then opened the *Wisden* to the place my thumb had been resting in. I dog-eared the page as I watched the letters swirl around in front of me.

This was the moment. This was the amazing gift that somehow I had inherited. While almost everyone else in the world who reads a *Wisden* sees words and numbers on the page, when I opened the book a sliding, swirling mess of letters and numbers swam giddily in front of my eyes, spiralling in a vortex towards the middle of the page but never quite disappearing. But with instruction from Jim, I'd learned to eventually slow and finally stop the movement. And when that happened, when the letters finally formed into the words that everyone else sees straight away, the real adventure began ...

I scanned down the page a little. The letters were small and hard to focus on, but in a few moments words started to appear. I was looking for a date, a place or any score. 'No bowler to match ...' drifted into my vision, like a fish suddenly appearing just under the surface of the water, '...demolished the Australian innings ...' Suddenly, from nowhere, 'Brisbane' swept across the page.

A familiar rushing noise like wind and fast-flowing water grew inside my head as more words settled on the page. Although it was never painful, it reached a point where I knew something had to give ...

Yuvraj Singh scored the fastest 50 in a match at Durban between India and England. He smashed his half-century in only 12 balls. The innings included 6 sixes and 3 fours.

2 Fire

THERE was a cry from all around. It wasn't a shout of joy, more one of surprise. I turned to the field. Players from everywhere were rushing in to congratulate the bowler. I swallowed and stared. It was Richard Hadlee. He was tall, with black hair and a small moustache. His shirt sleeves were rolled up. An Australian batsman was walking slowly back to the gate. I looked at the scoreboard. We were eight for 175. Hadlee had taken every wicket to fall so far — all eight of them.

There weren't many people about. Maybe the overcast and steamy conditions and the threat of rain had kept them away. Maybe they had a premonition about how the Test was going to unfold. I found a spot on a grassy bank and sat down. Like every other time I had travelled, I had arrived undetected. No one seemed the least bit interested in me having suddenly appeared, literally, from nowhere.

But the moment I had settled, I sensed that something wasn't right. I turned sharply, aware of a presence not far away, and saw a hooded black figure almost floating over the grass. No one else seemed to have seen it.

I jumped to my feet and started walking quickly in the opposite direction. Surely the other spectators wouldn't let anything happen to me? Unlike my dream, they were not disappearing or ghostly.

'You cannot escape me,' a voice rasped from just behind me.

It was time to leave. But my mind had gone blank.

'Please help!' I called, racing over to the nearest person. But he just looked at me and laughed. 'Nothing I can do, mate.'

The guy next to him laughed too. 'It's only a game, little feller. Be the same when we bowl.'

My head was spinning as I lurched away and onto a concrete path. I turned around again, stumbled and fell. I hauled myself up, but not before a hand had reached out and grasped my shoulder.

'I need help!' the voice hissed.

I swung out with all my might. My hand hit something hard and a stab of pain sliced up my arm. I broke free of his clutches and veered off, away from the ground.

The poem. I gasped for breath. The *poem*. I desperately tried to recall two lines that would get me back to the safety of home but no words came to mind.

My dream had become real. We were away from the spectators now. Only a group of kids playing cricket were in sight. I came up against a fence and spun around. The figure was right behind me.

'Stop,' it whispered. 'Stop running and listen.'

'Help!' I screamed.

A few kids turned to look at me. 'What are you doin'?' one of them called.

Suddenly the truth dawned on me. All they could see was a kid, all alone, backed up against the mesh fence, obviously looking like a complete idiot. The cloaked figure was invisible to them.

'Is it a bee?' another kid called, heading over to me.

I rolled to the left and started to run again, but had gone only a few metres when I was pulled back by a tremendous force.

I thrashed out again, this time more in anger and desperation. But the claw-like grip on my shirt wouldn't let go. I felt the pain of sharp nails tearing at my stomach and froze in terror.

'Help me, and I will leave you alone.'

I couldn't look into the face of the figure that held me.

'Don't look, just listen,' the voice hissed. I kept my head down. The hold on my shirt slackened and the pain from the scratches across my stomach eased.

'I am a time traveller, like you. But something terrible happened. I died out of my time.'

Briefly I looked up. His face was partly shielded by

the hood covering it, but I saw enough to realise it was the face from my dream.

Slowly the words sank in. Died. Out of time. The words of the poem flooded back:

> *Be aware that time moves on —*
> *Your time, this time; none short, or long.*

'I am in a lifeless zone of nothingness,' the figure went on. 'No one from here can help me. I am invisible to all except other travellers.'

But I had stopped listening.

The rushing noise began and quickly grew to a deafening roar. Something was tearing at me again. The grip of the hooded figure tightened and a searing pain ripped across my stomach. I swung my right arm out and it thudded into a box.

I found myself lying curled in a heap on the garage floor, shivering in fright. Slowly I opened my eyes. Apart from the upturned box, everything was as it should be.

'C'mon, Toby. Hurry up!'

Nat had reappeared at the door. I looked up. She was holding her yellow plastic cricket bat.

'Natalie, throw me the bat and run. Quickly!' I whispered.

'Toby, what's —'

'Just do it!'

She tossed the bat towards me and backed away. 'Is it a spider?'

'Yes!' I shouted, raising the bat above my head and creeping over to the left side of the garage. Had he followed me back? Had I carried him through to my time? I stood there, frozen, counting every second that there was no movement.

Slowly, one step at a time, I retreated, my eyes darting about. The bat was still raised when I bumped into the door. I squeezed myself through the doorway and out into the early morning sunshine. Perspiration dripped from me onto the square of cement I stood on. I closed my eyes.

'Toby! Did you get it?'

Dad burst out the back door and raced towards me. Suddenly he stopped, then came the rest of the way like he was walking over glass. 'Got to be quiet when spiders are around. Is it a biggy?' Dad had always had a thing about spiders. He was actually pretty scared of them.

I swallowed, then nodded.

'Right. Okay, let's be sensible about this. Can you walk?'

'Dad!'

'Right. Now come on.' Dad motioned with his arm for me to follow him as he started walking backwards towards the house.

'Did you get a good look?'

'Dad, I need to tell you —'

'I think perhaps we should leave this one to the experts.'

'Yep, but —'

'Wait on, Tobes. Let me grab some equipment first.'

I opened my mouth to speak but Dad waved me away and headed into the laundry.

Inside, Natalie was sitting on the stairs, chin in her hand.

'I haven't forgotten, Nats.'

'Breakfast, Toby,' Mum called from the kitchen.

'Coming, Mum. I've just —'

'Actually, that wasn't an invitation. More of a command.'

I sat at the table and started buttering a slice of toast. I wolfed it down, along with some orange juice, then got up again.

'Where are you going now?' Nat called.

'Just to check I shut the garage door.'

'But —'

'In case the big, hairy spider comes into the house.'

'Oh, okay.'

I slipped back outside and dashed over to the garage. I had to go back and check that I hadn't been followed.

I snibbed the door locked before realising that a small pile of magazines under Dad's soldering bench was on fire, smouldering and smoking. Somehow, they must have caught alight. Instinctively, I put up one hand to cover my mouth and thrashed about with the other to clear the smoke in front of me. For a few moments it worked. I took a step forwards, desperately hoping I was the only one in there. It was hard to see. I grabbed an old curtain lying on the far side of the garage and rushed towards the flames, but the material caught under my feet and I tripped and crashed to the floor.

I lay there, vaguely aware that I needed to get up and out. But my body wouldn't move. How long had I been lying there? Then I noticed the petrol cans for the mower. The fire was spreading along the boxes of old magazines and books, and flames were licking up the wooden walls — and the door!

My eyes fell on the open 1987 *Wisden*. I edged my body towards it and opened the book to the dog-eared page — the Test match from Brisbane. The swirl of words was faster than ever. The smoke was getting thicker and I was finding it difficult to breathe, even down low against the floor.

Just then a box of tools crashed down from a ledge above, smashing into the floor just metres away from me. There was a shriek from outside.

I stared at the swirling page, willing it to settle. I closed my eyes then opened them. Nothing had changed. The noise from the flames and the heat and smoke were overbearing. Someone was screaming and banging on the door outside. I trained my eyes on one section of the page. It blurred. Wiping away tears, I tried again. I feared the garage was about to explode.

I looked down, willing a word — any word — to appear. Surely that was one! I followed it till it slowed, and finally stopped. I clung to the *Wisden*, clutching it to my chest. With a scream I curled instinctively to protect myself from the flames that were about to engulf me.

A moment later I was rolling on damp moist grass. The relief from the heat was bliss.

I looked around. Same day, same Test match, but the ground was deserted. It was dark and thick grey clouds hung overhead. I turned to look at the scoreboard. I had arrived at the end of the first day's play. Australia were four for 146.

I fell back on the wet grass.

I knew that Mum and Dad would be desperate with the garage alight. They wouldn't be able to get near it and they would assume I was in there. Natalie would have told them. Their cries for me would be frantic.

Two lines of the poem and I could be back there. But should I go now and risk being burnt alive? Or should I wait, praying that neither would risk their life by racing into the fire to find me?

Maybe I could travel back to a different place? Same time, but somewhere else, like the other side of the house? But it seemed too risky. I decided to count to 300, then say two lines of the poem to get me back. I had the *Wisden*. I would just have to get out quickly.

I stared across at the grandstand opposite me and started counting. One, two, three ... I matched a seat for each number, row after row, until I had got to the front row. I tried to keep the pace even: 184, 185 ...

I got to 231 and couldn't wait any longer. I spoke aloud the two lines that had been competing for space in my head ever since I'd started to count. I could have chosen any of them — Jim had forced me to learn the whole poem by heart.

> But every word that boasts ahead
> Means lives unhinged, broken, dead.

The heat was overwhelming. I stayed low and crawled towards the door. My hand bumped something hard. The 1987 *Wisden*. I picked it up and, without another thought, jumped to my feet and lurched towards the door which had been smashed open. I staggered out and rolled to the ground.

'Toby! Oh, my God, Toby!'

I looked up into Mum's panic-stricken face.

'Mum?'

'Oh God, Toby,' she sobbed, kneeling beside me. I saw Natalie behind her, sobbing and shouting for Dad.

I closed my stinging eyes and listened to the sound of sirens approaching. I held onto the book firmly. I'd saved Dad's *Wisden*.

3 Jim's Tale

Tuesday — afternoon

I spent the whole day at home. We all did. It was amazing how quickly the fire brigade got on top of the fire, though there wasn't much left of the garage except charred wood and various unrecognisable items.

Official-looking people came throughout the day to inspect the remains and talk to Mum and Dad. I pretty much kept to myself. Mum's instructions. My throat stung, my arm ached and Dad put drops into my eyes every few hours. But I would have taken *triple* the pain if I knew I'd never see the spooky guy in the black cloak again.

It was nice having the whole family at home for the day. We played Scrabble and Monopoly, made milkshakes and went through an entire loaf of raisin toast. Mum started crying at one stage, saying we needed a good burning every month to bring us together, though Dad told me later it was the thought of having to play 'Test Match' doubles for an hour after dinner.

Wednesday — afternoon

Georgie, Rahul, Jay, Jimbo and I had planned another visit to the MCG. For the others, the excitement was going to the ground itself, but I was hoping to see Jim in the cricket library again.

Jay and Georgie had been to the library before, but had not time-travelled. They were probably my closest friends. Georgie lived just up the street from us and her mum was a good friend of my parents. We had known each other for years and had spent hours together playing games and mucking around. Georgie was almost as passionate about cricket as me. Jay loved cricket too, but he wasn't stir-fry crazy about it like I was.

Rahul had also been to the library. He'd time-travelled with me from there. He was a gentle guy who kept to himself a bit more than the others, but the travelling had changed him.

And Jimbo — who was also like Rahul in that he kept to himself and didn't seem to care much about having friends — had time-travelled too. It was with Jimbo that I had seen the hooded figure for the first time. Now that Jimbo was going to be a part of the Riverwall Cricket Team and playing games on Saturdays he was spending more time with us all.

We met outside the MCG as arranged. I pulled the card that Jim had given me from my pocket and showed it to a man wearing a colourful striped jacket.

'It's okay,' I told my friends, noticing their surprised faces. 'This little card is our ticket into the whole members' stand.'

The man nodded. 'Come along, I'll take you there myself.'

We set off up a long ramp. Huge pictures of footballers and enormous wooden boards with famous names written in gold covered the corridor walls. Every now and then we caught a glimpse of the oval itself. Finally, we reached the library door, with Georgie and Rahul arriving half a minute behind Jay and me.

'Where's Jimbo?' I asked.

He arrived a few moments later, his eyes sparkling and a look of wonder on his face.

I hadn't brought so many friends to see Jim before. He always appeared happy to see us when we arrived, though.

'Hello, Toby!' he called, putting his glasses down on the large oval table and getting up. 'And Georgie. How are you?'

Jim seemed in good spirits and not at all put out that there were five kids there. The same guy with glasses who I'd seen a number of times, but who I didn't think actually worked there, was sitting in his usual chair. His head was down and he had two *Wisden*s open on either side of him. He didn't pay us any attention.

'Now sit down here and tell me of your adventures.'

'We don't have adventures, Jim,' Georgie said. 'Well, except for Toby, that is,' she added.

Jim raised his eyebrows. 'Adventures, Toby?'

Georgie, of course, knew about the garage incident, and I'd rung up Rahul, but the others hadn't heard. So I spent the next 10 minutes going through the drama of the fire, leaving out the hooded figure and the bit of time travel that happened in between. But I think Jim sensed there were gaps in the story.

'How did the fire start?' he asked.

'Dad left his soldering iron on and I think it must have dripped onto some old magazines.'

'No one else was with you?' Jim asked quietly.

'I thought I'd carried him back,' I said. 'Remember you said that I'd only see him if I carried?' The words were rushing out. 'But I didn't carry, Jim. Not the first time I travelled —'

'What are you talking about?' Jay interrupted. I looked at Jim; I'd told him before about this evil, freaky guy. Jim nodded.

'Tell them, Toby,' he said.

The other kids were looking at me intently. Even the guy in glasses over by the secret door (it was a door into another part of the library that looked like a plain wall on this side) had looked up, his head to one side.

I looked at Jim. 'Are you sure?'

Jim nodded.

'Okay, here goes.'

Everyone leaned forwards. It had always bothered me that some of my friends, like Rahul and Jimbo, knew heaps more about the time travel because they'd actually gone with me. I looked around at the curious faces. It would be good to put my friends in the picture. But there wasn't anyone else I wanted to let know. Not yet, anyway.

'You've heard a few things lately about weird things going on with *Wisden*s, Jim here, time travel and stuff,' I began.

I paused and looked across at the guy with the two *Wisden*s. He was staring at me. He held my gaze a moment, then yawned and bent back down to his books. I lowered my voice.

'You see, Jim and I, we have this ... um, this ability to use *Wisden*s to travel back to cricket matches of the past.' I was talking to Jay, but the others seemed to be listening. 'And now, a couple of times, I've met this really spooky guy wearing a long, black cloak. But he's not like us, you know — not human. He's ... well ... '

No one moved. I looked across at Jimbo. Our eyes met. For a moment I thought he wasn't going to say anything. Then he spoke.

'It's true. I went too — back in time. I saw my dad. It's because of Toby's time travel that I'm going to be playing this weekend. And I saw this spooky guy too. It was really scary.'

For a moment no one said anything.

Then: 'You sure, Jimbo?' Jay asked.

'Yep.'

I looked at Jim, then nodded in the direction of the guy sitting a few metres away.

'Phillip, would you like to check that box that came in this morning?' Jim called over to the man.

'Yes, Jim. A pleasure.'

It was the first time I'd heard the man speak. He took his glasses off, closed the *Wisden*s and moved to the other side of the library. He was just an average-looking guy, not much older than Dad, though there was something almost *too* nice about him. I couldn't help feeling his politeness was masking something else. Still, he couldn't be all bad if he helped look after old cricket books.

Jim leaned forward. 'Now, this figure spoke to you?' he asked.

I nodded. 'He wants me to save him. Something about him dying out of time and being in a timeless zone.'

'Toby, are you serious?' Georgie looked from me to Jim.

'Yes!' I said firmly. 'Georgie, this is for real. I promise.'

'I've travelled too, Georgie,' Rahul said quietly.

'You as well? What about me, Toby? When do I go?' Jay asked.

'Maybe soon, Jay.'

'Good, because it all sounds like a major put-on, if you ask me.'

I knew Jay would be the hardest to convince, but that wasn't really my job. I couldn't control what he thought. I shrugged. 'That's cool, Jay. It would to me too,' I said, trying to make my voice sound light.

'I mean, come on. You really expect —'

'This is *not* a game,' Jim said firmly, interrupting Jay. He sighed, then shook his head slowly. 'I'm sorry, Jay.' He took another deep breath. 'Toby, this figure you speak of must be desperate if he has got to you while you were not carrying.'

'But what does he want?' I asked.

Jim thought for a moment. 'I think he wants his life back, Toby.'

'And how is Toby expected to organise that?' Georgie asked, sounding exasperated.

'I have heard of such people, trapped outside their own time. But I've never known of an actual encounter before. I wonder ...'

'What, Jim?' I breathed.

'Perhaps he has got to you because of your age,' Jim said, and sighed. 'I'm not sure. But not everything we encounter that is awful to look at means us harm. Try and listen to him, Toby. Find out what he wants.'

'Hey!' Jimbo called, changing the mood. He jumped out of his chair. I turned to see what he was looking at. Someone had come through the secret door. Jimbo walked over to it to take a closer look, and the others followed.

'Toby,' Jim leaned forwards slightly, 'I might not always be here when you come, so I want you to have this. It's a small thing but I think you will agree it will open a door to many adventures.'

Jim had pulled a small key from his jacket pocket and was holding it out to me.

'For the cupboard where the *Wisden*s are kept?'

He nodded, smiling.

I took the key from him and looked at it for a moment before closing my hand around it.

'Toby, be extra careful though, especially if you travel. This figure may just be one of many.'

'Jim, do excuse me.'

We both looked up. The guy called Phillip was standing at the door with a parcel wrapped in brown paper. He was holding it like it was some special prize. He looked at me briefly, then turned to Jim.

'From England. Addressed to you. Shall I open it?'

Just as Jim was about to reply, the secret door opened again. Rahul and Jay appeared, grinning and waving their hands, accompanied by a tall young guy with an MCG badge on his shirt. He wasn't looking as excited.

'Phillip, you're here,' the guy said. 'Can you give me a hand with some unloading downstairs?'

Jim took the parcel from Phillip, who looked disappointed that he wasn't going to be the one to open it. When he'd left, we all crowded around Jim, curious to see what the parcel contained.

Slowly Jim undid the string around the package, unwrapped it carefully and took out what looked like a very old book. We all noticed the change in Jim's expression the moment he opened the cover.

'Good Lord,' he whispered.

'What is it, Jim?' Georgie asked.

'Good Lord,' he said again, not hearing her question.

'Jim, what is it?' I repeated.

Jim was licking his lips, looking excited but tense. He took off his glasses and looked at each of us in turn. Even Jay was leaning forwards expectantly. Jim's eyes stopped on me. I held his gaze.

'Toby, forgive me. You deserved to know this sooner perhaps than now.'

I smiled, not knowing what to say. We waited a few moments then Jim spoke again.

'This book is a diary, written by my grandfather, James Oldfield. James was born in England in 1851. He grew up with a tremendous love for the game of cricket and was indeed a very good cricketer himself. Alas, he was not chosen to play for England in the First Test match in 1877.'

The secret door opened again and someone put down a box to keep it ajar. I don't think Jim even noticed.

'On James's 30th birthday he was given a *Wisden*. One of the very earliest editions. An extraordinary thing happened. When he first opened the *Wisden*, a small scorecard dropped out and fell into his lap. On that scorecard was written a strange message.'

Jim closed his eyes and recited:

> *'This one scorecard of thousands*
> *Will in any Wisden book*
> *Reveal the players' names*
> *And take you there to look.'*

'Well, of course James was a little surprised, and greatly sceptical, but when he placed the scorecard on the page of the *Wisden* showing the scores of that first Test match played between Australia and England in Melbourne, sure enough, the names mysteriously appeared on the scorecard that was completely blank a moment before.'

Jim shut the book and closed his eyes again.

'Without a hint of warning, James was transported 10,500 miles across the world to Australia and that first Test here at the Melbourne Cricket Ground.'

Jim chuckled. 'You can imagine the stares this overdressed Englishman got, stranded as he was in an Australian summer. He managed to see some of the cricket — cricket, I might say, that you would hardly recognise now. But of course he was horribly shaken and quite desperate to get home. The story goes that it took some convincing for him to finally understand and acknowledge just what had happened. Perhaps he thought he'd been drugged, or lapsed into some unconscious state, yet had somehow been taken to a game of cricket somewhere in England. Of course, he still held the scorecard in his hand and people around him were able to confirm the players actually out on the ground.

'Eventually, he must have turned the scorecard over and read aloud the two lines written on the back.'

Jim smiled and looked at me.

'Two hours is all the time
So before it's up, read these lines.'

'So did he get back safely?' Rahul asked.

'Oh yes, and he returned. Many times,' Jim replied, smiling again. 'James was so excited. He wanted to share his secret. And he did. Suddenly James was very popular. But he quickly realised his mistake. He suffered for his greed and loose tongue. Eventually he disappeared with his *Wisden*s and his precious scorecard to some remote part of England and the matter died down. But it took many years.'

'What about the scorecard?' Georgie asked. 'Is it in the diary?'

Jim sighed. 'Now, that's an interesting possibility. But no, I doubt it very much. James discovered that he didn't actually need the scorecard to time travel with the *Wisden*s. Just like you and I, Toby.'

'But maybe he's left some sort of clue about where it is?' Jimbo said.

'Yeah, like in the diary,' Jay added.

'Perhaps,' Jim said. 'But it is something best left alone. No good would —'

Jim was interrupted by a noise near the secret door. We all turned. Phillip was there, bending down to pick up a book he'd dropped. No one had noticed him come in. He grunted, nodded briefly and walked straight past the table without even looking at the diary in front of Jim.

For a moment no one spoke. How long had he been standing there, listening to Jim's story?

I stared at the old brown diary. It looked like the cover was made of leather or some kind of material. Jim picked it up gently and passed it to me. It was soft and about the size and thickness of an average paperback. Rahul and the others gathered round me. I opened the book a few pages in. The writing was tall and sloped in black ink and hard to read even though it was very neat.

'It even *smells* old,' Georgie breathed, holding her hand out to touch it.

'Now *there's* a relic, Jim. Just come in?' It was the young guy in the MCG shirt.

'Yes, just this afternoon,' Jim replied. I handed the diary back to him. 'I'll have a look at it tonight and see if it's of any interest or value,' he added, carefully wrapping it in the brown paper again.

'But Jim, you just —' Georgie was frowning.

'I think perhaps it's time you young people were off home, don't you?' he suggested, the smile never leaving his face.

'C'mon, guys,' I said, getting up. 'We'll call back again some time, Jim.'

The others followed me out.

4 Mini Cricket

Thursday — afternoon

AFTER the drama of the last few days it was good to be back doing what I liked best: playing cricket. Mr Pasquali, our teacher and cricket coach, seemed pretty pumped about the game coming up — a one-dayer against Benchley Park.

He spoke to us after cutting short our nets session.

'A win on Saturday probably means we'll stitch up a top-two position on the ladder. That means we avoid a semi-final against the Scorpions.'

'We're gonna have to beat them some time.'

'True, Scott, but I'd rather knock them off in the final, wouldn't you?'

'I guess,' said Scott, shrugging.

'Now, a one-dayer means we need control, concentration and tightness in the field. We're going to spend the last 20 minutes fine-tuning that. Ally, put on the gloves. Jono, set a field for a tight finish.

Let's say 20 runs needed off the last three overs.' Mr Pasquali clapped his hands. 'Let's do it.'

Most of the kids raced over to Jono (our captain) to get their favourite fielding position. I caught Jimbo's eye.

'You rapt to be playing on Saturday?' I asked him.

'Can't wait.' He grinned. It would be his first game with us, even though he trained each week.

Finally Jono had set his field and we waited for Mr Pasquali to belt the ball to wherever he chose. He had organised Rahul to pad up and act as the runner. Mr Pasquali stood at the batter's end and smashed the ball out into the off side.

'Yes!' he shouted, and Rahul came haring down the wicket. But Scott had snapped up the ball and hurled it flat and hard to Ally behind the stumps. She swiped off the bails.

'Howzat?' she yelled as Rahul lunged forwards, stretching with his bat towards the line.

Mr Pasquali stood for a moment, straightened, then raised his finger. We roared our approval. Scott was doing some silly dance, shaking his hands and waving his two first fingers in the air. Rahul jogged back to the other end of the pitch.

'They're seven down now. Seventeen balls, 20 runs. On your toes, everyone.'

We were all expecting another crashing shot, but Mr Pasquali just dropped the ball in front of him.

'Yes!' he yelled again.

Ally scampered from behind the stumps, dived at

212

the ball and flicked it underarm behind her while still in midair. It was a spectacular effort. Rahul wouldn't have made half the pitch if she'd hit the stumps. But she didn't.

'Again!' Mr Pasquali roared. Rahul spun around and raced back up the pitch.

'Wrong option, Ally. And why weren't you running in to cover the stumps?' he bellowed at Jay, who was fielding in slips.

'Yeah, idiot,' Scott called.

'And you!' Mr Pasquali said, pointing to the stumps at the bowler's end. 'C'mon, everyone. We need to back up and cover the stumps every time there's a run on.'

It was a tense last few minutes. Mr Pasquali and Rahul missed out on winning, but only just.

'That was almost as good as a real game,' Georgie said, as we packed up our gear.

'If you don't get yelled at,' Jay mumbled.

Friday — morning

Mr Pasquali had put up the team list for this weekend's game. I didn't spend too much time looking at it. The local paper, delivered on Friday afternoons, would be there when I got home after school. It had the teams as well as the previous week's results and ladder.

It was a boiling hot day and after lunch Mr Pasquali let us play games.

'Educational games,' he added wryly, giving us a wink.

'Jimbo and I — we've been working on a new game, Mr Pasquali,' I said.

A few other kids raised their heads. Jimbo was smiling.

'Oh?' said Mr Pasquali.

We'd played plenty of dice cricket, 'Test Match' and computer games, but I wanted to do something different. Something with a bit of action. Jimbo and I had been working on 'Mini Cricket'. You played it with a table-tennis ball, a mini cricket bat and run-scoring areas similar to the nets in indoor cricket.

'Would you like a demo?' I asked.

Five minutes later we had moved the tables and cleared a space in the middle of the room. Only Scott Craven and his mate, Gavin Bourke, hung back, pretending to be more interested in something they were doing on the computer.

We divided into two teams, with Mr Pasquali as captain of one and me of the other. You had to stay on your knees at all times. Catching a table-tennis ball smashed at you proved way harder than most people thought it would be. Hitting any cricket poster or book in the room meant you got a free life.

Rahul was the only one to do that. When he was finally out, he insisted that Mr Pasquali should get two lives himself on account of his old age, failing eyesight and slower reaction time.

'Shouldn't that be three lives?' Mr Pasquali joked before knocking up a cool 47 runs.

I noticed Gavin looking around often, but Scott

214

remained glued to his computer, not turning around once. He'd missed out on a fun game.

'So, you want to hear the grand plan, everyone?' Dad asked us at the dinner table that night. Mum was rolling her eyes. 'Thought so. We're going to build a studio.'

'We are?' Nat asked.

'Yep. Best thing that could have happened, that fire. That garage was full of junk anyway.'

'What about all your books and stuff?' I asked.

'Well, the *Wisden*s were saved,' Dad said, reaching across for the sauce. He seemed very excited about his new project. He'd already drawn up some plans and they were spread across the entire far end of the table. We were obviously going to get a full briefing after dinner.

Later, I took the newspaper up to my room and checked out the teams. Jimbo was in, Ahmazru out. He'd made a duck last week and only three in the game before. It looked like Mr Pasquali had put us in batting order. Scott was due for some runs and was opening the batting with Cameron.

I checked out Benchley Park's form. They'd beaten TCC by 13 runs, so they'd be feeling confident. But the ladder showed us 16 points clear. Jono was right, though, when he'd said that the bottom four sides were all close together. Only three points separated third place from sixth. Benchley Park would be *really* keen to do well tomorrow.

Ladder	P	W	L	Bat P	Bowl P	Win P	Total
The Scorpions	3	3	0	20	19	15	54
Riverwall	3	2	1	19	14	10	43
Motherwell State	3	1	2	14	10	5	29
St Mary's	3	1	2	12	11	5	28
Benchley Park	3	1	2	12	10	5	27
TCC	3	1	2	11	10	5	26

(NB 5 points for a win — 1 point per 30 runs —
1 point every 2 wickets)

I stared at the ladder, the teams and the draw for
Round 5 for a few more minutes, then pulled down a
few cricket books from my bookshelf and settled into
bed for some reading.

A monster innings was completed by a batsman
in Tasmania in 1902. Charles Eady smashed a
huge 566 runs for his club team, Break o'Day.
He made the score over three afternoons, and hit
13 fives (that's what six used to be worth) and a
cool 68 fours. On the first day of the game,
Eady took 7/87. I wonder if he was
man of the match!

5 Benchley Park

IT was the usual madness of a Saturday morning, with Mum and Nat racing around the kitchen looking for tennis gear, me hunting for my lucky socks and batting gloves, and Dad absolutely nowhere to be seen.

I found him eventually out by the fence, pacing out distances for his studio.

'Mum and Nat gone?' he asked.

'Yep. C'mon, Dad. If you're doing your usual stop at the —'

'No stops today. Look!' Dad held up an enormous book. '*The Complete Guide to Do-It-Yourself Makeovers.* There's a whole section on turning an unwanted room into a room of your dreams that you won't ever want to leave. It even —'

'*Dad!*'

'Yep. Right. Let's go, Toby.'

He marched purposefully towards the street, where the car was parked.

'Keys? Lock the house?'

'Good idea.' He spun around and headed back.

'Meet you at the car,' I called.

It was another perfect summer morning. We were playing at Benchley Park's home ground. For some reason they had switched venues. The draw said we should be playing at home, but Mr Pasquali had told us all to meet at Benchley Park.

It was a tiny oval in a quiet neighbourhood. It was surrounded on three sides by streets, though in the two times I'd played there before I couldn't remember seeing a car travelling on any of them. We often joked about hitting a car. I'd seen plenty of hits land on the road — on the full!

I watched Jono shake hands with the opposing captain. Hopefully one day I'd get to captain a team.

We gathered round as he walked back to us. 'Remind me not to call tails again. We're batting.'

Not a bad move by their captain. It would be hotter fielding later in the morning and a few early wickets could put us under pressure. At least batting second you knew what your target was and could adjust accordingly. Then again, we would have the runs on the board and they couldn't be taken away from us.

'What you puttin' the pads on for?' Scott asked Georgie. He asked her every week and got the same reply.

'Same reason I told you last time.'

Georgie was batting seventh but liked to be prepared.

'Hey, Martian. You playing?' Jay asked.

Martian shrugged. 'One more week and they reckon I'm back. That is, if I can get back in the team,' he added, looking at Ally.

Ally held up her hands. 'Hey, no worries there, Martian. I'm no permanent fixture.'

'No one is,' Mr Pasquali said, rubbing sunscreen onto the back of his neck. 'Now, you know the rules. Good, strong, sensible batting. Rahul, Jimbo, Scott — look to take advantage of the short boundaries. We should be aiming for a good score to put pressure on their batters later in the morning. Good toss to lose, Jono.'

'Mr Pasquali, do you know those guys over there?' Rahul asked. We all looked. Two men were leaning against a car, one with a clipboard in his hand.

'Well, I can tell you that the man with the sunglasses is Trevor Barnes.'

'As in Trevor Barnes who coaches the rep side?' I asked, looking again. He had the cream of all the players under 18 in the area. They trained for three hours on Sunday morning and played in a big carnival at the end of each season against the best teams from the State.

'The very one.'

'I'd say they're here to check out the talent, wouldn't you, Mr Pasquali?' Georgie asked.

'Well, they won't be looking at you then,' Scott chuckled.

'No, they're here to check out Jimbo,' she replied, completely ignoring Scott's pathetic joke.

'Bull. They wouldn't even know he was playing,' said Scott.

'Maybe someone told them,' Rahul suggested.

'They'll look at all of you, and the opposition too,' Mr Pasquali said, and walked over to talk to the other umpire.

'You want a hit, Scott?' I asked, picking up an old cricket ball. Although I didn't like him, we were on the same team and at the end of the day I'd do anything to help the team. (*See Tip 2.*)

'I'll tell you what I want. I don't want to be run out, you hear?'

'Hey, Toby,' Martian called. 'Do you know how to score?'

'Sounds like much more fun,' I said, dropping the ball at Scott's feet. I was getting sick of his arrogance. Anyway, scoring was still helping the team. I went over and sat with Martian and the 12th man from Benchley Park.

Scott did what he'd threatened to do all season: he smashed the bowlers all over the park. After only five overs he was striding back off the field, cursing the rule that said batters in one-day games had to retire at 30. He was on 35, the highest possible score.

'Why don't you leave your pads on, just in case?' Jay asked him. 'You can go back in if —'

'Mate, if I have to go back in, that would mean

we'd have lost nine wickets in half a morning of batting. I'd walk out on this team if that happened.'

He hurled his bat at his kit and tore at the velcro to undo his pads.

'I'd be that angry too if I'd just knocked up 35 runs with three sixes and four fours,' I whispered to Martian, looking at the scorecard in front of me.

'Well, *he* won't be dropped for the last game before the finals.'

'You never know,' I said.

Actually, we did lose a few wickets, six in all. I'm not sure that Mr Pasquali was totally pleased with some of our shot selections. I was one of the offenders, slashing at a wide ball and being caught in the gully. It was an awesome catch, maybe even a fluke, but it was still a bad shot.

Georgie said that it was Scott's fault for making it look too easy, though she didn't say that to his face. Jimbo walked out after a mini middle-order batting collapse when we'd lost three wickets for 17 runs. He blocked his first two deliveries, then smashed the next one back over the bowler's head and onto the road. It bounced on a driveway and clattered against a garage door. It was a spectacular way to score his first runs for Riverwall Cricket Club.

A car horn tooted away to our left. It was Jimbo's family. He made his 30 too, with some fantastic drives and one massive pull shot that ended up in a playground another oval away on the park side of the ground.

We'd had 35 overs bowled at us and we'd made 191.

'Only five and a half an over for them to win,' Rahul called from the little table where the scorecard was. 'Quite possible on this ground.'

'Absolutely. Remember our training session last Thursday? Let's get out there and do it,' Jono called.

Only twice has a team defeated its opposition by 10 wickets. This is a result where the second team batting passes the first team's score without losing a wicket. South Africa scored 0/130 to pass Pakistan's total in a game in 2007 and Austrlaia made 0/102 to defeat Sri Lanka on 20 September, 2007.

6 So Close!

WE all lathered ourselves with sunscreen and jogged out for a few catches before the Benchley Park innings started.

'Toby and Scott are opening the attack,' Jono announced. 'Three overs each. We'll see how things look before I decide on the next bowlers.'

Mr Pasquali tossed me the cricket ball. I loved the feel of a brand new shining red cricket ball. The white stitches stood out hard. I rubbed it on my trousers, more out of habit as it couldn't be any shinier, and watched Jono set the field.

'A couple of slips?' he called across to me.

'Yep, third man too, no mid-off.'

'You sure?' he asked.

'Yep. Bring cover around if you like. I want them driving.'

'Okay.' (*See Tip 3.*)

It was great how Jono let you have your say if you were bowling. He respected that we had our plans too. Normally I'd ease into it, my first few balls more like warm-up deliveries. But this time I decided to go flat out from the first ball and see what happened.

I'd measured my run-up and was waiting at the top of my mark for the batter to take his stance. He looked around the field once more then settled over his bat, tapping it against the crease. (*See Tip 6.*)

I strolled in, trying to make it look like this was a warm-up ball. But in my final strides I sped up and sent down a fast delivery heading for off-stump. I don't think the batter even saw it. The ball clipped the outside of the off-stump and sped away between Ally and Jono at first slip.

The batter looked at the bail lying next to the stumps, shook his head a few times and started the long walk back.

The team raced in, cheering and yelling and high-fiving me and everyone else.

'Save some for me,' was all Scott said.

We got back to our positions quickly, Jono asking me if I wanted any adjustments to the field. I wondered what Brett Lee would do now? Bang in a short one? Go for the yorker?

'Maybe bring mid-wicket in heaps closer,' I said. 'Make it Jimbo and put Jay at square leg,' I added. 'Yeah?'

'Sure, you got a plan?' Jono asked.

'Yep.'

I called Jay to come in closer from where he was standing next to Mr Pasquali at square leg. Jimbo was already hovering at short mid-wicket. I also called Scott in another five metres at cover. He walked in three.

I charged in. It was a classic set-up, but needed the perfect delivery to make it work. The batter's right foot was nudging backwards as I delivered the ball. Everything suggested something short. A bouncer that would be attacking his body. Following him and maybe crashing into his chest. But it was nothing like that. He was taken totally by surprise.

It was a perfect yorker, the ball rattling into the base of the middle and leg stumps. The batter was nowhere near it.

Once again the players rushed in to congratulate me.

'You don't have to kiss him!' Scott said to Georgie, who was patting my shoulder.

'No, I guess I'll save that for when you get your first wicket,' she said, sounding totally sick of his useless comments.

'Merv Hughes kissed,' said Jimbo.

'Who?'

'Merv Hughes. That big guy with the monster moustache. He kissed a couple of players on the field,' Jimbo said. It was the most he'd spoken all day.

'It's true,' Rahul added.

'Just shut up, would ya?' Scott sneered.

'You brought it —'

'Guys, Toby's on a *hat trick*. What's the plan?' Georgie asked.

'Obvious. Bring everyone in. That's what they do on the TV,' said Scott. Scott was an awesome cricketer, but I wasn't sure if he knew heaps about tactics. Still, he was basically right. The batter, facing a hat trick, wasn't going to go the slog. (*See Tip 12.*)

Jono brought the fielders in closer, though no one was allowed to be nearer to the batter than half a pitch length.

'Maybe the slower one, Toby,' Jimbo whispered to me as I walked back to my bowling mark.

'Just what I was thinking,' I said, and grinned. I'd never got a hat trick. I'd been *on* one a few times, but never taken three wickets in three balls. I stole a look at Dad. The DIY manual was on the ground next to his chair and he was leaning forwards. He held up a hand, his fingers crossed. The two guys by the cars also looked like they were paying careful attention.

I steamed in, a bit quicker even than the last delivery. I tucked my right big finger underneath the seam, the way I'd been shown. The ball was on a good length. The batter pushed at it early and it spooned into the air. (*See Tip 4.*)

I was celebrating even before Scott had taken the catch. Everyone was set to charge in. Mr Pasquali had one foot in the air, anticipating the wicket about to fall. But somehow Scott managed to drop it. He swore loudly and kicked the ball away towards Ally. She wasn't looking and the batters scampered through for a run.

'You shouldn't have run towards me!' Scott yelled at me, shaking his head.

'What?' I said, disgusted.

'I thought you —'

'C'mon, heads up,' called Jono. 'Let's have another one, Toby.'

I couldn't believe what had happened. It was the easiest catch I'd ever seen. And Scott Craven had put it down. On purpose?

After the drama of the first half of my first over, things settled down. I didn't take another wicket, but Scott took two in his three overs. After six overs we had them 4 for 23. But after that the game changed.

'You know what they've done, don't you?' Jimbo said at the first drinks break. It was getting hot and Mr Pasquali had arranged for a couple of breaks.

'What?' Ally asked, having downed half a bottle of orange juice.

'They've put their best batters into the middle order.' It was true. They certainly looked confident and comfortable out there.

'Maybe it's because Scott and *that* aren't bowling,' said Gavin Bourke, nodding towards me. I was obviously *that*.

'Maybe,' said Jimbo. 'But I don't think so.'

Their next three batters each made their 30. We then took the remaining six wickets within the space of four overs. It was pathetic. There were two run-outs, which looked so set up it wasn't funny. And the stumping was a joke. Ally had fumbled the ball, but the kid just kept on walking. Not even the batter at the other end yelled at him to get back into his crease.

227

All of a sudden the two middle-order players, who had knocked up 30 runs each, were back in the middle and hitting us around everywhere. We'd been sucked in big time. Scott and I each had one over left to bowl.

At the next drinks break Jono asked us for our thoughts.

'Give me the ball and I'll knock 'em both over,' Scott told everyone. They were 8 for 142 with eight overs left.

'I reckon we do it now,' I said. 'No point in waiting.'

'I agree,' Jimbo said, nodding his head.

'Rahul?'

'Yes. They haven't faced Toby or Scott. Even if we don't get the wickets, we should slow up the run rate. They need 50 runs off eight overs. That's six an over. We should be able to hold them if we can get it out to eight an over.'

Jono tossed the ball to Scott. We shouted some words of encouragement and went back to our positions. Scott bowled fast and accurate, but they kept him out. Still, only one run scored meant that now it was up to seven an over.

The ball had lost most of its shine and the stitches were flatter. I worked hard on one side, rubbing it vigorously up and down my leg as Jono positioned the field. I looked around. There was cover on the boundaries for me on both sides of the wicket as well as a deep mid-on. (*See Tip 7.*)

The first three balls were dot balls; no score, but no wickets either. The fourth ball I sent down a bit quicker, outside off-stump. The batter flashed at it and missed.

'He's rattled!' yelled Scott from the covers. Mr Pasquali glared at him. I sent the next one down a little wider. Again he flashed at it. This time there was a noise. Ally took the catch and I charged down the wicket, my arms in the air.

I was just about to high-five with Ally when I heard Jono's voice.

'What?'

I turned around. The umpire had his arms outstretched. A wide! I couldn't believe it. It was wide enough, but the kid had definitely got an edge.

'Howzat!' I yelled at the umpire, thinking that maybe no one had appealed and for some dumb reason he needed one to give the batter out. But he just smiled at me and shook his head.

'Two more, Richard, then we're clear,' the umpire called smugly to the batter at the other end.

The next ball was maybe the fastest ball I'd ever bowled. But it did nothing but smack into Ally's gloves. It hurt too, though she disguised it well. I looked across at Jimbo. He pointed to his chin. I nodded. I wasn't out to hurt him, just make him know that he was in a cricket match. And maybe get a dot ball out of it too.

I ran in hard and hurled the ball down. It bounced early and careered up towards the batter's face. He fended it off and the ball ballooned off the splice of his bat. The runner and I took off together. We both seemed to be heading for the ball. He was blocking me. I shoved him aside and dived full stretch, catching the ball centimetres off the ground.

'Toby! Bowler!' Jono was yelling at me and pointing to the bowler's end. I swung around and hurled the ball at the stumps as the batter scrambled back. The umpire had his arm out for a no ball. I fell back onto the ground as the ball smashed into the stumps, knocking the middle stump flying and causing the umpire to jump out of the way.

Everyone yelled, 'Howzatt!!!'

We looked at the umpire. Reluctantly he raised his finger. You can't get a wicket by catching someone off a no ball, but you sure as heck can run someone out. (*See Tip 10.*)

We won the game by 21 runs. Mr Pasquali didn't mention anything about the weird events of Benchley Park's innings, but I noticed him having a serious talk to their coach after the game. I also saw him chatting to Trevor Barnes. The other guy had gone.

'Fantastic, Toby. Well bowled. A bit stiff, I thought, not getting your hat trick.'

'Thanks, Dad,' I said. 'You ever get a hat trick?'

He shook his head. 'But you'll get one.'

'You think so?'

'I'm sure so. You keep bowling like that, and it might even be for Australia as opposed to Riverwall.'

230

I stared out the window imagining what it would be like to take three Test wickets in three balls. The crowd would be going berserk. And then I'd be walking down to fine leg at the end of the over. And the crowd would be roaring and chanting, 'Jo-ones, Jo-ones!' And I'd give them a little wave...

'Oh, by the way, a nice chap from the MCG turned up about half an hour ago,' Dad said to me in the car on the way home. 'Asked me to give you this.' He passed over an envelope.

I tore it open. It was an invitation to go to the MCC library and receive an award for rescuing the *Wisden* from the fire.

'Dad, did you organise this?'

'What?'

'This invite to the library at the MCG. To get an award?'

'No.' He kept his eyes on the road, but he seemed curious about it. 'Read it to me.'

Dear Toby,
Brave deeds deserve rewards.
You are invited to the MCC Library
at the MCG
next Monday
at 5.30pm
for a small ceremony
to mark your efforts to save a *Wisden*.

'And?' Dad asked.

'And what?'

'Who's it from?'

'Jim, I guess. There's no signature. Who gave you the envelope, Dad?'

'Not sure. Pleasant-looking guy. Said he worked in the library up there at the MCG. He just said, "Mr Jones? A letter for your son."'

'Did he stay for the cricket?'

'Don't think so. Never saw him again. You might have to go alone, mate. Mum and Nat have ballet class starting this Monday so they won't be there. I've got a builder coming round, you know, to see the site and —'

'It's okay, Dad.'

'But listen, I can cancel. Maybe put him off —'

'Dad, it's cool. Georgie will come.'

'Now that's a good idea. She'll love it. And while we're on the subject of bravery and *Wisden*s, can I ask you just one question?'

I knew what was coming. I'd been waiting all week for it.

'Why in heaven's name did you go into the garage to rescue a book?'

'It was a *Wisden*, Dad.'

'I don't care if it was the only surviving copy of the bloody Dead Sea Scrolls, Toby,' Dad roared. He was upset but trying hard to stay in control. For a while neither of us spoke. I turned and gazed out the side window.

'It was the only *Wisden* with your name in it,' I said lamely.

232

Dad seemed about to speak, then stopped. He shook his head a few times.

'Hey, Dad?'

'Hmm?'

'I reckon we should have a little plaque made — maybe a *Wisden* page or something? You know, for your new studio?'

'And that's a dumb idea too!' But he was smiling — just.

> If you'd seen the game played between South Africa and West Indies on 11 September 2007 at Johannesburg, you would have seen the most runs scored in boundaries in a game. Thirty-six fours and 18 sixes were struck during the match for a combined total of 252 runs scored in boundaries.

7 Being Chased

'WILL you come?'

'Of course I will, idiot,' said Georgie. 'But I'll meet you there, okay? Mum's having a panic attack about your birthday. We've gotta go shopping after school and it could get ugly. Don't wait. I'll get in somehow. Take your phone.'

I did wait, for about 10 minutes, then at five-thirty exactly I made my way through the glass door and up the ramp. No one seemed to be paying me much attention. Perhaps they were used to seeing me around by now.

The library appeared deserted, which was strange for an award ceremony. I pulled out the invitation and checked it again.

'Toby?'

I jumped at the sound of his voice.

'You got the message then?' It was the guy called Phillip who was always hanging around the library.

234

'Y-yes.'

'Good. Well, come in then. Let's get on with it, shall we?'

This wasn't sounding right.

'Where's Jim?'

'Oh, Jim said he wasn't going to be able to make it. He's not well, you know, Toby. He's very old.'

The knot in my stomach tightened.

'I'd better go.'

'What, and not get your prize? Jim has told me all about it. He's just so sorry he can't be here to watch.'

I looked into Phillip's face. 'W-who are you?'

'Me? Oh, I'm just a collector of books. Help out in the library sometimes. In fact, I think I've seen you before, yes? With a few of your friends?'

Maybe this guy was okay. Maybe I was just imagining things. Still, it would be nice if Georgie — or even better, Jim — turned up right now.

'Come along then and I'll fetch your reward.' He moved quickly over to a trolley by the main desk where a computer sat. 'Hmm, now where did he put it?'

'So Jim organised this?' I asked, not moving any closer.

'Oh, we all thought it was a good idea. Here we are.' He turned around and handed me a small parcel.

'Well, open it,' he said excitedly. 'You'll like it, I'm sure.'

I unwrapped the package. It was a green-covered *Wisden*. Thinner and shinier than the yellow ones I knew so well.

'Thank you,' I said, staring at its cover. It had the same writing as the yellow books.

'It's the Australian version. Go on, open it.'

I hesitated, wondering whether I'd see the swirls or normal writing. I opened the front cover. Someone had written my name on the inside.

'Thanks,' I said again, not looking up. I placed it on the table in front of me, closing the wrapping paper around it.

'A pleasure. Now, Jim said that you might like to look in the *Wisdens*' cupboard. I'm here till six o'clock if you'd like to dip in there and browse. I was supposed to have the bookcase open and ready for you, but I left my keys in the car. But I know Jim has given you a key. You must be a very special boy.' He went back to the main desk and started typing on the keyboard.

I stood there a moment, wondering how the man knew I had a key. Had he seen Jim pass it to me that day in the library? Or maybe Jim had told him I had a key when he'd organised the reward? I put my hand into my pocket and felt the small key there. I'd carried it with me constantly since Jim had given it to me.

The key fitted the bookcase lock perfectly and turned easily. There was a little click, and the glass-panelled door gently opened outwards. Row upon row of first brown and then yellow *Wisdens* were lined up along the shelves.

Almost the last thing Jim had said to me was that he might not always be here when I came. I reached into the cupboard to take out the 1931 *Wisden*. It was old and brown. This was the *Wisden* that would describe the Test match that Jim had missed as a 10-year-old boy. The 1930 Test match at Leeds. The game he longed to return to, but couldn't. He'd tried, but had only travelled from the hospital to the library here. There must have been some force stopping him. He'd had all his life to go back.

There was something hidden in the gap behind the *Wisden*.

'Hey, um —'

'Mr Smale,' the man said softly, walking towards me.

'Mr Smale. It's the old diary Jim was sent.'

'Well, well, so it is,' he whispered, holding his hand out. 'Best you give that to me, Toby. It's very precious. I can't imagine why Jim would hide it in there.'

I'm not sure what prompted me — perhaps the fact that no one else seemed to know about the invitation and the award or maybe because Mr Smale seemed to know too much about the *Wisden*s and yet not quite enough — but suddenly I bolted. I had the 1931 *Wisden* in one hand and the diary in the other as I charged towards the door.

'Toby?' Mr Smale sounded surprised. For a moment I hesitated.

'Stop!' This time I heard his anger. I ran.

I belted round the corner and headed for the stairs. I could hear his footsteps not far behind. I tore down the steps, three — four — at a time, almost overbalancing.

'Stop him! He's stolen a valuable book!' Phillip Smale cried from the top of the stairs.

'Hey!'

I had cannoned into a lady coming up. But I was past her before she could do anything. I got to the bottom and spun around. I heard more footsteps coming from the opposite direction. A voice called from behind. I tucked the diary inside my shirt and bolted to the right. I was in the long tunnel that ran around the ground.

I glanced back over my shoulder, still running. A man stood at the bottom of some steps, talking into a phone. Maybe he was security, organising for all the exits to be closed.

I ran on until I was out of his line of sight, then ducked behind a drinks stand and pulled out my mobile. I pressed 2, then hit send.

'Georgie? Is that you?'

'Toby, geez, I'm sorry. Have I —'

'Doesn't m-matter,' I said, panting. 'I'm in strife. Listen. How far away are you?'

'Toby, I'm here.'

'Where?'

'In the library. But where —'

'Doesn't matter. Come down those stairs just near the kitchen, but watch out for the guy with ... Georgie? Georgie?' I shouted.

'Toby? Is that you?' There was a new voice on the phone. 'You silly boy, what on earth has got into you? Now come on up and return those books. I'd

238

hate to think what Jim would say if he knew what was going on.'

I turned the phone off. Was it time to call in help? Or was I the person at fault here? I mean, what had the guy actually done? Sure, he'd acted a bit weird. But maybe guys who collected old books were a bit weird. Or maybe it was me that was acting weird. Maybe the *Wisden*s were doing something to me.

Still, there was no choice now that Georgie was up there with him. I'd go up to the library, give him the diary and then Georgie and I would clear out fast.

'Well, thank heavens for that,' Phillip Smale said, holding out his hand for the diary. He was smiling pleasantly. I didn't even get to open it, I thought, as I went to pass it to him.

'Wait!' called Georgie. 'Did you find the scorecard in there?' she asked me.

'Wha —'

'It's very precious to Jim, and you promised him you'd never let it leave your sight.' Georgie had just put her foot in it, big time. I didn't have the scorecard and she knew it.

We were both looking at her now.

'What are you talking about?' I said.

'Let me look!' Phillip Smale grabbed the diary and flicked through it quickly, holding it upside down.

'Where is it?' he snapped.

'I don't know,' I said, making a face at Georgie. It was the truth.

'Jim must have it,' Georgie said. 'We've never actually seen it.'

'You're lying!' Smale shouted.

'We *aren't* lying,' Georgie said. She was starting to sound frightened.

'Look, I think for Jim's sake we'd all better have a quick hunt for it. He *is* getting a bit forgetful. What do you say? Five minutes?' The cheeriness had come back into Mr Smale's voice but now I could tell it was fake.

I licked my lips and nodded. Georgie didn't say anything.

'C'mon, Georgie, let's start on the *Wisden*s,' I said.

But Georgie seemed to be in a panic. Her face went white and she began breathing in gasps.

'Why don't you just sit down, young lady, while Toby and I search,' said Smale.

I couldn't understand Georgie's behaviour. Normally she was the brave one. The first in for a dare; the first up for a challenge. But now she was sobbing. Her shoulders heaved as her breathing became more hysterical.

'Goodness me!' Phillip Smale cried, sounding exasperated, but trying to keep some calm in his voice.

'Georgie,' I said, grabbing her shoulders and shaking her gently. She moved a little so that I was standing between her and Smale, who was rummaging through Jim's desk. She looked down, still gasping and wheezing. I followed her gaze. Somehow she had got hold of the diary while Smale was distracted by searching for the scorecard. She nodded slightly towards the *Wisden* in my hand.

'C'mon, Georgie, we'll be fine,' I said, opening it and staring intently at the page. If I could do it to escape fire, I could do it from here. I still held her shoulders and my grip tightened as the words began to appear.

Georgie kept on sobbing, but more quietly now. I was almost there. The word 'Leeds' flashed into my consciousness, then disappeared. Then, suddenly, '334'.

No, it can't be! I thought, my eyes racing across the page to see more words.

'Right. Calmed down, has she?'

Ignoring Mr Smale, I locked onto that one number again — maybe one of the most famous scores in Australian cricket history. The numbers spun, merged, then formed again: '334'. I could even make out the name close by: 'Bradman'.

'Hold on, Georgie.'

'Hey! Where's the ...'

But Mr Smale's voice drifted away into the distance, or else we did. For a moment I was aware of Georgie and me and nothing else.

8 The Great Don Bradman

'TOBY?' Georgie's voice sounded in my head. I opened my eyes and made a quick survey of the scene around me.

'Come on!' I said, hauling her to her feet.

'Toby? What happened?' She turned to look at the crowd behind us. 'Why is everyone ...' Her voice trailed away.

We were standing next to a square brick building that looked like a shelter. Everyone was crammed in, their backs to us, facing the oval. And suddenly I realised why.

'Georgie, it'll be Don Bradman out there.'

'Good. Can you wake me up now?'

I grabbed her by the arms and turned her to face me.

'Listen, Georgie. We've done what I've been telling you about for the last five weeks. We've just travelled

242

back in time. Back to a cricket match. I just happened to be holding the 1931 *Wisden*.'

A bit of colour was coming back to her face. She still clutched the diary to her chest.

'Georgie? It's okay. We can't go back now. Smale will be waiting for us. C'mon.'

Georgie tucked the diary under her T-shirt and followed me into the crowd. The spectators were packed in close and spilling out onto the oval itself, where hordes of people sat in the bright sunshine enjoying the cricket. There wasn't the usual noise of a modern Test match. It was quieter, with lots of chatter rather than shouts and chants.

'Toby, look at us!'

'What?'

'What we're wearing.'

I noticed a guy with a cloth cap and waistcoat, a cigarette dangling from his mouth, looking at me.

'Where's tha been? A fancy dress party, eh?'

'Yes,' Georgie said, her head lowered. 'Very fancy dress.'

''Ere, Eddy,' the man went on. 'You think our John down at the mill would like a look at this get-up?'

I looked at Georgie. She smiled and shrugged.

'Well, we'd better be going,' I told the man, trying to sound English.

'Aye, that's a right queer accent too,' he chuckled.

We both pushed into the crowd. I was desperate to get a look at Don Bradman. What would Jim say when I told him *this*?

'Toby, I don't think this is a good idea,' Georgie whispered as I squeezed myself into a small gap between two kids. They were giving us strange looks.

'How much is he?' I asked the kid next to me. He was wearing long shorts, socks and a cap. He looked like he'd walked straight out of school.

'Tha what?'

He also talked in a funny way.

'D-o-n B-r-a-d-m-a-n.' I spoke the two words slowly.

'Look at the scoreboard,' he said, nodding to his left, still staring at me. I went to tuck in my T-shirt but I couldn't cover the words 'Go Aussies' splashed across the front in green and gold.

There was a buzz of noise, then a ripple of applause. It didn't last long. One of the batters had just smacked a four.

'Was that Bradman?' I asked.

'Aye,' the kid nodded.

Georgie was looking more relaxed now. The whisper was going round a portion of the crowd nearby that we were just back from some fancy dress party.

'We'll give it three overs then head back,' I murmured to Georgie. 'We can't be away forever.'

'But won't that guy at the library be waiting for us?'

'Probably. And he's got all night, but we haven't. We're going to have to chance it. Whatever happens, we can't stay here for long. We'll get stuck, like that hooded guy I told you about.'

There was another rise in crowd noise, though people didn't shout, they just clapped then started talking again. I looked at the scoreboard. It was a big wooden box. Bradman had scored 81 and the other batter, Woodfull, was on 18.

Bradman was awesome. He was so quick to move, dancing down to make a half volley or stepping back to cut a ball for four. He didn't seem to hit the ball hard, but worked the ball around. He must have had really strong wrists.

I think Georgie had finally realised where she was, though she couldn't decide between looking at the cricket and staring at the faces around us. There were plenty of fairly grim-looking people, but they seemed engrossed in the cricket. Maybe they were looking glum because of Don Bradman.

'C'mon,' I said to her, starting to move away.

'Is tha comin' back?' the boy asked me.

'Probably not for a while.'

He was holding something out to me.

'They're boiled lollies,' Georgie whispered. 'Take
one.'

He offered them to Georgie too. She reached into her pocket and pulled out something.

'Georgie, no, you can't!'

'What's it matter?' She had a packet of pink fluoro bubble gum. She unwrapped one, popped it in her mouth then passed the packet to the boy. He took it, but looked nervous.

'Georgie, *no!*'

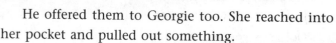

245

She blew an enormous bubble. It splashed back onto her face, covering her nose and mouth. Everyone around was watching. Georgie grinned. 'See you later, guys!' she called.

We weaved a path back through the crowd of people, all dressed in browns and blacks, with the odd splash of white, until we reached the edge.

'Be ready, okay?'

'Ready to what?' she asked.

'I dunno. Just be ready.'

I grabbed her hand and said aloud the first two lines of the poem.

At once the sound of clapping was drowned out by a whooshing sensation that raced up my body, finishing in my head.

Instinctively I ducked as we found ourselves on the carpet of the library. Georgie scrambled behind me. We held our breath. Everything was silent. I looked around the room. The *Wisden* was still lying on the floor, where it had fallen when we travelled.

'It's clear,' I whispered.

'Just wait a few moments.'

'No! Let's get out of here.'

'What's the time?'

'Ten to six. C'mon.'

I got up and crept over to the door, waving at Georgie to follow. We heard the knock at the same time and darted back to the table.

'No, over here!' I whispered, urging Georgie over

to a trolley stacked with books. We crouched behind it as the door opened.

'Toby?'

'Dad?'

'I guess I'm too —'

'Hi, Mr Jones,' called Georgie, getting up.

'Not interrupting anything, am I?' he asked, looking at us oddly.

'Boy, are we glad to see you!' I cried. I rushed over to him. 'Did you see him anywhere? The guy who gave you the invitation?'

'Who? No, I haven't seen anyone up here. Has he left already? You in some sort of strife?' Dad must have sensed my panicky voice.

'Don't worry, Mr Jones. Toby's pretending we're in this big crime thingo. That's why we were hiding. You see, there's this guy who's out to get us. But then you arrived.'

'Okay. I get it,' Dad said thoughtfully. 'So, how did the presentation go?'

'Well —'

'It was great! He got this!' Georgie pulled out the diary from under her shirt.

'Wow, that looks impressive,' said Dad, as Georgie placed it on the table in front of him. 'Oh, I'm with you now. The baddy was after this. So that's why you were hiding?'

'Exactly!' we said simultaneously. I looked at Georgie, who smiled.

247

'Can we go home now? I'm starving,' I said, picking up my 'prize' from the table.

'Good idea. Everyone left pretty quickly then?' Dad asked as we headed off down the stairs. 'I didn't think I was going to be that late.'

I didn't answer. I was too busy peering around, expecting someone to jump me at each corner.

'Tobes, you can probably stop acting now,' Dad suggested as I took a last quick look around before getting into the car.

'Yeah, I think we've won, Toby. Your Dad saved the day.' Georgie gave me a thump in the ribs as we settled into the back seat.

When we got home Dad went straight over to the site of the burnt-out garage and Georgie and I walked slowly towards the front door.

'Hey, Georgie, what exactly *are* mills? You know, that pommy guy said something about a mill?'

'I think it's where they make clothes. They'd probably never seen anything like our clothes before. And maybe in 1930 no one wore these colours,' she said, pulling at her shirt, which was a hot pink. 'We'll have to make sure we dress less conspicuously next time.'

'What do you mean, next time?'

'Well, we have to go back.'

Oh, no. I thought of Rahul and his urge to return to India.

'Why?'

'Are you kidding? We've got to see Don Bradman

again. And Jim too. We can take him with us. He'd be rapt!'

I was getting worried by all the 'we' talk. But she was so excited, I let it ride. 'You going to tell anyone?' I asked.

'Der! Why do you think I got you out of trouble when you were about to blab to your dad?'

'So why did you go all asthmatic with Smale? I thought you were going to spew or faint or ... or something!'

'Geez, Tobes. That was a put-on, to distract him, and so I could get a bit of time travel myself. It worked, huh?'

I nodded. 'That guy was weird.'

'No, he's just greedy. He doesn't know us from squat.'

But that's where Georgie was wrong. I sensed that Smale knew a lot about me.

Only once has a player bowled two maiden overs in an innings — that is, bowling an over without having runs scored. Dewald Nel, playing for Scotland against Bermuda, had bowling figures of 4 overs, 3 maidens, 2 wickets for 12 runs.

9 A Birthday Away

Tuesday — afternoon

TUESDAY. My birthday. It was pretty low-key. I got to jump into Mum's and Dad's bed in the morning to open my presents.

Dad gave me a copy of the 2001 *Wisden*.

'You remember Hobart?' Dad said, opening the book. 'When we sat downstairs and watched Gilchrist and Langer put on that huge partnership to win the game? All *you* wanted to do was go and play cricket.'

I had a vague recollection, and I'd certainly read heaps about that partnership. I nodded, said my thank yous and turned to look at my other presents.

'Found it, Tobes! Look!' Dad had the *Wisden* open and was shoving it under my eyes.

'Excellent!' I said, nodding again.

'Can Toby open mine now?' Nat asked.

'Good idea. Come on, you've got the rest of your life to look at that book. And judging by the thickness of it, you'll need it too,' Mum laughed.

I turned my attention to Nat's present, which turned out to be a 12-coloured pen with a light at the top that glowed the colour you were using. It was just the distraction I needed. 'Awesome, Nat, that's the best,' I told her, flicking buttons to make the light change colour.

To celebrate my birthday, all the guys were coming around later for some cricket, takeaway food and a couple of DVDs. We Joneses were going to go out to the movies as a family on the weekend.

We left Dad in bed reading about the Hobart Test and got ready for school.

Mr Pasquali always started the Tuesday training session with an update of the weekend's matches, even though he said that our destiny was in our own hands and that he, personally, wasn't that interested in the results of the other matches.

'But I acknowledge that you are all *very* interested and, of course, you can never really find out until the following Friday. So, no surprises that the Scorpions were comfortable winners at home to St Mary's: 213 to 7 for 106.

'Wow, a hammering!' Jay said.

'A pasting!'

'A shellacking!'

'Yes. As I said, a comfortable win. One piece of news though — the Scorpions' opening bowler has broken down and won't be playing for the rest of the season.'

There were a few low whistles at that little bombshell. I'd heard that one of their bowlers was playing senior cricket in the afternoons. Maybe he was bowling too much.

'And our nearest rival, Motherwell State, beat TCC. I'm not sure of the scores, I just know the result.'

A few kids started chatting, but Mr Pasquali broke it up. We were soon toiling away in the nets. I noticed Mr Pasquali take Scott into the far net for some batting coaching. Scott was lunging forwards and blocking each ball thrown at him by Mr Pasquali, who was standing about five metres away from him. Maybe he was teaching him about defensive strokes.

Jay and I were bowling to Jimbo. He was being very polite, gently stroking our deliveries back to us or just occasionally letting them go through.

'He should be smacking us all over the place,' Jay said as he walked back to his mark. Jay was a good player, but he didn't really star as a batter or a bowler. He wasn't as passionate about it as a few of us were.

'Anyway, when's it my turn?' he asked me. He ran past and bowled a full toss at Jimbo, who punched it gently back to him. Jay fumbled the ball and I picked it up.

'Your turn for what?'

'You know. The *Wisden* thing. I reckon everyone else has been, haven't they?'

Jay was right. He had a right to go, especially as he was one of the group, and now Georgie, as well as Rahul and Jimbo, had gone.

'I thought you didn't believe in all that stuff,' I said, running in to bowl. It wasn't a bad delivery, moving away, but just a little wide and Jimbo let it go.

'Nice, Toby!' he called, scooping the ball up and tossing it back.

'Jimbo, have a dip!' I yelled to him.

'You reckon?'

'I reckon.'

Jimbo smashed and crashed the ball into and over the nets for the next five minutes until Mr Pasquali put a stop to it by calling time.

'Was that fun?' I grinned at him as he strolled past a moment later.

'Heck, yeah,' he replied, taking off his helmet.

Jay and I threw a few low catches to each other while we waited for Cameron to face.

'Well, I've thought about it a bit and I'm willing to give it a go,' Jay said, scooping up a neat one-hander centimetres from the grass.

'Jay, that's hardly the point. I'm the one who'll decide whether or not I take you. Or anyone else,' I added. 'You haven't said anything to anyone, have you?'

'Course not,' he said indignantly, throwing the ball hard at my shins. I caught it in the ends of my fingers. 'Trust me.'

We worked for an hour and a half in the nets, but the Esky of cold drinks Mr P had organised for us afterwards made up for it. Meanwhile, an idea had been forming in my head. There was a catch, but I thought we could overcome it. I kept the plan to myself for now.

By six o'clock everyone had arrived for my birthday. We played a bit of backyard cricket, with Dad insisting that any shots into the studio building site were out, no questions asked. It cut down on off-side play, but we adapted well enough.

After dinner we went upstairs to my room — Rahul, Georgie, Jay, Jimbo and me. Nat followed us.

'Hey, Nat. We're gonna come back down soon. Can you set up for corridor cricket? We're going to play a Test match,' I explained.

'Me too?'

'Of course. You're opening the bowling!'

'Cool.' But she kept on following us.

'Nat?'

'I'm coming in to get all your socks.'

She gathered up an armful, dropped a few, which Jimbo picked up for her, and finally left us.

'I've got a plan, but first I want to tell you something,' I said to the others.

I spent the next 10 minutes explaining everything I could about Jim, the *Wisden*s, the weird hooded figure and the guy with glasses Georgie and I had encountered the day before at the MCG. No one interrupted. Although I'd told them some of it before, in the library with Jim, I didn't think anyone knew just how monumental this whole time travel thing was.

'I just reckoned it was time for all of you to know everything. That way you might be able to help me out.'

'The gift mightn't last forever, Toby. We've got to take advantage of it now,' Rahul insisted.

'I mightn't last forever, you mean! There's a disgusting creepy figure after me and now the guy in the library with the glasses —'

'We don't know about him,' interrupted Georgie. 'He's probably harmless enough.'

'How do you *know* that?' I asked.

'Well, he hasn't pulled a knife on us or anything, has he? Anyway, what's your plan?'

They all looked at me eagerly.

'Hang on.' I raced out and came back a moment later with the 2001 *Wisden*, which Dad had left on his bedside table.

'Beauty,' Jimbo breathed as I settled down on the carpet. The others quickly joined me, Jay looking expectantly at me.

'All of us?' Rahul asked.

'Why not?'

'Toby, isn't that a bit risky?' said Georgie.

'Well, I could just take Jay and you guys could cover for me.'

Rahul looked at Georgie and smiled. 'Let's give it a shot, eh?' he suggested.

'Ten or 15 minutes, tops. No more!' Jimbo added.

'Let's do it!' Georgie said, grabbing my hand. Jimbo raised his eyebrows.

'Travel, you idiot!' she retorted.

I got up and closed the door.

We linked arms in a circle on the floor. I laid the book open in front of me.

'What does it say, Jimbo?' I asked. 'Just read a few words.'

'*Hobart, November 18, 19 —*'

'Yep. Get to the bit about Langer and Gilchrist. Their partnership.'

'Okay, got it. *They had been on the ropes at 126 for five, but Langer and Gilchrist —*'

'Okay. Where does it say 126?' I asked. 'Point at it.' This help was making it all happen much quicker. I followed Jimbo's finger into the swirl. It was on the left-hand side. The top of the page was a mess. I'd never seen anything like it. I stayed focused on the writing.

'What's up the top?' I whispered as the number '1' appeared.

'A picture of them both. Gilchrist pumping the air with his fist.'

'Can't he see it?' Jay said. But their voices were like echoes now as the letters and numbers gathered and finally settled.

'Got it,' I breathed. I concentrated on the score. The whooshing sound rose up from nowhere and spread over me. I tried to keep my eyes open but I saw nothing but blackness.

'Toby?'

'*Nat!*' I swung around. Nat was standing at the door, looking shocked.

'What are you doing?'

'Um, we're —'

256

'Playing truth or dare,' said Georgie. 'You want to play?'

'No way. What about corridor cricket? It's all ready.'

'Yep, 15 minutes, okay?' My head was thumping.

'Yeah, and don't come back 'cos Rahul might have his pants down,' Jay called out for good measure.

'You okay, Toby?' Jimbo asked.

I rubbed the side of my head. 'Yep. You guys?' I asked, looking around. Everyone nodded. Maybe they hadn't been pulled back halfway through.

'Okay, point again, Jimbo.'

It didn't take long at all. One moment we were sitting there in my bedroom, the next we were bundled into two rows of white seats in a big stand off to one side of the ground. A few people sat scattered about but it wasn't a big crowd.

'Oh, my God,' Jay gasped, picking himself up. He'd landed on his back and tumbled into the back of the seat below him.

'*Oh, my God*!' he said again, looking around. I grinned at Georgie. She was still holding my hand.

'Toby, you are the best, man. *The best*!'

'Let's just watch the cricket a bit, hey?' Jimbo said, settling himself in. Australia were 5 for 312 and a spin bowler was about to bowl to Gilchrist. He pushed it out to mid-on. He did the same with the next ball, and then he drove the next through the off side for four.

'Nice!' I said, turning to look at the others. Except for Jay, they were all concentrating on the cricket. Jay just sat there with his jaw slack and his eyes bulging. I guessed he would settle soon.

There was another burst of applause as Gilchrist belted another four through the off side.

'How many do they need?' Jimbo asked.

'I think it was 369,' I said.

'Geez, not far to go then.'

Gilchrist hit a single off the last ball of the over.

'Nope. Forty-eight'll do it.'

I turned around to see what Jay was doing.

'Oh, no! Jay!' I shouted. He was talking to a kid a few rows away. 'Jay!' I yelled louder, racing over to him.

'Toby, this is Jason. I've just been asking him who he reckons will win the Grand Final next year.'

'Come on, Jay.' I grabbed his arm hard and pulled him away. Jason was looking a bit bewildered.

'Idiot!' I hissed into Jay's ear. 'You can't do that sort of stuff. You've just got to sit here, shut up and watch. That's the point. This gift is for people who like cricket. Remind me to make you read the poem when we get back, okay?'

I was really angry and Jay looked shocked at my outburst.

'Sorry,' he mumbled. 'You can let go of me now. I'm not going to run away.' I took a deep breath. 'Jay, this is serious, man. Big time. If I take you, you can't stuff up on me...'

'What?' Jay said.

'Oh, God!'

'What?' he repeated.

258

'Don't turn round. C'mon!' I grabbed his arm as he turned to look at what I'd just seen. I pulled him back to the others. The hooded figure stood tall and silent, only six or seven rows down from us. It wasn't moving, which somehow made it even more sinister.

'Grab on, quick!' I yelled, clutching at Georgie and saying words from the poem at the same time. 'Rahul, hurry!' He and Jimbo both grabbed for my hand.

'Then find yourself a quiet place ...'

Now the figure was moving towards us.

'Wh-what is it?' Jay gasped.

'Hold on!' Jimbo screamed at him.

'Where shadows lurk —'

As the last word left my lips, Georgie screamed and was yanked away from me.

'Hold on, Georgie!' I shouted, clutching for her hand. I leaned over, crashing my other hand down on the figure's bony arm. There was a cracking sound, a hissing, then silence.

From miles away I heard someone clapping. Why was everyone in the crowd so oblivious to what was happening? Why weren't they rushing towards us? I raced through the two lines as quickly as I could:

> *'Then find yourself a quiet place*
> *Where shadows lurk, to hide your trace.'*

10 Surprise Visitors

WE fell in a bundle onto the carpet in my bedroom. At once we jumped up, expecting the hooded figure to be on top of us, but he wasn't there. Four frightened faces looked at me.

'I can explain,' I gasped, getting up to sit on the bed.

'Th-that was h-him?' Jay stuttered. 'Why didn't anyone h-help us?'

'No one can see him. You only see him if you are travelling.'

'But someone must have seen us disappear?' Rahul insisted.

'Maybe —'

'Toby?' It was Mum.

'Coming, Mum.' I got up and opened the door.

'Is everything all right? Where have you been?'

'What do you mean?' I said, pretending innocence.

'Well, Scott Craven's here and I told him —'

'Scott Craven?' I gasped.

'Yes,' Mum said, looking surprised. 'I sent him up, but he said no one was in here.' She looked at the others.

'We were playing — um, hide and seek, Mrs Jones,' Georgie mumbled. Rahul was looking at his feet. 'Very cleverly too, I might add,' Georgie said, nodding her head. 'Right, guys?'

We all nodded.

'You'd never have found me,' Jay piped up.

'Well. That's great. Now come down and say hello. There's a man with Scott and I think they're doing a very nice thing.'

I had no idea what Mum was talking about, and by the look of the others, neither did they.

'Toby?' Nat said, tossing a sock in the air.

'In a minute, all right!' I snapped. It was like I'd slapped her. Her bottom lip quivered. 'Oh, I'm sorry, Nat,' I said, holding my hand out for the sock.

'Come here, Nat.' Georgie grabbed her hand. 'You and me against the boys, okay? We'll kill 'em.'

I got the shock of my life when I walked into the living room. Scott Craven really *was* standing there.

'Scott! Hi,' I said. 'Um, sorry we missed you upstairs. We were ...' I didn't finish the sentence. I sensed Georgie stiffen beside me and I looked to the kitchen door.

Dad and Phillip Smale came into the room. My face must have gone white. I felt my hands become

261

sweaty. Georgie's hand brushed mine, but she didn't take it.

Dad and Smale were both laughing at something Smale had said.

Mr Smale looked over to us. 'Hello again, Toby,' he said. 'And how's your girlfriend now?' Georgie gave him a dirty look.

'Ah, the disappearing five return,' Dad exclaimed heartily. 'Where on earth did you get to?'

'They were playing hide and seek,' Mum said. I saw Scott snigger. Yeah, and we were too smart for you to find us, I thought.

'Scott probably did see us,' I said suddenly. 'He couldn't be that blind.'

I looked at him. He seemed about to say something, then clearly thought better of it. My heart sank. I sensed he knew something was going on. Maybe he'd seen us come back, or leave. And the open *Wisden* on the floor of the room — what would he make of that?

'Well, never mind,' Dad said. 'Scott has some news for you all. He's already spoken to Mr Pasquali. This is Mr Smale. He's the manager of the Scorpions team.'

This was too much.

'The Scorpions?' I said, before I could stop myself. 'But you work in the library!' My mind was racing. '*Scorpions*!' I said again, looking from Scott to Smale.

'Now, steady on, young feller,' Smale said. 'You've probably heard we've lost our strike bowler, Greg Mackie, but I think Scott will more than adequately fill his shoes.' He looked over at him. 'Scott?'

262

'Yeah, well ...' Scott stopped for a moment and looked at Smale, who was standing next to him. 'Phillip reckoned I should come over and tell the team members personally, and since you were having your party here, I thought I'd get most of you in one hit.'

No one said anything, though I saw Georgie mouth the word, 'Phillip'. Why would Scott be calling Smale Phillip?

'It's not till the finals. We've got to organise the transfer and clearance,' Mr Smale added. He was wearing a dark blue sports jacket with his glasses tucked neatly into the top pocket. He avoided all eye contact with me, spending his time looking at Scott or Jimbo.

You're not taking him as well, I thought, suddenly having the awful thought that he'd got his eye on Jimbo too.

'Well, then,' said Mr Smale. 'We'd best go. Thanks, Peter, for allowing us to talk to the team, and I'm sorry to intrude. But I do feel it was the right thing to do, don't you?'

I didn't hear Dad's reply. Mum and Nat followed them out. The rest of us sat down on the couches.

'You look really bummed off with the news,' Jay said to me. 'I reckon it's great. We don't need him on the team.'

'Jay, we do,' I said.

'We've got Jimbo as a newy and Martian is set to return. We're okay,' Jay continued cheerfully. 'Now, what say we head back to —'

'No!' we all said together.

Rahul was thinking it through. 'Okay. Down side? We lose one of our top three batters and probably our best bowler. Up side?' He paused.

'We're waiting,' said Jay.

'Up side: we'll be a happier team, and maybe play more *as* a team.'

'I agree,' Jimbo said. 'That catch he dropped on Saturday from your bowling, Toby — I reckon it was spite, to stop you getting a hat trick. He never drops catches.'

The thought had crossed my mind a few times.

'Well, it's done now,' Georgie muttered. 'Come on. We owe Nat a game of corridor cricket.'

Thursday — afternoon

'Can we talk, Toby?'

'Hey, Rahul.' I thought I knew what was coming.

'I was thinking about India and my brother. I think we should maybe try once more.'

'Rahul, no way —'

'This time *you* would be in charge, totally.'

'I was in charge last time and look what happened! You left me for dead in that whacky hospital and went looking for your family. It was a disaster!'

'Toby, I *saw* my brother. How can that be a disaster?'

'Rahul! As soon as we got to Chennai you changed. It was like some force had taken you over. You were out of control. It was crazy. We were lucky to get away with it.' I held his gaze. 'Listen, I know what you want to do. But the chances of getting back to the right time to save your brother are remote. There's probably not a game in *Wisden* near enough in time —'

'Ah, well, I have —'

'Nor in space,' I added. 'And anyway, that's not the main reason. You can't change things that have happened. The poem, Rahul — remember?

> *'But every word that boasts ahead*
> *Means lives unhinged, broken, dead.*
> *Don't meddle, talk, nor interfere*
> *With the lives of those you venture near.*
> *Respect this gift. Stay calm, stay clever,*
> *And let the years live on forever.*

'It's not right. You're trying to change things in history. Think about it. There'd be an extra seat in a classroom somewhere. Another bed in your house. It can't just happen. We'd be making a new life.'

'Yes. My brother!' Rahul shouted. 'How can that be wrong?'

'It doesn't matter. It just would.'

'What do you mean?' Rahul snapped. 'It counts for everything.'

I took a deep breath. 'Rahul, I can't explain, I just know it's wrong.'

'And if it was Nat you were trying to bring back to life?'

'I wouldn't know about her to bring her back.'

'But that's just it. I know about my brother.' Rahul was shaking. I looked away across the ovals.

'Toby,' he said, quietly. 'You've already changed time.'

My eyes were fixed on a sprinkler pumping water in an arc on the other side of the pitch.

'Toby?'

I thought back to the trip I'd made with Jimbo to watch his father get hit on the head by a vicious bouncer, bowled by Scott Craven's father of all people. Jimbo's dad had vowed from that day on never to play cricket again. His vow had applied to Jimbo too.

'Jimbo wasn't playing cricket matches last week. You've changed the past. Now he *is* playing cricket matches.'

'That was a little thing,' I said.

'Not for Jimbo.'

I said nothing.

'Well, can I ask one thing then, since you're being so stubborn about it?'

'What?'

'Talk to Georgie about it.'

'Why?'

'Just talk to her. Ask her what she thinks. We . . . I mean, *I* think there's a way to do this.'

'*We?*' Rahul sure had let that one slip through to the keeper.

'Well, we thought that if we did go, she could be my guardian. She would make sure I didn't do anything stupid.'

'Rahul . . .'

'Yes?' he said eagerly.

'Forget it. *Totally* forget it.'

He stood still, looking away from me.

'Rahul?'

'Okay, okay. Forgotten.' He drifted away from the bench outside the gym where we were chatting. And then I had the most amazing thought.

'Rahul,' I called. He turned around hopefully and headed back towards me.

'No, not that. Listen, I've just realised something. Even if we did go back — well, it never worked!'

'What do you mean?'

'Right now, in this time, you aren't with your brother and you haven't seen him. So it never worked.'

He was still looking blank.

'Okay. Say I agree to take you to India. We try and rescue your brother. If we'd *managed* to rescue him, he'd be here, or somewhere, and you wouldn't be asking me to rescue him.'

I saw his face drop as he realised the truth in what I was saying.

'If we did get back and somehow saved him from the river, then he'd be here now, a part of your family. Or else we did go back, but we didn't save —'

I'd gone too far. Tears were brimming in Rahul's eyes and he turned away.

'Rahul! I'm sorry.' He headed away towards the nets. 'Rahul, I'll work on it, okay? I'll talk to Georgie.' He didn't respond. 'And Jim!'

I watched his drooping shoulders as he walked away, made my decision and ran after him. I didn't know if I would ever go through with it, but maybe it would make him feel better to talk about it anyway.

'Rahul, wait up.' I walked alongside him. 'What happened? Where? When, exactly? All I know is that he pulled you out of a river and saved your life. But then ...'

Rahul stopped walking and leaned against the wire mesh of the cricket net.

'Of course I remember nothing about it. I was three. Sunni, my older brother, was eight. We were having a picnic. A *family* picnic, by the river. Dad said that we wandered too close to the water. Sunni was carrying me on his shoulders. He was strong.'

Rahul paused. He was trying hard to keep his emotion inside.

'He must have slipped near the edge. He screamed. Maybe I did too. My father heard his cry and rushed down to the river's edge. A great wall of water had appeared from nowhere. Like a tidal wave. Sunni held me up above the water as he struggled himself. Dad plucked me from his arms and put me down on the ground. When he turned back to the river there was no sign of Sunni. He jumped in, but Sunni had gone.'

'Gone under?' I asked, swallowing.

The bell went. It seemed so out of place at that moment.

Rahul shook his head.

'He disappeared. Completely. They never found his body.'

I was about to ask if he might have survived, but stopped myself. Kids were running in from play, laughing and yelling.

'Gee, I'm sorry, Rahul. I don't know what to say. I can't imagine what it would be like to lose a brother.'

'Sometimes I feel I'm not completely me. Like there's a bit missing.' Rahul squinted in the sun's glare. 'C'mon, Tobes. Let's go.' He thumped me on the back and we walked towards the classrooms.

'You coming around tomorrow?' I asked. Since the party had ended on such a flat note on Tuesday, Mum and Dad had said that whoever wanted to could come around again on Friday.

'Think so.' He looked at me and smiled. 'So, any travelling?'

I shook my head. 'Not tomorrow. Probably not for a while.'

The only hat trick to be taken in an international Twenty20 match was by Brett Lee. He picked up three wickets in three balls against Bangladesh on 16 September 2007 in Cape Town, South Africa.

11 Nash Street

Friday — evening

WE sat around the table, the diary in front of us.

'Don't you think you should tell Jim you've got it?' Rahul asked.

'I've tried, heaps of times, but no one's seen him anywhere. It's happened before. He just disappears.'

'Time travel?' asked Georgie.

I shook my head. 'I doubt it. Remember, you've only got two hours to travel before bad things start to happen. And he's not at the hospital either. I've checked.'

'What bad things?' Jimbo asked.

'Not exactly sure, but Jim really drummed it into me that you only ever have two hours out of your own time.'

'You don't think ...' Jay started.

'What?' I turned to look at him.

'Well, he's old, isn't he? I mean ...'

'What?' I said again.

'Nothing. So let me get this straight. Someone sends Jim this old diary which belongs to his family. And then for some reason he leaves it in the library behind the old *Wisden*s. Toby here gets an invite to a fake award ceremony —'

'We don't know it was fake,' Georgie interrupted.

'Oh, come on —'

'Maybe that explains why Jim's not around,' Rahul said quietly. 'Maybe Jim *did* organise the award thing but never made it.'

I looked at Georgie.

'It's possible,' she admitted.

'Yeah, well, as I was saying,' Jay went on, 'this creep Smale, who we now discover is manager of the Scorpions, forces you to give him the diary and looks for the scorecard.'

I nodded. 'That about sums it up.'

Jay pulled the diary towards him. He seemed transfixed by it. 'Come on,' said Georgie, getting up. 'Let's go see if the paper's arrived. Maybe Smale was fibbing about Scott not playing with the Scorpions till the finals. Maybe he's already in their team.'

The paper hadn't arrived so we decided to walk down to the milk bar to grab a copy. Jay stayed behind to read the diary.

There was a game of street cricket going on in the laneway behind the milk bar. The Nash brothers, all four of them, often got games going and kids from round about would wander across and join in. Their eyes lit up when they saw us stroll by.

'You want a hit?' the oldest Nash called out.

I shrugged, then looked at Rahul and Georgie. They nodded.

'We'll take you on,' I called.

They were tough kids who seemed to spend most of their life outside playing. They 'owned' the laneway. They'd even changed the sign from Noel St to Nash St. Their dad had laughed and left it.

We batted first. One batter, 18 balls. Side fences were worth a run, two on the full. Any shot getting back past the bowler was four. And if you hit the ball past the bowler before it hit the ground, it was six.

The Nash kids scampered and scurried, diving to stop the ball, laughing and joking even though after 10 minutes they were all cut and bruised. I didn't think our team was going to show the same dedication in the field.

I'd just gone out, with the score on 57, when Jay turned up.

'You're in!' I called to him, handing him the old, splintered bat.

He lasted four balls. The extra fielder didn't really help us either, though Jay managed to knock down a full-blooded drive and deflect the ball over to me. I swooped on it, picked it up with one hand, and threw down the stumps while I was still turning. The stumps at the bowler's end went flying. The Nash boys knocked up 81 before we decided it was time to leave.

'You want to play tomorrow?' the littlest one said to us.

'We're playing *real* cricket tomorrow,' Rahul said, a little too strongly.

'Anyway,' Georgie said as we headed back, 'the oldest Nash kid's gotta be about 16!'

'Yeah, but the youngest is about seven,' I added.

Jay seemed preoccupied — quiet, but jumpy. 'Did you read all the diary?' I asked him.

'Yeah,' he said.

We looked at him.

'Discover anything interesting?' Rahul asked.

'Nah.'

'Hey, we forgot to get the paper!' Georgie said.

A car was pulling away as we arrived back home.

'Oh, Toby. You just missed the man from the library —'

'Jim?' I called, racing back down the drive.

'No, no, the man who works with him. Phillip Smale.'

'The diary!' I cried. 'Jay, tell me you didn't leave the diary sitting out on the table?'

'You don't have to worry about the diary,' Jay said. 'I gave it to your mum before I left to meet you guys.'

'Yes,' said Mum, 'and I gave it to Mr Smale. He said that he was working on old documents and books with Jim in the library and that they wanted it back to verify it and make copies. I think perhaps it's in safer hands over there, don't you?'

I looked at her, horrified, but before I could say anything Georgie bustled past me and went inside.

'Spot on, Mrs Jones,' she said. 'C'mon you lot.'

'It wasn't my fault,' Jay wailed when we got up to my room. 'What was I supposed to do? Bring it down to the milk bar and chuck it behind the stumps while you played?'

'I'm not saying it was your fault, Jay,' I snapped.

'Anyway, like I said, you don't need to worry. It doesn't have the scorecard in it.'

'We know that,' Rahul muttered.

'We've got to find Jim,' Georgie said. 'He's been missing too long. We've got to find out the truth about this guy, Phillip Smale. Maybe we should sneak a visit to the Scorpions' training. I wonder when they train?'

'We could always ask Scott,' Rahul suggested.

'Oh, goody. Toss you for it,' Georgie muttered.

Nat walked in with the paper. 'Mum said you wanted this.'

Georgie took the paper from her and ruffled her hair. 'Thanks, Nat, you're a star!' she said, as she opened it. 'There you go. Scott Craven is still one of us.'

I checked the ladder. There was only one round to go before the finals. The top four teams would be playing.

Ladder	P	W	L	Bat P	Bowl P	Win P	Total
The Scorpions	4	4	0	27	22	20	69
Riverwall	4	3	1	25	18	15	58

Motherwell State	4	2	2	19	15	10	44
Benchley Park	4	1	3	17	13	5	35
St Mary's	4	1	3	15	13	5	33
TCC	4	1	3	14	12	5	31

Benchley Park were the movers. Not big movers, but they were hanging on to fourth spot and a semi-final against the Scorpions.

'Well, whoever wins that game between Benchley Park and St Mary's will be in the finals,' Rahul said, looking over my shoulder.

'Unless we get flogged by TCC,' Jay said.

'Hey, look, Martian's in.' I pointed. 'And so is Ally. Wonder who'll keep?'

'Mr Pasquali might give them both a go. Ally deserves the finals though,' said Georgie. 'She's done all the work.'

I nodded but didn't say anything. Nor did the others.

We went downstairs to watch a World Cup one-dayer I'd taped, settling in on the beanbags to watch the game. I couldn't wait to see Andrew Symonds' innings. Dad and I agreed that it was the best innings of the whole tournament. He blasted 143 not out. But that wasn't all. He came in when the Aussies were 4 for 86 and struggling.

'Now this is one innings we should go and see,' laughed Rahul, as Symonds belted another four through mid-wicket.

'What do you mean? You're seeing it now,' Dad said, flopping onto the couch next to Georgie. He rolled his eyes at her. She shook her head and smiled. The rest of us kept our eyes glued to the TV.

Have extras even been the highest scorer in an innings in a Twenty20 game? Yes! When the West Indies lost to South Africa in a game in the 2007/2008 series, South Africa conceded 29 extras while the West Indies struggled to a total of 7/131. The next highest score was 24.

12 TCC Get Belted

Saturday — morning

SATURDAY was another really hot day. There was plenty of cloud cover but it was steamy and sticky. I felt washed out. Splashing cold water on my face hadn't helped. I grabbed my drink bottle out of the freezer, collected my gear and waited outside for Dad.

'Where to?' he asked, throwing his stuff in the back.

'TCC,' I said.

'Hey, that's near that new mega-hardware store, isn't it?' he said, reversing out of the drive.

'Think so.'

Dad was awesome when it came to supporting me. He never missed a game. And it wasn't as if he built himself a studio every season.

'Dad, why don't you duck down there during the game?'

'That's not a bad idea, Tobes. Sure you don't mind?'

'No, that's cool,' I said, smiling.

'Can I get you something?' he asked.

'From the hardware store?'

'Yeah.'

'No, I'll be right, Dad.'

This time Jono won the toss. Or maybe the other captain lost it. Whatever, it was a good toss to win. It was a two-dayer, which meant they'd be fielding in hot, steamy conditions. Maybe it would be as hot next week for us. Then again, a cooler day was probably more likely. I liked thinking about the decision to be made at each toss.

'We're batting,' Jono called. 'Here's the order. Scott and Cameron, opening. First drop me, then Rahul, Martian' — there were a few claps and whistles when Ivo's name was called — 'Jimbo, Ally, Georgie, Jay, Toby and last is Minh.'

Mr Pasquali gathered us in for his usual pre-match talk.

'Now, you know I haven't been that pleased with your form recently. There have been some good individual performances, but I think there's room for improvement. Scott, this is your last game with us. I've spoken with you and worked with you in the nets. Let's see you show that form out in the middle today. Then you can promptly forget everything I've told you,' Mr Pasquali said, smiling.

Scott looked tense. 'Can you throw me a couple?' he asked me.

I grabbed two old balls and tossed them hard on

half-volley length. He played them straight back to me. It was textbook forward defence.

'Openers, please!' the umpire called.

'One more,' he said. I tossed a slightly shorter ball at him. He stepped back and clubbed it away into the school yard to the right of the oval.

'Just had to blow the cobwebs out,' he said, watching the ball clatter against some drinking taps about 100 metres away. 'Go fetch,' he added.

'Well, that's a relief,' Georgie said, hearing Scott's comment as she walked past with Ally. 'I didn't think it was Scott for a moment, the way he was paddling those tiddlers back to you. We'll get it!' she called over her shoulder.

I settled down to watch the opening overs. It was probably my favourite part of the game. New ball. Everyone excited and fresh and ready to go. Everyone with a chance of winning or doing something spectacular. And with Scott out there, you couldn't afford to miss one delivery.

Martian was on the scorecard. I gave him a pat and grabbed a deckchair.

Scott scored a gentle two runs off the first over. How long would that last, I wondered. On the last ball of the second over Cameron was amazingly caught by the kid at square leg. Cam had cracked it like a rifle bullet and knocked the kid over. I was looking for the ball out near the boundary until I heard shouts from the field. They were running over to congratulate the fielder, who was still lying on the ground.

The bowling didn't look difficult and Jono and Scott put on a steady 25 runs without attempting anything spectacular. But just as they started to crank up the pace, Jono was out-stumped trying to force the spinner over the top. It didn't look good.

I took over the scoring from Martian as Rahul went out to bat. Martian was looking extremely nervous as he padded up.

Then Scott started to move. He'd had enough of defence. Now and again he played a defensive shot back up the wicket, as if to show us he hadn't forgotten. But in between he blasted the bowlers everywhere.

In no time at all he had raced to 44. Mr Pasquali, who was keeping his own scores, called him in. We stood up and clapped as he strode towards us. There was sweat pouring from him and his shirt was drenched. It was probably the longest he'd ever batted in a game.

Two run-outs — one really embarrassing — and two catches in the deep kept TCC right in the game. And poor Martian went for a duck, clean bowled. Only Jimbo held up an end until Georgie ran him out, calling for a risky third run. (*See Tip 20.*)

When I walked out to bat, we were 8 for 122 with still almost an hour of batting time left.

The very next over Jay was out, bowled for eight. Our only hope was that Scott would come back in. Minh or I would have to try and bat with him until the innings closed or two and a half hours were up.

I batted carefully, trying to hit the loose ones. But TCC had brought their opening bowlers back on, so it was harder to score. I noticed Scott standing on the boundary line, gloves and helmet ready, waiting to come back.

'Toby, I'm going for it,' said Minh. 'If I score a few, good. If I go out, Scott comes back.'

It was probably a good call, though I wondered if Mr Pasquali would agree. Minh was clean-bowled next ball. Scott marched to the wicket. I went out to meet him but he breezed past me.

'Leg stump,' he called to Mr Pasquali, who was standing at the other end. Mr Pasquali looked a bit surprised but gave him leg stump. Scott scratched his mark and settled over his bat. (*See Tip 14.*)

For the next 40 minutes we were treated to some of the most powerful and clinical hitting I'd ever seen. It was phenomenal. I scratched around at one end, feeding Scott the strike while he blasted the attack all over the ground. Even the TCC coach was getting involved, shouting instructions at his bowlers and fielders.

At one stage someone yelled out 94, and then there were a whole lot of shushes from everyone, but Scott hadn't heard. He was in another zone. At the end of each over, though, we'd meet mid pitch and I got the same message each time. 'Keep it going, Toby.' And I did.

When the innings was over, the kids and parents made an impromptu guard of honour as Scott walked off the ground, not out 134. I had made 31. Scott had made half our runs from his own bat. I eyed the massive willow lying on the grass while Scott celebrated with a drink. The rest of the team packed up after congratulating him. Mr Pasquali was talking with a couple of the dads. Scott stood alone, staring out at the pitch. It didn't look like any of his family was here.

I crept closer to his bat. I'd just had an idea. I picked it up and, before anyone saw what I was doing, shoved it into the back seat of our car. Guiltily I glanced about, but no one seemed to have noticed. But I realised a moment later how stupid that would be. Scott would go berserk and there'd be a huge search for it. I placed the bat carefully back on the grass. I'd talk with Mr Pasquali about it. Maybe he could organise something.

'Hey, you know what?' Dad said to me in the car.

'What?'

'Mr P was saying that if you'd reached your 40, he would have had to retire you and Scott mightn't have got his 100.'

I hadn't thought of it that way. Now we were back on equal terms after the run-out a few rounds before. Scott had only said a few words to me after our innings. 'Smart batting, Jones. See you in the final.'

Yeah, you will, I thought. I couldn't wait to bowl to him. But we had to come back next week and get TCC out first. Hopefully for less than the 256.

282

13 Jim Returns

Monday — afternoon

MR Pasquali had set us a new project to work on. I had managed to link cricket in to mine even though it had been set during English. We had to write about an inspired event that influenced and changed the outcome of succeeding events. I made my choice at once. It was Andrew Symonds' 146 not out in South Africa. Dad said that it set the course for Australia. They went on to win every match they played in the 2003 World Cup.

'Did you try and ring Jim?' Georgie whispered to me during class. I nodded. 'And?'

'He's okay. I didn't really have much time to talk.' We both bent our heads low as Mr Pasquali walked past.

'Did he travel?'

'Nup.'

'What about that other guy?' she hissed. 'Smale.'

'I didn't ask about him.'

'Don't blame you.'

'Hey, I spoke to Mr Pasquali and he's going to get Scott's bat so we can all sign it.'

'What do we want to do that for? Do you think he'd bother signing a bat if you made a hundred?' Jay asked, overhearing our conversation.

'Probably not, but Mr Pasquali reckons it's a good idea. He's asked him to bring it to school tomorrow. Made up some excuse.'

'Fair enough,' Rahul said, joining in. Mr Pasquali was now talking with someone at the front of the room. 'It was a brilliant innings.'

We settled down to work on our assignments. I'd found a website with a ball-by-ball description of Andrew Symonds' innings. I was going to present a summary of his innings and then put together some questions to ask him in an interview. All I had to do was find him. Rahul had managed to find Ray Bright and Dean Jones for his last assignment, and they'd played that tied Test match about 20 years ago. So it shouldn't be too hard to track down Andrew Symonds.

Maybe I could arrange to meet him when the Aussies played in Melbourne. Maybe I'd get a free pass into the dressing room during a one-dayer. Maybe I'd get to chat to all of them.

'Hi, Andrew!'

'Hey, Toby. How's things?'

'Yeah, not bad. How's the bowling arm?'

'Good, thanks. It's a seamer today. Would you mind if I just bowled a few at you? Can you watch my form?'

'Toby, throw a few my way too, would you? Not too fast, though.'

'Sure, no probs.' Matthew Hayden was always after my flippers. 'And I'll toss a few at you afterwards, okay, Ricky?'

'Yep, great, Toby.'

'Toby? TOBY!' Mr Pasquali was staring at me. I shook my head and smiled.

'Yes, Mr Pasquali?'

'Would you like to start writing now?'

'Okay, Mr Pasquali. Yep, no worries.'

He shook his head and moved off.

Monday — evening

When I got home, a taxi was parked outside the house and a guy with the most humungous gut was leaning against the bonnet, smoking. He nodded at me but didn't say anything.

I went into the house, dreading another visit from Mr Smale. But the first person I saw when I walked into the kitchen was Jim, smiling contentedly in the big chair by the bookcase and sipping a glass of cold water. 'Jim!' I called, dropping my bag and rushing towards him. He got up awkwardly and shook my hand. His old face broke into a broad smile.

'Hello, Toby,' he said. 'Peter has just been telling me about your heroics on Saturday. Well done. We might have another Jones in *Wisden* not long into the future.'

I was bursting with questions and tried to read every expression on his face as he chatted away happily about cricket, the MCC library and a few other things. He seemed healthy and in good spirits.

'Can Jim stay for dinner, Dad?' I asked, finally seizing on a break in the conversation. Dad had given Jim a full-blown version — *his* version — of the garage fire and how I'd gone back in to save a *Wisden*.

'Well, that's up to Jim, Toby.'

'Jim?' I asked.

'That's very kind of you, Toby, but no, thank you. I have my meals cooked for me and dear Andrea would be most upset if I missed one of her culinary pleasures. Perhaps you could walk me out to my chariot.'

I closed the front door and started explaining, the words tumbling over each other. Jim held up a hand.

'Jim,' I started again. 'The man who's often at the library. The guy with the glasses. His name is Mr Smale and —'

'Phillip, yes. He helps us out in the library. With the archives.'

'The what, Jim?'

'Archives,' he repeated. 'He helps with the old records and documents. Files them. He does a marvellous job. Actually, his father made a very generous gift to the library: some quite rare cricket scorebooks. Phillip has mentioned that he is in possession of many more old cricket documents. We're rather hoping that Phillip might bring them across to the library.'

'Jim, I'm not sure about him.'

Jim stopped and looked at me. 'Pardon?'

'When Georgie and I were at the library getting my award ... Jim, did you invite me to receive an award for saving the *Wisden*? Did you know about it?'

'I did hear something about it,' he said slowly, shaking his head.

'But did you organise it?' I asked, searching his face.

'Well, no. But you certainly deserved your reward, Toby.' It sounded like Jim was embarrassed that he *hadn't* organised it.

'Jim, I don't mind about the award. It's just that Mr Smale was very interested in the diary.'

'Well, that doesn't sound odd. Phillip would be interested in the diary, but I hid it carefully away —'

'Behind the 1931 *Wisden*,' I interrupted.

'Take your time,' the driver called, lighting up another cigarette.

'Which leads to another thing, Jim. He's got it.'

'Phillip Smale?'

'Yes.'

'He's got the diary?'

'Yes. He came here to get it.'

I told him about my and Georgie's adventure on the night of the 'award ceremony' and how Georgie and I had found the diary behind the 1931 *Wisden*. I was hoping Jim would explain it away as some silly sequence of errors that amounted to nothing. But when I'd finished, he was clearly worried.

'Phillip suggested I take a break while he sorted some things out at the library,' Jim said quietly. 'I wonder . . . Toby, I fear it's time for action. Perhaps our Mr Smale is a little too taken with the diary and where it might lead.'

'But what about the scorecard?'

'Well, we must just hope that Phillip doesn't find it,' Jim said, slowly, still looking concerned. 'Or perhaps that no one finds it,' he added. We were silent for a moment. Then I remembered another important thing I had to tell him.

'Jim, I went back to 1930. I saw Don Bradman. Me and —'

'1930? Leeds?'

'Yep. First day. It was amazing, Jim. We've got to go — you and me. I can get you there easily. They talked funny, but they were —'

'You talked to people?'

'Well, we couldn't help it. Georgie was wearing this —'

'Toby. Take care. Especially when you take those long journeys back in time. Come along to the library on Wednesday if you can manage it.' Jim took a few steps towards the taxi. 'And I would like to hear more about Leeds too,' he said with a smile.

I waved and watched the taxi until it had disappeared around the corner.

14 A Chase in the Car Park

Tuesday — afternoon

MR PASQUALI had told each of us during the day to get to training early.

'I've also arranged for Scott to be delayed at the office,' he told me. 'I'm going to ring Mrs Grimes there when we're ready.'

'The bat?' I asked.

Mr Pasquali nodded. 'It's been engraved and there's a place for our signatures up near the splice.'

We all gathered together before training and Mr Pasquali made the presentation. Scott had no idea it had been planned. He seemed a little stunned.

The engraver had carved a short inscription: *Scott Craven scored 134 not out with this bat. U–13 Southwestern Division,'* and below was the date. We had signed our names neatly down each side of the splice, up near the top of the bat. Mr Pasquali had too.

I think Scott was genuinely happy with what we'd done. He didn't even bowl pace during centre-wicket practice and everyone was rapt with that. Although Jimbo said later that he probably did that deliberately so we wouldn't gain confidence from playing him before the finals.

Wednesday — afternoon

Jay insisted on coming along on Wednesday to meet with Jim. There was something Jay had discovered about the diary that he'd been holding back, ever since we'd left him with it when we walked up the street to get the paper. Maybe he would tell Jim.

We'd just reached the outside glass doors when I saw a familiar face. Mr Smale and two guys, dressed like security, were standing on the other side of the doors, talking. Mr Smale looked straight at me then turned to the guards.

'Oh no, not again,' I yelled, turning to run. Jay just stood there, mouth hanging loose, a stupid grin on his face.

'I wonder who they're after?' he said.

I grabbed him by the arm. 'We're not hanging around to find out. C'mon!'

We dashed off around the outside with me a couple of metres ahead of Jay.

'Come on, over this way!' I yelled.

'But, Toby —'

'Jay! Come on!'

I started running across the car park. Jay followed. We dashed between a few cars, Jay almost getting smashed by a door that suddenly opened in front of him.

'Watch it!' a lady shouted at him.

'The station!' I yelled, pointing away to the left. A silver train was snaking towards us. 'It's over there! Come on, Jay!'

We scrambled forward, weaving between the cars. I heard Jay yell out behind me. He'd fallen next to a van. Maybe it had started moving and knocked him.

'Jay? You okay?' I raced back.

Jay had tripped over a basket someone was unpacking.

'C'mon!' I cried. I grabbed Jay by the arm again and together we stumbled down a path that headed towards the station. A train thundered in as we raced past the small ticket office.

'T-tickets?' Jay gasped.

'Forget it,' I said, dragging him towards the train. The automatic doors closed as we fell inside. Jay tumbled into the lap of an old lady. He excused himself and jumped up.

'Wow, that was close,' I sighed, holding the metal bar.

'But, Toby. There was no one chasing us!' Jay had finally got his breath back.

The train started up, then immediately slowed. We raced to the window as it came to a stop.

'What's happening?' Jay asked.

'Maybe the security guys have radioed ahead and stopped the train.'

I opened the door and leaned forwards carefully to look out. To my amazement, a policeman was climbing aboard.

'Jay, we're gonna jump, okay?' The doors started to close. 'Quick — *now*!'

I jumped and Jay squeezed through and followed. We stumbled onto the platform, then turned to watch the train pull out of the station.

'Won't he follow us?' Jay asked.

'He won't be able to open the doors.' A moment later I saw the policeman and defiantly stared at him through the window as the train passed by. But he hardly appeared to notice me. He seemed more interested in the passengers inside the train.

'Let's go,' I said.

'Home?'

'No, the last place they'd expect to find us. Back to the MCG.'

There was no sign of Mr Smale but the two security guards were still standing in the same spot they'd been in 15 minutes ago.

'See,' Jay hissed at me as the doors closed behind us.

'Hey, boys?' one of them called out as we tried to slink past. We both froze.

'Your class headed that way — you'd better hurry.' He was pointing up a ramp to the left.

'Th-thanks,' I mumbled. There must be a school group visiting the museum.

We hared up the ramp and into an awesome display of sporting history. We kept a low profile for another 10 minutes, mingling with the school group and checking out the displays before heading towards the library.

'Smale's probably up there now, knowing our luck,' I said to Jay as we got closer. 'We'll take the secret door.'

I looked down the corridor, checking that no one was around, then pulled the door open. There was no sign of Mr Smale as we entered, but Jim looked up from his desk and waved us over.

'Well, now, come along and sit yourselves down and tell me everything again,' said Jim.

I repeated what I knew, going into detail about everything Mr Smale had done. I sensed Jay was agitated and wanting to butt in, but I finished without interruption.

'Well, this does change things, I'm afraid,' said Jim. 'I must admit, it has surprised me that Phillip has persisted for so long here. It would appear he is after something. Perhaps he knows a little more about the *Wisden*s, time travel and scorecards than he would like everyone to believe.'

'There's something else,' Jay said quietly.

We both looked at him. The tone of his voice suggested something important.

'I've got the scorecard.'

Jim looked completely stunned. I jumped up from my seat. But at that moment the door opened and the group of school kids we had snuck in with surged into the room. In no time they had filled up all available space in the small library. Luckily David, the main librarian, was with them and soon organised them into a group in front of the *Wisden*s bookcase.

Jay and I pushed our chairs in to make more space. David introduced Jim, talked about the *Wisden*s, and then the group moved on. One of the kids hung back.

'Would you like to look at one?' Jim asked the boy. He nodded. I had the weirdest feeling as I watched Jim and the kid look at an old *Wisden*. That had been me just a short time ago. I studied the kid's face closely: there was obviously no strange stuff happening. A minute later he joined the rest of the group.

'There's always one or two who want a look,' Jim said, smiling, as Jay and I sat down again. 'Now, Jay. You were saying?' Jim licked his lips and leaned forwards eagerly.

Jay reached into his pocket and pulled out a small faded yellow card. It had words near the top and numbers down the side.

Jim held out his hand. 'Please?'

But Jay was leaning back, smiling. 'Now, just let me —'

'Jay!' I hissed. 'It's not yours. Give it to Jim.'

Reluctantly Jay passed the card across to Jim. Jim held it in his hands, almost tentatively, then slowly turned it over and read aloud what was written on the back:

> *'Two hours is all the time*
> *So before it's up, read these lines.'*

'Where'd you find it, Jay?' I asked.

'Well, I had this idea, but I wanted to see for myself. So when you guys went off down Nash Street the other day, I carefully made a slit in the back cover. And there it was! I saw it on a movie once — these guys had hidden this map in the inside cover of a book. And it was an old movie, so I thought maybe it would be the same.'

'Well, well. Bravo, Jay. Goodness me.' Jim seemed amazed at the discovery.

Jay was looking very pleased with himself.

'So, who have you told?' I asked.

'No one!' he retorted, sounding offended.

'I hope not, Jay,' Jim said gravely.

'Well, only Rahul, but he —'

'Rahul!' I cried. Some of the kids turned to look at us. *'Rahul?* He'd want it more than anyone. He'd try and go back to India.'

'There's no one who wouldn't want it, Toby,' said Jim. 'And we know that there are people who are determined to get it. Jay, may I look after it?'

'Sure. Anyway, I had this idea,' Jay said. 'Toby and me, we could go into business. A travel business. We could use the scorecard to take people to games of their choice. I'd collect all the money and Toby could be the tour guide.'

Jim straightened. 'Do you know what would really happen, Jay?'

'I'd be making us bucketloads of money and Toby would be a worldwide sensation,' Jay replied quickly.

'Exactly!' Jim said.

'He'd be on the front covers of newspapers and magazines,' Jay continued.

'You are right, Jay. He'd be talked about, interviewed, quizzed, hounded and followed for the rest of his life. He'd have his brain scanned and all sorts of scientific tests done so this extraordinary phenomenon could be explained. His life would be a misery.'

Jay was defiant. 'Well, yeah, maybe, but we'd be rich.'

'Money doesn't create happiness, Jay. That comes from within.'

There was a commotion at the door and Mr Smale burst in. 'Ah!' he cried, pointing at us. By now the class, with their teacher and David, had left via the secret door.

'Phillip. Do join us,' Jim said, managing to hide the scorecard just in time.

Smale looked from me to Jim then back to me.

'Jim, I brought in some of the family cricket archives. The 1912 programs we were talking about, do you recall?'

'Well, certainly, Phillip. I'd be most —'

'It appears that one has gone missing. I think perhaps before the children leave we should check them both.'

'Phillip, I hardly —'

'Those programs are very valuable, Jim. You said so yourself. I certainly won't be bringing in any more of the cricket material under these circumstances.'

Jim looked at me and Jay. 'Is that all right, boys?'

We stood up and turned out our pockets.

Smale looked disappointed. 'Well, everything seems to be in order. Jim?'

'Phillip, are you suggesting that I —'

'If everyone is searched then I will be satisfied that the fault lies with me and that perhaps I have misplaced one of the programs,' Smale said coolly.

Somehow he'd latched onto us and he wasn't letting go. Did he know the scorecard was only a metre away?

'Phillip, I understand your concern,' Jim said evenly. 'However, I will not be searched in front of visitors to the library.'

Smale looked like he was about to argue, but Jim held his gaze. Suddenly he smiled.

'Thank you, Jim. I'm sorry about all this. I'm just rather upset at the thought of one of those 1912 programs disappearing. I shall go and speak with David and the teacher of the group currently visiting.'

Jim nodded and turned to us. 'Well, boys, thank you for coming to see me.' He held out his hand and I felt the scorecard, cool against my palm.

'Goodbye, Jay.' Jim shook his hand too.

I kept my hand in my pocket, closed gently but firmly around the scorecard, until we had left the building.

'Got it,' I muttered to Jay as we left.

When India played Australia in a Twenty20 match in Melbourne on 1 February 2008, they managed a rare feat. It was the first and, so far, only time that 10 of the 11 batters didn't reach double figures. Only Irfan Pathan managed to get to double figures, making 26 out of a total of 74.

15 How Much Does Scott Know?

Thursday — morning

I put the scorecard in a tight plastic pocket — the type card-shop owners sell expensive cricket cards in — and, thinking it would be safer if it was with me all the time, I took it to school. Big mistake.

It must have happened during the lesson before recess. We were playing touch football out on the oval. I didn't want the card to get creased or damaged, so I put it in my pencil case and left it in my bag. When I checked on it at the start of recess it had gone.

I immediately thought of Jay and set off to find him, but no one had seen him. Then I started to panic. I flew up to the library, thinking he might have borrowed one of the *Wisden*s that the school had recently bought. None of them were on the shelves.

'Miss Thomson, can you tell me who's got the *Wisdens?*' I said urgently. 'It's just that I'm about to give a talk and I've got to check on some info. I was —'

'Well, I can tell you who's got one of them. Jay Barclay. He borrowed it about half an hour ago. Hang on, I'll check the other one.' She pushed some buttons on the keyboard, but I didn't wait to find out. 'Thanks,' I called, running out again.

Where would he go? I headed down to the boys' toilets. I saw the *Wisden* straight away. It was lying open on the floor in the farthest cubicle.

I dashed forwards and picked it up, desperately trying to read any of the words. I didn't notice the sound of footsteps till they stopped just outside the door.

'Catching up on a bit of reading, are we?' Scott Craven snarled. 'Why you gotta do it in the toilets?'

'Forget it, Scott,' I said, folding the corner of the page to bookmark it and moving to get past him.

'Forget what?'

He moved to block my path.

I opened the book again. 'Scott, what's it say on this page?'

'Can't you read, Toby Jones?'

'No. Not this book. The writing's too small. Just give me a few words. Please?'

In spite of the desperation in my voice, he wouldn't help.

'You know, you really annoy me, Jones.'

He edged closer, backing me against the far wall of

300

the cubicle. 'You think you're the world's best cricketer, but you're not. You get all the attention —'

I'd had enough. I pushed him away so hard that he reeled into the door, banging his head against it before crashing to the ground. The *Wisden* landed next to him.

He got to his feet, blazing with anger. 'We're gonna keep this quiet, eh, Jones?'

He came at me, his hands raised. I ducked, then body-slammed him straight back into the door, which was slowly opening. Again he crashed to the floor, this time dazed.

'Use your fists and fight properly,' he said, struggling to get up.

'Can you just read this one bit for me?' I asked again. He flung out his right arm and I saw his fist heading for my face. Without knowing quite how, I threw up my right arm, deflecting his punch.

'There's no need to fight. I'm just asking you to read a few lines from the *Wisden*,' I said.

Lunging at me, Scott tripped and crashed to the floor. He doubled over, struggling for breath. I grabbed him by the shirt and yanked him up, then pushed him against the cubicle wall.

'You want to help, Scott, or what?'

He swore, then came at me again, but I was ready. I put up my arms again, but this time surprised him by throwing out a hard punch. It caught him unawares. He staggered back.

I picked up the *Wisden*, found the right page and thrust the book beneath his face.

'*Read*,' I hissed.

'11 M-march,' he whispered. 'World C cup semi-final.' He looked up at me. 'What is it with —'

'Just read!'

'Australia v New Zealand. Madras —'

'The date?' I hissed. 'When was it? Point!'

His eyes searched the page.

'Here. I *said*, 11 March —'

Suddenly Scott slammed the book closed and barged past me. He was out of the toilets in a flash. I set off after him but at the end of the corridor almost knocked over Mr Beechworth, the vice-principal.

'Why the rush, Toby Jones? Just *walk* back to class.'

'But —'

'*Immediately*!'

I walked as quickly as I dared back to the classroom. As I'd suspected, neither Rahul nor Jay was there. Mr Pasquali raised his eyebrows at me but didn't say anything. I scrawled a message on a scrap of paper and tossed it across to Georgie when Mr Pasquali's back was turned.

Where's Rahul and Jay?

She shrugged.

When I caught up with her at lunchtime, I told her all about the scorecard and that I thought they might have travelled to India.

'Well, if you're dumb enough to leave the scorecard lying around, and knowing what we know about Jay, it was bound to happen.'

It wasn't the answer I'd expected. She must have seen my look of disappointment.

'Don't worry,' she said. 'Leave it till the end of school.'

'But they've only got two hours. They'll probably forget that in their excitement.'

'Well, maybe they're back already. Why not go and look?'

I hung around the toilets all lunchtime but there was no sign of them. For the last 10 minutes I actually shut the door of the far cubicle and sat there. It felt weird to think that any minute I might get squashed by two kids coming through from another time. Maybe I'd actually see them reappear.

After lunch, as happened on every other day, the class roll was taken.

'Anyone seen Jay and Rahul?' Mr Pasquali asked.

'I think they might still be helping out with some jobs in the office,' Georgie said quickly. 'Mr Beechworth said to say they'd be a bit late.'

'Okay. Thanks, Georgie. Right, maths books out, please.'

The afternoon lesson dragged on.

Finally I said to Georgie: 'I've got to tell him.'

'Don't be stupid. What on earth can Mr Pasquali do? Just tell their parents, your parents, the whole school —'

Mr Pasquali interrupted our whispers. 'Georgie, go and see how Jay and Rahul are getting on, would you?'

'Can I go too, Mr P?' I asked.

'I think Georgie can handle this mission solo, right, Georgie?'

'Guess so, Mr Pasquali.'

A few minutes later she returned. I watched her closely. The day was becoming a series of lies.

'Um, they said that Jay was sick and he's gone home. But since there wasn't anyone at his place, Rahul's parents came to collect him and they took both Rahul and Jay home.' She stared at Mr Pasquali a moment, almost daring him to challenge her, then went back to her seat.

'Looks like they'll miss training,' I added, a bit lamely.

'Let's hope they're both well enough for Saturday,' said Mr Pasquali, who looked puzzled.

Georgie put her head down, as though her maths had suddenly become totally engrossing. I looked over at Scott Craven. He also had his head down, but his eyes were roving about, taking in everything. I was pretty sure he wouldn't say anything about what had happened in the toilets.

After school Georgie and I were called into the office.

'Now, no more games, you two. Where are Jay and Rahul?' demanded Mr Beechworth.

'We don't know. They've left the school, that's all we know,' I explained. And it was the truth — though not all the truth.

'This is very serious. Their parents —'

There was a sudden commotion in the hallway outside and we all turned to look. We heard raised voices and Mr Beechworth went to investigate.

'So, what else do we say?' I muttered to Georgie who was looking worried.

Then: 'It's them!' she cried. We hurried to the door and looked out into the corridor. Mr Pasquali was also out there and so were Jay's and Rahul's parents.

Jay and Rahul both looked wrecked. Their clothes were torn and their faces were filthy. They also looked spooked.

Mr Pasquali turned to Georgie and me. 'Off to training, you two. We'll deal with your side of the story later.'

I went through the motions at training. Georgie was equally distracted and even Scott was subdued. Rahul and Jay never turned up. Mr Pasquali finally arrived, 15 minutes late. He thanked Jono for organising the nets and didn't say anything more about it.

I hung around with Georgie afterwards, helping pack up the kit, knowing that it would be better to cop it from Mr P now rather than later.

'You have disappointed me, both of you,' he said. 'Don't you ever, *ever* let that happen again. It was totally irresponsible of you to lie for them the way you did. We have a hard enough time as it is looking after students *within* the boundaries of this school, let alone when they take it into their heads to run off on some silly adventure. Do I make myself clear?'

'Yes, Mr Pasquali,' we both said. I looked up at his face as I spoke. He was obviously very upset. He nodded curtly, pointed to the kit, then headed off. After ten or so paces he stopped and turned. Neither of us had moved.

'I hope Mr Beechworth isn't thinking cricket when he speaks with you tomorrow morning. He wants to see you at 8.30 in his office. Don't be late.' He walked back towards the school buildings.

I turned to Georgie when Mr Pasquali was out of hearing. 'Get into CROC tonight, 8.30, okay?'

'Couldn't you pick another time?' she said sarcastically.

I didn't get what she meant until I was halfway home.

Thursday — evening

CROC (cricket online chat) was a chatroom we had devised to discuss cricket, and other things too. Only a few kids had the password. I just hoped that Jay and Rahul would log on. I'd rung a few times before dinner but both phones were engaged.

Georgie, Jay and Rahul were on when I logged on just after 8.30. I was afraid to ask Rahul directly about his brother and his whole family situation. Hopefully it would just come out.

Toby:	well?
Jay:	sorry
Toby:	what happened?

Rahul: i'll tell, jay. we tried to go back to india
Jay: it was my idea
Rahul: true, but i encouraged it
Georgie: did you achieve anything?
Rahul: save my brother, no. it was dumb, i think we
            were about 2 days out
Toby: you were away for more than 2 hours
            though
Rahul: i know, we got stuck on a bus. the freak guy
            with the cloak saved us
Toby: what?
Georgie: the same one that almost killed toby?
Rahul: yep, it was soooo weird
Jay: he gave me a message for you toby
Rahul: dad's calling
Georgie: you guys in trouble?
Jay: not so bad, my folks reckon i deserve what
            punishment i get at school
Rahul: i'm grounded on top of that
Toby: where's the scorecard?
Jay: i've got it, and i'm giving it back to you
            tomorrow toby, promise
Toby: bloody hope so jay
Georgie: jay?
Rahul: guys, talk tomorrow, okay?
Georgie: cya, rahul
Toby: yep. bye rahul
            well, jay?
Jay: what can i say? it was dumb and i did
            wrong. big time. i'm sorry, toby.

	toby?
	you there?
	toby ... c'mon, man.
Georgie:	toby?
Toby:	what was it like?
Jay:	shocking. horrible. smelly. we walked
	forever. there were people everywhere, on
	buses, walking on the roads. it was like
	rahul was possessed. if i'd known there's no
	way i would have gone.
Georgie:	it was dumb, jay
Jay:	so you've said, both of you, i know. you can
	have the stupid scorecard toby.
Toby:	jay, you are bloody lucky
Jay:	what?
Georgie:	you might not have come back at all
Jay:	yeah, i know
Toby:	i'm going, jay, tell me everything tomorrow
Jay:	we still friends?
Toby:	course we are, idiot
Jay:	bye
Georgie:	bye guys

16 Rescue at the Station

Friday — morning

GEORGIE and I received a spray from Mr Beechworth and three lunchtime detentions. Rahul and Jay copped it worse. They had 'a Friday': an hour and a half detention after school, as well as litter duty for three lunchtimes.

They filled us in on the details during recess, and Jay handed me the scorecard.

'So what happened, you know, when the two hours were up?'

'We'd completely lost track of the time. We'd got on this crowded bus and were heading towards the outskirts of town where this river supposedly was,' Jay said.

'Yeah, then suddenly, like he's walking out of a mist, the same guy who was after us at Hobart is calmly walking down the bus towards us,' said Rahul. 'No one else seems to notice him. He like, just walks straight past them.'

'*Through* them, remember?' said Jay.

'Whatever. Then he's talking to us. "You're in trouble now, boys. Look at yourselves."'

'What did he mean?' asked Georgie.

'We were sort of disappearing ourselves. We couldn't feel it, but it was true. We were getting paler and paler. "Soon you'll disappear completely," the guy laughed.'

'Didn't you realise yourselves? How come you didn't notice?' I asked, amazed.

'We were so distracted and excited and worrying about everything that was going on around us. It was all so noisy and bumpy.'

'Yeah, and you don't really feel anything. It must happen really slowly,' Rahul added.

'How long over the two hours were you?' I asked.

'I reckon it must have been about three, maybe four hours by then — yeah, Rahul? So he says, "Get back now. You're wasting your time here. And tell your friend it's time our paths crossed again. Tell him, bring a 1984 *Wisden* and find me if he doesn't want to end up like me." Then he keeps walking, right through the back of the bus.'

'And then we came straight back,' Rahul said, breathlessly.

'God, what does all that mean?' Georgie asked.

I looked at her. 'I've gotta do this, Georgie. Or else I'll never travel again. And there's one more place I want to go.'

'1930?' she asked. I nodded. 'And I'm coming too,' she added.

'Georgie, I don't think —'

'Toby, there's no way you're not letting me go back to that place in England. Anyway, you need me there.'

'We could all —'

'NO!' we both yelled at Jay.

'No, guess not.'

'I'm going to the library to look up fashion in the 1930s in England,' said Georgie. 'Anyone want to come?'

We shook our heads.

'Not this time, Georgie,' I said.

Friday — evening

I sat on my bed staring at the front cover of the 2001 *Wisden*. I'd met the ghostly hooded figure in many places, but somehow the Test match in Hobart made me feel more secure and at home than the other places I'd visited.

I leaned over to turn the music up a bit louder, grabbed hold of Dad's 1984 *Wisden*, then opened the 2001 edition to the page with the picture of Adam Gilchrist, his fist clenched and raised, with Justin Langer alongside him.

I wanted the last day. I knew the date: 22 November. The numbers and letters on the page drifted and swirled but I quickly latched onto a sequence of numbers. I focused on the right side of the page, just beneath the picture where the last number should be. Gradually the 2s materialised. The music faded as other noises took over.

I sat alone on a patch of grass at the Bellerive Cricket Oval, watching Gilchrist and Langer batting together on that last day in the 1999 Test match. I'd tried to arrive earlier than last time, but I couldn't help looking up into the stand every now and then to see if I could catch a glimpse of a group of kids being chased by a hooded ghost.

One minute I was alone, the next I knew he was nearby. I didn't turn my head. I stared out at the oval, reassured by the cricket and everyone's rapt attention. I didn't even jump when I heard him speak.

'We have to travel again. Listen carefully to me now.'

His voice was low and calm. I didn't look at him. I knew no one else could see him. I took comfort in watching Adam Gilchrist and Justin Langer pound the attack and tried to concentrate on what they were doing.

'Have you got the *Wisden*?'

I nodded.

'Give it to me.' I put the *Wisden* on the grass next to me. '1982,' he breathed, the pages of the *Wisden* flapping open. He was just behind me. 'Melbourne. The Melbourne Cricket Ground. 30 December. The final day.'

I closed my eyes. Allan Border and Geoff Thompson. The day Dad, and plenty of other Australians, cried. One of the greatest Test matches played between Australia and England.

'You must arrive before 11 a.m., before play starts. I will show you which word to focus on. As soon as you arrive, you must walk away from the ground and towards the station that runs parallel to Wellington Road. Do you know it?'

I nodded.

'Look for me. I will be wearing black trousers and a grey shirt. I am tall and thin. I am nothing like what I am now. You will not find it difficult to recognise me, but you must find me. The station will be crowded, but only after a train arrives.'

'But it'll be impossible to find you,' I said, listening to the polite applause around me as Justin Langer clipped a ball down to fine leg for a single.

'No, it won't.'

'Why?'

'Nearly all the people will be getting off the train to go to the cricket. I will be getting on the train.'

'Why? Why were you *leaving* the cricket?'

'Greed.'

I waited for him to continue. Maybe there was a curse on the poem. If you did non-cricket things, maybe it somehow made fate go against you.

'What happened?' For the first time I turned to look at him. But he continued to stare out at the game, his face hidden by the cloak.

'Someone or something — some force — pushed me onto the train tracks and I was crushed by the train that was supposed to take me to the racecourse.'

'So you died?'

'Yes ... and no.'

I swallowed.

'A time traveller who dies out of time does not die a mortal death. I am a spirit in a decaying body. My world is timeless; my future is endless. I am invisible to the real worlds I travel in. But I am visible to you, another time traveller.'

All the anger and hatred had gone out of his voice. I felt sorry for him, even though he repulsed me with his injuries, his black cloak and the hood. My body relaxed slightly and I half turned again to face him.

'Then what happened?'

'Enough.' His impatience had returned. 'It will not be easy. But somehow you must prevent this accident from happening.'

'Sounds like it wasn't an accident.'

He passed me the *Wisden*, open at the right page.

'If we never meet again, you'll know that you've achieved your task.'

I felt like saying that if I'd achieved my task, then maybe I should never have met him anyway. But the whole time thing was now so confusing that I didn't know what was or was not possible.

'Wait,' I called, wondering if anyone had heard me. But the cricket had everyone's attention.

'Can I travel from here?' I asked.

'Yes, but remember your two hours,' he called, drifting away.

'What happens if I go over time?' I knew part of

the answer but I was desperate for more information. He stopped and turned to face me.

'Look at me,' he said darkly. 'This is what happens.'

I took a last look at the cricket. Gilchrist and Langer were only 10 runs shy of the target. Langer would soon go out, but I kept that little piece of knowledge to myself. I stood up and headed towards the rear of the ground.

I found a quiet spot by a fence and opened the *Wisden* at the page the ghost had marked. I felt with my finger to the spot at the bottom of the page where the number 15 swam about, scattered like bits of dirt. I focused on the time of day and closed my eyes as the tug and pull took hold and the rushing noise started somewhere in my head.

He was right. Crowds of people were streaming towards the ground. White floppy hats, yellow T-shirts, enormous eskies and lots of bare skin surged past me as I started jogging away from the concrete stand I had arrived outside.

I quickly recognised where I was and darted towards the station. It was the same station where Jay and I had made our 'escape' from the security guards, a few days before — or about 22 years later.

The car park was full as I walked towards the station. I looked closely at as many people as I could before I remembered that the man would be heading in the same direction as me. I turned to look back, but no one else was going in my direction. There weren't many people at the station: only an old lady, maybe going to the city to do some shopping, a family, a couple of young guys and a group of men who stood waiting near the exit. Maybe they were meeting people coming in on the next train.

I edged closer to the track and looked down the line. I heard the tingling of the rails and saw the front of the train at the same time. I moved back, turning to see if there'd been any new arrivals. There hadn't.

The train let off so many passengers that suddenly the station was filled with people streaming towards the exit. I moved back and watched them disappear. The train departed and in no time the platform had emptied. Only one man was left.

'Excuse me, do you have the time?' I asked him.

'Ten to 11,' he answered, glancing at his watch. 'Another couple of minutes, mate.' He was obviously talking about when the next train was due in.

I waited nervously for some minutes, looking closely at the people who were drifting into the station or were visible just outside it.

Then I saw him. He was looking nervously up and down the platform. I hadn't thought about how to convince him not to get on the train, to get him to move away from the edge of the platform.

Tentatively, I approached him.

'Excuse me, but you shouldn't get on the next train.'

He looked down at me, frowned, then looked back up the line.

'Excuse me —'

'Are you talking to me?'

'Yes. You told me to —'

'Listen, little feller. I don't know who you are or what you're playing at but just stop it, okay?'

Just as I heard the next train approaching, he moved away, walking slowly down the platform. I didn't know what to do. In a moment there would be a crush of people and this guy was going to end up on the tracks.

'You've got to leave — *now*!' I yelled, dashing up to him.

'Shove off!' he snarled, pushing me away. We both turned together as two kids ran towards us.

'Watch it!' someone called as they pushed their way through.

I could hear the train roaring towards the station. It didn't sound like it was going to stop. I backed away, fearful. The man looked confused.

'Hey, mister!' I shrieked, desperate now.

He turned to face me and made a threatening step towards me. Suddenly his face changed and he moved towards the edge of the platform, as if someone was calling to him.

The two kids careered past in front of us, one bumping the man so that he stumbled and fell to the ground. I threw myself forwards and grabbed his leg, but still he moved towards the platform edge. I held on grimly, feeling myself being dragged towards the approaching train with him.

My shoes scraped the concrete as I tried desperately to get some sort of grip. I yelled in terror as the wind from the rushing train whipped my hair and clothes. I squeezed my eyes shut and suddenly everything went into slow motion.

We toppled over the edge of the platform. My head landed on the track. I heard and felt the ringing vibration of the train through the rails as it disappeared out of the station. Arms reached over and hauled the two of us back onto the platform.

'Bloody idiots!' someone yelled at the two kids who'd bumped into us.

The man was brushing himself down, looking embarrassed and confused.

'You okay?' someone asked him.

He nodded, avoiding eye contact with everyone. I sidled away, then jogged to the back of the station, fearful of any more attention.

A few minutes later another train arrived. This one stopped and let off another horde of people. For a moment I lost the guy I'd just saved. Then I saw him stepping onto the train and taking a seat by the window in an almost empty carriage.

As the train eased out of the station, our eyes met. I waved, then looked away quickly, thinking what a dumb thing it had been to do.

17 Georgie's Surprise

Saturday — morning

JONO threw me the new ball and for the first time in my life I wished he'd thrown it to someone else. I felt tired and lethargic. I was bruised and sore from the train station fall and hadn't slept well. Even Dad had noticed, asking me if I was sick as we were driving to the game.

I was opening the bowling against TCC. It was the second half of our game and we were defending 256 runs.

After three overs I'd got no wickets and had been hit for 13 runs. Not a disaster, but Jono must have realised I didn't have my usual pace and zip running in to bowl. (*See Tip 1.*)

'I'll hold you back till later when we might need some tight bowling against the lower order,' he said. 'Take slips, I'll go out.' Normally I fielded at mid-off and then third man or fine leg so that I didn't have to jog too far between overs. (*See Tip 21.*)

It was a slow morning. The TCC batters were solid. They had good defence but weren't scoring quickly.

'They won't make 257, will they?' Ally said to me between deliveries after the first drinks break.

'No way. They'll struggle to get to 150 at this rate.'

'You'd think they'd be going all out for as many batting points as possible.'

The next ball from Rahul zipped through and Ally took it cleanly before tossing it over to me. I threw it long to Jono at mid-off.

'Is Martian going to have a keep?'

'Yep, Mr Pasquali told us to swap after 20 overs. I think he's looking forward to it.'

The next ball was pushed back to the bowler.

'Toby?'

'Yeah?'

'Is Georgie your girlfriend?' asked Ally.

I looked at her, but she was staring down the pitch, already crouching and waiting for the next delivery. I bent over myself, but kept my hands on my knees.

'Um, no. We're just really good friends.'

The next ball was a repeat of the previous one.

'C'mon, James!' someone yelled from the boundary.

'Yeah, I know, I was just wondering whether there was anything more to it. You don't see many boys whose best mates are girls, that's all.'

'Who says she's my best mate?' I asked. I had never thought of Georgie in terms of 'best friends'. She was just a great friend, like Rahul and Jay.

James took a swing at the next ball. It caught the edge of his bat and flew towards my face. More out of self-defence than an attempt to catch it, I threw one hand up in front of my eyes. The ball struck the base of my thumb and popped up into the air.

I spun round, desperate to make amends and catch it. It had bobbled out to my left, but I was too late. By the time I saw it, the ball was on its way down. But just before it hit the ground a pair of gloves came swooping from nowhere and grabbed the ball just centimetres from the grass. Ally. (*See Tip 24.*)

Everyone rushed in to celebrate the wicket.

'Looked like you were dozing there, Toby,' Jono said.

'Chatting up Ally, more like it,' Scott sneered.

'Nice teamwork, you two,' Georgie called, slapping us both on the back. I felt myself go red.

I came on for a bowl and picked up two wickets late in the game. Scott bowled out his eight overs during the middle part of the innings and picked up three. We won by 84 runs in the end.

'Well bowled, Rahul,' I said as we all left the ground. 'I rate those medium pacers of yours.'

'Yeah? Thanks, Tobes. Actually, you know, you did well to get a hand onto that. It was flying.'

'I'm not sure I was concentrating as hard as I should have been.'

'Yeah, if I was fielding in first slip next to Ally, I reckon I'd struggle too,' joked Jay, who had joined us.

'Good work, Martian!' I called, watching him carefully packing away his wicket keeping gloves.

He smiled. 'Gee, it was good to be out there again. You reckon I'll get picked for the semis next week?'

'Who knows?' said Jay, shrugging.

Ally and Georgie joined us and we all sat on the grass enjoying the sunshine and the sandwiches, drinks and ice-creams that our parents had provided. Jimbo's dad had brought an Esky full of food and no one seemed too keen to leave.

'Toby!' whispered Georgie, as the others became involved in an argument about whether you scored two runs or nothing if you were run out taking a third run. She jerked her head quickly to one side. I moved over to the Esky by Jimbo's dad's car and pulled out another drink from the ice.

'Hey, I've got two awesome outfits!'

I had no idea what she was talking about.

She noticed my blank look and went on, 'I went to the fancy dress shop yesterday. You know — the 1930s look? You want to check them out?'

'They're here?'

'Yep. Hang on.' She came back a moment later with a bag, but just as she was opening it, Ally came over to say that she was going.

'What are you two up to this arvo?' she asked.

Georgie shrugged. 'Nothing much. You?'

'Same.'

I wanted to say something but took a swig of my drink instead.

322

'Oh, okay, well, I guess I'll be seeing you,' she said, moving off.

'Yeah. Hey, Ally, I'll call you tonight, okay?'

'No worries.'

Georgie reached into the bag and pulled out some of the clothes.

'Who gets to wear the cute cap?' I asked.

'We both do.'

'Yeah, well, you don't have to get it all out now,' I said, looking around nervously. 'You coming to check out the Scorpions?'

'You mean, see if we can get any dirt on Mr Smale?'

'Yep. I wouldn't mind finding out if he really is involved with them.'

James Anderson, playing for England against Australia in a Twenty20 match at Sydney in 2007, conceded a whopping 64 runs off his four overs. His economy rate (average amount of runs hit off each over) was 16.

18 Caught!

Saturday — afternoon

THE Scorpions' home ground was only about a ten-minute walk from my place. I hadn't ever been inside their clubrooms. I wasn't exactly sure what we'd find, if anything, but it was something to do.

I picked up Georgie on the way. She still had the bag of clothes with her.

'Don't worry,' she said. 'I know we're not going for a while. I've got a few other things in here I thought I'd show you.'

'Like?'

'Like ... Hey, look. Isn't that Scott and Gavin?'

Two kids were skate-boarding in the car park on the other side of the ground.

'I think so. Let's go around the back, just in case.'

We sneaked around behind the clubrooms. They were deserted. All the senior teams must have been playing away. The doors were locked.

'It would have been easier if they were playing at home,' I said.

'Yeah, we could have just had a nose around, then left. So what now?'

'There's a window over there that's open.'

I took a last look around, then hoisted myself up onto the ledge and slid the window open further. A curtain billowed in my face as the wind got hold of it. I pushed it away and looked inside.

'It's the main room. Here, pass me your bag.'

Georgie passed the bag up and a moment later we were standing in a long room with lots of chairs and tables, a bar and a pool table. There were heaps of photos, flags and premiership pennants on display as well as a trophy cabinet with some nice-looking silverware inside. The room was dark and smelt stale.

'Look!' Georgie was staring at a sign on a door next to the bar. '*The President. Strictly No Admittance*,' she read.

'You reckon that's our Mr Smale?'

'Gotta be,' Georgie said. She tried the door. 'Locked. Well, that's hardly surprising. You want in?'

'Into his office?'

'Of course. Hang on.' Georgie pulled out the most massive bunch of keys I'd ever seen. 'Used to belong to Gran. Haven't failed me yet.' She started on the lock.

'How many times have you used them?' I asked, thinking this was a side to Georgie I didn't know about.

'Just the once.'

A lot of the keys fitted but none worked. We both turned when we heard some shouts from the other end of the room, outside the window.

'Did you shut the window?' I whispered.

'Almost. Hey, wait ... *yes!*' I heard a click and Georgie pushed the office door open slightly. A second later, the window behind us slid open.

'Quick!' We scuttled into the office, and I eased the door closed as quietly as I could.

'My bag!'

'Forget it,' I told her. Gently I pushed the button on the round door handle to relock the door. We both waited silently for the intruders to look around, then, we hoped, disappear again. For a while there was no sound, then we heard the hiss of a can being opened, followed by another. Georgie grimaced. A few moments later there was a click of balls.

'They're playing pool,' I whispered.

Georgie came closer. 'Seems like they haven't bothered with the bag. Let's have a quick look, then maybe sneak out this window.'

At first it looked like a normal office, but we soon noticed things that were surprising. On the desk there was a draft of a brochure with the heading 'Tests in Time' scrawled across the top. It was partially hidden beneath a Scorpions' scorebook.

'Weird clothes,' I muttered, pointing to a long black coat and other items hanging on a rail inside a cupboard opposite the window.

'Yeah, and look at this!' Georgie had spotted some more papers. 'It looks like some sort of price guide. Wow! $9000. You don't think —'

We both froze as the phone on the desk started ringing. The clunk of balls outside stopped. After four rings there was a click and Mr Smale's voice began speaking.

'You've called the Scorpions' head office. No one is in the office at present so we are unable to take your call. Leave your contact details and we will call you back shortly.'

There was another click and then a long beeping sound. Someone wasn't leaving a message.

'C'mon, we've seen enough, haven't we?' Georgie said.

'And heard enough too … Ssh, listen!'

A car had pulled up outside. We both raced to the door. I opened it slightly and peered out. The room was empty — aside from two cans left on the edge of the pool table and a cue lying on the floor.

'Someone's coming in,' I hissed at Georgie. Keys jangled outside the main door of the clubroom. Georgie darted out, grabbed her bag and shot back in. Again I closed the door quietly, pushing in the button of the lock. I followed Georgie over to the window.

'It's deadlocked!' she whispered hysterically, shaking the locks.

'Maybe it's just a cleaner or —'

There was another jingle of keys, this time outside the office we were in.

Click.

We both bolted for the desk and scrambled to get a place beneath it. Too late.

'What the blazes!'

'We can explain,' I stammered, edging around from behind the desk. 'You see —'

'I see two intruders in my office. How dare you! I wonder what the police will have to say about this? And your parents. How did you get in?'

Mr Smale moved over to the phone and picked up the receiver.

'W-we had something we wanted to say ...' Georgie's voice petered out.

'What?' He scowled at us.

The situation was hopeless. My stomach lurched.

'It's about the scorecard,' I said.

He paused, put the phone down and looked at me. 'Well?'

'We just thought you would be interested in it. Maybe you are the best person to have it.'

'I wasn't born yesterday,' he stormed. 'What were you doing here?'

Then the phone rang again. Instinctively we both made a move towards the door.

'Stop!' he roared.

The phone rang four times like last time and then Mr Smale's message came on. He smiled unpleasantly and his voice echoed around the room, louder now that he'd turned up the volume. But this time there was no click after the single beep.

'Phillip? Jim here. I'm afraid there are a number of

matters we need to discuss, including your involvement with the library —'

Mr Smale pressed a button on the phone, activating the speaker.

'Well, that suits me fine, old man. You see, my time there is finished, but for one task that you will help me with. Say hello to some friends of yours.'

'I beg your pardon?' Jim said in his quiet voice.

'Speak!' Mr Smale shouted at us.

'Hello, Jim,' I said tentatively.

'Toby?'

'Y-yes.'

'What's this about?'

'Your friend Toby is actually a thief,' Smale replied. 'He and his young lady friend broke into my office here, Jim. Now, I will lay no charges and forget this entire episode if you come over to the Scorpions' clubrooms and hand me the scorecard.'

I could hear Jim breathing into the phone.

'Are you all right, Toby?' he asked.

An idea occurred to me.

'Yes, Jim. I'm fine. But I think you'd better do as Mr Smale says. Bring the scorecard. It's in the *Wisden* you placed the scorecard behind originally. Do you remember?'

There was another pause.

'I think I do, Toby. Yes.'

'And don't think about ringing the police, Jim,' warned Smale. He pressed another button to end the call.

'Well,' he said, turning to us, 'and what have we in the bag, eh?' Striding over, he wrenched it out of Georgie's hands. His eyes narrowed. 'How quaint.'

Georgie grabbed some of the clothes and shoved them into her pockets. 'Well, that's just it. You see, we thought —'

'Oh, don't try your lame excuses on me,' he cried, throwing up his arms dramatically. He grabbed the bag again and this time we all heard the jangle of keys. He pulled out the massive bunch and threw them onto the table. 'Well, we are little detectives, aren't we? Now sit over there by the wall and keep your traps shut.'

The first men's international Twenty20 match was played between Australia and New Zealand on 17 February 2005 at Eden Park in Auckland, New Zealand. Australia won by 44 runs.

19 Trapped!

GEORGIE and I sat there for what seemed like ages, occasionally making eye contact but not daring to talk. The one time I leaned over to whisper something, Mr Smale looked up and pushed his chair back as if to come over and tackle me, so I shut my mouth.

A taxi pulled up. Mr Smale walked over to the window.

'Good. The old man has arrived. You can tell him that if he's thinking about involving the police or anyone else, then you'll have your own criminal behaviour to explain.' He pointed towards a small security camera in the corner of the ceiling. Then he left the room to go and meet Jim.

After a minute or two of silence, Georgie asked, 'What now?'

'Listen, I'm hoping Jim's brought —'

'Enough!' Mr Smale strode back into the room. Jim shuffled slowly behind him.

'I'm so sorry, Toby. And Georgie. This is —'

'Save it for later, Jim. Just hand me the scorecard,' Mr Smale said crisply.

Jim looked at me, then turned to Mr Smale. 'You don't know what you're doing, Phillip. This is something more powerful than you could possibly imagine.'

'What do you know about power, old man? Sitting up there in your tower of dust and relics. Just GIVE ME THE SCORECARD!' Smale was shaking, his face burning with anger.

There was silence for a moment. Then Jim said softly, 'I don't have the scorecard.'

Mr Smale smashed his fist onto the table, then moved threateningly towards Jim.

'Toby!' Georgie squealed, turning to me.

'I've got it!' I yelled, pulling the scorecard in its plastic sleeve out of my pocket. Everyone froze. Jim was looking pale, leaning on the desk for support. I held the scorecard out for Mr Smale.

'But first let Jim walk over to us,' I said.

Mr Smale nodded reluctantly. Slowly Jim straightened up and tottered over to our side of the room.

'Georgie, take Jim and get out of here,' I said. 'Now!' I still held the card out in front of me. Georgie slowly picked up her bag, took Jim's arm and walked with him out of the office.

'Now give me the card!' Smale said tensely.

I bolted for the door. But Smale was there before

me. In a flash he was around the table and had lunged at me, catching my legs and tripping me.

'Toby!' Georgie yelled from outside. 'Just give him the stupid card and let's get out of here.'

I kicked out with both feet, but his grip was tight. I was being dragged away from the door. I clung onto the card, stretching my arms out to keep it away from him.

Suddenly a tremendous weight fell on me. I gasped for air. I couldn't believe it — it was Scott Craven! He got up and raised his fist. As I flung up my arm to protect my face, Mr Smale swiped at the card, knocking it out of my hand.

'Now go — all of you!' he shouted, pushing me and Scott out of the office and slamming the door shut.

Georgie and Jim were near the main door. I was halfway across the clubroom when Scott's elbow crashed into the back of my head. The force of his blow knocked me to the floor.

'We've been standing outside the door there, hearin' about your scorecard. And waitin' for payback time, scumhead,' Scott sneered, close to my face.

'You want me to hold him down?' Gavin said, strolling forwards.

'Georgie!' I yelled.

'Ya girlfriend's not gonna save you, Jones.' Craven dragged me to my feet and threw me against the wall. 'But first, you're gonna tell me what all this scorecard crap is about.'

'Leave him alone, Scott,' Georgie yelled from the doorway.

'Get her,' he snarled at Gavin. But Georgie hoisted her bag and Gavin ran straight into a swinging blow across the side of the head. He swore as Scott laughed. In Georgie's other hand was the *Wisden* Jim had brought: the 1931 edition.

'Stop this!' Jim called, his voice quivering. 'Please.'

Scott's grip loosened slightly. I tried to move away, but he still clutched me firmly.

'This is none of your business, old man,' Scott snarled.

'Oh, but it is,' Jim said, walking slowly towards Scott and me. 'You see, it was me —'

'Don't, Jim!' Georgie called, moving forwards, fearful of Jim getting caught up in the struggle. Gavin had recovered and charged at her. I struck out again at Scott, aiming a kick at his shins. He yelled in pain and his grip slackened. This time I broke free, gave him a shove and ran towards Gavin, who looked as though he was about to belt Georgie.

'Run for it, Jim!' I yelled. 'We're right behind you!'

'The *Wisden*, Toby. Quick!' Georgie called.

She threw the book at me. I caught it. I didn't want to leave them but it was the only way I was going to find the correct spot in the *Wisden*. Scott was still nursing his bruised shin, lying near the pool table as I dashed to the main door. I slammed it behind me and searched desperately for the Leeds Test match.

334

It was easier than I thought. There were other marks on the page — perhaps someone's notes about the game. I noticed that I could see these markings clearly. With one finger glued to where I thought the dates of the Test match were written, I entered the clubrooms again.

The *Wisden* closed onto my finger as I hurled myself at Gavin, who was sitting on top of Georgie. I pushed Gavin aside and helped Georgie to her feet. Jim had managed to grab Scott's attention and neither appeared interested in the rest of us.

I called to Jim and he turned slightly. I sensed Scott's attention was distracted as I headed towards them. I flicked the book open with one hand and concentrated on the spot where my fingernail had scored a small scratch.

I reached out for Jim's hand as the number 11 crystallised on the page. The *Wisden* wobbled in my left hand as I fought to hold the heavy book steady. It was the date of the first day's play. Bradman's day. I squeezed Jim's hand more tightly.

'Georgie!' I called, straining with concentration. Someone swore. I felt my hand clasped and a sudden painful blow in the chest. But Jim's grip was firm.

20 Jim's Dream

'JIM! Wake up. Oh please, Jim.'

He lay on the grass, unmoving, the hint of a smile on his face, wisps of hair across his forehead. Georgie pushed them aside gently and called his name. Slowly Jim's eyes opened.

'My dear boy, you'll be the death of me yet,' he chuckled, trying to raise himself up. Georgie and I helped him back to his feet, but he was looking wobbly.

'Tha all right?' a voice called. Jim turned to the man who'd spoken, looked past him, quickly turned one way, then the other.

'Oh, good Lord,' he whispered, blinking in the sunshine. 'Toby, what have you done?'

'It's 1930, Jim,' I told him. 'Leeds. Don Bradman ...'

Jim walked as if he was in a dream, dazed and disbelieving. We took an arm each and walked with him slowly towards the oval.

'Tha'll be wantin' the doc, lads, eh?'

336

We paid no attention to the man calling after us. Jim was shaking.

'Jim, are you okay?' I said.

Jim stopped and turned to face me. 'Toby, my dear boy, we've done it. *You've* done it.'

A burst of applause came from the crowd below and Jim appeared to forget what he was saying. 'Perhaps we could stay for a quick look?'

'Jim, we can stay as long as you like.'

'Toby!' cried Georgie. 'The bag didn't come through, but I've got a couple of things. Look!' She held up a cap, a pair of shorts, an old grey shirt and a small waistcoat. 'C'mon!'

'What?'

'We need to change! Jim, we'll be back in a tick.'

But I don't think Jim heard. We found a bench in a small stand and Jim settled at the end of a row, staring open-mouthed at the game. His face had taken on a look of amazement and wonder — like a little boy. I had a quick look out to the pitch.

'That's Bradman at the non-striker's end,' I said.

'Yes, and ...' Suddenly Jim's voice changed. 'Toby!' he said urgently. 'You've been here before. Who was batting with Bradman?'

'Woodfull.'

'What was his score?' Jim sounded anxious.

'Um, I think he was on 18, or maybe 22. Not that many. Bradman was doing most of the scoring.'

Jim turned to look at the scoreboard. Woodfull was on 11.

'Toby,' he said. He sounded like the old Jim again — calm and in control. 'We have ten minutes or so.'

'But don't we have a couple of hours?'

'No. You can't afford the risk of seeing yourself. Remember, you arrive again later this morning.'

'But —'

'Toby, the risk is too great. If you should see yourself within a small location, such as here, an irresistible force will bind your two bodies together, like magnets. It is a power greater than the power of time travel itself. There is no escaping it.'

I thought of the man I'd saved at the station. A powerful force had been dragging him towards the tracks. And then suddenly it dawned on me. Maybe the man had been on the train speeding through the station too, and so the man I'd saved had been drawn to the train as it sped past. But instead of meeting each other, he'd been dragged beneath the train and killed.

'Toby, are you okay? You've gone white,' Georgie said. I ignored her.

'Jim, what happens if you do meet your other self?' I asked in a croaky voice.

Georgie looked nervously from me to Jim, then back again. 'Toby, you haven't —'

'No, he hasn't,' Jim said quickly. 'Yet. Two bodies desperate to become one ...? I am not entirely sure myself.'

There was a roar from the crowd and we turned to look. Bradman had just belted another four.

'*C'mon*, Toby,' Georgie pleaded. 'Let's go now.

There's obviously not much time.' She turned and jogged away.

'Georgie, we have to be careful, remember?' I yelled, running after her. 'Back in a tick, Jim,' I called.

'Toby, remember the words of the poem,' Jim shouted. He turned back to the cricket as more applause broke out. This time the bowler had got one past the bat. I put my head down and raced after Georgie, brushing past a kid running from the opposite direction.

'Toby! Come *on*!' Georgie cried. She ducked into a toilet but came straight back out again, looking embarrassed.

'What?'

'It's the men's. There were boys in there. And a man. There's all these weird —'

'Yeah, well never mind that. I don't see many girls here. You're going to be a boy, aren't you?'

'I guess.'

'Well then?'

'You come in too.'

We both went in together. Georgie grimaced and she quickly turned away as a boy approached the brown urinal.

'Stand in front of me,' she hissed, almost tripping over herself as she tried to take her trackpants off.

'C'mon, Georgie, this is —'

'George!' she snapped, buttoning up the waistcoat. She adjusted her cap and turned to face me. 'How do I look?'

'Cute,' I said.

A little boy was standing at the urinals, staring at us. He was making a big mess, having lost concentration on what he was doing. Georgie didn't know where to look.

'Da?' he called, looking worried. We edged along the back wall, carefully avoiding the spillage on the floor, then raced out the doorway.

I crashed into a guy standing just outside.

'Um ... er, sorry,' I mumbled. Looking up, I almost fell over with shock. Georgie screamed.

'Well, that didn't take long,' sneered an all too familiar voice.

'B-but how ...' I stuttered.

Phillip Smale stood there smugly, his long black coat almost reaching the ground. He wore a large hat with a dark band around it, making him look like a gangster from an old movie. He was horribly convincing.

'You left the *Wisden* open, you silly boy,' he jeered. 'Very convenient. And I'd heard enough about the scorecard to know how it works. Very simple, really. Intriguing too,' he added.

A groan came from behind Smale.

'Come along, Scott,' he said. 'Get up. I've a little job for you.'

Scott Craven! He was dressed in a similar outfit to Georgie, except he had the long socks and shoes as well. He looked pale and stunned. 'Is ... is this r-really —?'

'Yes. Now take this girl here and keep out of

trouble. Toby and I have an appointment to keep.'
Smale's chuckle was not comforting.

Scott grabbed Georgie's arm and half dragged her
away towards the oval. She threw his arm off, planted
her feet and stood firm.

'Uncle Phillip,' said Scott, 'maybe we'll just stay
here and wait for you.'

'Uncle?' I gasped.

'That's right. Is there a problem?' Scott said.

I turned to run but Smale grabbed me hard and
pulled me back. His other hand went to his pocket.
He bent down close.

'Not much anyone can do about a boy lost in time
75 years ago, eh? Now turn and walk,' he said,
smiling meanly. 'Scream, and I'll kill the old man too.
I know exactly where he is.'

I managed to catch Georgie's eye. She nodded
quickly. I tried to slow Smale down, but he pushed
me firmly away from the toilet block and the old
stand nearby. He was right behind me, one hand on
my shoulder as though we were father and son,
guiding me away from the ground.

When we were outside we turned left and
walked more quickly. There were fewer people out
in the street, and those we passed paid us little
attention.

'Where are we going?'

'Shut up and keep walking.'

There was a shout from behind as we turned the
corner. 'TOBY!' Our pace quickened.

Georgie raced up and flung herself onto Smale's back. I stuck a foot out as he stumbled forwards and all three of us went sprawling on the pavement. Smale pulled himself to a squatting position. He was obviously shaken. I dragged myself out from beneath him as he reached for his pocket.

'Watch out, Georgie, run!' I yelled, struggling to my feet. But Georgie was lying there, not moving. She'd hit the pavement hard.

'I've had enough of this!' Smale began.

But before he could say another word, I threw myself on his shoulders, toppling him over so that he banged his head on the pavement.

I turned to Georgie. 'Come on!' I yelled, shaking her. She groaned. 'C'mon, we've gotta go!'

Smale tried to haul himself up, but he was looking dizzy. Not wanting to lose my advantage, I drove a knee into his neck, once more pressing his face into the pavement. Reaching into his pocket, I felt around for whatever it was he'd been after. My fingers closed on the scorecard.

By now a small crowd had gathered around us.

'He was trying to steal our money!' I shouted, helping Georgie up. Blood streamed from a cut on her forehead.

'Tha deserves all tha gets,' one guy growled, nodding at Smale who was looked blearily from one face to another.

I grabbed Georgie's hand and pulled her through the ring of bystanders. Scott was jogging towards us, but he took one look at me and flattened himself against the fence. He must have spotted his uncle lying at the roadside, surrounded by bystanders.

I looked down the street, then ran onto the road, still holding Georgie's hand. An old open-seated car honked at us but we got across safely. There were shouts from behind. We turned left and raced down a narrower street. Georgie was struggling and gasping for breath; blood covered her face and shirt.

'C'mon, Georgie,' I cried, but even as I spoke she stumbled and fell.

I hauled her up again and we took another turn, this time to the right. The houses here were smaller and darker. A woman was hanging some washing over the railing of a short flight of steps that led up to her front door.

I looked up at her. 'Please,' I panted. 'Can I borrow a cloth or something? My friend here —'

The lady had seen Georgie and even as I was speaking, she took a shirt from her basket and pressed it against Georgie's forehead. I touched the shirt. The fabric felt cool and wet. Georgie clutched it gratefully.

'You okay?' I asked.

Tears streamed down her face. She didn't say anything, just nodded.

The woman shook her head when she saw the blood soaking into the shirt. 'You keep it, lad. It's not much use to our Bill now 'e's in London. Tha's all right, eh?'

'Thank you so much,' I said, and turned to look down the narrow street. Smale and Scott came tearing around the corner.

'Toby,' Georgie began, 'why don't we just —'

'C'mon, we gotta go.'

I turned to the woman. 'Thank you,' I said again. I couldn't imagine what she was thinking, but there wasn't time to explain.

We ran on, diving down tiny laneways and running across streets. Mostly the roads were empty. We turned another corner and stumbled onto a game of cricket in one of the lanes. The boys were using a wooden crate for a wicket and the ball looked hard, small and black. They all stopped and stared at us grimly.

'Sorry,' I said, walking backwards. It didn't look like we were welcome.

'Tha can field,' said the oldest-looking kid. He tossed the ball from one hand to the other.

'No, it's okay, we were just —'

'Covers,' he added, pointing to a spot by the paling fence that ran along one side of the lane.

'C'mon, Toby,' panted Georgie. 'Let's just get out of here. Right out.'

'No, it's okay.' I saw Scott appear at the top of the lane and ducked down. Seeing me attempt to hide, the boys turned.

'Wha?' one kid shouted.

Smale jogged by a few seconds later. Georgie and I ducked again, pretending we were part of the game.

344

'Bowl it!' I hissed at the kid with the ball.

He shrugged, walked back to his mark and ran in to bowl. I stared at the batter, praying that Scott and his uncle wouldn't venture back to check the game.

Three balls were bowled and nothing happened. It looked like Georgie's bleeding had stopped.

The batter hit the next ball hard to my left. Sensing that the runner at the bowler's end was on the move, I bent down quickly and, without thinking, I grasped the ball, spun round and hurled it at the crate at the bowler's end. It smacked into the crate so hard that it toppled over. The kid, who was about my age, was run out.

I froze and looked over at Georgie. Open-mouthed and frightened she returned my stare.

'Nash Street,' she breathed. 'That was the exact same ...' Her words trailed away. I followed her gaze.

Scott and Smale were leaning against the fence, smiling. I glanced back at Georgie. This time there was real fear in her eyes. She was staring at Smale. He had something in his hand and was waving it about. All the players backed away, but none of them ran.

Slowly he raised his arm and levelled it at me. I stood, transfixed.

'The poem!' Georgie shrieked.

Suddenly the ball fizzed past me and crashed into Smale's hand. Whatever he was holding went flying, and so did three of the kids, diving for it. Smale started walking slowly towards us. He looked scary with his grim expression, black coat, hat and bloodied face. The cricketers bolted.

'Now, let's be sensible and reasonable about this, shall we?' Smale said, edging closer still.

I grabbed Georgie's hand.

'Noooooooooooo!' he shrieked, lunging at me.

'Uncle Phil!' Scott's voice died as I yelled aloud the words:

> *'But every word that boasts ahead*
> *Means lives unhinged, broken, dead.'*

The highest total by a team in a Twenty20 match was scored by Sri Lanka when they knocked up a massive 6/260 against Kenya on 14 September 2007.

21 Scott Lends a Hand

RECITING two lines of the poem while you're running is not the best way to return. We both crashed into the wall next to Smale's office door.

'Why didn't we do that —'

I held up a hand for Georgie to be quiet. The room was eerily silent. Nothing had changed.

I sat up slowly and looked around. 'He's not here,' I whispered.

'Who?'

'Smale. He grabbed at my leg. I felt the tug. But maybe he slipped.'

We waited another few moments. Then I got up and walked over to the drinks machine just outside the little kitchen door. I thumped at a few of the buttons.

'Jim!' I cried suddenly, turning around.

'Can't he just say two lines of the poem?' Georgie asked.

'No. I'm sure he told me once that if you get carried through to a new time, the only way back is to be carried.'

'Even if he has the power of travel?' Georgie asked.

'Yep.'

Georgie started taking off the waistcoat. 'Maybe he meant it to happen like this. Maybe he's where he wants to be.'

'Georgie! What if he's waiting there now for us? And remember, he's only got two hours. I've gotta go back.'

'Won't you need a *Wisden*?' Georgie asked, looking around.

'Smale had it — you know, to put the scorecard in.' I groaned. 'You reckon he would have taken it with him?'

'No idea. Can you do that?'

'I don't think so. I never have.'

We spent the next few minutes hunting about the place. Smale's office door was locked; Georgie's keys probably sitting on his desk inside.

'What now?' I called from the kitchen. 'Georgie?' There was no answer. '*Georgie!*' I charged back into the room.

'You could have killed me!' Smale roared, shaking with anger.

So I had dragged him through, but obviously only just. He must have held on for long enough to get through, but not at the same time as we did. He took a few more heavy breaths trying to calm himself.

'Give me the scorecard,' said Smale, stepping towards me.

'Give me the *Wisden*,' I replied.

He hesitated. I pulled the scorecard from my pocket and held it out. Georgie wasn't in the room. Nor was Scott.

'Where's Georgie?'

He shrugged and reached out his hand.

'You put the *Wisden* in Georgie's hand and I'll give you the scorecard,' I said firmly.

Smale looked around.

'Oh, for God's sake, girl! Where are you?'

Georgie appeared at the door a moment later. She took in the scene immediately, crossing behind Smale and coming round beside me.

'Give Georgie the *Wisden*,' I repeated, holding the card up for him to see. He looked from the scorecard to me, then back to the scorecard. Reaching deep into his coat pocket, he pulled out the *Wisden*. Georgie took a few steps forwards and he slapped it into her hand.

'Now, Mr Jones, the scorecard,' he hissed.

For a moment I thought of trying another escape, back to 1930, but we'd been lucky the first time and I couldn't leave Georgie to face Smale's rage alone. I held the scorecard out. He snatched it out of my hands.

'C'mon, Georgie,' I said. 'We're out of here.'

'Where's Scott?' she asked as we headed for the door.

'No idea. Do you care?'

She stopped at the door and repeated the question to Smale.

'He's waiting for you,' he chuckled, striding over to his office.

We jogged out the door and headed back to the other side of the oval, stopping behind a small scoreboard halfway round.

'What did he mean that Scott is waiting for us?' Georgie asked. Cap in hand, she was shaking out her hair.

'I'm not sure. But Scott is still back in 1930. Surely Smale isn't going to leave him there.'

'Scott'll probably go looking for Jim,' Georgie said.

'Yeah, and Jim can't travel. They're both stuck. Smale has to go back. Maybe he'll meet himself,' I said hopefully.

'There's a bigger chance that you will, Tobes. Just be ready to say two lines of the poem, okay?' Georgie said. She knew what I was going to do. I nodded.

'Georgie, hold the *Wisden* for me. I'll come back soon, hopefully with Jim. Will you wait?'

'Of course, idiot. I might go and wash my face though, if that's okay,' she said, nodding towards a toilet block further round the oval.

'Yep. Right. You okay?'

She looked up from the blood-soaked shirt still wrapped around one hand. 'Hey, this shirt is over 70 years old.'

'No, it's not. Think about it.'

'I have. If it was made in 1925, then that makes it —'

'Georgie! C'mon, open the book. Jim'll be getting anxious.'

Georgie thumbed through the *Wisden*, then turned it over for me to see.

'You keep holding it, okay?' I said, staring into the misty swirl of black on white.

'Watch out for . . .'

Georgie's voice faded as the two number 1s pulled together and locked into position.

I landed smack bang in front of Scott.

'Scott! Sorry, can't hang around,' I said, getting up.

'You took ya time,' he snarled, getting up from the ground himself.

'You got plenty of that on your hands now, eh?'

'Whaddya mean?'

'Who d'you reckon's gonna take you back, Scott?'

'Uncle Phillip, of course. He said I've got exactly one —'

'Scott. Right now your Uncle Phillip is trying to explain himself to two policemen and Georgie is heading back to the MCG to hand in the old 1931 *Wisden* and the scorecard. The *scorecard*, Scott.'

He looked at me, his eyes narrowing. 'You're bluffing, Jones.'

'Maybe. Maybe not. But don't mess with me, Scott, or you'll definitely lose your last chance of getting back.'

Scott's eyes darted about. He seemed to be searching for a solution.

'Mind if I head off then?' I said.

'Where?'

'To find Jim.'

'Wait!' he called, jogging after me.

I raced down to the stand where we had left Jim. It seemed like hours ago. I looked up at the scoreboard. To my horror I realised that I had returned at pretty much the exact same time as my first visit. Don Bradman was 45, Woodfull 11.

'Scott, you're going to have to go and get Jim,' I said, as we passed a crush of people and reached the edge of the stand where Jim was sitting.

Then, from nowhere, I suddenly remembered the kid I'd brushed past when I'd left Jim to go off to the toilet block with Georgie. I stopped dead and looked at Scott, who almost crashed into me.

'Oh, my God,' I whispered.

'What?'

I swallowed fearfully. Right now another version of me was up in the stand with Georgie and Jim. I hadn't felt any pull yet, but I started to step cautiously backwards, away from the stand.

'Um ...' I caught my breath. 'Scott, go up into the stand here and tell Jim it's time to go. Tell him Toby says *now*. It's vital.'

Scott looked baffled.

'Go!' I felt like adding, 'And don't look at the two kids who race past you,' but he was gone, heading for

352

the stand. I looked about me, then decided to head deep into the crowd in front.

'Hey, lad, mind yerself, eh? The cricket's not going anywhere!'

'Sorry, sorry,' I apologised, slowing down. I had to force myself not to turn around. There was a sudden buzz in the crowd. A ball had got through Bradman and had been taken by the keeper, Duckworth.

'Aye, tha's human, after all,' someone joked. A few people laughed.

'Bloody never 'appens when ball's in line to stumps,' another spectator said.

Their accents made it hard to understand just what they were saying, but I thought they were cursing their luck with Don Bradman. What if I quietly told them what he'd end up scoring? They wouldn't believe me — not till tomorrow anyway, when England finally got him out. It would be awesome for any *team* to score 300 runs in a day. But Don Bradman scored 300 runs *himself* in one day!

I watched him flick a ball out through point and head off for another run, and wondered whether another Toby Jones was watching the same stroke from somewhere else in the ground.

At the end of the over I made my way up to the back of the crowd and looked over to the stand. Scott and Jim had disappeared. Panicking, I barged through the last few lines of spectators and burst out into an open space where only a few people stood around.

'Jim!' I called. 'Scott?'

'Over here,' Scott waved, calling from near the toilet block. I raced over.

'Toby,' said Jim. 'What's happened?'

'Quick, we've got to move away!' I called, keeping my head down.

I set off, staring at the grass below me, Scott and Jim following. I didn't turn, fearing I'd see myself behind the others. We pressed on, walking quickly, until we reached another stand.

'Jim, are you with us?' I called, still not turning back. There was no answer. 'Jim?'

'He's stopped,' said Scott.

'Jim!' I yelled, turning around.

'Toby, go on, I'll follow you shortly,' he called.

I walked back to him. 'Jim, you can't. You didn't *do* the travel. Didn't you tell me that no one who's carried is able to return themselves?' I stood looking at him. Scott, who wasn't letting me out of his sight now, was just behind me.

'Toby, you have brought me back to 1930. This is my dream come true. It was meant to be.'

'But Jim, your real life is —'

'Toby, I'm home. These are my people — here, around us.'

They looked totally alien to me and I couldn't understand where Jim was coming from. He must have seen the concern on my face.

'Toby, please, trust me.'

'But, Jim, you've only got two hours. You told me yourself.'

'Toby, those two hours will be a long time for me. I've been waiting for this for over 60 years. Goodbye, my boy.' Jim held out his hand.

I looked up into his kind, wrinkled face. He smiled gently. I took his hand, then rushed forwards and hugged him. I felt tears brimming in my eyes.

'Toby, you and your father are as close as family to me. Take care, dear boy.'

I bent close to his ear. 'Smale's got the scorecard,' I whispered quietly so Scott couldn't hear.

'I know he has, but it's going to be all right,' he whispered back. 'Now off you go. Hurry. I'm missing the innings of a lifetime!' With one last wave, he turned and headed back towards the stand.

'You heard him. Let's go,' Scott said, looking anxious.

I wiped the tears away, not caring that Scott had seen me crying.

'Do you have any idea who's batting out there at the moment?' I said.

'Who cares?' he replied. *'C'mon!'*

I turned and started walking back towards the exit.

'Hey, what're you doin'? We've gotta —'

'Scott, just hold my arm,' I said, stretching it out horizontally as I recited the lines from the poem:

> *'Respect this gift. Stay calm, stay clever,*
> *And let the years live on forever.'*

22 Tobler

Thursday — afternoon

SCOTT was away from school the first two days of the following week, and I couldn't get near him on the Wednesday. But on Thursday I cornered him. He'd been avoiding me.

'Scott, what's going on with everything?' I asked him.

'What's it to you?'

'Have you told anyone about what happened?'

'What do you think?' he sneered.

'What about Gavin?'

'What about him?'

I sighed.

'Don't worry. He doesn't know anything,' he added.

'And what's your uncle up to?'

'Listen, Jones, I'll make a deal with you. I say nothing, you say nothing. Got it?'

The old Scott had returned. I nodded and walked away.

'Good luck Saturday!' I called, as an afterthought. He didn't reply.

The atmosphere at training was different without Scott. Everyone was more cheerful and people were queuing up for a hit in the nets — a part of training that was never much fun with Scott steaming in to bowl.

I watched Ally and Martian have a solid workout with Mr Pasquali out in the middle. Jimbo's dad was looking after the net session. He was a good coach too. He helped me with my grip and showed me how he held the ball when he bowled. (*See Tip 5.*)

Then Mr Pasquali called the whole team over for some outfield catching. We had to take five catches each before we could go home. A dropped catch meant you had to take three extra catches. I managed to take my five cleanly and waited around, watching the others finish.

After training, Georgie and I got together with Rahul, Jimbo and Jay to tell them the whole story. We'd given them snippets of info during the week, but they were impatient for the rest.

'Smale is Scott Craven's *uncle*?' Jay still couldn't believe it.

'So this guy Smale has got the scorecard, and you reckon he's planning some sort of business to make money?' Rahul said when we'd finished our tale.

I nodded.

'And we'll never see Jim again?' Jimbo asked, looking a bit confused.

'Well, I don't think so.'

'He can't just go and start that sort of business. They'll be on to him in a shot,' said Rahul.

'Who will?' I asked.

'Well, everyone. The media, the police, scientists. You name them.'

'Smale's a weird guy, but he won't do anything for a while, I don't reckon,' Georgie said.

Our parents started arriving and we broke off the conversation. I waved at Dad as he pulled up and started walking over to meet him.

'Hey, Toby, can I get a lift?' It was Ally. 'Mum said she can't be here till six,' she added, holding out her mobile phone.

I looked at Dad, who shrugged.

'I think it's on our way, isn't it, Ally?' I asked, hoping that it actually was.

'Fine then,' Dad said, opening the boot. I threw my stuff in and then Ally's bag.

I wanted to tell Ally everything about the *Wisden*s and Jim and the scorecard, but with Dad in the car chatting away about the game coming up, the chance didn't come. In no time, we were parked outside Ally's house.

'Thanks, Mr Jones. See ya, Tobler!' she called, dragging her stuff out of the boot.

'Tobler? That's a new one, isn't it?' said Dad, pulling away from the kerb.

'Yeah,' I mumbled. 'Dad?'

'Hm?'

'I guess we won't be seeing Jim for a while.'

'Oh, why's that? Have you seen him recently?'

I smiled, thinking how dumb it would sound to say *Not since 1930.* 'Yeah, you know, when we went up to the 'G the other day? He said he'd be away for a while.'

'Probably out chasing old books,' Dad said, smiling. 'Dear old guy. We'll get him around for that barbecue, Toby. I'll show him my studio. You know what I'm going to call it?'

I shook my head.

'The *Wisden* Studio. Hey, we'll get Jim to open it! He'd love that.'

'Sure. That'd be cool.'

I sat back and wondered if I would ever see Jim again. It seemed ridiculous that he was gone from this life, my life. And even weirder that he was living in a different time.

I took the paper to bed with me that night and stared at last week's results, the ladders and the teams for tomorrow's game. There was Scott Craven, vice-captain for the Scorpions. His uncle would probably make him captain for the grand final. And then I saw Smale's name: *Team Manager — Phillip Smale.*

He just couldn't keep his name out of the limelight.

I flicked off the light and lay wondering what the next turn of events would be. But for all the drama and action of the last few weeks, my last thought before falling asleep was of steaming in to bowl the first ball of the semi-final tomorrow. It would be just short of a length, pitched just outside off-stump and moving away slightly off the seam ...

The most runs scored by an Australian off one over was 30. Ricky Ponting achieved this in a game against New Zealand in Auckland, in 2005. The bowler was Daryl Tuffey. His scoring shots were 6 – 2 – 6 – 6 – 4 – 6.

See page 603 for more details about Toby's Under-13 competition.

BOOK 3

Toby Jones

—— AND THE ——
MYSTERY OF THE
TIME-TRAVEL TOUR

IT'S NOT JUST A GAME – IT'S TIME TRAVEL!

1 Runs on the Board

Thursday night — late

'READ the poem to me again, Toby,' said Ally.

'Again?'

'Yeah. Slower.'

Pushing my bedroom door gently closed, I settled into the desk chair, adjusted the phone and started reading.

'Wow,' she sighed when I was finished. 'So, this all began on that excursion? Why didn't I pick the MCG?'

'Dunno. But that's where I met this amazing old guy in the library called Jim. He also has the gift — the ability to travel back to cricket matches in the past using *Wisden*s. They're those yellow cricket books I brought into school for my sports project, remember?'

'I remember.'

'Yeah, well, a few of us — Georgie, Rahul, Jay, Jimbo ... even Scott Craven — have actually travelled back in time. And I thought it was about time you knew — especially since you're one of us now, playing cricket and everything. Jim was sent a diary and Jay found an old scorecard inside it. Anyone can travel with the scorecard; it's awesome. But Scott's uncle, Phillip Smale, has it now, and I know he'll use it. Sooner rather than later too.'

'He'll use it to travel back in time to a cricket match?' Ally asked. 'But isn't that just what you do, except you use a *Wisden*?'

I sighed. 'I do it to watch the cricket. Well, mainly,' I added, thinking of the scary times I'd had. 'Phillip Smale will do it to make money. To become famous.'

'Can he time travel without the scorecard?' Ally asked.

'Nope.'

'So, let's get the scorecard *from* him,' she said, like it was the easiest thing in the world.

'Well, it's not quite as simple as that,' I explained. 'Anyway, there's someone else I want to get back first.'

'What do you mean?'

'Jim is in Leeds, at the 1930 Test match he's dreamed of going to all his life. I took him there, and I left him. I'm really worried about him, Ally; he's like a grandpa to me.' Neither of us spoke for a moment. 'Anyway, I hope that fills you in.'

'Toby?'

'Yeah?'

'Thanks,' Ally said quietly. 'I'm really glad you told me.'

I smiled. 'No worries, Ally.'

'Okay. We're batting first,' Mr Pasquali announced to the team. It was the semi-final against Benchley Park, the team we'd struggled against a few weeks ago. I was going to have to wait another day before I'd be steaming in to bowl that perfect off-cutter — the one I'd been dreaming about last night. 'Jono and I have discussed the batting order,' Mr Pasquali continued, nodding to our skipper.

'Yep,' Jono said, picking up the cue from our teacher and coach. 'Cameron and I are opening. Then Rahul, Jimbo, Toby and Ivo. Seventh is Ally, then Jay, Georgie, Gavin and Jason. Any volunteers for scoring?'

I wanted to watch the cricket without the hassle of keeping track of runs. Minh, our 12th man, finally put up his hand.

Both our openers were warming up with some parents. I put my pads on carefully, then walked around the oval to sit behind the bowler. It was good playing at school, on our home ground. Mr Pasquali had been plugging the game all week: there was a note in the school newsletter and he'd even mentioned it at assembly on Friday. Quite a few kids had turned up to watch.

365

'If you make it through to the final we'll parade the entire team in front of the school assembly next week,' he'd told us.

'But not Scott Craven,' Ivo burst out.

'He's been a part of this team,' Mr Pasquali replied. 'Perhaps I'll give him the choice.' Scott had been our number-one strike bowler before he switched teams. Given the way his new team, the Scorpions, had played during the season, there was every chance they'd make it through to the grand final. Now that Scott had joined them, that seemed even more likely.

We made a solid start with our batting. There was good, sound defence from our openers against the accurate deliveries but also some attacking shots on the looser ones. When Jono mistimed a pull shot and holed out to mid-wicket, we had already scored 43 runs at more than five an over.

Rahul played fantastically, fluently driving balls to the boundary. The Benchley Park umpire moved his fielders all over the place, but Rahul kept on finding the gaps.

When drinks were taken out, we were 1/81 and looking good. Both Rahul and, soon after, Cameron retired when they got their 40, and each got a huge clap as he came off the field.

With the score at 1/121, I strode out to the wicket to join Jimbo. There were still plenty of overs left, but I sensed that now was the time to crank up the scoring, especially with wickets up our sleeve. Jimbo agreed. He was already on eight (from two fours)

when I joined him, and he hit another three boundaries before scoring his first single.

Each of his fours was greeted with beeping car horns and cheering from the boundary. Dad honked when I nudged my first two runs through point. For the next four overs we belted 37 runs off the tired Benchley attack.

'Looks like they're bringing on their openers again,' I said to Jimbo at the end of that fourth over, recognising the tall blond kid walking back to his mark.

'Good,' Jimbo said. 'Let's try and keep the tempo up.'

He hit two fours and a single from the next over and then had to retire. I found the fast bowlers harder to put away than the medium pacers and spinners. Martian belted a quick 11, but then Ally, Jay and Georgie went in fairly quick succession.

I was still in when Gavin marched out.

'Get out or retire,' he said to me. 'There are some big hitters waiting to come back and we haven't got much time.'

I was caught at deep mid-wicket that over, but Gavin only poked at the ball with Jason. I think Benchley Park preferred to keep them in; their fielders dropped two catches and their bowlers often bowled wide of the stumps. Finally, Gavin was caught off the last ball of the second last over.

'Your call, Jono,' I said. Rahul, Cameron and Jimbo were all padded up, ready to go.

'Jimbo, get out there and smash them,' Jono said.

And he did. After Jason scrambled a single to put Jimbo on strike, Jimbo blasted a two, three fours and a six off the last five deliveries.

Mr Pasquali was pleased, but reminded us that only half a game had been played. We'd scored 7/231. Batting was our strength, definitely. But tomorrow was going to be a lot harder, as we were without our strike bowler.

'Toby will be carrying a big load,' said Mr Pasquali, 'as will our other bowlers. We'll need outstanding support for them in the field. That's our focus for Saturday. Now off you go and have a relaxing evening — you've all earned it. Well done!'

Georgie elbowed me. 'Oh, my God,' she said. 'Look!'

Walking straight towards us across the oval were Scott and his uncle, Phillip Smale. No one said anything as they approached, until Mr Pasquali noticed them.

'Scott! How was your game?' he asked. Scott was playing in the other semi-final at the Scorpions' home ground, against Motherwell State School.

He shrugged. 'Got a few,' he said, looking down.

'A few! He took 7 for 17 off eight overs, with three maidens. It's got to be a record; I'll be checking the files this evening. In *my* office,' Smale boasted, looking at Georgie and me.

I won't ever forget the ordeal Georgie and I had

been through in Smale's office at the Scorpions' clubrooms the previous weekend.

'Well done, Scott. Terrific,' said Mr Pasquali. He sounded genuinely pleased.

'We'll be pressing for the outright win, of course,' Phillip Smale persisted. 'We've already won the game. Got them all out for —'

'Uncle Phillip, leave it, okay?' Scott muttered.

The rest of the team went about packing up. No one was taking much interest in Scott, though there were a few curious glances at his uncle.

Smale turned towards Dad. 'Peter, how are you?'

'Oh, hello, Phillip.'

'I just wanted to mention that we're looking at making some changes over at the library at the MCG. Actually, I thought I'd be pulling out of there, you know. That was my intention, but they really do need me.'

I caught Scott's eye before he looked down again.

'Yes, we're doing some upgrades, so unfortunately there'll be no visitors for some time.' Mr Smale looked at me. 'But I'm sure Toby here will find other things to do.'

'Well, I'm sure he will, Phillip. We've got the *Wisden* Studio to work on, haven't we, son?'

'The *Wisden* Studio?'

'It'll be a step back in time, won't it, Toby? We're looking to get as many copies of *Wisden*s as we can. And Jim Oldfield is going to open it.'

Smale's jaw dropped. 'B ... but, well, th ... that's —'

'C'mon, Dad,' I grumbled, dragging him away. 'You don't want to listen to him.'

'Bye, Phillip!' Dad called over his shoulder. There was no reply.

'Nice one, Dad,' I murmured under my breath in the car on the way home.

'What's that?'

'Want some help in the studio after tea?'

'Sure,' Dad replied, looking pleased.

But I didn't end up helping out because Georgie phoned me after dinner.

'Toby, there's supposed to be a poster up on Smale's office window about a virtual cricket machine. Ally and I are going to check it out. Are you coming?'

'What, to the Scorpions' clubrooms?' I said doubtfully, thinking of the swarms of Scorpion kids and parents who would be celebrating their semi-final thrashing of Motherwell that afternoon. 'Georgie, I don't know — Scott and Smale and everyone else'll be there.'

'So? We'll just look in the window, then leave. What's the big deal?'

'Nothing, except that Smale mentioned his office in a funny way after the game this arvo. I didn't like the way he said "In *my* office".'

'Tobler, you're getting paranoid. C'mon.' Georgie was beginning to sound frustrated.

'Since when have you called me Tobler?'

'Since you've started taking girls home from cricket practice,' she sniggered.

'What do you —' But I was talking to a long, high-pitched beeping noise. I could imagine Georgie chuckling as she put down the phone.

'Just going for a quick ride!' I announced, to no one in particular.

'Can I come?' Natalie, my younger sister called.

'No,' I yelled back, banging the front door shut. I opened it again, feeling a bit guilty. 'Next time, Nat. I'm just going up to Georgie's.'

'Then why don't you walk?' she shouted from the living room.

'Because!' I shouted back, lamely.

The last Australian to take all 10 wickets in an innings was Ian Brayshaw in 1967. He was playing for Western Australia against Victoria, in Perth. His figures were 17.6 overs (there were eight balls per over), 4 maidens and 10 wickets for 44 runs.

2 Virtual Cricket

Friday — evening

'WHAT'S the camera for?' I said, exasperated. Georgie was forever bringing along extra things: a camera, clothing, keys, binoculars ... Mind you, they'd mostly come in handy before, but I didn't think the Scorpions would want someone taking photos around their club.

'Relax, Tobler,' she said, packing the camera into its case.

'My name's not Tobler.'

'Yeah? You don't say that to Ally.'

'I never get a chance —'

'Hi, Tobler,' Ally called, as she stepped out of Georgie's house. 'I'm glad you could come.'

'Oh, hi, Ally,' I said, wondering if she'd heard me.

'See?' Georgie hissed.

'Well, let's go and check this poster thing out,' I said, hastily changing the subject. I wish I could just talk cricket, 24/7. Life'd be so much easier.

372

Sure enough, there were plenty of kids and adults gathered around the Scorpions' clubrooms enjoying a barbecue as we rode up. A few of the kids were playing cricket with some of the dads, but most of the crowd were sitting around in plastic chairs, drinking beer or cola. A new scoreboard, displaying the afternoon's scores, stood prominently by the main door to the clubrooms.

'Motherwell all out for 53. Scorpions 2 for 89 in reply,' I remarked, quietly.

'Well, let's hope the scoreboard looks totally different next week,' said Ally.

We rode up to the building, where a large and colourful poster took up half of one of Smale's office windows. Georgie pulled out her camera and took a quick photo, but we'd hardly had time to look when Scott Craven himself marched out of the clubrooms and over to us.

'So, what brings you all here?' he sneered, before taking a swig from the can he was holding.

'We just missed you, Scott, that's all,' Georgie said, airily.

'Yeah, well, beat it. I told you, Jones, that it's all over. Maybe you didn't get the message clear? Maybe you want me to give it to you a different way?'

Scott had been involved the last time we'd travelled back to 1930, and he was spooked by the whole thing.

'Gee, Scott, thanks for the thought.'

'C'mon, let's go,' Georgie said, as Scott seemed about to reply.

We spun around and sped off.

'Hey, I never even got to read the poster,' Ally cried once we were several streets away from the Scorpions ground.

'Nor me,' I added.

'That's why I brought this, sillies,' Georgie laughed, holding the little digital camera up in the air. 'Toby, can we do this at your house? Mum'll be on the computer at home.'

We downloaded the photo of the poster onto the computer in the living room. It looked awesome. There was a big TV screen, a cricket pitch with real stumps and a complicated box of gadgets and dials, switches and buttons. There was also a picture of a headset.

'Survive the Master Blaster at Lyndale Shopping Centre!' I read.

'So how does it work?' Georgie asked, looking at the fine print.

'State-of-the-art futuristic technology puts you into a virtual game of cricket. Go up against the might of the greatest bowlers in the world,' Ally read.

'Cool,' Georgie and I sighed at the same time.

'Face the world's fastest deliveries coming at you at over 150 kilometres per hour. Completely safe, Master Blaster is set to sweep the world in the next few years. But trials are continuing, and luckily for you they are about to happen in *your* home town.'

'That'd be like facing Brett Lee. How is that safe?' Georgie asked.

'It's virtual — that's the thing. You don't get hit, you don't get hurt. It's all pretend.'

'No way.' Georgie sounded very impressed. 'This sounds so cool. When is it?'

'Next Friday. Hey, why hasn't Mr Pasquali told us about this? Why doesn't anyone know?' Ally said.

'Scott knows. Mr Smale knows. Probably all the Scorpions know,' I said, looking out of the window. 'Gosh! Imagine facing up to Brett Lee.'

'You can have him. I'll wait for someone a bit slower, thanks.'

'Maybe Michael Clarke? I thought you said you fancied him,' Ally said, teasing Georgie. 'You like the blonds, don't you?' Georgie gave her a shove, and suddenly they were cavorting about on the floor. I read, then reread the poster, until someone grabbed my leg and hauled me over onto the carpet.

'Spoilsport,' Ally cried, as I bounced back to the chair in front of the computer.

I logged onto the Net to see if I could get any more info about this Master Blaster thing; I was hooked. I looked up Master Blaster, virtual cricket, even Lyndale Shopping Centre, but nothing of interest came up. For a few minutes I fiddled around with some dodgy-looking cricket games with cruddy graphics and basic layouts. They weren't at all what I was imagining virtual cricket would be like.

'Ally,' Mum called from somewhere. 'Can you give your mum a ring?'

'So, Toby, Jim is stuck in England —' Ally said.

'He's not stuck,' Georgie protested. 'He's just there.'

'He *is* stuck,' I muttered.

'Toby, that's where he wants to be. He said so himself.'

'How is he stuck exactly?' Ally asked, looking curious.

'Haven't you got a phone call to make?' Georgie asked.

'It can wait five minutes.'

I looked at Ally. 'Jim is in England because —'

'Toby! You might as well write something in the school newsletter,' Georgie interrupted, throwing up her hands.

'Sorry, am I out of line here or something?' Ally asked.

Georgie sighed. 'Sorry, of course you're not. It's just that I reckon the more people that know, the more dangerous this is for Toby and anyone else who knows.'

'Well, go on,' Ally said, looking at me, not sounding at all concerned about anyone's safety.

'Jim never got to see the famous Leeds Test match from 1930, the one where Don Bradman made over 300 runs in a day. Jim was a kid, living over there, but he was too sick to go to the game. So I took him —'

'But, Jim's a time traveller too, isn't he? He has the same gift as you?'

'Yes. And I know what you're going to say: why didn't he go back on his own?'

'Exactly,' Ally said.

'He was warned never to return to that particular time alone. It was like, really serious. And he never did.'

'So, Toby took him there,' Georgie said, like she wanted to close the matter.

'And left him there,' I added. No one spoke. Ally pressed her lips together. She was stewing over something.

'Well, why don't you go back and check if he's okay?' she asked, finally.

'Ally, that's the dumbest idea in the world. Don't you get it? Toby *can't* go back. Nor can I. We've already been back twice ... three times ... how many times, Toby?'

'Um —'

'Exactly. It's impossible. If you see yourself or get close to yourself, which is what could happen if we went back, then there's supposed to be this powerful force that smashes your two bodies together.'

'And then?' Ally asked.

Georgie looked over at me. I shrugged.

'I think it's bad,' I said, quietly.

'*I* could check on Jim,' Ally said, almost in a whisper.

'Ally, you haven't got this gift,' Georgie moaned, closing her eyes.

'How do you know?' Ally asked.

'I could take you there,' I said, slowly.

'Toby, you know you shouldn't,' Georgie scolded.

'You know what some of the last words Jim said to me were?' I asked her.

Georgie shrugged.

'He said that Dad and I were like family to him. And families stick together, right?'

'Right,' Ally said, eagerly.

'Families look out for each other, yeah?' I looked over at Georgie.

She nodded. 'I guess.'

'So, I've got to go back.'

'Then I'm coming too,' Georgie said, jumping to her feet. 'We just need to arrive at the end of the day.'

'You been thinking about that?' I asked her, grinning.

Georgie looked at me sheepishly.

'Yeah, well, it crossed my mind,' she chuckled.

Ally went to make her phone call while Georgie and I hurried upstairs to my bedroom to find the 1931 *Wisden*. I reached up and pulled it down from my shelves. It was by far the oldest and rarest in my growing collection. The cover was a faded yellow, old, softish and a bit leathery.

We came out of the room to find Ally at the foot of the stairs, a smirk on her face.

'You often go into Tobler's bedroom, Georgie?'

'Since I was about three years old,' Georgie fired back, quick as a flash. Georgie and I had been

378

neighbours and best mates for about 10 years now; she lived only a few doors down. I don't think it had occurred to either of us before that there was anything weird about her being there. But maybe, from Ally's point of view, it seemed a bit odd.

'Come on up,' I called to her.

'Everything okay?' Georgie asked Ally as she entered the room.

'Yep. Mum's coming round to pick me up in an hour,' she said, looking around. I felt a bit self-conscious with her gazing about at my things like that.

'C'mon, Ally, over here,' I said, sitting down on the floor. 'Georgie, the Leeds Test is on page 33. You've got to find a bit where it talks about the end of the day. Just read —'

'What about our clothes, Toby?' Georgie asked, stretching out her light blue singlet.

'Do you remember ever seeing three kids in blue, red and off-white tops running about the place at Leeds?' I asked her.

'Nope,' she said, with a sly smile.

'Nor me. That means we made it without being noticed. C'mon, start reading. There's usually a bit of an intro and then it gets into the summary.'

I watched Georgie scan down the page, mumbling to herself. Georgie saw words, just as she should. But when *I* looked at *Wisden*s the words and numbers were lost in a swirling confusion that dipped and spun in a slow, twisting spiral. With effort, I could focus on a date, place or score, and then the fun would begin.

'Can I try?' Ally asked, reaching out for the book. Georgie passed it to her.

'Well?' we asked simultaneously.

'Looks pretty boring to me,' she said.

'Can you read it?' I asked.

'Which bit?'

'Here, give it to me. I'll do it.' Georgie snatched the *Wisden* back. Ally shrugged, put her chin on her hands and waited. I guessed she hadn't really taken in what was about to happen. I turned back to Georgie, who held her finger to a spot well down the page.

'Here you go,' she said.

'You sure this is the right spot?' I asked. 'What does it say?'

'Yes,' she said. 'Bradman's already made 105 runs. You can't do that before lunch on the first day of a Test match, can you?' she said.

'Don Bradman's different,' I replied. But I didn't recall seeing him with that many runs on my previous visits.

'Ally, this'll feel really weird, but trust me, it works. Grab Toby's hand.' As Georgie reached out for my other hand, I leaned in closer to see where her finger was pointing.

Almost straight away a capital 'B' emerged from the mess, then disappeared. I stared at the spot where it had vanished till it emerged again, this time with some more letters after it. I looked to the right for Bradman's score. A number appeared.

'How many runs?' I whispered, staring at the page.

'105,' Georgie replied.

'One ... hundred ... and ... Georgie, are you sure ...'

My voice trailed away, becoming separate from my body. I felt Ally's grip tighten, her fingernails digging into me. I squeezed back, a whooshing sensation surging over and all around me like a breaking wave. Just as quickly as it had come the rushing noise stopped and we were sitting in the sunshine on a patch of grass by an old wooden fence.

The best bowling figures ever recorded were produced by Englishman Hedley Verity. Playing for Yorkshire against Nottinghamshire in 1932, he achieved the amazing result of 19.4 overs, 16 maidens, taking 10 wickets for only 10 runs.

3 Come Back, Jim

'TOBY?' Ally breathed, still holding my hand. 'We're in Leeds?'

'Yes,' I said, looking round.

'Where is Leeds?' she asked tentatively.

'Leeds? In England, Ally. You are standing in England, over 75 years ago. What do you think?'

Not surprisingly, Ally stood there silently, amazed, staring at the crowd in front of her. I, on the other hand, was getting very familiar with the surroundings. The entrance to the ground was away to our right, the stand where Jim was sitting a little further around.

I nodded at the scoreboard. 'Look, Bradman's on 113 already. And Woodfull's still in. Georgie, maybe it still is the first session. Let's not do anything stupid,' I said, turning back to the girls. 'You stay right here, and I'll go and check on Jim. I want to give him one last chance. That's all.'

'That's *all*?' Georgie queried, tilting her head.

'Yes, I promise. I'll be back in three minutes, tops. Then we're out of here, okay?'

'I'm freaked,' Ally shivered. 'Three minutes is three too many if you ask me.'

'Ally, it's cool. I promise,' Georgie said, squeezing her arm, trying to reassure her. Ally looked pale.

'Won't be a moment.'

I raced off towards the stand as a burst of applause swept around the ground. Another Bradman boundary, I thought, noticing a fielder jogging out to retrieve the ball. I reached the steps of the stand, and suddenly felt a violent tug. It was as if someone had grabbed me round the waist and was hauling me backwards. The air was forced out of my lungs and I gasped for breath.

''Ere lad, c'mon.' A man was talking to me, but the pain was terrible and I couldn't answer. I fell back, crashing onto the first step. It seemed like a gigantic vacuum cleaner was pulling at me and sucking out my insides. I wrapped my arms tightly around myself as other arms reached down to move me. I was dying inside. Something was leaving me and I was scared witless. I tried to open my eyes and respond to the concerned voices but they became distant.

Then suddenly everything became quiet and calm. The fever that had gripped me eased and I drifted away. I seemed to be floating. Hundreds of images flashed across my mind, a speeding whir of snapshots from my life: Natalie crying; Mum driving; Dad standing in the back yard, hands on hips; the view from my bedroom window ...

'Toby?' The images slowed. I saw a yellow *Wisden*; Scott Craven's head slamming into a toilet door ...

'My dear boy, look at me.'

And Jim. The stooped, gentle figure with his lined face, smiling at me in the library at the MCG ...

'Please, Toby.' A hand was grasping my shoulder. Slowly I opened my eyes, the pain in my head awful. The pale, ghostly image of Jim's face hovered over me.

'Jim?' I felt my lips moving, but no sound came out. I licked them and tried again.

'Look at me, Toby,' Jim said, sternly. But his face disappeared, and with relief I again closed my eyes, sinking back into the wonderful sleep that was overtaking me.

'*Toby Jones!*' Something tickled my face, and I felt my eyes being prised open.

'Jim?' I gasped.

'Be strong, Toby. Open your eyes and look at me.' I knew he was shouting, yet his voice was barely a whisper. He seemed so far away.

'J ... Jim? W ... what's happening?' I couldn't move. Other faces started to appear and I could hear faint noises of life around me. Jim put a hand to my face and wiped away the tears. There was blood on his hand, which he cleaned with a handkerchief.

'What happened?' I asked again.

'You met yourself,' he grimaced, 'and I've brought you back.' He pursed his lips.

'*I saw myself?*'

384

'Perhaps for a moment there were *two* Toby Joneses present in the same time and space. And of course there is only room for one. But possibly not,' Jim replied, standing up. He held out a hand for me. The onlookers had drifted away, lured by the cricket. 'Come along. You obviously came back to fetch me, hmm?'

'Jim, I couldn't leave you here. What about the two hours? What would have happened to you after two hours?'

'Well, it would appear that this time travel is actually invigorating me, Toby. I think perhaps that I am immune to the dangers of staying too long. But, believe me, if I weren't, then quietly slipping away without burdening anyone wouldn't be too bad.' Jim saw my look of horror. 'Well, I saw Bradman play some beautiful strokes. Not the 300 runs in a day that I might have, but one takes what is offered. Isn't that right, Toby?'

'Will you come back with me, Jim?' I asked, struggling to my feet. I felt like I'd just gone 10 rounds with Scott Craven in a certain toilet block.

'Of course,' he said. 'Lead the way.'

Jim put an arm on my shoulder and we walked back to where Georgie and Ally were still standing, trying to blend into the background in their bright red and blue tops.

'Georgie girl, how good it is to see you again. It's only been half an hour since I saw you last, but how much time has gone by in your life?' Jim asked. Ally was looking totally bewildered.

'Not long, Jim. About a day,' she chuckled.

'Ah, good. These old bones are used to a bit of travel, so a day away won't be too much of a bother. Nothing new, then, for me to learn?'

'Well,' I said aloud, thinking of the virtual cricket machine, 'there may be one thing. But I'll tell you about it later. Come on, everyone. Hold on.' I felt better by the minute.

'But won't someone see us?' Ally asked, taking my hand again.

'That is an interesting question,' Jim chuckled. He didn't seem at all put out that I'd come back to rescue him.

'Jim, you don't mind coming back, then?'

'My dear boy, I've been waiting for you,' he said. 'Perhaps hoping you might arrive a little later, but alas. Now, let's be gone.'

> *Then find yourself a quiet place*
> *Where shadows lurk, to hide your trace.*

I recited the words aloud — and in a flash we had returned to my bedroom.

'So, no one saw us?' Ally asked, looking from me to Jim.

'Jim. Jim Oldfield,' he said to Ally, smiling. 'Delighted to meet you, my dear,' he added, holding his hand out to her.

'Oh, hi. I'm Ally.' She shook his hand.

'No one saw you, my dear,' said Jim. 'It's one of the peculiar things about *Wisden* travel, quite unexplained. Some sort of time warp takes place. Those in the area temporarily cannot see into the space occupied by the travellers. I'm afraid I don't know much —'

'Toby? Are you in there?' Natalie called from the hallway.

'Just coming, Nat. You wanna play corridor cricket? Ally here wants to play on your team.'

'Oh, cool. I love Ally,' she yelled. We heard her footsteps retreating down the hall.

'She's not the only one,' Georgie mumbled. At least, that's what I thought she mumbled. We all ignored her.

'Well, now,' said Jim. 'There's just the small task of removing myself from your home, Toby Jones. I think it would be most unwise for me to stroll down your stairway and greet your dear parents at this point, don't you?'

'Um, yes. I guess so,' I said.

'That wouldn't be good,' Georgie laughed. 'Ally and I will go and suss it out. Ally, get Nat to show you how to play corridor cricket. I'll wait at the bottom of the stairs and signal when the coast's clear, okay?'

'Good old practical Georgie,' Jim said, nodding approvingly. Ally just looked at each of us in turn, shaking her head in wonder.

'Don't worry, Ally,' I told her. 'You'll get used to it.'

'Oh, well, that's a relief. For a minute I thought I'd shifted to another planet.'

Georgie opened the door, and Jim took a few steps back to be out of view of the hallway, just in case.

'Ally, are you okay?' I asked her quietly.

She took a deep breath. 'Yep, I think so. Toby, I was totally freaked out. But you know what?' I had a feeling I knew what she was about to say. 'I want to go again.' I was right. 'Weird, huh?'

'Yep. Very strange.'

Ally nodded and headed out the door to follow Georgie downstairs.

'I met myself, didn't I, Jim?' I said.

'Yes, Toby, you did. Luckily for us travellers, it's an experience that we are more able to deal with than those we carry.'

'You mean like my friends?'

'Yes. They are far more vulnerable to the problems that can arise.' Jim had picked up a cricket ball from my desk and was gently fingering the seam.

I had grown really close to Jim in the time that I'd known him. There was something vulnerable about him that needed protecting. He was old, and no amount of wisdom could make up for the fact that he was fragile. But I needed him. The time travel was part of my life, and I wanted Jim to be a part of it as well.

'Jim, would you come and live with us?' I said. I had no idea where he lived. His life outside the library at the MCG was a complete mystery, and maybe he had nowhere to go. The only other place

I'd seen him was in a hospital. He never spoke of a family.

'One thing at a time, Toby,' Jim said, smiling at me.

'Hey,' Georgie called from down below.

I stuck my head round the door, and she gave me the thumbs up. 'Let's go, Jim.'

He picked up the 1931 *Wisden* lying on the floor and shuffled out. I raced ahead of him, bounding down the stairs. I'd just reached the bottom when the phone rang.

'Got it,' shouted Dad. A door banged shut.

I spun around, urging Jim to follow me. I took his arm and gently guided him towards the back door, then steered him away from the house and to the little side gate next to Dad's new studio.

'This is where the fire was,' I said quietly. 'It used to be a boring old garage. Now Dad's contemplating a permanent move.'

'Most impressive,' Jim said, eyeing the bookshelves behind the double-glass doors.

'Jim, can you make it to my game tomorrow? We're in the semi-final against Benchley Park, up at the school oval.' The words were just tumbling out of my mouth.

We'd made it to the laneway. 'How will you get home?' There was a pause. I looked into Jim's eyes. 'Where is home?'

The question hung between us. He smiled, then turned away.

'Jim?'

'You get a good night's sleep, Toby Jones,' he called without looking back. 'You've got a lot of bowling to do tomorrow.'

I watched him walk away, wondering where and when we would meet again.

I also wondered how he knew that I'd be bowling tomorrow. Maybe it was a 50/50 bet. But then Jim didn't seem the betting type.

I turned and jogged back inside for the promised game of corridor cricket.

The best bowling figures in a Test match are held by Jim Laker of England. Playing against Australia in Manchester in 1956, he took all 10 wickets in Australia's second innings (and nine in the first). He bowled 51.2 overs in that innings, with 23 maidens and 10 wickets for 53 runs.

4 Can It Get Any Hotter?

Saturday — morning

'IT'S a boiler,' Dad sighed, strolling into the kitchen the following morning. 'It's going to be an absolute belter. Toby, get Benchley Park out nice and quick, you hear me?'

'You bet, Dad.' I searched his face for any clues that he suspected anything was up after last night. But he padded about in his bare feet, boxer shorts and straggly hair, as on most other mornings, totally focused on getting his breakfast organised.

'Hey, Dad. There's a new virtual reality machine down at the shopping centre. Can we go and check it out sometime?'

'Virtual what?' he asked, attending to the toaster.

'Virtual reality. You know — real, but not real.'

'Real, but not real?' he repeated slowly.

'Well, yeah. Almost real. Virtually real. You know.'

'Hmm, not exactly, but I guess I'm going to find out soon enough, aren't I?' He winced as his finger touched the hot edge of the toaster.

'Thanks, Dad.' I looked at the clock. 'Ten minutes and we're out of here, okay?' I called, getting up.

'Ten minutes,' he said, licking his finger.

I couldn't believe the heat. The air was still, and it was hard to breathe. Even at 8.20 in the morning the temperature was 27 degrees, and Dad said it was expected to climb to 42 degrees. You could smell the dryness as well as a faint hint of smoke.

'Let's hope we don't have to worry about a bushfire,' Dad said, sniffing the air as we got out of the car. 'Total fire bans bring out the total idiots.' He looked at me. 'Sounds dumb, I know, but make sure you do a proper stretch.' Dad hauled out his deckchair and the enormous Saturday newspaper, and settled down in the shade of a large gum tree.

I grabbed my gear and walked over to Mr Pasquali's car to help him with the kit.

'It's a hotty, Mr P,' I said, pulling out the stumps.

'Short spells today, Toby. Hats and zinc too,' he added, looking up at the sky. 'Thanks for helping.'

More cars arrived and soon the team was in the outfield tossing a ball around. I went to measure my run-up, though I could easily see where I'd scuffed a mark in the grass lots of other times during the season.

I strolled in to the middle and rolled my arm over

392

a few times until Mr Pasquali called us together for the traditional pre-game pep talk.

'Now I don't need to tell you to be sensible out here today. I want you to wear hats, sunscreen, even sunglasses if you've got them,' he began. Already there were beads of sweat on his face. 'It'll be hard work for their batters too, but we must support our bowlers. Short spells, Jono,' he said, turning to our captain. Jono nodded.

'I'm not going to interfere with bowling changes or fielding positions,' Mr Pasquali continued, 'but I'll say this. Any suggestions should go through the captain, and I want there to be suggestions. I want you to be alert to what the batters are doing, alert to any weaknesses you see, alert to anything at all.' He paused, looking around at each of us in turn.

'I've coached a few Riverwall teams in my time, but none quite as good as this one. Let's show the parents, and the opposition, what sort of a team you are.'

Jono tossed me the new ball. How would our bowling line-up rate now that Scott Craven wasn't a part of it? Time would tell. I had to stand up and take over the responsibility for leading the attack. I'd been in Scott's shadow all season — now was my big chance to lead from the front.

My start couldn't have been worse. I should have pulled out of my run-up, but instead I stuttered up to the crease, my rhythm and strides all over the place. I overstepped the popping crease by a mile and bowled a wayward delivery that Ivo took in front of Jono at first slip.

I slowed down for the rest of the over and wasn't even thinking of taking wickets; I just wanted to put the ball in the right spot.

'Okay, you've got that one under your belt, Toby. You've got to attack now,' Jimbo said. He'd jogged all the way over from the covers to fire me up.

'It felt shocking,' I told him.

'Mate, it looked shocking. But that's because you weren't relaxed. Next over, just let it go and see what happens.' I nodded, feeling better for the advice.

Our top four bowlers — Cameron, Jono, Rahul and me — were in the top six of the batting line-up as well. We were a team that fell away quickly. Ivo was a really good keeper. He had won his spot back from Ally, who had filled in for most of the season after Ivo's bad accident, when his bike collided with a car. Ally was an awesome softballer with great reflexes and a strong throwing arm, but she didn't appear very comfortable without the keeper's gloves on.

Georgie, Jay, Gavin (who was really grumpy now that his best mate, Scott Craven, had left the team) and Jason loved their cricket but were really just filling up the numbers.

I looked over at Jimbo as I took the ball for my next over. He gave me the thumbs up. I tried to clear all the negative thoughts from my mind. I'd run in to bowl a thousand times without ever thinking of my stride pattern, yet suddenly I was feeling like a total loser.

'C'mon Tobes,' Jimbo called from the covers, clapping his hands. A few others joined in. 'Time for some action.' The batter nonchalantly looked around the field, then settled down over his bat.

I took a deep breath, made one final check that the small plastic disc I use to mark my run-up was exactly where it should be, then steamed in. Somewhere, someone was clapping but I pressed on, striding out, my paces lengthening as I approached the pitch.

This time it felt perfect. The seam of the ball stayed upright and the ball cut back fractionally from the off side, thudding into the batsman's pads. It was probably 15 kilometres per hour faster than any ball from the previous over.

'Howzat!' I screamed, jumping in the air and turning to the umpire. I could tell straight away by his grim look that he was going to put up his finger. And he did.

'Yeah!' I roared, turning round and charging down to the slips.

'Bloody beauty!' Jono cried, clapping me on the shoulder. The rest of the team charged in.

'That's more like it, Toby Jones,' Jimbo said, his fists clenched.

The rest of the over played out uneventfully — the kid who went in for Benchley at first drop, a guy called Edison Rocker, was easily their best batter — but I felt much better. Every ball was on target.

It's amazing what a wicket can do for your confidence. Suddenly I was feeling on top of the world again, desperate to get another crack at the batsmen.

'Two more overs, Toby, maybe three if you snag another wicket,' Jono called as we changed ends. And then the day improved even more when I noticed Jim sitting in Dad's chair with Dad nowhere to be seen. He was probably off scrounging another chair. I gave Jim a wave and he waved back.

I didn't take another wicket in that spell. By the first drinks break Benchley Park had still only lost the one batsman and were looking settled, though they weren't scoring quickly.

'We've just got to dry them up,' Jono said, guzzling down some ice-cold cordial. 'It's really important that we keep the runs down. No wides, no misfields.'

'And we need to back up in the field,' Jimbo said. 'They're probably going to start looking for the quick singles to break things up a bit.'

It was great how Jimbo was getting more involved. This was only his third game for us. Years earlier his dad had banned him from playing cricket because he'd walked away from the game himself after being hit by a vicious ball. His anger had carried through to poor Jimbo, but luckily Mr Temple, Jimbo's dad, had had a change of heart. Lucky for us too. Jimbo was a brilliant batter and his knowledge of cricket was amazing.

And he was right about backing up too. During the second over after drinks, the batters sprinted through for a single. Jimbo charged in, scooped up the ball and took a shot at the stumps at the bowler's end, missing by centimetres. Cameron tried to gather in the ball, but it flew past him.

'Again!' Edison Rocker screamed, not realising that I had actually stopped Jimbo's throw from going to the boundary with an enormous dive to my left. I flicked the ball back to Cameron, who was still by the stumps at the bowler's end.

Edison's batting partner was run out by about eight metres.

'I'm going to call you Prophet,' I laughed at Jimbo. He'd predicted exactly what had just happened.

But as the morning grew hotter, some of us started to drag our feet. Two catches went down, and several misfields and sloppy throws crept into our game.

Jono, Jimbo and I tried to keep everyone positive and motivated but it was an effort, particularly because Benchley Park didn't really look like a threat.

Edison Rocker got his 40, but there weren't any other quality batters in the team. And although Jay and Jason were belted for a couple of fours each, it was just a matter of time before Benchley collapsed.

With ten overs left Jono tossed the ball to me.

I decided to put the heat out of my mind and concentrate on line and length. There was a chance for some wickets as the batsmen were starting to play loose shots to up the scoring rate.

My first two balls were off target, but the third was spot on. Aimed at off-stump, it caught the seam and deviated left, catching the bat's outside edge. Martian took a ripper catch low down in front of Jono.

I slowed up the next two deliveries and the new guy played them easily enough. Ambling in for the last ball of the over, I was hoping the batter was expecting the same again, but I swung my arm over quickly, pitching the ball on a shorter length.

At the last moment he hoicked his bat to keep the ball off his chest. The ball ballooned away to my left and I dived, catching it just centimetres from the ground.

The game died quickly after that. The Benchley Park coach made sure all his team got a brief hit, retiring a couple of the batters early. One kid was so annoyed that he swore then threw his bat about five metres into the air.

Benchley Park had fallen short of our total by just under 70 runs, but our celebrations were pretty subdued. Maybe it was the weather. Maybe it was the fact that we hadn't really won anything — yet. Scott Craven and the Scorpions were on most people's minds as we packed up the gear, folded away the chairs and headed off to our cars.

'Dad,' I said, 'can Jim come around to our place this arvo?' But as I spoke I saw a taxi turn into the ground and Jim wave an arm at it.

'I already asked, Tobes. But he said he'd come around tonight if he can.' Dad smiled, ruffling my hair. 'You're really very fond of him, aren't you?'

'He's shown me some very interesting things,' I said, watching Jim walk towards us.

'Well played, Toby. Your bowling is most impressive,' Jim said.

'Not my first over,' I mumbled.

'No, indeed. But that too was impressive. You were able to put it behind you and bowl from then on with good pace and rhythm.'

Jim said goodbye and walked slowly over to the taxi. Watching him, I remembered that he really was an old man.

'Toby?' Ally called, holding up a bottle. 'You want the last drink?'

I didn't, but I headed over to her anyway. 'Um — er, Toby?' she asked quietly, looking up at me from beside the Esky. 'You reckon I can go on another cricket trip?'

'Well, I guess,' I said, cautiously. My experiences of taking friends to faraway places weren't all good. Rahul in India was the scariest: he'd paid me no attention at all, wanting to go off on his own. It was like he'd been possessed.

'You don't look so sure,' she said, eyeing me closely.

'Well, it's just that —'

'You think Georgie'd get a bit upset?' Her voice had risen slightly. I looked around but nearly everyone had gone or was in their car about to leave.

'You see, I took Rahul to the Tied Test —'

'The Tied Test? Cool, that would have been exciting. Did you see the run-out?'

'Run-out?' I asked.

'There's that famous photo of the West Indian dude who did that amazing run-out,' Ally said.

We were talking about different games. She was thinking about the Test match between Australia and the West Indies in 1960, played in Brisbane. It was another of Dad's favourites. And he had that *Wisden* ...

'Toby?'

'What?' My mind had wandered. 'Sorry?'

'The Tied Test?'

'Oh, yeah. Well, I took Rahul back to India. To 1986 and the game in Madras where Dean Jones made 210 runs and almost died doing it. But you know what? That Brisbane game's a possibility,' I said, nodding slowly.

'Yeah?'

'What are you doing this afternoon?' I asked, helping her tip the mostly melted ice out of the Esky.

Ally shrugged. 'Maybe going back to 1960 with you?' she suggested, her face brightening. 'Hang on!' She jogged over to her car, had a few words with her dad and came back grinning. 'We're on! Dad's gonna drop me around later. He's got to go and pick up my brother. About three?'

'Okay,' I said. 'See you then.'

George Lohmann, playing for England against South Africa in 1896, managed these amazing bowling figures: 14.2 overs, 6 maidens and 9 wickets for 28 runs in Johannesburg; 9.4 overs, 5 maidens and 7 wickets for 8 runs in Port Elizabeth. He took 35 wickets in three Tests with a bowling average of 5.80! (That's a wicket for every 5.8 runs scored off his bowling.)

5 All Tied Up

Saturday — afternoon

'IT'S got to be cooler than this in Brisbane,' Ally said, when I opened the door to greet her.

'I forgot to mention about fashion and stuff,' I said, letting her in.

'Fashion?'

'Shut the door, Tobes!' Dad called. The heat outside was like that in a furnace and Dad must have felt the temperature rise a few degrees in the kitchen.

'You know,' I looked at her, 'blending in. Not standing out in a crowd.' I paused, then shouted into the living room. 'Ally's here!' Dad was settled in watching the cricket on TV in the only air-conditioned room in the house, while Mum and Nat were shopping in comfort down at the supermarket.

'Hi, Ally,' he called, as we headed for the stairs. 'Are you guys coming in to watch?'

'Nah, we'll listen in on the Net.' I signalled Ally to follow me upstairs.

Although Mum had closed my window and pulled down the blind, it was still hot in my room. 'Maybe watching the cricket with Dad would be better,' I suggested, suddenly nervous as I stood in the middle of my bedroom while Ally hovered at the door.

'No way, stupid.' She smiled. 'We won't be here, remember?'

'That's all very well until someone comes looking for us.' I headed over to the bookshelf to find the 1962 *Wisden*.

'So, we'll just say we stepped outside for an ice-cream,' Ally said, walking over to me. 'Now what's this about clothes?'

'It probably doesn't matter. We'll just have a quick visit, okay?' I thought back to India and Rahul's dramatic behaviour when he ran off to see the brother he'd never met. And then pictured Jay, in Hobart, trying to tell a kid the result of the game and who'd win the AFL Grand Final the following year.

'Ally, you've got to promise me one thing, okay?'

'Of course, Toby. What is it?' She looked at me expectantly.

'The trouble is, it's really easy *now* for you to say, "Sure, Toby. No worries." But when we get there, it'll all change.'

'Toby, I'm a girl. I'm totally trustworthy. Don't doubt me on this, okay? Now, what is it?' She was looking at me challengingly. I shrugged. I knew how easily it could all go wrong.

'Ally, when I say it's time to go, we go straight away. Have you got that?'

'Sure, Toby. No worries.' She grinned.

'Okay. Time will tell.' I picked up the *Wisden* and offered it to her. 'You'll have to look for the section called "West Indians in Australia". It'll be towards the back.'

Ally flicked through the book. 'Got it. Now, we want the First Test, yeah?'

'Has Georgie told you about this?' I asked. Ally seemed pretty confident with what she was doing.

'A bit,' she said. 'Here we go: page 842. Wow! They're fat books, hey?' She looked up, smiling. She was so cool about it all.

'Right. What you've got to do —'

'I know. Find a date, place or score, hopefully one that's near the end of the game.' Ally muttered to herself, her head buried in the text. 'Will any number do?'

'I think so.' I felt the familiar adrenalin and excitement surge through me with the thought of more time travel. Dad often spoke about this game; he'd only bought this particular edition of *Wisden* for this series and Richie Benaud's Aussies reclaiming the Ashes from England in 1961. Dad said that both series were awesome, especially because there'd been heaps of boring cricket during the 1950s.

'Ally, go to the scorecard. It's easy to see all the scores there.'

She gently turned the page. 'Ah, okay. So, Australia were batting at the end. Here you go.'

I followed her finger into the wash of numbers and letters spilling and swirling on the page.

'Quick,' I whispered, reaching out a hand as numbers appeared, then retreated again. 'Which one?' I breathed.

'There. Look at one of those twos.'

Sure enough, a '2' emerged from the mess and I latched onto it with all the concentration I could muster. A drop of sweat fell from my forehead and landed in the swirl beneath me. I felt the squeeze of Ally's hand as I heard her gasp.

'Two ... two ...' I said over and over — and we were gone.

We 'landed' on a hill of grass, slightly away from the arena itself. I immediately sensed the tension in the crowd, although the number of people was amazingly small. Everyone's attention was hooked on the drama unfolding out in the middle of the ground 80 metres away.

I turned to Ally. There was a look of wonder on her face. I wasn't sure how she'd react, but she didn't seem too fazed by the fact she'd just travelled back in time over 40 years, as well as more than a thousand kilometres north in the space of a few seconds. Perhaps Georgie had told her more than just a bit about the wonders of time travel. And she had taken a quick trip to 1930s England.

'Ally?'

She turned to me, her smile dazzling, and with a squeal of delight she kissed me on the cheek. 'Toby, this is brilliant,' she gasped, clapping her hands as she took in the scene around her. 'Let's get closer and watch —'

'Ally? Remember your promise?'

'What promise?'

I groaned.

'Kidding,' she said, weaving a path towards the action.

'There's Richie Benaud,' I whispered, awestruck with the thought that we were seeing Channel Nine's master commentator batting.

'What's going to happen?' Ally asked as we watched an enormously tall West Indian walk back to the top of his run-up.

'I *don't* know,' I said pointedly.

Ally turned at the tone of my voice. 'Oh yeah. Sorry,' she said sheepishly, hunching her shoulders. She turned back to the cricket, and I checked the scoreboard. The Aussies were doing okay: Richie Benaud and Alan Davidson had added over 100 runs to the total and were going strong.

'How much ...' Ally started. 'No, it doesn't matter. I'll just shut up and enjoy the cricket.'

'Good idea.'

We watched a couple of overs. The situation was getting more tense with every delivery. Davidson and Benaud had piled on a massive partnership and the crowd was sensing that something special was about to happen. From a hopeless 6 for 92, the two batsmen had steered the Aussies to 6 for 226. They were only seven runs short of pulling off a stunning turnaround.

But then disaster. There was a shout from the pitch.

'He's run out, Toby,' Ally said. We watched Alan Davidson walk back towards the dressing room.

A man pushed past me, snacks in hand. 'Bloody awesome, isn't it, mate?' he said, and then moved closer to the fence.

One over left and seven runs to win.

'Okay, Ally. It's time,' I said, expecting some excuse from her. She didn't move. 'Ally?' I said more firmly as we watched Alan Davidson walk back towards the dressing room. He'd just been run out by a direct hit from one of the West Indians. The people around us seemed shocked, but still confident.

'Hmm, what's that?' she said, vaguely. She was enthralled, like everyone else.

'I think it's time.'

This time Ally turned to face me. 'Toby,' she said evenly. 'I am in total control here . . . '

'Ssh,' I hissed, although no one seemed to be paying us the slightest attention.

'. . . and we are about to see the most amazing over.' There was a dreamy look on her face.

'Ally?'

She turned her head from side to side, looking dazed.

'Ally? What is it?' I cried, alarmed, as she grabbed onto a post she had been leaning against.

'Nothing,' she sighed, shaking her head. She was looking behind her every few seconds. 'Just feeling a bit in awe of what's going on. One more over and then vamoosh, okay?' There was sweat on her forehead, and her knuckles were white from gripping the pole.

'Yep, okay. But relax.'

Gritting her teeth, Ally nodded, turning to look behind her.

I looked out to the ground. The West Indies were setting up for the last over. It was to be an eight-ball over, but three wickets going in the one over — as I knew was about to happen — was still incredible.

Australia was six runs from levelling the scores, and needed seven to win. Even though I knew the result I still felt the electric atmosphere of a close game. You often got this situation in a one-dayer, but in a Test match it was very rare for the teams to be so close after five days of cricket.

'Who's bowling?' Ally asked.

I checked the scoreboard, even though I already knew the answer. 'It's Wes Hall. He's the fastest bowler going around at the moment,' I replied as I watched him charging in to bowl. The ball hit the

Aussie batter high on the leg and they raced through for a single. The crowd roared in approval; they knew exactly what was required for victory.

Ally had her head down, one hand covering her eyes. 'Toby? I think someone's calling my name.'

It was the tone of her voice that told me it was definitely time to go. Something was really freaking her out.

'C'mon, Ally,' I said, unhooking her hands from the pole. For a moment it seemed like she wanted to pull away from me, but I hung on firmly.

Once more she turned, her mouth gaping as though she'd just seen a ghost.

> *What wonders abound, dear boy, don't fear*
> *These shimmering pages, never clear.*

I quickly said the first two lines of the poem as I pushed through the spectators and into some space away from the crowd. I heard screams and groans, and I turned for one last look at the field. Richie Benaud had just been caught by the keeper, attempting a big hit.

When we arrived back in my bedroom, Ally thanked me, though she wasn't as excited as she'd been before we left.

'I told you weird things happen.'

'Yeah, something strange *was* going on. But I'm glad I went.'

In 1972, Patrick Pocock took five wickets in six balls. He was playing for Surrey against Sussex in the English County Championships.

6 Georgie Snaps

Saturday — evening

'I'M not sure that I've ever contemplated such a fine array of food, Jane,' Jim said, beaming as he surveyed the plates in front of him.

A cool change had arrived and a fresh breeze was pushing the hot air out of the house. Dad had just walked in with a huge plate of chicken kebabs, hamburgers, prawns and lamb steaks, which he set down on the table alongside the rice salad, potato salad and about five other green salads.

For a while no one spoke as we all tucked in. Ally, Georgie, Rahul, Jimbo and Jay had all turned up to celebrate our semi-final victory. And to top it all off, Mum had even allowed Dad to manoeuvre the TV so that every now and again we could get a look at the one-dayer in Sydney.

'We're very glad you're able to stay with us tonight, Jim,' Mum said, smiling at him.

'He could stay for ever,' I interjected.

'Well, it's very kind of you to have me.' Jim smiled.

I wanted to know about what had been happening at the MCC library but I wasn't quite sure how to ask. Perhaps Jim sensed my curiosity.

'It would appear that my time at the library is over, but when one door closes there's sure to be another that opens somewhere.'

'Why can't you stay there?' Jay blurted out, reaching for another kebab.

'It's called downsizing,' Jim said. 'Our friend Mr Smale ...'

'He's no friend of anyone here,' Jay said.

'Jay, can Jim finish what he was going to say?' Dad asked.

'Sorry, Mr Jones.' Jay looked a bit embarrassed.

'Well, I was just going to say that David, the main librarian, and Phillip Smale are in the process of making a number of changes, and quite frankly I'm rather glad I'm not there.'

'What sort of changes, Jim?' Dad asked, looking up from his plate.

'Well, bringing in the electronic age for a start. And he is removing all the significant works and older pieces. He's concerned about their safety.'

'Removing them to where?' Georgie asked.

'Away from the eyes of the public,' Jim said sadly.

'How dumb is that?' I spluttered. 'What's the point of having fantastic old books and scorecards and photos and cricket bats and caps and stuff if people can't see them?'

'You might as well just bury them away in a vault,' Jimbo said, shaking his head.

'Exactly,' Jim said.

'It does sound rather odd,' Mum commented. 'What does everyone else at the library think?'

'They are all somewhat swayed by Phillip Smale's offering.'

'Which is?' Ally asked.

'Which is, I'm told, the most significant and valuable collection of cricket memorabilia in the Southern Hemisphere.'

I noticed the sceptical look that passed between Dad and Jim.

Rahul let out a low whistle. 'Wow!' he gasped. 'Really?'

'Evidently,' Jim said, though he didn't sound convinced. 'Though one would think that such a significant collection would have been known and already on display somewhere by now.'

We took dessert — a choice of chocolate-ripple cake, fruit salad or a waffle cone — back into the lounge to watch the rest of the cricket in comfort, but after about ten minutes it started raining in Sydney. As a fill-in, Channel Nine put on a replay of an old game. Dad always gets excited when this happens.

'This is a cracker,' he said. 'This innings has got to include one of the best-ever one-day knocks. Do you know how many sixes Ricky Ponting hit?'

'Dad, don't spoil it,' I begged. But he'd certainly got everyone interested; even Mum came in to have a look.

'You keep going in the kitchen,' Dad chuckled to her. 'I'll tell you when Ponting's innings starts.'

Mum tossed the tea towel in Dad's general direction and sat down on the couch. But we only got about 15 minutes worth of highlights before Channel Nine switched back to the end of the live Sydney game. Still, it was great watching Adam Gilchrist and Matthew Hayden smashing the Indian attack all over the place.

Dad was really disappointed.

'Well, I'm sure the game is available on DVD,' Mum told him, heading back to the kitchen.

Dad got up to follow. 'I guess so, though what I'd give to have been there to see that game,' he said.

'Maybe Toby ...'

'Jay!' I snapped.

'... could buy it for your birthday?' he concluded lamely.

But luckily Dad hadn't heard.

'Why don't you take your dad?' Jimbo asked, as the guys and I headed for the door a little later. Some of their parents had arrived to pick them up.

'Yeah. You've taken all of ...' Ally stopped short.

I looked over at Georgie, who raised an eyebrow then lashed out.

'Well, Toby. Who else do you plan to take? Jimbo to Melbourne, Rahul to India, Jay to Tasmania, me to England. You've taken Jim and now Ally. Why don't you take the whole team on a trip to —'

'Why don't you shut up?' Jay snapped. 'Toby can take who he likes.'

'Toby can speak for himself too,' she said, looking at me.

'I took Ally 'cos she wanted to go. She seemed to know plenty about it anyway,' I said defensively, staring at Georgie.

'Hey, what's the problem?' Ally asked, throwing her hands up.

I walked to the door and opened it. Rahul's dad was waiting.

'Well, see you all tomorrow,' Rahul said, escaping. 'Thanks for the great night, Tobes.'

The others left soon after.

'Sorry for snapping,' Georgie said as the two of us headed back inside. 'I did tell Ally about it. She deserved to go again. I'll be honest with you; I was jealous ... I guess I wanted this to be just our special secret, you and me!'

'It always will be, Georgie.'

I told her about our trip to Brisbane, though I didn't mention Ally's odd behaviour. Georgie then left for home after we'd made plans for me to call by her house tomorrow on the way to practice.

In 1972, Australian Bob Massie took 16 wickets in his first Test match (against England at Lord's). He took 8/53 in the first innings and 8/84 in the second innings. Only four other bowlers have taken 16 or more wickets in a Test match.

7 Toby Jones Opens on Boxing Day

Sunday — morning

MR Pasquali had arranged to hold our Sunday morning practice at the Scorpions' home ground. I guess he thought it would be good for us to familiarise ourselves with the pitch and surrounds.

'Geez, I hope they're not training there too,' Georgie said as we rode to the ground. But the place was deserted, or so we thought.

As we stowed our bikes over near the clubrooms we noticed a sleek black car parked in the rear. Edging around the front of the building, we crashed into Phillip Smale, who was carrying bundles of papers.

'You,' he snarled, bending down to pick up some of the papers that had fallen. 'What are you doing here?'

'Practice,' I said, defiantly.

'Give me that!' he snapped, snatching a small card from Georgie's hand. 'I don't need your help.' He looked at both of us sternly, discreetly trying to hide the card that Georgie had picked up for him.

We all turned at the sound of Mr Pasquali's car approaching from the other side of the ground.

'You just stay clear of my affairs, do you hear me?' Smale hissed, leaning closer. Georgie and I took a step back. He spun around and walked towards his car.

I began to turn away but then sensed Georgie stiffen next to me.

'What now?' she sighed.

Smale was storming back towards us. He brushed past Georgie on his way up to one of the windows, where he ripped away the Master Blaster poster, muttered something then charged off again. He sped out of the car park a few moments later, almost colliding with a car coming in.

'Did you get a look at the card he was so stressed about?' I asked Georgie.

'It looked like some sort of business card with a website address on it,' she said. 'Nothing to get too anxious about,' she added.

'Unless he doesn't want us knowing about the site. I wonder what it was?'

Georgie smiled. 'I knew I shouldn't have looked,' she giggled.

'You saw it?'

'Yep, it was w-w-w dot scorpions dot com dot a-u.'

'Cool. We'll check it out later,' I suggested, watching two more cars arrive. 'He obviously doesn't want us knowing about the Master Blaster either,' I added.

Mr Pasquali took us through some light exercise and fielding drills, emphasising the importance of total concentration in the field. Everyone dived and darted about, knowing that there were only 11 spots up for grabs for the grand-final team. Maybe the first six spots would be filled automatically, but people like Ivo, Ally, Georgie, Jay, Gavin, Jason and Minh were all trying their best to impress Mr Pasquali with their catching, throwing and ground fielding. Damian and Trent from a lower-division team had also turned up; it was good to see them here supporting us ... though maybe they were secretly hoping for a couple of us to get injured so they could have a shot at making the team.

'Okay,' Mr Pasquali shouted, calling us in. 'Ally and Ivo, put your gloves on and meet me out in the middle. The rest of you, take a breather.'

We watched Mr Pasquali throw some short, firm catches to both of them. Ally looked as sharp as ever, catching everything that came her way. Ivo was also good, but at one stage he hurled his glove into the ground after he'd dropped one.

'Maybe he injured his hand?' Jay said, looking concerned.

'Injured his pride, more like it,' Georgie said. 'He's okay.'

Martian put his glove back on, slapped his gloves together and continued catching.

'Do you want to tell the others about the business card?' I asked Georgie quietly. Mr Pasquali and the two keepers were heading in and it looked like it was the end of the session.

'Nah. Let's see if we can find anything first. Ally's brother is a total legend with computers if we need the extra help ... You should enjoy that,' she added, smirking.

'Ally's brother?' I asked, surprised.

'No, idiot. Involving Ally.' She stared at me. I tried to look confused. 'Forget it,' she said, whacking me on the shoulder.

'Hey, are you guys coming into town to check out that virtual cricket machine?' Jimbo asked, walking over to us.

'You bet,' I said.

Only four of us were able to make it. Jay and Ally were really annoyed because they had family events organised.

'Oh, my God, look!' Georgie said, as we turned a corner and walked into the central square of the shopping centre. Standing next to a big sign which read 'Cricket Master Blaster' was none other than Phillip Smale. He was talking with a young guy, who appeared to be the owner or operator of the machine.

'What's Smale doing here?' I asked.

'He's probably going to buy it and keep it

420

exclusively for the Scorpions,' Georgie grumbled.

'Or put it in a vault with all the old cricket stuff,' Rahul suggested.

'How much?' I asked. The young guy had seen us coming and moved a step away from Mr Smale, who had his back to us, apparently fiddling with something.

'We'll have a little chat later, all right, Alistair?'

But the guy, Alistair, didn't appear to hear Mr Smale. 'Hi there. It's 20 dollars for three six-ball overs,' he said. 'Fancy a hit?'

'Fancy a hit?' I repeated excitedly, reaching for my wallet.

'Well, well, looking for some extra practice, are we?' Mr Smale had turned round, no doubt recognising my voice. He had a mobile phone to his ear.

'How does it work?' Georgie asked, ignoring Mr Smale.

'Okay,' said Alistair. 'We program in your challenge and then you put this headset on and see how you go.'

'Challenge?' Georgie queried.

'You pick your opposition, the bowler you're facing, whether it's a one-dayer or Test match, the ground you're playing on, the situation in the game, even the commentators you'd like to have calling your innings.'

I was licking my lips in anticipation. I couldn't wait — I knew exactly what I wanted. 'Can you buy this machine?' I asked, stepping forwards with my wallet open.

'Ha, ha.' Alistair smiled. 'As far as I know this is the only one in the world, so I'm afraid —'

'Everyone has his price,' Mr Smale chuckled, but I don't think Alistair heard him.

'Okay, you want a hit?' he asked me. I pulled out a 20-dollar note.

'Do I get a free go if I survive?' I asked.

'Let me know your challenge first and we'll see. What's your name?'

'Toby Jones. And I'm at the MCG, facing Shoaib Akhtar in the Second Test match —'

'Whoa, hang on there, Toby,' Alistair chuckled, frantically feeding the data into the machine via a touch screen. Suddenly an image appeared on the huge screen. It was the MCG, and there was Shoaib Akhtar standing at the top of his run-up, his black hair blowing in the breeze as he tossed the ball from one hand to another. I suddenly felt very nervous.

'Is he really going to bowl to me?' I asked.

'C'mon, Toby. He can't actually hurt you. He's not really here in the shopping centre,' Rahul said.

'Isn't he?' Alistair said, quietly. 'You ask Toby that in 10 minutes' time. Okay, Toby, what's the situation?'

I'd been planning a tight finish, but seeing Shoaib standing there waiting for me made me rethink.

'Um, can he bowl off his short run-up?' I asked.

'Toby!' Rahul and Jimbo said at the same time.

'Okay. It's the first day of the Boxing Day Test match.' I swallowed. 'I'm opening with Justin Langer.

422

Matthew Hayden's got a stomach bug and couldn't make it.'

Alistair was typing away madly. A dull roar could now be heard coming out from the speakers behind the screen. A small crowd was gathering around us.

'Who's in the commentary box, Toby?' Alistair asked.

'Richie Benaud and Bill Lawry,' I said without hesitation.

'Okay, that about does it.' He took the 20 dollars from me and handed me a pair of batting gloves, some pads and a bat.

'What about a helmet?' someone called from the crowd, laughing.

'Yep, but not the sort you're thinking of. This one's worth just a little more.' Alistair carefully lifted a big silver helmet that looked like the one Darth Vader wore.

'Any last requests?' Jimbo said, helping me seal the Velcro ties on my pads.

I had a thought. 'What happens if I go out?'

'Guess,' Alistair chuckled.

'I go out?'

'You go out. And Australia loses an early wicket on the first day of the Boxing Day Test match.'

Now my stomach was really churning. Alistair walked me over to a patch of green where a set of stumps stood and two white lines were marked out. Ahead of me was a full-length pitch, and beyond that was the enormous screen, which was almost the size of a movie screen. I was facing away from the growing shopping-centre crowd and looking at Shoaib Akhtar standing in the distance. Boy — maybe he was getting impatient.

Alistair gently placed the helmet over my head. I could hear a crackling sound, then the unmistakable voice of Bill Lawry:

'*Does it get any better than this? It is the opening day of the Boxing Day Test, and the young talent Toby Jones is out there to face the music.*'

'*Bill, this will be a baptism of fire,*' Richie remarked in his understated way.

I swallowed again, and licked my lips. The crowd noise was electric. I could hear the Pakistani players geeing each other up and clapping their hands. This was turning out to be the most thrilling moment of my life. It was one thing to travel to Test matches; it was another thing altogether to be playing in one.

Inside my helmet I could see the same scene that everyone in the shopping centre plaza could see on the big screen. I took guard, looked around the field, then tapped my bat on the pitch, waiting for Shoaib to begin his run-up. The crowd noise became deafening. I jumped as Bill Lawry's voice came on again:

'*It's all happening!*'

Shoaib roared in like a train. I almost passed out as he came closer, gaining speed with every stride.

'It's just a game. You're in a shopping centre, idiot,' I muttered as he stormed past the umpire.

Suddenly a red dot was heading straight for my head. I ducked, almost falling over.

'*Oh, what a beauty!*' Bill called, delighted.

'All right for you,' I muttered, picking myself up. The Pakistani players were chatting and jumping about, supporting Shoaib.

'Keep your eyes on the ball, Toby,' Justin Langer called out, walking down the pitch.

'Justin?' I tried to say, but no sound came out.

He just smiled at me encouragingly. He pointed to his eyes, reaffirming his advice.

I settled over my bat. The noise was deafening. There was chanting and clapping as Shoaib ran into bowl. This time I watched the ball rocket past, well wide of the off-stump.

'*It's a beautiful day, Richie,*' Bill said cheerfully.

'*It most certainly is, Bill,*' Richie drawled.

I pushed blindly at the next ball. It flicked the edge of my bat but there was a great roar from the crowd. I looked around to see the ball racing away through a vacant fourth slip and down to the third-man boundary for four. Then a replay was shown inside the head piece.

'*Well, it's a glorious day!*' Bill laughed. He sure was chatting about the weather a lot.

'*Nice work. You kept that down well,*' a voice said. Was that meant to be Justin Langer speaking?

The next ball was short, but much faster than the first three deliveries. Again I ducked, my arms and bat flailing in the air, but unfortunately I knocked my stumps. Shoaib and his team-mates raced into the middle, hugging and yelling.

I felt a hand on my shoulder as the screen went black.

'Toby?' The helmet was taken from my head and Alistair stood there smiling. 'Are you okay?' he asked.

I was a little unsteady on my feet but amazed by the game all the same.

'That was the most awesome thing in the world,' I cried, tearing off my gloves. At that moment I would have given up *Wisden*s, time travel and the grand final next weekend for a fistful of 20-dollar notes.

'Nice going, Toby,' Rahul said, grinning. 'My turn.'

I sat down to take off my pads and watch on the big screen as Rahul took guard. Bill's voice blared over the loud speakers. I turned to see a crowd of about a hundred people gathered round.

'C'mon, Rahul,' I murmured as Shoaib charged in.

Suddenly the screen went black. Alistair worked frantically on the touch screen and then on a keyboard, but after a minute he gave up.

He looked up sheepishly. 'There are still a few things that need ironing out,' he said, handing Rahul his 20 dollars back.

The crowd slowly moved away but we hung around, hoping that Alistair might be able to fix the glitch.

'There!' he cried, a few moments later. 'But there won't be any commentary. Now, who's up for one more shot? No charge.'

Georgie shot her hand up and raced over before we could get a word in.

We waited impatiently for Georgie's challenge to appear on the screen. She was chatting to Alistair and putting on her gear at the same time.

A few of the onlookers had wandered back. 'It's Lord's,' someone called as an image appeared.

'And Michael Clarke,' a girl squealed. Sure enough, Michael Clarke, with his cheeky grin, appeared on the screen. He was spinning the ball from one hand to the other and barking out instructions to the fielders.

'Remember, you promised!' Georgie said to Alistair as he placed the helmet over her head.

'Promised?' I said, turning to Rahul, who just shrugged in reply.

'Is she playing for England or what?' I asked.

'Must be. Look!' Jimbo was nodding at the batter at the other end, dressed in light blue. It was a one-dayer between England and Australia.

'Cool,' I said, under my breath.

The first ball was a slow full toss. Georgie swung it away through mid-wicket. The crowd roared as the ball raced away to the boundary for four, and then hushed as Michael Clarke walked in to bowl again. It was another full toss, exactly the same as the first. Georgie swung again, this time sending the ball behind square leg for another four.

'Look, the score's appeared,' Jimbo said, pointing to the top corner of the screen.

Australia: 7/324. England: 9/315. And only four balls left.

'She's set herself 18 to win,' Rahul said, smiling.

'And just one over to get them,' added Jimbo.

'And with Michael Clarke bowling full tosses.' I laughed. 'She's programmed him to bowl six slow full tosses at her. What a ripper!'

'*Well, surely Australia can't lose the World Cup from here,*' Ian Chappell said, sounding worried. Even the crowd behind me groaned.

Georgie belted the next three balls — all full tosses — for four. Michael Clarke stood there, his hands on his hips, looking totally shattered.

Everyone in the plaza was clapping Georgie as the helmet came off.

'You guys are such nongs! Why would you want to face up to Shoaib Akhtar when you could win a World Cup against the young blond Aussie star at the home of cricket?'

We all just stared at her.

'At least we were playing for *our* country,' I said.

'Yeah, well, that was one sacrifice I had to make so I could have Michael Clarke bowling at me. Neat about the full tosses, huh?' She slapped me on the back.

BANG!

A short, sharp explosion had everyone jumping and ducking for cover. A small trail of smoke from a big black box near Alistair drifted into the air.

'Oh, no,' he sighed, though he was grinning. 'I guess we've overworked the Blaster.'

Before we left we managed to get a card from Alistair with his phone number on it.

'Actually,' he said as he handed it to me, 'I'm not really supposed to have gone public yet, but I just wanted some kids to try it out.'

'Well, if you want a permanent volunteer for the job of testing the Master Blaster, I'm your man,' Jimbo said.

'Thanks,' Alistair said. 'I'll remember that.'

In the first over that Ralph Phillips ever bowled in a first-class game, he took a hat trick. He was playing for Border against Eastern Province in South Africa during the 1939/1940 season.

8 The Double-wicket Comp

Tuesday — afternoon

'I didn't have any luck with that Scorpions' website,' Georgie said, as we headed to the ovals for training.

'Yeah? What was the site like?'

'Pretty normal. It just had some photos, team lists, statistics and stuff like that.'

'Anything about the Master Blaster?' I asked.

'Nope. Why?'

'I dunno. I'm just suspicious about Mr Smale being at the shopping centre, talking to Alistair and speaking continuously on his mobile phone.' I looked across the cricket ground. It was one of the few parts of the school that still had green grass; the summer had been long, hot and dry. 'I dunno,' I repeated. 'He's up to something. Plus he's got the scorecard — there's no way he'll be putting that down in his precious vault.'

'Yeah, well I gave the website address to Ally,' Georgie said. 'Her brother, Ben, is going to check it out and see if he can find anything.' She picked up an old cricket ball from the long grass behind the practice wickets.

'I looked up Master Blaster on the Net,' I said, holding out my hand for her to throw the ball to me.

'Anything?' she said, tossing it.

'Music systems, cricket bats and Viv Richards,' I told her, catching the ball.

'So, nothing about virtual cricket?'

'Nup, not a sausage.'

We went for a warm-up lap of the oval, then joined the rest of the team for some stretching. I was really looking forward to this practice. Mr Pasquali always organised a special game on the second-last practice of the season. It had become a bit of a school tradition and there were plenty of school kids, parents and teachers who had come to watch.

'Okay, people. This is the double-wicket competition,' Mr Pasquali called, coming over to where we'd gathered. 'You're probably familiar with the rules but I'll go over them quickly while you finish your stretching.'

All we really wanted to hear were the pairings Mr Pasquali had decided on, but no one spoke as he went through the rules.

'There will be six overs per batting pair, and every pair will face six different bowlers, each bowling six-ball overs. A wicket costs the batter 15 runs and also means a change of ends for the batters. A wicket is worth 10 runs for the bowler. A run out is worth five runs for any fielder and a catch is also worth five. I'll organise your bowling, fielding and keeping duties so everyone gets a fair go. And there will also be bonus points.'

'Bonus points?' Jono asked.

'They'll be awarded to anyone I see doing worthwhile things on the cricket field: backing up, supportive play, a fine piece of fielding or maybe an act of sportsmanship. That's all at my discretion.'

'And so every run is worth ... one run?' Jay asked.

'Exactly that, Jay,' Mr Pasquali replied.

'But what if my overs are against Jimbo or Jono ...'

'Jay!' about six kids exclaimed at the same time.

'It's just practice. We're a team, remember. We've got a big game on this Saturday,' Mr Pasquali told him patiently.

Jay's outburst didn't surprise me. I guess like everyone else he wanted to perform well so he'd get picked for the grand final.

'Righto,' Mr Pasquali said, opening up his blue clipboard. 'Here are the teams. Pair One: Jono and Jason; Pair Two: Rahul and Gavin; Three: Ally and Toby; Four: Jimbo and Jay; Five: Minh and Cameron; and Pair Six is Ivo and Georgie. Pair One, go and pad up. Jimbo and Jay, you're bowling first — grab a new ball from the kit and organise your field. Cameron, you're starting as keeper.

'Ripper!' Cameron said, racing over to the kit.

'Martian looks really happy,' Georgie muttered to me, sarcastically.

'Well, I'm happy. And I'd be happy swapping with Martian too,' I told her.

'Fat chance of that,' she said, jamming her cap down on her head. 'And look at Ally, all excited.'

'You and me, Tobler,' Ally called, giving me the thumbs up.

'See what I mean?' Georgie said.

Jono and Jason did a great job, knocking up plenty of runs despite Jason losing a couple of wickets. It was a similar pattern with Rahul and Gavin. Rahul must have gone close to scoring 20 himself but, like Jason, I reckon Gavin would have ended up with a negative score.

Ally and I batted fourth. Our first two overs were pretty quiet, with Rahul and then Jono bowling. But no one could complain about Mr Pasquali's organisation. The next three bowlers were not as strong and during the third, fourth and fifth overs we managed to knock up 21 runs without losing a wicket. But we were going to need a big last over to put ourselves in contention.

'Okay, we're right up there, Ally,' I said, as we came together in the middle of the pitch.

'We've got plenty of bowling and fielding points too,' she added. We watched to see who would bowl our last over.

'I reckon it'll be Cameron,' I said. Sure enough he walked across to the bowler's end, passing Mr Pasquali his hat.

'Ally, don't do anything stupid. We lose 15 runs now and we're sunk,' I said, pulling my gloves back on.

Ally blocked the first two balls and we scampered through for a single from the third. Cameron's next ball was a slower delivery outside off-stump and I swished at it. The ball clipped the outside edge of the bat and flew away over point. Jason hurled himself into the air but the ball just grazed his fingertips before racing away to the boundary for four.

'You were saying?'. Ally smirked as we met mid-pitch.

'It was there to be hit,' I said. She rolled her eyes.

We scored another three runs off the last two balls, but only Mr Pasquali knew what the exact scores were as Pair Five went to put batting pads on.

By 10 to six everyone had batted, bowled, kept wicket and fielded in just about every position on the field. We collected the gear and pulled bottles of soft drink from Mr Pasquali's big blue Esky as we waited for him to add up the final scores.

'Right!' he said, looking up from his clipboard. Jay passed him a bottle of iced water.

'Do I get a bonus point for that?' he asked, grinning.

'Why not?' Mr Pasquali said, making a little note on his clipboard. I looked over at Jimbo. He shook his head slightly and smiled. We both knew Jay wouldn't get a bonus point for that.

Mr Pasquali took a long drink from the bottle, slowly screwed the lid back on and put the bottle down on the grass. The spectators moved in closer, while we sat down and waited for Mr Pasquali to speak.

'That was perhaps the best double-wicket competition I've seen at this school in all my years here,' he began, looking around at each of us. 'And it demonstrated well the importance of protecting your wicket when batting — only one pair survived their six overs without losing a wicket.

I looked over at Ally, who beamed at me. Georgie was picking grass angrily. Mr Pasquali held up his clipboard, and we all crowded around to see the results.

Players	Points	Place
Jono	58	
Jason	−12	
Pair One total	**46**	**4th**
Rahul	57	
Gavin	−5	
Pair Two total	**52**	**3rd**
Ally	12	
Toby	63	
Pair Three total	**75**	**1st**
Jimbo	68	
Jay	−14	
Pair Four total	**54**	**2nd**
Minh	9	
Cameron	35	
Pair Five total	**44**	**5th**
Ivan	15	
Georgie	25	
Pair Six total	**40**	**6th**

'Tobler, we would have won even if we'd lost a wicket,' Ally said, as we looked at the final totals.

'You can see all the batting, bowling, catching and bonus point scores on the sports notice board tomorrow,' Mr Pasquali said, tucking the clipboard under his arm. 'And I shall see you here at four o'clock on Thursday, warmed up and ready to go.'

'Will we be in the nets or out on the centre-wicket?' Jono asked.

'Nets,' Mr Pasquali replied. 'I've got a little treat for you.' He smiled, waved goodbye and headed over to the kit.

'Wow, I wonder what he's got in mind?' I said to Jimbo.

'I think I know,' he muttered.

'And that would be?' Rahul asked.

But I didn't hear Jimbo's answer. Ally was motioning me over to her dad's car.

'Tobler, Georgie told me about that card.'

I looked at her blankly.

'You know, the business card? The one you guys saw when you ran into Mr Smale at the Scorpions' rooms? Look!' Ally handed me her mobile phone. 'Read the text message,' she said excitedly.

I read it softly to myself.

hey ally, u were right, website weird,
bring yr friends over – esp Georgie –
got s'ing to show u, B

436

'Especially Georgie?' I said, looking at Ally.

'I know, weird, huh?'

'What, the Georgie bit or the website thing?' I asked.

'Nah, the website. Ben's always had a soft spot for Georgie,' she laughed.

'Yeah? How old is he?'

'Fifteen, going on 11,' Ally said. 'So, do you want to come around and have a look tomorrow night? Georgie's calling round after tea.'

'You bet,' I said, trying not to sound too eager. But before that I wanted to go and have one more look at the Scorpions' oval and clubrooms. Especially the clubrooms.

Richie Benaud — who was the Australian captain in the 1960 Tied Test — achieved the bowling figures of 3.4 overs, 3 maidens and 3 wickets for 0 runs in a Test match against India in Delhi during the 1959/1960 season.

9 The Crazy Ride

Wednesday — afternoon

I left the bike at home, opting for my skateboard, which I hadn't ridden for weeks. I stuck to the pavement, enjoying the sound and rhythm of the board as it sped over the cracks in the concrete.

There was only one stretch where I had to pick it up: the dirt and gravel road that was the entrance to the Scorpions' ground. I thought of taking the path that wound its way through the cemetery that was next to the oval but I didn't want to be here for too long.

There was no one about apart from a guy jogging with his dog on the far side of the ground and an old couple heading into the cemetery with some flowers.

I walked over to the clubrooms, leaned my skateboard against the wall but decided to keep my helmet on. I placed my palms against a window and pushed to the right. Luckily it opened. Taking one last glance around, I moved the curtain aside and quickly climbed through the opening. I found myself in the main room, which I recognised from when Georgie and I had snuck in here a few weeks ago, trying to find out more about Smale.

I'd only just slid the window closed when I heard a truck approaching. I crouched below the sill, thinking that it was probably another visitor to the cemetery — maybe the gardeners. I craned my head up to look through the window and saw the truck edge past the cemetery entrance, coming towards the clubrooms. I heard it come to a stop around the corner of the building, out of sight.

I ducked away from the window and tried the door to Smale's office. Predictably it was locked and so too was another door nearby. I was just heading over to a notice board where a huge Master Blaster poster was pinned when I heard keys jangling over by the main door.

I darted back to the window, wrenched it open and jumped out, half expecting a voice to shout at me as I scrambled over the edge.

I stood still outside the open window, my back stiff against the warm bricks of the building. My heart was thumping as the main door creaked open. I carefully pulled the curtain aside a few centimetres and peered through the gap.

Phillip Smale was entering the room backwards, pulling a trolley with three silver boxes piled up on it. He struggled with their weight as he unloaded them. A few moments later Alistair followed him in, carrying a large cardboard box.

'It's good of you to look after the Blaster, Phillip,' Alistair said, putting the box down.

'It's an absolute pleasure, Alistair,' Smale said. They both headed out and I waited a few minutes, concealed as I was from the truck and the main entrance. The two of them soon returned, this time Alistair with the trolley in tow.

'Now I have something to show *you*,' Smale said as they began stacking up the boxes.

'Oh, actually —'

'No, no,' Smale interrupted him. 'You have no choice, Alistair. You've shown me the Master Blaster. I've got something even more impressive.'

'Well, thanks, Phillip, but —'

'There,' Smale continued, totally ignoring Alistair. 'It's all completely safe here, I assure you. Now come along. You were telling me about that one-day game you went to in Sydney, when Michael Bevan hit the winning runs?' Smale's voice trailed off as the two left the building again.

The truck's engine started up. What was Smale up to? I wondered. Was Alistair in trouble? I stayed hidden as the truck slowly headed back out of the grounds. It stopped at the exit, waiting for some traffic to pass.

I tucked the skateboard under my arm and sprinted down the driveway. The truck pulled out, turning left onto the street. It accelerated away, but almost immediately slowed down again. I dropped my skateboard, wheels down, and jumped on, pushing quickly with my right foot.

In no time I had caught up to the truck. Careful to stay on the left (and hopefully out of sight of Smale's outside mirror), I edged up alongside it. A bank of cars, all with their headlights on, was coming down the other side of the road; it was a funeral procession. The truck came to a halt — maybe Smale wanted to turn right? But there was no way he was going to get across unless someone let him through.

I jumped when Smale honked his horn, obviously impatient to get moving. The truck jerked forwards then stopped. There was a screech of brakes, another horn blast and the sound of crunching metal and shattering glass.

The truck moved forwards again, and I grabbed onto a thin pipe at the back. Suddenly I was being towed along, the skateboard wheels crunching and grinding through the broken plastic and pieces of glass that were spread all over the road.

I stole a glance at the angry and surprised faces of the people in the damaged car then concentrated on staying on my board as the truck swung right into Hope Street.

We quickly left the blaring horns behind us and raced up the street. For a moment everything was going smoothly and I had time to wonder what on earth I was going to achieve by hanging onto the back of a truck.

Then it hit a road hump and my hands flew off the pole. I threw my arms out to balance myself, crouched low and sailed off the top of the bump.

But Smale had stopped the truck. I ducked, instinctively throwing my arm out to protect my face as I smashed into the back of it. My shoulder took the force of the collision, the skateboard skidding out from underneath me and flying beneath the truck.

I lay on the road, slightly dazed, then picked myself up and ran around to the passenger side. Jumping onto the step, I opened the door. To my amazement, the cabin was empty.

Readjusting the straps of my helmet, I clambered in, desperately searching for something: a *Wisden*, the scorecard, anything to give me a clue as to what had just happened. But there was nothing but food wrappers and empty drink cartons.

I climbed back down, looking left and right. The line-up of funeral cars was still visible at the bottom of the street, crawling towards the cemetery, but Hope Street was deserted.

I dived beneath the truck and kicked my board back towards the gutter.

'When will you bloody learn?' Smale snarled, suddenly appearing as I picked myself up.

'Where's Alistair?' I asked.

'*Where's Alistair?*' he mimicked. 'Look, this is not some Famous Five adventure, you interfering little creep. Now get into the truck.' He stood over me threateningly, quickly glancing up the street.

'Where's Alistair?' I repeated.

'Oh, for God's sake, he lives here.'

As Smale spoke, I glanced down at my skateboard, but he must have noticed my look and thrust his leg out just as I jammed my own foot onto the end of the board to flick it up. We both kicked it at the same time, and it shot forwards, straight into Smale's shins.

As I stooped down to pick it up Smale grabbed me by the collar, swore viciously and dragged me smartly to the back of the truck. His grip was vice-like. He pushed me up the steps and I was hurled into darkness as the doors slammed behind me.

I yelled and thumped on the metal, praying someone would hear. But the street had been deserted and a moment later I heard the driver's door close.

'Alistair!' I yelled, hoping like hell that he'd noticed something from his house. But the truck lurched forwards and I was flung into the side, banging my head against some wooden boards.

I stumbled to my feet and bashed away at the lock, even using my skateboard as a hammer, but the doors didn't budge. There was no way I could open them; I'd heard Smale slide bolts across on the other side after he'd tossed me inside.

A wave of panic flooded through me as I realised the situation I was in: trapped in a truck, going to some unknown destination and, worst of all, no one knowing I was here — except the weird, crazy man who was driving. Smale was probably taking me out to the edge of town, away from people. What was his plan?

The truck came to a halt; maybe we were at some traffic lights? Suddenly someone was working on the lock, and I threw myself to the back of the truck. The enclosure filled with light as the doors swung open.

'Well, Toby Jones, I always like to give someone a sporting chance. Get out!'

We had pulled over at the top of a hill, on the steep road that ran past the old cement works. A thin path snaked its way down the left side of the road, while to the right there was a steep drop. Scrubby bushes, dirt tracks, rubbish, old fence wire and discarded signs lay scattered about, all covered with white cement dust.

I swallowed. My throat had gone dry.

'Oh dear, what a silly thing for you to do,' Smale chuckled. 'And in the week of the grand final too.'

'You can't make me go down there,' I said, looking over the edge of the path. The first 20 metres were very steep before it levelled out slightly. I glanced around, preparing to make a dash for it.

'And you can think again about running away. I'll find you — you and the old man. I can make your life a misery, and I will.'

'We just want the scorecard back,' I said.

'Oh, save me. Take the drop, Toby Jones, or I will haul you off to the police.'

'What for?' I yelled, turning on him. 'I'll just tell them that you kidnapped me!'

'How about breaking into the Scorpions' clubrooms, for one?' he sneered. 'Now hop on your

444

silly skateboard and get out of my sight.' A cool wind blew across the top of the hill.

'I'm going to sit down,' I mumbled, walking to the edge.

'Sit down, stand up — do I really care?'

I took one last look around, then slowly sat down on the board, gripping either side and rocking gently to get evenly balanced.

Suddenly Smale's foot slammed into my back. I swore loudly as I wobbled to the left, then over the top of the rise. I jerked back to the right to regain my balance as the board plunged over the precipice.

Smale's laughter faded quickly as I tore down the first section of concrete path. For a split second I thought of purposefully falling off; what were a few scratches, or maybe a sprained wrist or ankle? But within seconds my speed was so great that I knew I'd be hurt badly.

Oh, God!

I was frozen in terror as I hurtled down the steepest hill in town. The whistling of the wind and the screeching roar of the wheels being torn and shredded by the rough path drowned out all other sounds. There was no rhythm in the cracks in the pavement — there was just one crazy, frightening blur of noise as the wheels tore over the path at a million miles an hour. I held on in desperation, my fingers stiff from the tension of gripping the edges of the board so tightly. I had it balanced, but one slight stumble, one little wobble, and I'd be crashing at 40 kilometres per hour.

I screamed as I picked up even more speed on a short drop that was almost vertical. Somehow I managed to keep all four wheels on the path. There was nothing for it but to hold on — and pray.

Just when I thought the hill was never going to end, the track started to level out, weaving to the right. I leaned into the curve and the board responded, taking the bend at a frightening speed. I leaned back suddenly to the left to avoid a small rock that was sitting in the middle of the path. The board wobbled right, then left. For an awful moment I thought I was finally going over. I closed my eyes, my last thought being a desperate prayer for no major injury that would cause me to miss the grand final.

The board ran straight over an empty bottle which exploded into hundreds of shards. Some of the pieces must have jammed in the wheels, which sent out tiny splinters of glass.

By now I was totally out of sight of the top of the hill, and I was finally slowing down. I swung back onto the middle of the path and rode along for several more metres before steering the board off to the right.

Straight away I heard it — Smale was driving the truck slowly down the hill, no doubt to see what had happened.

I kicked the skateboard off to the other side of the track, and threw myself down into the dirt, lying spread-eagled. I held my breath and waited.

Pressing my face into the dust, I heard the truck

idle past, slowly, before disappearing down the street. I stayed where I was for another few moments then carefully staggered up, grabbed my board and started the tough walk back up the hill. It was long and steep but still the shortest way home.

That could have been a whole lot worse, I thought to myself as I turned at the top of the hill and looked back at the slope I'd just ridden.

'Is that you, Toby?' Mum called when I finally got home.

'Yep,' I answered, heading for the bathroom. I washed away the blood and grime, then gave Georgie a ring. I had to tell someone about my skateboard ride, and better her than Mum.

Taking 100 wickets in a season is a fantastic achievement, and Englishman Wilfred Rhodes did it 23 times! *Wisden* records that he took 4187 first-class wickets during his 33-year career, with an amazing average of 16.71 runs per wicket.

10 Ben, the Good-looking Geek

Wednesday — evening

'BEN, this is Toby,' Ally said, as we entered Ben's room. 'And of course you know Georgie,' she added.

'Hi, Toby, Georgie,' Ben said, smiling and waving us in. 'Are you guys gonna tell me what this is all about?'

I couldn't take my eyes off the setup in Ben's room. He had a massive flat-screen computer with what looked like every possible accessory you could want. There were CDs and DVDs all over the place, as well as speakers, microphones, a scanner, digital camera, printer and even what looked like a three-in-one phone, fax and copier.

'Neat, huh?' Ben was watching Georgie eyeing the room.

'You live up here 24/7?' she asked him.

Ben laughed. 'I'll give you a tour sometime.'

'That'd be neat.'

Ally broke into the conversation. 'I think Ben is running about three dodgy businesses from up here,' she said, grinning at my awed look.

'Only three?' Ben joked. 'You've been out of the loop way too long, Ally McCabe. Now shut up and check this out.'

Ben hit a few buttons on the keyboard and suddenly the Scorpions' website was on the computer screen, larger than ever. Ben cruised around the site, clicking a few links and showing us some of the scores and pictures that were posted there.

'It's nothing special, agreed?' he asked, clicking the 'Home' button.

We shook our heads, curious to see what Ben had discovered.

'But watch this!' Ben held the pointer over what to me looked like just another section of white background.

'We're watching,' Ally sighed impatiently.

'Wait on, another ... couple of seconds ... there!'

Suddenly the pointer changed from an arrow to the hand symbol. I took a sharp breath as Ben clicked his mouse.

'I had to check the HTML to verify it, but someone's put in a time-delayed hover link here that takes you away to a secret site. Check out the URL!'

'How did you find that?' I asked, amazed at his skill, or luck.

Ben chuckled. 'I'm not telling *you* my secrets, Toby Jones.'

I noticed his wink at Georgie.

A moment later and we were staring at a completely white page.

'There's nothing there,' Georgie said. 'It's blank.'

'Great minds think alike,' Ben whispered. 'That's what I thought too, George, but look closer.'

We all leaned in.

'There, down the bottom!' I cried, causing Ally to jump.

'Exactly!' Ben said. He hit a button and the faint, blurry image got slightly bigger.

'I can hardly see anything,' Ally muttered, leaning in even closer.

'And you a state softballer,' Ben joked.

'Can you make the image darker?' I asked.

'I already did. I just wanted to see if you guys could make anything of it in its original form. I copied and pasted it into a new doc. then fiddled a bit. Here you go,' Ben said, opening up a file.

'What is it?' Georgie quietly asked, looking at the new image displayed on the screen.

'That's what I was hoping *you* guys would tell *me*,' Ben said, turning round. 'Spit it out, Toby Jones. You're the one who seems to be in the know about all of this ... according to Ally,' he added, winking at Georgie again.

I was quiet for a moment, staring at the picture. I recognised it straight away. Now that it was clearer

I could easily make out an old man bent over a set of cricket stumps. You could even see his walking stick, or whatever it was he was leaning on.

'It's Father Time,' I breathed.

'It's what?' Ben asked, peering up at me.

'Father Time; it's maybe the oldest and most famous of all the symbols to do with cricket,' I said, as I stared at the old man with his long beard.

'Oh, yeah,' Ally said. 'Look, he's putting a bail back on. Maybe he's the first-ever cricket umpire?'

'What else do you know about it?' Ben asked, ignoring his sister.

'It's a weather vane,' I replied. 'You know, it tells you which way the wind is blowing. This one sits up on top of a stand at Lord's.'

'Lord's!' Georgie cried. 'As in Lord's, the famous cricket ground where I won the World Cup?'

I nodded. 'Don't ask,' I said, looking at Ally and Ben.

'Lord's — even I've heard of Lord's, the home of cricket,' Ben said. 'Well, okay. So, we've established that this is old Father Time.' He made his way back to the original website. 'Now we've gotta work out how to get in. Watch this.'

Ben clicked on the original faded Father Time image and a new page appeared, as plain as the one before. Two words stared at us:

Username:
Password:

'Any ideas?' Ben asked, leaning back in his chair.

'That's why we're here in your bedroom, stupid,' Ally said, straightening up.

'Bummer! And I thought it was for my good company and great looks,' Ben scoffed, pushing the keyboard away and getting up.

'Wait!' I said, hoping Ben wouldn't disappear. 'I know a few things we could try.' Everyone turned and looked at me. 'C'mon, let's think. This is Phillip Smale's site, right?'

'Yeah, so?' Ally said. 'How does that —'

'May I?' I asked Ben. I pulled the keyboard drawer back out and sat in his chair.

'Hey, make yourself at home, Toby,' he said, throwing his hands up. He moved away to sift through a stack of CDs.

I started entering some combinations.

```
Username: Phillip
Password: Smale
```

The reply wasn't encouraging: 'Your username is not recognised.'

'Does that mean you got the password right?' Georgie asked, excitedly.

'Nup. Not at all,' Ben said, walking back to us.

```
Username: Time
Password: Travel
```

The same screen appeared.

```
Username: Father
Password: Time
```

'That was a bit obvious, wasn't it?' Georgie said, when that attempt also failed.

'Are you guys going to tell me what this is all about?' Ben asked, looking at each of us in turn.

Georgie sighed.

Ben noticed our hesitation. 'Actually, forget it. Come and look at my CD collection, Georgie. Those two can work it out.'

I shrugged as Georgie followed Ben to the other side of the room.

'So, this guy, Phillip Smale,' Ally said, squeezing herself onto the seat next to me. 'He's a bit arrogant, isn't he?'

'A bit?' I laughed, turning back to the screen.

'Wants power? Wants to do things? Wants to impress people?'

'All of the above,' I replied, typing.

```
Username: Wisden
Password: Wisden
```

No.

'Just type "Smale",' Ally suggested.

'No password?'

Ally shook her head. I put it in and hit Enter. No go.

'"Smale's"?' Again, no luck.

'Try it without the apostrophe,' Ally suggested, though less certain.

'We might as well try everything,' I said as I entered 'Smales'. 'Should we be writing all these down?'

I felt Ally's hand land on my wrist. 'Georgie!' she yelled.

All four of us crowded around.

Type in your password.

'Bad security,' Ben said, hitting the back button. 'Do it again.'

I typed in 'Smales' and pressed the Enter key. The same screen appeared.

'We're halfway there,' Georgie cried.

It took another seven tries with different passwords to get in.

Username: Smales
Password: Travels

'Oh, my God, Toby. You did it!' Ally shrieked.

The screen was covered in writing. Ben was obviously reading faster than the rest of us, because he nudged my shoulder.

'Toby, move — quick!' he said.

'What, Ben?' Ally snapped. 'He's the one who —'

'Hurry!'

I shrugged and nipped out of the chair.

Ben hit the Print icon and his printer sprang into action and started churning out paper. Then he closed the website.

'Ben?'

'The guy running that site might be able to trace our computer. Only five people were meant to access it, and the owner has probably been told the five IP addresses of their computers. We weren't one of them.'

I grabbed the three pages from the printer. 'Thanks for helping out,' I said, folding them in half. Ben had already seen enough.

We raced into Ally's room, leaving Ben behind to clean up the files on his computer and try to remove the evidence of our visit. I spread the printouts on Ally's bed.

Wednesday

I have now had contact from four of you. I confirm that your interest has been received. I am just waiting for acknowledgment from one of you.

Saturday

I am still waiting for one of you to sign in and confirm your interest. I

455

must repeat: this is the only mode of communication accepted. Do not try to contact me except by the 'Submit' link above.

Monday

I am sorry to inform the fifth person – who knows who he is – that no confirmation of entry has been received and that from 8 a.m. Friday I shall make alternative arrangements to find a suitable candidate for travel.

I should also remind all of you that you are sworn to secrecy – not only now, but for life ...

Wednesday

Of course, I am being reasonable beyond all belief in allowing you fine people this once-in-a-lifetime opportunity – you will not be disappointed, I can assure you. And, naturally, your identities are being kept secret.

There was a knock on the door and a moment later Mrs McCabe appeared. I gathered up the papers, trying to look relaxed.

'Toby, your dad's here.' She looked at the three of us sitting on the bed. 'What's been happening?' she asked, with a smile.

'Team tactics,' I smiled back, waving the folded pages in the air.

'Got it all worked out, Mrs M,' said Georgie, bouncing up to her feet.

'Well, that's great,' Mrs McCabe said and ruffled Georgie's hair.

In 1978, Chris Old took four wickets in five balls when playing in a Test match for England against Pakistan in Birmingham. Unfortunately he bowled a no ball between his first two and last two wickets. On the scorer's page, Old's over read 'o w w nb w w 1'.

11 The Surprise

Thursday — afternoon

'NOTHING flashy or fancy tonight,' Mr Pasquali said crisply to us at training. 'Everything we do, we do well. Efficiency, economy, concentration: keep those three words in the front of your mind for the next two hours.'

We warmed up with a drill called 'Five 'n Alive'. Mr Pasquali had us stand in a tight half-circle and threw fast, hard catches to us. If you dropped a catch or misfielded a ball, you had to go to the end of the line on the right. If you did something special, like taking a tricky one-handed catch, Mr Pasquali might advance you one or two places to the left.

He had an old egg timer set to ring every two minutes. Whoever was the leader of the group when the timer rang — that is, the person at the far left-hand end — got five points. The next in line got four points, then three, two and one for the next three kids. No one else scored.

In the original version of the game only the top five kids stayed in after the timer went — everyone else would just sit and watch till there was a winner. No way was that Mr Pasquali's policy; he'd changed the rules slightly so that everyone stayed in, even if you never scored any points. He had us all participating as much and as often as possible.

The catches were always harder if you were one of the top five. Ally was a freak at this game, gobbling up everything that came near her — and sometimes balls meant for the person next door.

'No problems there,' Mr Pasquali grinned, indicating Ally should swap places with Martian after she'd plucked a one-handed catch from in front of his right knee. 'I've seen Ricky Ponting do exactly the same,' Mr P said. 'He wants the ball. He wants the catch. It's as if he's willing the ball to come to him. If you don't like the ball coming at you fast, then don't ever field in the slips. You'll be a nervous wreck.'

The bell jangled for the fifth time.

'Okay, did anyone score over 15 points?' Mr Pasquali asked. No one said anything. 'Over 10?' Ally and Rahul put their hands up. 'Ally? How many did you score?'

'Thirteen,' she said, looking at her hand and rubbing her thumb.

'Rahul?' Mr Pasquali asked.

'Me too, Mr P.'

'A can of drink for each of you,' Mr Pasquali said.

'What about the surprise you mentioned, Mr P?' Jay asked. We stopped and looked at Mr Pasquali, who looked at his watch.

'Another half an hour,' he said, smiling. 'Don't look forward to it too much, though,' he chuckled.

We spent another 20 minutes fielding, practising long throws and catching as well as doing short work around the pitch, including trying to knock the stumps down and backing up the wicket. It was as exciting as the first practice months ago when the season was starting and Jimbo and Ally weren't even a part of the team.

In the nets we focused on playing down the 'V' — aiming our shots in the space between mid-on and mid-off — and positioning the front foot to the pitch of the ball, head still and over the shot with bat and pad close together.

'Play the good deliveries with respect. You'll still get enough loose stuff to put away,' Mr Pasquali said regularly as he watched each of us concentrating on good defensive technique.

'Here comes the surprise!' he called a short time later, as a small white car drove up.

'Oh, way cool!' someone yelled. Everyone stopped; balls and bats fell to the ground and a dozen kids charged towards the car. A tall guy with blond hair emerged from the passenger side.

'Danny Chapman?' Georgie gasped. She'd got there first.

He removed his sunglasses and smiled.

Danny Chapman was only 19 but he was already a local legend and fast becoming a state one too. This season he'd taken two hat tricks, as well as 10 wickets or more three times in the local premier-grade cricket. He'd played in two one-dayers for the state, taking a 'three-for' in the second match. He was always in the local papers, being interviewed or photographed, and he'd even appeared in a TV commercial. On his day, they said, he could bowl as fast as Brett Lee.

'That's me,' he said, grinning. 'I hear you guys have a pretty important cricket match coming up this weekend.'

We all started babbling at once. Finally Danny held up a hand as Mr Pasquali joined us.

'Awesome, Mr P,' Jay cried. 'This is the *best* surprise.'

'This isn't the surprise,' Mr Pasquali said. 'Or, at least, not all of it.'

'What?' I cried.

'No, no. The real surprise is that Danny will be bowling to some of you.' Mr Pasquali tossed him a brand new cricket ball. 'Pace,' he added, nodding his head at Danny.

'P ... pace?' Jay stuttered. 'As in from the top of his run, flat-out pace?'

'They will have full gear and protection on, won't they?' Danny asked, looking at Mr Pasquali.

'Oh, yes,' he said, nodding. 'Absolutely. It's school rules.'

I caught the faintest hint of a smile on Danny's face.

'Okay. Rahul, Jimbo, Cameron, Jono, Toby, Martian and Georgie, can you head over to the nets please?' Mr Pasquali said. He took the rest of the team out onto the field for some fielding drills. We were the 'lucky' ones chosen to face up to Danny Chapman.

'He won't bowl express, will he?' Georgie asked.

'Geez, I hope he does. What an experience,' Jimbo said. He hadn't taken his eyes off Danny Chapman since he'd arrived.

'No way,' I told Georgie. 'We're about to play in a grand final. How stupid would it look if half the batting line-up was out with hand injuries and cracked skulls because the coach decided to make them face up to the fastest bowler in town — maybe in the state — two days before the game,' I said, hoping I sounded convincing.

'It'd be the master stroke of all time,' Jimbo said, his eyes flashing with excitement. He was already putting the pads on! 'He's too professional to hurt us. He won't bowl bouncers. But imagine how confident we'll feel against Scott Craven if we've been able to face up to Danny Chapman?'

'Are you Jimbo?' Danny asked him.

Jimbo dropped a pad in surprise. 'Yeah,' he said, shaking the hand that Danny had stretched out towards him.

'Your coach said that you were to bat last.'

'Oh, okay,' Jimbo said, looking disappointed.

Danny winked. 'That's when I'll be warmed up and at my quickest.'

'Oh, right. Excellent! Who wants the pads?'

'Are you gonna start off with a bit of spin?' Georgie asked, one hand out for the pads Jimbo was offering.

'Maybe,' Danny laughed. 'Okay, sit down for a moment, guys, and I'll give you a few tips on facing fast bowling. I hear you've got a good bowler heading your way this Saturday?'

'Scott Craven,' I muttered. The others nodded their heads, mumbling.

'Not looking forward to it?' Danny said, eyeing each of us in turn.

Only Jimbo offered up anything positive about the looming showdown.

'And therein lies your major problem,' Danny said, squatting down. 'You guys are the batters of the team. Your job is to score the runs, but you won't score anything if you don't want to be out there in the first place. Okay, this guy can bowl. Maybe he can bowl fast. But you guys can bat — you've proved that all season. You're in the final, you're up to this.'

He paused, looking at each of us closely. 'When you walk out there to bat on Saturday, you want to be going out there licking your lips in anticipation. Focus on rock-solid defence but look for runs, especially boundaries. Defy this Scott guy with good batting technique and a positive attitude. You've got to look like winners even before you start playing like winners.'

His words were stirring and the passion in his voice was evident. Danny Chapman, the town's fast-bowling sensation, maybe a future Australian fast bowler, was talking to us — the Under-13s from Riverwall. By the time he'd finished we were all bursting to get the pads on and show him what we could do.

'I'll look at your technique, but that's not going to change too much over the next 36 hours. What can change, though, is your attitude. Maybe it already has?'

'Well, I can't speak for the others, but I reckon mine's done a 180-degree flip in the last few minutes,' Georgie said.

For the next 20 minutes we took turns in the nets, facing Danny's deliveries. We hung on his every word about what we were doing well and how we could improve. Rahul needed to get his back foot positioned more effectively for the shorter deliveries. Jono had a tendency to step onto his front foot as his first movement, so Danny dug a few balls in short — not super fast ones, but they got Jono stepping back better. Cameron was told to roll his wrists more for his cross-bat shots and Georgie to hit through the line of the ball; she'd probably spend half the night in front of a mirror working on her follow-through.

'Toby, you're lazy with your back lift.' Danny had come down the wicket to talk to me. 'I think you're sometimes jamming down on the ball because you're a little late. With fast bowlers this could get you into a bit of strife.'

'Like it did with Shoaib,' I said, tossing Danny the ball that had whizzed past my off-stump. Danny was just ambling in, taking a few gentle paces, and yet he was sending round, red bullets down the wicket!

'Shoaib? As in Shoaib Akhtar?' he laughed.

'Yep,' I nodded. I told him all about the virtual cricket machine. 'I could have faced up to you,' I added, suddenly feeling a bit guilty. 'You could bat against state or international bowlers, but I wanted to play for Australia.'

'Fair enough. I want to play for Australia too.' He rubbed the ball on his trousers. 'The dream always comes first,' he added.

'C'mon, Toby. Let's have a look at you,' Mr Pasquali said, walking across to our net. I told him what Danny had said about my lazy back lift. After five minutes with Danny Chapman in front, bowling to me and Mr Pasquali behind, offering more advice, I felt like I could play anyone, even Danny Chapman at top pace!

Mr Pasquali didn't mind us all watching Danny bowl to Jimbo last. After a few early words of encouragement from Danny, their battle turned into a quiet, determined game. Jimbo wasn't there just to survive — he was actually putting a few balls away.

'Coach?' Danny called, indicating a longer run-up with a nod of his head.

'Jimbo, are you okay in there?' Mr Pasquali asked quietly.

'I'm ready,' Jimbo said, determination etched on his face. Mr Pasquali went and stood as umpire.

Danny moved back another 10 paces or so then ran in, smooth as ever.

Jimbo let the first two balls go through to the keeper then clipped the next one off his pads into the side netting. Everyone cheered when Mr Pasquali signalled four by waving his left arm around. The next ball, even quicker, smashed through Jimbo's defence, knocking over the yellow stump set. Danny eased up after that but he was still full of praise for Jimbo when they'd finished.

I spent the last 15 minutes of practice bowling while Danny watched. We worked on my outswinger and my slower ball as well as accuracy. He told me I had heaps of potential as a pace bowler, and with my batting maybe I could be a future all-rounder for Australia!

After 10 minutes spent signing autographs Danny said goodbye, and we watched the white car disappear down the road.

Mr Pasquali had pulled off the biggest surprise of all time. We promised him he wouldn't have to touch a piece of cricket equipment for the rest of the season.

'But that was our last practice!' he moaned, throwing his hands up.

'You're just going to have to plan a bit better next year, Mr P,' Jimbo said dryly, sitting back and closing his eyes. He'd had the practice of his dreams. The Scorpions had their trump card: Scott Craven, bowler. But we had ours: Jimbo, batter.

Mr Pasquali smiled and looked at Jimbo. 'Even

with all the planning in the world some things just come out of the blue.'

'Like Jimbo?' Cameron asked.

Mr Pasquali just smiled.

During the 1972 tour of England, Ian Chappell took 10 wickets at an average of 10.6 runs per wicket. He topped the Australian bowling averages for players who bowled in 10 or more innings and took 10 or more wickets.

12 Who's Pixie?

Thursday — evening

AFTER tea I went up and stared at the computer. I desperately wanted to go back and look at the secret Father Time site, but was worried about what Ben had said.

It wouldn't hurt to go to the main Scorpions page, I thought, opening it in my browser. I scrolled down and left the cursor hovering over the blank area, as Ben had done the previous evening.

And anyway, my IP address was different to Ben's, so there was nothing to worry about as far as tracing the computer went, I tried to tell myself.

The new blank screen appeared and I scrolled down to the faint watermark of Father Time.

My hand paused on the mouse. I stared at the image, its ghostly lines almost invisible on the white background. Then, before I could change my mind, I clicked on the picture.

When the new page appeared I quickly punched in the username and password, then spun around to check that no one was at the half-open door. I hurried over and kicked it shut. My heart was racing.

'Toby!' Mum called from downstairs. 'Phone!'

I looked back at the screen, the page only half loaded. I sighed and closed the browser.

'Coming!' I met Mum on the stairs and headed back up to my room with the phone.

'Toby, it's me, Ally,' came the breathless voice on the other end.

'Ally?'

'I'm in. I've confirmed that I'm the fifth person and —'

'Ally!' I screamed. 'You've what?'

There was silence. Her voice was a lot quieter. 'I ... um, you know, I went into the site and wrote in that text box up at the top, saying ...'

'Saying?' I tried to make my voice sound calm. I guess I shouldn't be sounding so high and mighty — after all, what had I been about to do? Though maybe I wouldn't have had the courage to do what Ally had just done ... or was it stupidity?

'I've stuffed up, haven't I?' she said.

'Not yet,' I told her, trying to sound confident. 'Smale doesn't know who you are, does he?'

'Nope.'

'And I'm not sure he's smart enough to work out all that IP stuff Ben was talking about.' Silence. 'And even if he did, well, what have you done wrong by going into a website? I mean, you haven't broken any law, have you?'

'Exactly,' Ally said, not sounding reassured at all.

'So, what happened?' I asked.

'Well, nothing. Nothing at all. I just wrote that I was making contact. You know, that I was the fifth person.'

'Did you say who you were?'

'Of course not, you idiot. I used your name.'

'WHAT?!?'

'I'm joking,' she giggled. There was another pause. 'So what happens now?'

'How long ago did you do it?' I asked, wondering whether there might be a change on the website.

'An hour, maybe an hour and a half. Why?'

'I'm going to check the site. Don't do anything. I'll call you back soon, okay?'

'Okay, Tobler, whatever,' she sighed.

I tossed the phone onto my bed and logged back in, scrolling down to the bottom of the page.

Once again I was interrupted, this time by a gentle tapping on the door. I quickly hit the 'Print Screen' button as Jim poked his head around the door.

'Jim!' I cried, jumping up, but closing my browser first. He entered, his eyes immediately going to my small collection of *Wisden*s on the bookshelf by the window.

'Hello, Toby. I just called by to see how your father's studio is progressing. And, of course, to say hello to you as well.'

'Jim, I think we've got a problem,' I told him, offering him my seat. Instead he plonked himself onto my bed.

'Our friend Phillip Smale?' he asked, raising his eyebrows.

'How did you know?'

Jim smiled. 'An old man's intuition. What's concerning you?'

Grabbing the printed sheets from Ben's computer, I told Jim about the card we'd seen and the Internet site we'd hooked into. Jim took the pages and studied them, looking darker by the minute.

'Well, I think this needs investigating,' Jim said. 'I warned Phillip of the terrible potential for danger in playing with all of this, but he doesn't seem to have heeded my warning, does he, Toby?'

I shook my head. 'But what do we do?'

'We reveal a secret weapon,' Jim said with relish, rubbing his hands together.

'A secret weapon?'

'Pixie,' he said firmly, slapping his thighs and standing up.

'Pixie?' I asked.

He nodded. 'Pixie, though by name only. She looks and performs like no pixie you will ever encounter, Toby Jones, I can assure you.'

I had no idea what Jim was talking about. 'Well, Pixie will have to get a move on,' I said to him, turning back to the keyboard. 'Have a look at this.' I opened up Word, and pasted in the webpage I'd copied. Jim walked over to the screen and read the final entry.

Thursday

Well, now we have confirmation from all. Number Five, I shall arrive tomorrow morning before 7 a.m. to deliver your instructions. You have made a wise decision that I know you won't regret.

'Well, it looks like an early start for one of us,' he chuckled, shuffling towards the door.

'One of us?'

'Toby, let me handle this one. Phillip Smale is a dangerous man. I've a good mind to alert the authorities, however I fear they'd take me for a doddering old fool who was talking through his hat. Our friend Smale is a slippery customer, but I'm not sure he's done anything illegal.'

'Yet,' I said, quietly.

'Yet,' he repeated. 'Come along, Toby. Peter sent me up to see if you were in bed ...'

'But what about the scorecard? He forced you to give that to him!'

'He did, but the fewer people who know about this the better. Now, come along —'

'Jim,' I interrupted. 'What will you do? Who's Pixie? Can't I come too?'

'I shall follow our intrepid friend; Pixie is a car;

472

and no, you can't come too. Now, I believe you have some teeth that need attention, then it's bed.'

'Is Dad taking you home now?' I asked.

'That's right. We'll talk some more tomorrow, okay?'

Jim headed for the door. I waited a few moments, grabbed a small notebook and pencil, then followed him. Creeping downstairs, my back scraping along the wall, I listened for the sound of adult voices. They were coming from the kitchen, and I could hear the jangle of keys.

I snuck out past the laundry, sped around the side of the house and arrived at the back of the car. It was a big four-wheel drive with loads of room in the rear section. Would the car be open? I wondered. Yes! I opened the hatch a little and slipped in as quietly as possible, closing it behind me. I commando-crawled over to the enormous blue tarpaulin Dad used for tip runs and scrambled beneath it. A few seconds later I heard the front doors open and Dad and Jim get in.

The engine started. I stayed still, pencil at the ready to describe as well as I could the trip Dad was about to take. The plan had only half-formed in my head as Jim was leaving my bedroom, and even now I didn't know quite why I was doing this, but somehow I knew that Jim was too old to tackle Phillip Smale alone. If he was going to follow Smale in Pixie, then I was going to be there with him. But first, I needed to know where on earth Jim lived. Hopefully it wouldn't be too far away.

Dad broke the silence. 'He is really very fond of you, Jim.'

'And I of him, Peter. But I can't possibly impose on you like this. You are a young family. You have so many things that you'll want to do without the burden of an old man ...'

'Jim, I'm not quite sure you understand. We've all discussed this at length. Jane, Toby, Nat and I would dearly like you to join us, perhaps on a trial basis if you like — a month with the Joneses. I'm sure that would be enough for you anyway!'

'I shall indeed think about your very generous offer, Peter.'

There was silence for a while then Dad spoke again. 'You know, you and Toby have an amazing affinity ... some sort of connection.'

I held my breath, wondering whether Jim would spill the beans.

'He has a passion for cricket and a knowledge of the game quite remarkable for one so young. He reminds me so much of myself when I was his age.'

'Well, it would seem you benefit from him as much as Toby benefits from you, Jim.'

'Oh, I've no doubt about that, Peter. No doubt whatsoever.'

Their chat moved on to other things and I concentrated hard on noting down left turns and right turns, but it was difficult. Finally, after about 10 minutes we came to a stop and Dad turned off the engine.

Walk Jim to his door, Dad, I thought to myself. Luckily I heard both doors open and, very slowly, I lifted my head to sneak a look. Dad and Jim were standing by his door. It was a tiny little house, one in a row of them. There were no front gardens, just a long thin porch that connected each building. A dim light glowed over Jim's front door, but the rest of the street was dark and I couldn't see any road signs anywhere.

Before Dad returned I angled myself better beneath the tarp, leaving myself a line of sight through the back-left window. All I needed to see was a street sign or a special feature — something recognisable.

After only a minute of the return journey I got my break: a service station with a big green and gold sign. Then it was gone. But I knew where we were.

In 1999, Wasim Akram took a hat trick in two consecutive Test matches against Sri Lanka. The first was in Lahore, Pakistan, and the second was in Dhaka, Bangladesh, in the final of the Asian Test Championship. Wasim Akram was named Man of the Series.

13 I'm Not the Paperboy

Friday — morning (early)

I woke up to the muffled ringing of my mobile phone, buried beneath my pillow. Last night I'd texted Georgie and told her my plan. I looked at the digital clock on my bedside table: 5.50 a.m. I swore, and grabbed the phone, pressing the 'On' button.

'Georgie?' I whispered.

'No, it's your fairy godmother. C'mon, you lump. I thought you said half past five.'

I jumped out of bed. 'Okay. Where are you?'

'Two doors up, on my bike, freezing. Hurry.'

For the second time in eight hours I was skulking down the stairs like a burglar, then sneaking out the back door. Dad's bike and then Nat's crashed to the concrete as I tried to retrieve mine from behind them. I might as well have rung the front door bell for the sound I'd just made.

I closed my eyes, swore again and waited for someone in the house to stir. Nothing. Somewhere down the street a dog barked. I decided to leave the two bikes lying there and hoisted mine over the top. Putting my helmet on, I wheeled the bike down the driveway.

'I'm still half asleep,' I whispered to Georgie when I met up with her a few moments later.

'Then someone else must be sleepwalking too,' Georgie said, nodding towards my house. A light had just come on, and the side drive was as bright as day.

'Let's go,' I murmured, mounting the bike and pedalling hard.

'How far is it?' Georgie said, catching up.

'It'll take us 10 minutes, tops,' I told her. I'd checked out the area on a map I'd downloaded from the Internet and there were a few laneways we could take to make the trip shorter.

It was cold and eerily silent. There was also a wispy fog that dimmed the streetlights.

'Hey, it's pretty good at this time of day, isn't it?' I said.

'What are we actually going to do?' Georgie asked, ignoring my question.

I hadn't really thought about that. Maybe we could sneak into Pixie, like I had into Dad's car last night, though big cars were not the first things that came to mind when I thought of Pixie.

'Here we go,' I said, ignoring her too. 'This is the service station I saw. I reckon Jim's place is straight down this street, on the right.' Somewhere ahead an engine was idling — the sound was a throaty rumble, deep and threatening.

'C'mon,' I called, speeding past Georgie. About halfway down the street was the line of houses I'd seen last night. An enormous car sat outside Jim's, shaking a bit and blasting out plumes of smoke from its exhaust.

'That's Pixie?' Georgie gasped, staring at the old car shuddering in front of us.

Jim's garage door stood open; I was amazed the car could actually fit inside it. 'It must be,' I whispered. We ran our bikes into the garage and dashed back to the car, stooping low to avoid detection. We needn't have bothered.

'I take it you'll be letting me drive,' a voice called from the front of the house. We both spun round.

'Jim!' I gasped. 'Um, well, me and Georgie, we were out —'

'Come along,' he said, looking at his watch. 'We may already be too late.'

'This is Pixie?' I asked, trying to open the passenger door.

'The very one,' Jim said, climbing stiffly into the driver's seat.

'I can't ... I can't open ...' Georgie grabbed the long silver handle with me and together we managed to open the door, which creaked and groaned.

'Better hold it while I get in,' she said, grinning as she shoved past me.

'I'm not sure when I last had passengers,' Jim said, reaching back for his seat belt.

'Maybe the 1960s?' Georgie suggested, hunting around for a seat belt herself.

'Hmm, you're probably right there.'

Georgie and I looked at each other. Maybe this wasn't such a great idea. 'Jim? Are you sure you ...' I began to say before we were both flung back against the seat as the car lurched and sputtered into action.

'It needs a bit more choke,' Jim muttered, pulling out a little lever by the steering wheel.

'Choke?' Georgie mouthed to me.

I shrugged.

Jim pulled hard on a thin stick poking out from behind the steering wheel and the car jolted again.

'Right then,' he said, gripping the wheel and staring straight ahead. 'I guess you two are wondering why you always see me in a taxi, and not in a Pixie.' Jim grinned, looking at us in the rear-view mirror. 'Well,' he continued, 'Pixie's been out of action for quite some time, but I've recently discovered mobile mechanics.'

I just hoped the mobile mechanic hadn't botched the job. Pixie certainly didn't sound well-oiled and tuned.

'Now, I take it you two are also keen to find out just where Mr Smale is heading this morning with his letter of information?'

'Er, yes,' I replied, feeling tiny on the brown leather seat, which was cold against my bare legs. I looked enviously at Georgie in her jeans. She had finally fastened her seat belt.

'And what's your assessment of the situation, Master Jones?' Jim asked.

'Well, I reckon Phillip Smale has organised five people to travel back to a game in the past, using the scorecard.'

'Just what we hoped he wouldn't do,' Georgie said.

'But knew he would,' I added. Pixie rumbled and grumbled as we waited for the lights to change.

'And now?' Jim asked, looking at me in his mirror.

'Well, we go to Smale's place and hopefully we can follow him to where he's going to hand over the letter. Then we —'

'Then we reassess the situation,' Jim said firmly. 'I take it your parents don't know you're driving across town with an old man at the wheel?'

'We didn't want to wake them, did we, Tobes?' Georgie said.

I shook my head. 'No, why worry them?'

Jim was working hard to negotiate a roundabout.

'How much further, Jim?' I asked.

'Almost there. We'll park a short distance away.' After a couple of minutes Jim pulled in behind another car.

'Which house is Mr Smale's?' Georgie asked.

'Three up on this side,' Jim said. 'I think we'll give our friend half an hour, then head back for breakfast.'

'What if he's already gone?' I asked. 'Why don't I just slip out —'

'No!' Georgie and Jim cried together.

Fifteen minutes later, having finally convinced Jim that it was time to do something, I had wrenched open the door and was darting from bush to bush. Jim had said Smale's garage would probably be locked but that I might be able to see, possibly through a window or under the door, whether his car was there or not.

Smale's house was big and modern, and a huge fence ran along the front of an impressive garden, but the gates were open. I didn't think this was a good sign, so I darted through them then crept along the side fence, avoiding some rose bushes as best as I could, until I reached the garage. The door was closed.

But just as I rested my ear against the door to see if I could hear anyone inside, it clanged and started going up. Wildly I searched for a place to hide. There were no trees or large bushes anywhere, so I belted across the front garden and hauled myself up the wooden fence on the other side. There was a three-metre drop to the neighbour's yard, but a sore foot seemed better than meeting Phillip Smale in front of his house.

I grabbed the top of the fence with both hands and gently lowered myself down, trying to reduce the distance between my feet and the ground. Letting go, I luckily landed on soft earth. I jogged back towards the road, careful to stay low.

'Oi!' a voice shouted from behind me. 'Are you the new paperboy? I said I wanted my paper delivered to the porch, here, not down in the garden.'

Smale's car was reversing down his driveway.

'Yep, right you are,' I looked around for the paper. 'Sorry.'

'It's over there,' the man growled, pointing to a bird bath on his open lawn. I grabbed his wrapped-up paper and took it up to him.

'On the porch in future, got it?' he snarled, snatching it from me.

I backed away, listening for Smale's car. It sounded as though he had backed out and was heading up the street, towards Pixie.

'Well, what are you waiting around for?' the guy on the porch asked, starting to get suspicious. 'Where are all your papers, anyway?' he said, moving towards me.

'Um, I ... I was just ... wondering ...'

Smale drove past and the mean guy gave him a wave.

I spun around. 'Okay, I'm off,' I called, running back to the pavement. Smale's car was well past Pixie by the time I started sprinting down the street towards Jim and Georgie.

'He's gone!' I panted, struggling to open the door. 'Did he see you?'

'We hid,' Georgie said. 'You?'

'Nup, don't think so.'

Pixie's engine grumbled deeply as it warmed up. Slowly Jim wheeled her around to face the other way, but he couldn't do it in one turn and had to reverse before heading off.

'C'mon Jim, floor it!' I yelled, doing up my seat belt.

'Hold on!' he called. Pixie quickly picked up speed and we charged back the way we'd come.

'There!' Georgie called, looking out her window. Jim hauled on the wheel and we spun to the right. I looked at Georgie, who had turned a bit pale.

'Don't worry. I did an advanced driving course some years ago, and you never forget these things,' Jim chuckled, a gleam in his eye.

We managed to stay a good distance behind Smale's sleek black car. A few times Jim backed right off and twice I thought we'd lost him, but Jim seemed to know what he was doing and a moment later there was Smale's car, 50 metres ahead.

'Ally lives around here,' Georgie said as we turned into a street with big trees along each side.

'And I think our friend does too,' Jim said, slowing down and carefully parking a safe distance from the black car's position. We watched Smale march up to the door and knock. Nothing happened.

'Did Ally choose this address?' Georgie asked, as Phillip Smale glanced about furtively.

'Nope. She just made contact. This must be the house of the fifth person,' I said, 'but no one seems to be home.'

As I watched, Smale became more and more frustrated, slapping an envelope against his thigh. Again he banged on the door, this time with his fist. Finally he left the front of the house and walked around the side. A minute later he reappeared, but without the letter.

'He must have found someone,' Georgie said.

'Time to go,' Jim said, reversing Pixie.

'But Jim, what about . . . '

'All in good time.' Jim launched Pixie back onto the road. We turned and headed up a side street where we waited for a few minutes, before crawling back to the mystery house.

This time we all got out. Jim hung back, pottering about near the front while Georgie and I dashed down the side. It was Georgie who found the letter, with a hastily scrawled note written on the back, under the doormat at the rear of the house.

'Right then, detectives. That was a successful mission, wouldn't you say?' Jim beamed as he took the letter from Georgie and we hurried back to the car. 'We shall reconvene this afternoon — at your house, Toby.' It appeared that Jim was going to get first look at Smale's letter. That was fair enough, since it was his Pixie that had brought us to it.

'Why do you call the car Pixie?' I asked, settling back in the enormous seat.

'Maybe it's got something to do with its size?' Georgie said, rolling her eyes.

'But this car is a monster,' I replied.

'Exactly,' Jim chuckled.

Charlie Turner holds the record for the most first-class wickets in an Australian season. Playing for New South Wales and Australia in 1887/1888, he took an incredible 106 wickets in only 12 games. That's an average of almost nine wickets a game!

14 Timeless Travel Tours

Friday — afternoon

'THE letter is on your bed,' Jim whispered to me in the kitchen that afternoon, a few minutes after Georgie and I had arrived back at my home from school. No one had missed us that morning and there'd obviously been no calls from Mr Smale or his neighbour about any funny things going on. Georgie and I grabbed a snack from the fridge and raced up to my bedroom.

> I'm pleased that you have made contact, Geoff. We shall depart from the Scorpion clubrooms at 9.00 p.m. this Saturday. We shall be gone no longer than an hour. I trust that you have been, and will continue to remain, fully discreet in this matter.

Please wear comfortable, light clothing
as befitting an Australian test-goer of the
1960s.

Phillip Smale
(Manager)
Timeless Travel Tours

'It doesn't say much,' I muttered, handing the letter over to Georgie.

'No, only where and when Smale is planning his little tour party,' Georgie said sarcastically. 'What did you expect?'

'I dunno.' I was starting to get nervous about the final, worried that I hadn't been thinking about it enough — though maybe that was a good thing. Probably the more I thought about it, the more worried I'd get.

'Georgie?'

She looked up sharply, noting something in my voice.

'We've got the grand final tomorrow. I reckon we should forget about this for a bit and, you know, focus on the game tomorrow. Do you want to set a field or maybe work out a batting order?'

Georgie folded the letter. 'Yeah, Toby. Good idea.'

We spent the next hour working on fielding positions and the batting order. I'd come up with a 6–3 fielding setup: six fielders on the off side and

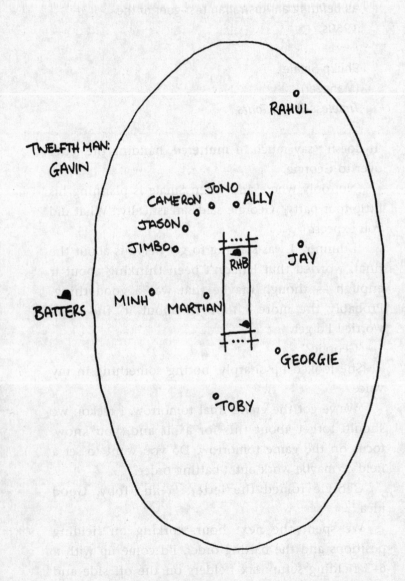

RAHUL

TWELFTH MAN:
GAVIN

JONO
CAMERON   ALLY
JASON
JIMBO   JAY
                RHB
BATTERS   MINH
           MARTIAN

                        GEORGIE

            TOBY

three on the on side. We could use it when I was bowling to a right-hander — though not necessarily to Scott Craven. The field would have to be spread more when he was batting.

Georgie and I had a long argument about Martian's position at silly mid-off. I would also have really liked to have a short leg, like they do in the Tests, but in our games no one is allowed to field closer to the batsman than a half-pitch length, unless you are the keeper or in the slips or gully.

'You're giving away runs down through third man,' Georgie argued, pointing to the big open area behind the slips.

'Well, if I'm finding the edge of the bat then that's good. With those two slips and a gully I might be getting a few wickets.'

'Not if their shots are going along the ground,' she replied.

'But I'm still finding the edge.'

'We might only have a few runs to play with,' she said, folding her arms.

We were going around in circles.

We finally agreed that the fielding positions depended entirely on the situation of the game. Maybe at the start of the innings, when we were on the attack, we could have this sort of field.

'Yeah, but what if we'd been bowled out for only 53?' Georgie said, as we headed into the kitchen for some food.

'We still attack,' I said loudly. 'Like Danny said: we've got to look and play like winners, whatever the situation.'

'He didn't say that —'

'One more sleep to the final, guys,' Dad called out from the next room, hearing us in the kitchen.

I grabbed a couple of nectarines from a bowl on the kitchen table and headed into the lounge. Georgie followed me in.

'Cup of tea, Jim?' Dad asked, passing us in the doorway.

I noticed Jim was also in the lounge, reading a book. 'We're going to focus on the game this weekend, Jim,' I explained, passing him the envelope with Smale's letter inside.

'Good, good,' he nodded, closing his book. 'An excellent decision. The last thing you need is this sort of distraction.' He slipped the letter into the inside pocket of his jacket.

'Will you be doing anything?' Georgie whispered to Jim as I gave her a nectarine.

Jim looked at me. 'Perhaps I'll go and have a talk with Phillip, though I fear his heart is set.'

'We have to get the scorecard back,' I said.

'Not yet, Toby. You have other cricket matters to attend to. Let's think about all of this after the weekend — after the grand final, hmm? What do you think?'

I looked at Georgie. She shrugged, looking thoughtful.

* * *

Four more people were finding out about the time travel, I thought as I lay in bed trying to sleep, wondering where Mr Smale was going to take the group that had signed up for his trip.

How many people knew about it now? Me and Jim. Then Georgie, Rahul, Jay, Jimbo and, of course, Ally. Also Scott and his uncle, Phillip Smale. Maybe Gavin, Scott's friend — and who knew how many others Scott might have told?

And now four complete strangers. Four adults. What would go through their heads when they were transported back through time to a cricket match in the past? They would freak out completely. There was no way they would be able to keep that sort of experience secret.

In a week's time it could be all over the town. All over the news. On everyone's lips. But Mr Smale didn't want that. He wanted secrecy. To what lengths would he go to ensure that time travel by means of the scorecard and the *Wisden*s remained a secret?

I glanced at the red numbers on the clock next to my bed: 10:34. In 10 hours I would be playing in the most important game of my cricket career and here I was lying in bed worrying about Phillip Smale, *Wisden*s, scorecards and four complete strangers about to go on the journey of their lives.

I bet Scott Craven was sound asleep, dreaming of cartwheeling stumps and high fives ...

The most balls bowled in a Test match by one bowler is 774 by Sonny Ramadhin of the West Indies. Playing against England at Birmingham in 1957, he bowled 31 overs in the first innings, taking 7 for 49. In the second innings he bowled a whopping 98 overs, taking 2 for 179.

15 Collapse

Saturday — morning

IT was another warm day. There were already plenty of people about when we arrived at the ground, setting up rugs, portable chairs and even barbecues.

'Finals atmosphere, son,' Dad said, looking excited. 'Come on, Nat. Help me out with all this gear. Toby,' he said, looking at me and holding out his hand. 'Best wishes, mate. Enjoy yourself. The result will look after itself.'

'Thanks, Dad,' I said, feeling nervous. I got a kiss from Mum and Nat, who also wanted to shake my hand.

Jim also gave me a handshake. 'I'm looking forward to the game, Toby. But remember, that's all it is — a game. A wonderful game, perhaps the greatest of them all, but still just a game.'

Mum, Dad, Jim and Nat watched me head across to the team area. I turned around once, halfway across the oval with my cricket bag hanging over my shoulder, and waved. They all waved back.

'We're batting,' Jono called, walking over to the team from the coin toss in the middle. I felt a tingly feeling in my stomach, especially on seeing Scott Craven warming up off a run-up that took him almost to the boundary line.

Positive, stay positive, I told myself. 'Great day for batting,' I said.

'Who won the toss, Jono?' Rahul asked.

'Scorpions.'

I looked over at Mr Pasquali for a reaction, but he was writing something into his scorebook.

'Jono, bring everyone over to the small scoreboard here, please, and I'll announce the team. Then you can read the batting order. After that I'd like you all together for the team photo and a quick chat, okay?'

All 12 of us, the squad Mr Pasquali had announced and introduced at our school assembly, followed him across to where a big magnetic scoreboard leaned against a wooden table that the scorers would use. One of us would also be sitting there, watching, ready to field if one of the team got injured.

Gavin, Georgie, Jay, Jason and even Ally and Martian would all be feeling nervous right now. No one spoke.

'It's been a long and successful season, regardless of what happens today and tomorrow,' Mr Pasquali said, rubbing sunblock into his arms. 'I said last week that you were a fine team. We agreed at the start of the season that you were happy for me to pick the in-form 12 for this game, and that's what I've done. Unfortunately, I have been faced with the difficult task of appointing one of you as 12th man, or woman, as the case may be.'

I glanced at Georgie. She was kicking at something and avoiding all eye contact.

'I wish it was a game for 12 or even 15 players. But it's not — cricket is played between two teams of 11. And this is the team of 11 that will take the field in this year's grand final.'

Mr Pasquali paused, looked up at us, then down at his clipboard again.

'Jono: captain. Toby: vice-captain.'

A shiver swept through me, this time of excitement. We'd never had a vice-captain before.

'Then in alphabetical order by first name, because that's how I know you all ...' Poor Mr Pasquali was finding this difficult. He hated the thought of someone missing out. And someone was about to not play in a grand final. He looked up. 'Ally, Cameron, Gavin, Georgie, Ivo, Jason, Jimbo, Minh and Rahul. Jay, you are our 12th man for this game.'

Jay was making a brave effort to hide his disappointment. Georgie, Martian and even Gavin weren't showing any signs of delight, though each would be feeling relieved.

Jono stepped forwards into the circle. 'It's pretty well the same as last week,' he said, unfolding a piece of paper that he'd pulled from his pocket. 'Cameron and I will be opening, then Jimbo, Rahul, Toby, Martian, Georgie, Minh, Ally, Gavin and Jason.'

We turned back to Mr Pasquali.

'We have all the time in the world. I will be very disappointed if there are any run-outs or wasted wickets. But keep the runs ticking along, let's not get bogged down. If the top order can see off Scott Craven, then I'm sure there are plenty of runs for the taking. Remember, there are no limits on batters or bowlers in a grand final. *But* we have to win the game. The Scorpions finished on top of the ladder so a draw is good enough for them to win the cup.'

I tossed a few deliveries at Cameron then went over to console Jay, who was sitting at the scorers' table with the Scorpions' 12th man and a couple of parents.

'You're a part of this team, Jay, and you'll be with us for the celebrations after we've won too,' I said, patting him on the back.

'Yeah, whatever,' he mumbled, not looking up.

'C'mon, Jay. At least you don't have to face Scott,' said Georgie, who had joined us.

'You wanna swap then? Here, you sit on your arse here and do nothing —'

'Hey, young feller,' one of the men at the table said, 'that's no way to talk. As it is, you've got your

496

part to play. Now, let's get this batting order into the book.'

I walked around to my usual spot, right behind the bowler's arm, to watch the start of the game. For a moment I was the closest person in the world to Scott Craven at the top of his mark.

'Good luck, Scott,' I called, sitting down on the bank.

He turned around and looked at me in amazement. 'Well, Toby Jones,' he drawled, 'luck doesn't come into it, mate.' He sniggered, spun around and headed off to bowl to Cameron.

We survived the first five overs before disaster struck. None of us expected the other opening bowler to do much damage; maybe our batters were a bit too relaxed when Scott wasn't bowling.

First to go was Cameron, caught at mid-off by none other than Scott Craven, who hurled the ball high into the air. Then Jimbo went, caught off the last ball of the same over, and I was making my way back to the group to put on my batting gear.

'C'mon, Rahul,' I called. 'Big knock from you.' At least give me time to get my gear on, I thought to myself, watching him stride out onto the pitch.

Jason managed to toss me a couple of balls before there was another shout from the field. Scott Craven had just got his first wicket, clean-bowling Rahul. We'd lost three of our top four batters in the space of about six deliveries.

I hadn't thought I'd be walking out to the middle so soon, and I felt flustered with the rush and the panic that had come over the team. Taking a few deep breaths to try and calm my nerves, I arrived at the wicket and paused to adjust my pads and tighten my gloves.

'Take your time,' I muttered to myself.

'Come on, Scott, let's have him,' a voice called.

I glanced up to see Mr Smale pacing about down near the third-man boundary. I turned away quickly.

I had one ball to face to see off Scott's over. I expected a bouncer and was ducking almost before he'd bowled it. The ball flew past my head.

'Toby, I don't care how slow we go, we've just got to survive, okay?' Jono said when we met mid-pitch at the end of the over.

'Okay. Just don't shield me from Craven,' I said over my shoulder.

'I have no intention of doing that,' he replied.

We survived the next six overs without too much drama, though Scott beat me twice in a row with two beautiful deliveries that moved away from me. After the second one, he came down the wicket a few paces and mouthed some swear words in my direction. I turned my back on him, just like some of the international players do when the heat is on.

I looked out past square leg to see Dad chatting excitedly with Jim, who was nodding as though in agreement. I then gazed at our players — they all

498

looked a bit dejected with the way the first hour had gone. The scoreboard read 'Riverwall 3/38'.

'It's better than 3 for 19,' Jono said at our first drinks break. Mr Pasquali watched from a distance. He was chatting politely to the other umpire but inside he would be feeling the disappointment.

Scott continued bowling after the break. I played his first two deliveries back up the pitch. He'd slowed down a fraction; maybe he was beginning to tire. His third ball, however, spat and flew from just short of a length. I fended it off my body. A short leg would have gobbled it up. Scott stood and stared, shook his head slowly and wheeled around.

'Stay focused, Toby,' Jono called from the other end.

'Stay alive, more like,' I muttered, tapping the crease.

The next ball was shorter. I was inside it in a flash, flaying it high and wide over deep backward square leg. I didn't even leave my crease. Car horns blared and the umpire raised both arms. I presumed Scott was glaring at me, but I ignored him and walked up to get a pat on the back from Jono.

Scott bowled another short one, though this time further outside the off-stump. But I was on fire. Again I tried to get inside the line, but the ball was onto me too quickly. It caught the top edge, flew over the slips and down to the boundary for four.

Ten runs in two balls. I stole a glance at Mr Pasquali out at square leg. Slowly he raised a hand. *Don't get carried away*, he seemed to be saying.

Where would Scott pitch this last delivery? Would it be another short one? I heard some clapping from the Riverwall supporters as he steamed in and bowled a fast in-swinging yorker. I jammed the bat down on it. Bat, ball and pitch all collided. The ball stopped dead and I kicked it away.

The umpire called the end of over and I headed up the pitch.

'I want one more,' Scott yelled at his captain, who was standing in the slips. He got his extra over. Jono glided the first ball down through the gully for a single and then I was clean-bowled with the next delivery. I hardly even saw it.

We had been five balls away from seeing out Scott's first spell and I'd blown it. I walked off the ground dejected and angry. I didn't speak to anyone and no one attempted to talk to me. I didn't care that I'd been bowled by maybe the best ball of the match so far. No ball is too good once you've spent some time at the crease, once you've nailed a few in the middle and hit the boundary two or three times.

Martian top-edged Scott's fourth ball over slips for six, but was caught in the gully on the next ball, fending off another short one.

Georgie survived Scott's last ball, but was out lbw for a duck in the next over. Three for 38 had turned into a disastrous 6 for 55.

How could you stay positive in a situation like this?

Tom Veivers holds the record for the Australian who has bowled the most balls in one innings. Playing in a Test match against England at Manchester in 1964, he sent down 571 deliveries. He bowled 95.1 overs, 36 maidens and took 3 wickets for 155 runs.

16 Out of the Blue

WE scrounged another 39 runs off the Scorpions' other bowlers. 'Extras' ended up being the third top scorer with 13. It was easy to see how frustrated Scott felt at not being able to bowl at our lower order. Perhaps the Scorpions' captain was being a bit generous in holding him back.

'I think the Scorpions have made their first mistake,' Mr Pasquali said, smiling as he threw a ball at us at the changeover.

And with that comment our whole attitude changed.

'Taking Scott off?' Jimbo asked, flinging the ball to Ally, who would be keeping.

'Exactly,' Mr Pasquali replied.

'The ball's doing quite a bit out there. Tight, accurate bowling will be rewarded, I assure you.' Maybe Mr Pasquali was just trying to get us to be positive. So what? It was working.

Jimbo nudged me and nodded towards a guy standing on his own 10 metres away to our left.

'It's Trevor Barnes,' I whispered. 'Coach of the Under-18 representative side.'

'The very same,' Jimbo said quietly.

I took the new ball and went out to measure my run-up. I thought back to Danny Chapman and the chat we'd had. The Scorpions hadn't had that experience. Surely that was an advantage for us?

But it wasn't Danny Chapman with the ball. It was Toby Jones. And that was going to be just as good, I thought, looking around at the field Jono had set. I'd shown him my plan and he was happy to go with it — for the first few overs, anyway. Like Georgie, he was nervous about not having a third man.

'Minh, go closer to point,' I shouted. I also directed Martian to go a bit squarer from his position at silly mid-off. That way I had opened up a nice gap through mid-off to tempt the batter into driving at a ball that was either swinging away or not at a length full-enough for driving.

'C'mon, Toby, go right through 'em,' a voice I didn't recognise yelled from the boundary. I didn't turn around.

'Play,' Mr Pasquali called.

I ran in hard, looking every bit like I was going to bowl the fastest possible delivery. Halfway to the wicket, though, I spread my fingers on either side of the ball. It was the perfect slower ball, straight and pitched fuller. The batter's eyes lit up, but he was into the shot way too early. He had already completed his stroke when the ball hit the bat. Gently the ball ballooned back towards me.

I took it in both hands at knee height. The batter banged his bat into the pitch and walked off, staring at me, while my team-mates all rushed in to celebrate.

'I thought you were a pace bowler,' Rahul said, high-fiving me.

'Not all the time,' I replied.

'Body language, everyone,' Jono said, clapping his hands. He wanted us looking confident and in control.

'Game on,' I whispered to Georgie as we headed back to our positions. She was at mid-on.

'It's not the only thing on,' she said, winking at me.

'C'mon, Toby!' Jimbo shouted from the gully, clapping his hands.

I let Georgie's comment slip through to the keeper — I didn't want any non-cricket issues getting in the way and distracting me.

I took a wicket in my third over, then another in my fourth. The moment we'd all been waiting for arrived when Scott Craven marched out to the crease. The whole team stared at him as he took guard from Mr Pasquali, calling for two legs.

'One more over?' Mr Pasquali called over to the other umpire, who looked at his watch, then nodded.

What would Scott do with one over to survive before lunch?

I brought Georgie and Minh in closer, hoping to tempt Scott to go over the top. The plan worked — sort of. I should have known better. Scott carved the first two balls over Minh's head and out to the cover boundary for four each. He clipped the third off his pads for a two. The fourth ball went right through him, but he belted the next back over my head for another four. The last ball he blocked. He'd just belted me for 14 runs.

'C'mon, guys,' Jono urged as we walked from the field for lunch. 'We're only one wicket away from being level if not ahead in this game.'

He was right, but Scott Craven was a big wicket. The scoreboard had the Scorpions at 3/36 and we were only 58 runs ahead. Splitting up, we headed over to our respective families for food and drink.

Jono gave me two more overs after lunch. The Scorpions had changed their tactics — they were obviously waiting for me to finish my spell, like we'd waited for Scott to finish his.

Slowly and steadily the Scorpions started to accumulate runs with first Jono and Rahul bowling, and then when Jason and Gavin came on.

It was the hottest part of the day and we were struggling, but Scott and his partner had taken their score from the 20s into the 120s without too much sweat or bother.

'Maybe we should try and buy a wicket,' I said to the team at the drinks break.

'Buy a wicket?' Ally asked. 'You want to bribe Scott Craven?'

'No, let's set him up. He's itching to put one away; so is the other guy. I reckon they've been told to grind us into the dirt.'

'Toby's right,' Jono said. 'We've gotta try something different. It's not happening for us at the moment.' He glanced at the scoreboard. 'They're 30 odd runs ahead and putting us out of the game. Remember, we've got to win.'

'What exactly did you have in mind, Toby?' Jimbo asked. He sounded positive.

'Give Georgie a bowl. She's accurate and can mix up her pace a bit.'

'She'll get pasted,' Martian said, shaking his head. 'No offence, Georgie, but you're up and down — no spin or movement.'

'Exactly! So they get lulled into doing something stupid.'

'Or get lulled into belting her over the boundary line,' Martian said dejectedly.

'Jono?' Rahul said, looking over to him.

'That's time, boys,' the Scorpions' umpire called.

'Okay. We'll give it a try. Two overs and then we'll review. Georgie, which end do you want?'

'Into the breeze,' she replied, pointing to the far end. 'Bloody ripper idea, Tobes,' she said, clapping me on the back.

'Thought you'd approve.'

The Scorpions pair played out Rahul's next over, taking only a couple of singles. Scott was on strike for Georgie's first ball, and I watched his face closely. He was looking smug, yet determined. He would hate to get out to Georgie. He padded her first ball back down the pitch.

'Bowled, George,' Ally said, clapping from behind the stumps.

'Right there,' Jimbo called from covers.

But Georgie's next ball was short and wide. Scott leaned back and hoicked it from outside his off-stump over mid-wicket. The ball landed just inside the boundary.

Jono told Minh to drop back from his position at mid-wicket. Scott watched lazily, chewing his gum and smiling. He put the next ball out over cover. Same result.

Now the field was spread. I didn't think Scott was interested in singles, and I was right. He blasted the next ball wide past mid-on. It produced four more runs, but the shot lacked control.

'On your toes, everyone,' I shouted, clapping my hands.

'Settle,' I heard the Scorpions' coach hiss through clenched teeth from his position at square leg. Scott looked towards him in surprise.

I made a quick movement of my hand to Georgie when she turned to look at me. 'Faster one,' I mouthed.

This one was onto Scott much quicker. He slashed at the ball, which was delivered short and outside off-stump, aiming to belt it over mid-wicket again. But instead, the ball shot directly into the sky.

'Mine!' I screamed, sensing it was coming in the general direction of square leg.

'Leave it for Ally!' someone called.

'Mine!' I yelled again. The ball had only just reached its peak. Time stood still. My mind went blank as I stared into space at the little red dot, now hurtling back towards me at alarming speed. I squinted. I was too far forwards. I took a step back, then another, then staggered three more paces.

I reverse-cupped my hands in front of my face. Still edging backwards, I caught the ball, then stumbled and fell over. I clutched the ball to my chest, closing my eyes in delight and relief.

'Told you it was a good idea,' Martian said, grinning.

I was hauled to my feet and we jumped about like galahs for a few moments before Jono held up his hands.

'We're in this game,' he roared at us. 'Two more wickets before tea, okay?'

We got him three. I came back on to bowl and snapped up Scott's partner, lbw, with a fast yorker that got him on the toe. Then Rahul got a lucky break when their number six batter played on. The ball spun back and clunked into the base of his off-stump, just dislodging the bail.

The Scorpions were rattled. Jimbo swooped on a ball played into the covers in the last over before tea. The batters stuttered and stumbled. 'No!' the non-striker finally shouted, holding up an arm. But the batter had committed. He turned and tried to regain his ground, but Jimbo's flat and awesomely fast throw to Ally caught him well short.

The dismissed batter flung his bat into the stumps in anger and frustration, and swore at his partner. Ally was lucky as the bat missed her by centimetres.

'Nicko, here — now!' The Scorpions' umpire demanded.

We went to tea a much happier group, though we could hear shouting from the other team's clubrooms during the tea break. I assumed the coach was getting stuck into them again.

By contrast, Mr Pasquali was quiet and friendly. He spoke to us individually, encouraging and giving each of us something to focus on for the next session.

The Scorpions' last three wickets put on about 40 runs, though, which was a bit disappointing. We dropped two catches during that last hour and I had what looked like a plumb lbw decision turned down too. The batter shouted straight away that he'd hit it, but it was unlikely that Mr Pasquali was influenced by that call.

We left the field as a tight group at the end of the innings. The day wasn't quite over for us, especially for our openers Cameron and Jono, who would have to face a very tricky three overs to see out the day.

Padded up and ready to go in, I sat down to watch the action and see if we could get through the overs without losing a wicket. We'd already decided that we wouldn't risk Jimbo going in tonight, so I was given the role of night watchman — the batter whose job it is to go in if someone gets out, and survive till stumps.

They almost made it!

Jono was given out lbw to a Scott Craven yorker — a vicious and amazingly fast ball that smashed into the bottom of his pads. Jono was trapped in front of his wicket, absolutely plumb.

That left me with three balls to face from Scott Craven.

'Survive, survive,' I said to myself as he ran in to bowl. The first ball whizzed past my off-stump. Scott threw up his arms and screamed in anger and disbelief. Maybe it had been closer to my stumps than I thought.

Two balls to go.

The next caught the edge of my bat and flew towards second slip. I spun around to see the guy thrust out his left hand. The ball bobbled, then dropped to the ground as he rolled over. To my amazement he jumped back up, shouting and holding the ball up for all the world to see.

I didn't move. Scott charged down the wicket yelling in delight. I looked over to Mr Pasquali, who'd swapped positions to be at square-leg for our innings, and gently shook my head.

'How's that?' Scott yelled, turning to the Scorpions' umpire.

I'd never felt so sick in my life. 'Don't do it,' I muttered.

The umpire looked over at Mr Pasquali, obviously not sure about the catch.

'That was not a catch,' Mr Pasquali said firmly. 'The ball hit the ground.'

'Not out,' the Scorpion's umpire called.

'What?' Scott said, looking dumbstruck and pointing to the fielder with the ball. The umpire was unmoved. Slowly the players returned to their positions, swearing and muttering.

I settled over my bat and waited for the last ball of the day.

'Cheat,' one of the kids mumbled behind me. I straightened up and pulled away from the wicket.

'Is there a problem?' the umpire asked. He obviously hadn't heard the comment.

'Just a bit noisy down here,' I yelled back. I glanced at Mr Pasquali. He smiled and gave a slight nod.

Scott charged in and bowled a bouncer. Surprise, surprise.

I ducked, but hardly needed to because the ball soared over my head as well as the keeper's and flew to the boundary for four byes. It didn't matter how the runs came, as long as they did.

In 1997, Glenn McGrath took 8 for 38 in a
Test match against England at Lord's. His bowling
figures for the first innings were 20.3 overs, 8 maidens,
8 for 38. These are the best bowling figures
for any Australian at Lord's. McGrath also took
8 for 24 against Pakistan in Perth in 2004.

17 Ally or Jessica?

Saturday — evening

'TOBY, we have a plan,' Georgie said excitedly.

'To stop Scott Craven taking all 10 wickets in the second innings?' I asked, just as Mum brought in a plate piled high with hamburgers stuffed with lettuce, onion, cheese, tomato, egg and sauce. She then disappeared outside where the adults were having drinks, while Ally, Georgie, Nat and I blobbed in front of the TV, ready to tuck in. Somehow I knew that the plan Georgie was talking about had nothing to do with the grand final.

'Ally did some checking out. She knows the people in the house that we went to with Jim. You know — to get that letter?'

I looked over at Nat, who was nibbling on her hamburger and feeding the odd bit to an army of Beanie Bears she had propped up against the couch. She wasn't listening to us.

'Who are they?' I remembered that Ally lived close to the area where Jim had driven us when following Smale.

'Well,' Ally said, putting her plate down, 'I don't really know them, only to say hi. Their name is Walters. They have a girl a few years older than me, called Jessica. The weird thing is they're on holiday.'

'How do you know that?' I asked, taking a bite.

'Their neighbours are collecting their mail.'

'And how do you know the neighbours are collecting their mail?'

Ally sighed. 'Because Henry lives next door to them and we often walk to school together.'

'You and Henry?' I asked.

'Is there a problem, Toby?' Georgie asked, frowning.

'No,' I said. I was still on a bit of a high after the day's play, and I would rather have talked about the fake catch or my catch to get rid of Scott, our decision to give Georgie a bowl or the state of the game.

I shrugged. 'Okay, so what's the plan?' I'd made a conscious decision, along with Jim, to put the time travel issue to one side while the grand final was on. It was after all, only two days of my life. But the girls had other ideas and their energy and enthusiasm was grabbing my attention.

'We think that the father is the fifth person — the fifth traveller to go with Smale to wherever they're going,' Georgie began.

'A cricket match in the past?' I suggested.

514

Georgie nodded, taking a drink. 'So, Smale thinks someone's coming because the fifth person has replied.'

'Only he hasn't,' I said.

'Exactly, but Smale doesn't know that. What if this guy's daughter, Jessica, went instead of him?'

'But didn't you say they're on holidays?'

'Yes, exactly,' Ally said, pointing at me.

'Riiiiight,' I said, slowly.

The two girls looked at me.

'But how does Jessica go if she's not here?' It seemed pretty straightforward to me.

'Jessica doesn't go,' Ally said quietly. 'I go.'

There was a shout from the TV. The Aussies had just taken another wicket.

'You go?' I asked. Ally nodded.

'Brilliant, huh?' said Georgie.

'Tell me how it's brilliant,' I said.

'Smale doesn't know me from Adam,' Ally explained.

'Don't be daft —'

'Wait on!' Georgie said, glaring at me. 'Let the girl finish.'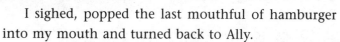

I sighed, popped the last mouthful of hamburger into my mouth and turned back to Ally.

'Smale won't recognise me,' she said. 'I'll explain that I'm Jessica, Geoff Walters' daughter, and that I'll be taking the trip on his behalf.'

'Told you it was brilliant,' Georgie repeated.

'Okay,' I sighed, grabbing another hamburger. 'First, you said yourself, Ally, that Jessica is two years older than you. Second, you say Mr Smale won't recognise you. Except he's just spent the entire afternoon watching you play a game of cricket. And third ...'

'Third?' Ally said, smiling and looking like she didn't have a care in the world.

'Third? Um, yeah, well, third is that there's no way Smale will let a girl travel with him and a group of adults. He's probably asking them to pay 10 thousand bucks each for the privilege.'

'Great. So let's just do nothing, hey?' Ally said, looking at Georgie. 'Let's sit on our backsides here, eat hamburgers and —'

'Okay!' I shouted. Nat looked up sharply. She had been talking happily to her 'friends'.

Georgie turned to her. 'Bet you haven't got Aussiebear,' she said out of the blue.

'Nope.' Nat was surprised. 'Have you?'

'It was the first one I got. You want me to get it for you?'

'Would you?' she asked, no longer troubled by my outburst. 'Cool!'

Georgie raced out of the room with Nat hard on her heels.

'Okay, so how do you plan to do it?' I said, turning to Ally.

'No probs. I ... well, *we* go down to the Scorpions' clubrooms, and I'll go in on my own and explain the situation. If I can't go on the tour, then we just go back home.'

'But what if he does recognise you?'

Ally shrugged. 'I guess I'll just skedaddle.'

'Yeah, and hope that Smale doesn't —'

'Toby, Smale will be occupied with the other people there. I'm going to be hanging around at first, like I just happened to be there. Then, if he does recognise me, we haven't given anything away. He'll simply tell me to run away.'

'And you will?'

'And I will.'

Georgie and Ally had the evening all planned. I headed to Georgie's house at 8.30 to 'watch a DVD'. Ally had made a similar arrangement, while Georgie was supposedly going over to Ally's. We all hopped on our bikes and rode towards the Scorpions' ground. Ally looked completely different. Her long dark hair was now bunched up on her head, and her eyes appeared darker. Maybe it was the make-up. She had neat-looking clothes on and seemed taller and older.

'You can stop staring at her,' Georgie hissed as we rode onto the street.

'I'm not!'

'Not what?' Ally called from in front.

'Totally preoccupied with the game tomorrow,' Georgie finished with a grin.

There were lights on at the Scorpions' rooms and four vehicles in the car park when we arrived.

'If he does look suspicious straight away,' Georgie said, 'just say you came back because you left your hat or something here.'

'Okay.' Ally leaned her bike up against the cemetery fence that ran behind the car park 'Will you wait for me?'

'If you're not back in 15 minutes, we'll assume you made it in.' Georgie looked at me.

'Which means it should be about an hour at the most before you're back,' I added.

'Hopefully not more,' Georgie grimaced.

I had a thought. 'Ally, listen! If it does look like you're going on this trip, see if you can sneak out just for a moment and tell us where you're going. That way, if there's any trouble, I —'

'We!' Georgie interrupted.

'*We* can come and help you.'

Georgie and I wheeled the bicycles behind a nearby old scout hall and sat down on the grass to wait. I guess we both expected Ally to be back pretty quickly, but after 10 minutes of chatting about the grand final and what might happen tomorrow, our conversation dried up as we thought of Ally and what might be happening.

'Should we go and take a look?' I asked.

Georgie nodded. 'If they've gone there'll be no one there anyway.'

There were fewer lights on in the clubrooms now, only a glow from a room behind Smale's office. We hadn't been in there before. All the outside doors and windows appeared to be locked, except for one window that was open just a few centimetres.

We crept over to the open window, freezing when we heard a man's voice.

'Brilliant!' someone exclaimed, and there was the sound of hands clapping.

'He must be showing them something,' I whispered. 'Maybe the scorecard?' I edged away from the building.

But Georgie wasn't listening. She'd picked up a piece of paper that had been half-pushed out from beneath the main door.

'Brisbane, 19 ...' Georgie stopped reading and looked up at me.

'What?' I said, snatching the paper from her.

'Toby!'

'Brisbane, 1960. Tied Test,' I read aloud. Ally had already been there. This was a disaster. I turned to Georgie.

'I know, I know,' she groaned. 'It was a slight chance.'

'*Slight* chance?'

'Well don't you get so high and mighty,' Georgie fired back. '*You* took her there. *You* knew as well as anyone else.'

We both paused, breathing heavily, staring at each other. I couldn't remember Georgie and me ever fighting before. Not once had we had a cross word for each other.

Georgie closed her eyes and sighed. 'Toby, we're not going to get anywhere standing here arguing. What will we do?'

519

'The problem is we don't know if she's in any trouble. She may be fine. If there's enough distance or time between her two selves ... oh, hell!'

'What?'

'When I took her to the game — it was near the end, obviously — there was something wrong ...'

'Toby, there's always something wrong with us when we go back in time. Rahul in India. Jimbo, watching his dad. And Jay! God, remember what he did down in Hobart?'

'No, this was different. Ally was really scared. She kept looking around, and she said something about someone calling her name.'

'Smale?'

I shrugged. 'I dunno. Maybe.'

Georgie pulled a pencil from her pocket and scrawled a note on the back of the one Ally had written.

'And how will we get that to her?' I asked.

'I'll just put it on her bike. We've got to try something.'

I sat down with my back against the brick wall of the clubrooms and watched Georgie walk along the fence line to the bikes leaning against the scout hall.

'Maybe we should give it a few more minutes?' I said, looking at my watch as she returned.

'How long has it been?' Georgie asked.

'Well, we don't know how long they've been away,' I replied, 'but it's nearly half past nine. Let's give it a few more minutes.'

While we waited, we checked out the cars parked nearby and paced around the clubrooms.

'Toby!' Georgie whispered, beckoning me over to the open window. She had pushed a section of curtain to one side, and I put my head next to hers and listened.

'They're back.' She spoke softly.

'Or they haven't gone yet. Can you see Ally?'

Holding up a hand, Georgie shook her head. There didn't seem to be the excitement in the room that we'd heard earlier.

'But what about Colin?' someone said, his voice rising above the others. A door banged shut.

'There's something wrong,' Georgie said, looking worried and backing away from the window.

'What?' I leaned in closer, trying to hear what was happening. I heard a few more shouts before Georgie grabbed at my sleeve. Something was about to happen. Crouching, we ran back to the fence, then along the side of the cemetery, to our bikes.

'We shouldn't have let her go, Toby,' Georgie said, slamming her helmet on and grabbing her bike. 'Let's go down to the end of the street and wait a few minutes.'

'I'd love to know what's happened,' I said.

'C'mon, Ally. Where *are* you?' she screamed into the wind as we tore off down the road.

'Guys!' came a shout from behind, just as the words left Georgie's lips.

We braked hard and swung our bikes around, amazed to hear Ally's voice. She was riding hard, trying to catch up with us.

Georgie dropped her bike and gave her a hug. We walked our bikes home, not only because it was dark and Ally was out of breath, but so we could hear the whole story before we got there.

In 1926, Clarrie Grimmett — playing for South Australia against New South Wales — had 394 runs scored from his bowling. This is the most runs scored off a bowler during a match in Australia, however his haul of 10 wickets (4 for 192 in the first innings and 6 for 202 in the second) was a great achievement.

18 Back to Brisbane

ONCE Ally began retelling her adventure, the words poured out like a torrent. She was still wound up by all the excitement.

'Guys, I was so nervous I thought Phillip Smale would hear my heart pounding, but I walked straight up to him and said G'day, because my disguise was pretty good and I knew I had to act like I was meant to be there.'

'And he didn't recognise you?' I asked as we picked our way carefully along the dim footpath.

'No. He just said, "Don't be ridiculous. I'm not taking any children. This isn't a game, you know."' Ally smiled. 'But one thing I didn't tell you guys, is that I'd typed up a fake letter from my "Dad", saying why he'd sent me along in his place.'

'Hey, that's a good idea,' Georgie said.

'Smale didn't want to look at it at first,' Ally continued, 'but when he read how much money my

"Dad" was offering, he decided it was okay for me to go — as long as I stayed in the background and didn't bug him.

'Then he got us all together, sitting on a big couch. There were two other men there, as well as a lady. Smale had this big screen set up, and he gave a speech, saying why we were all there. He'd asked one of the guys, Rick, along because he was a businessman; the other guy, Colin, because he'd worked in theatre and stuff; and the lady, Davina, because she knew the media.'

'And what about Mr Walters — Jessica's dad?' I asked. 'Why had he been chosen?'

'Apparently he's a really well-known guy in banking. I didn't really know what Smale was talking about, so I just nodded and played along.

'Anyway, then he showed a bit of the Tied Test on the big screen. The others didn't know what was going on, and they were pretty annoyed that he'd got them all there just to show them an old cricket match. That's when I slipped away to leave you the note — I said I was going to the toilet but I don't think Smale heard me, because he was too busy trying to calm everyone down.

'When I got back he asked us all to hold hands while he fiddled around with a *Wisden* and an old scorecard. It must have been that magic one, Toby, because the next thing I knew we were in Brisbane in 1960.'

'What happened when you got there?' Georgie said. 'How did they all react?'

'Well, at first they didn't realise that they'd gone back in time. They thought it was some kind of virtual reality. Then as it started to sink in, the guy called Rick started to freak out — he looked really frightened and turned white. Davina stayed calm, but the other guy, Colin, was so excited, until Smale told him they wouldn't be staying to watch one of the most famous overs ever played.'

'I bet he didn't like that,' I murmured.

'Smale tried to tell us all to stay put, but Colin ignored him and ran off into the crowd because he didn't want to leave. Smale spent about 20 minutes trying to find him, but he'd disappeared.

'And that was it. The rest of us came back and I got out of there as quickly as I could ... Oh, I almost forgot! Toby, you know that Master Blaster thing you guys played down at the shopping centre?' Ally added, as we reached her front gate.

'The virtual cricket?' I said.

'Yeah, well you were right, Toby. It was there in the clubrooms. I reckon Phillip Smale has bought that too.'

'Bought or stolen?' Georgie said, looking at me. 'And what about Alistair? Have you rung yet?'

'Yep, I finally got through, but the person who answered said he's out of town for the next few days and they're not sure when he's due back.'

'So, it's just as we thought,' Georgie said. 'Smale's going to open up a business.'

'Yeah, and it looks like he's gathering a few people around him to help out,' Ally said.

'Like that Davina woman?' Georgie asked.

'Yep.'

'But not Colin,' I muttered.

'Do you reckon Smale will go back and rescue him?' Georgie said.

'He was going to leave Scott, remember?' I answered. 'I wouldn't trust Phillip Smale.'

'I agree,' said Ally. 'We get the scorecard now and we kill this once and for all.'

Georgie and I looked at each other.

'How long have we got before Colin is in serious trouble?' I asked.

Georgie looked at her watch. 'An hour? Hour and a half, tops.'

'Okay,' I said, my mind racing. 'I'm going to get Jim and his car. You two, go home and grab your mobiles, then come back here and let me know what's happening. Stay down, but watch to see if Colin returns. Keep an eye on the cars, okay?'

'Have you got yours?' Ally asked, as I hopped onto my bike.

'My what?' I called.

'Your mobile!'

I pulled it out of my pocket and held it up behind me as I sped off.

Ten minutes later, just as I pulled up in front of Jim's, it rang.

'Anything happening?' I asked.

'Toby, all the cars have gone and the lights are all out,' Georgie said. 'We reckon he's packed up and gone.'

'He must have gone home. I'm going to head over there with Jim. We've got to nail this. Especially as that guy is stuck in Brisbane and I can't go back to get him because I've been there before.'

'That's why we need the scorecard, isn't it?' Georgie said.

'Yep. It's gonna have to be you, Georgie.'

'Okay, we'll meet you over there —'

'No! You guys stay low. I'll get back to you.'

'Hey,' Georgie cried, sounding annoyed. 'Since when —'

'Georgie. Just me and Jim, alright?' There was a pause. 'George?'

'Yeah, fine,' she mumbled.

Jim was delighted to see me and even more delighted to be getting back into Pixie, which was surprising.

'I thought you agreed it was a good idea to take a break from all this till the game was over,' I said, as we reversed out of his garage.

'Indeed I did, Toby. Indeed I did. But *carpe diem*, my boy.'

'*Carpe diem?*'

'Seize the day, Toby. Strike while the iron's hot.' Jim was raving on but he was genuinely excited. I just hoped not too excited — Jim was having adventures

527

that most people his age wouldn't want to know about. 'At least your mind isn't stuck on the game,' he added.

That was one good spin on all this, I realised.

As we drove to Smale's place I outlined the evening's events.

'So, this Colin chap is still at large in Brisbane?' Jim said, frowning.

I nodded.

'Dear oh dear,' he murmured, accelerating a little.

'I bet I know whose car that is,' I said, pointing to one parked outside Smale's house as we drew up to the kerb.

'One of Ally's travelling partners?' Jim suggested.

I nodded.

'I think we should simply take the direct approach, Toby. Straight to the front door.'

I followed a few paces behind Jim as he marched up the path and knocked on the door.

'Who is it?' a woman's voice called, a moment later.

'Jim Oldfield.'

'Are you a friend of Phillip's?' There was no sign of the front door being opened. Maybe this was Davina. I took out my phone and dialled Ally, moving a few steps away from the house.

'Ally? What was that Davina lady wearing?' I whispered into the phone.

'Um, grey trousers and a white shirt. Why?'

'There's a lady in Smale's house and, hang on ...'

Jim was walking back towards me. 'It appears our friend Phillip is out for the evening,' he said.

'I'll call you back, Ally,' I said, snapping the phone closed. 'Now what?'

'I'm not exactly sure,' Jim replied.

We both turned at the sound of shouting.

'Let's try the back,' I urged, setting off around the side of the house. 'The door's open,' I whispered to Jim, who arrived a few moments after me. I eased it open further and then we were inside.

Jim put a finger to his lips as we snuck into the kitchen. There were voices coming from the next room — Smale's and the woman's.

'A partnership,' Smale was pleading. 'You don't know how to operate the scorecard anyway,' he continued. Their voices stopped. Jim and I stepped cautiously back, away from the door. Suddenly it burst open. Phillip Smale stood there, glaring at us.

'You interfering old man,' he growled, moving towards Jim. I stepped in front of him, reaching into my pocket at the same time. 'Get out of my way, you snivelling little boy!' He pushed me to one side. I opened the phone, carefully felt for the second number along, and pressed it. It was the autodial number for Ally's mobile.

'Davina, call the police,' Smale shouted through the kitchen door.

'Yes, do that,' Jim said. 'I'm sure they will assist Toby and me to get back what is rightfully ours.'

'What are you raving on about?' Smale said.

Jim was standing upright and perfectly at ease beside the table. 'The scorecard, of course,' he replied firmly, not taking his eyes off Smale.

My heart was racing, and, I guessed, despite his outward calm, so was Jim's.

'Jim, maybe we should just leave,' I whispered.

'Not this time, sonny,' Smale said.

'Are you a friend of Jessica's?' Davina asked, coming to the door, a phone in her hand.

'Who?'

'You heard me.'

'I don't know any Jessica,' I said, trying to sound calm.

'Just ring the bloody police,' Smale said, his anger rising.

'I'm not sure that's such a good idea,' she replied, eyeing Jim closely. 'What do you know about this scorecard?'

'Quite a bit,' Jim said. 'It was sent to me, you see —'

'Don't listen to this senile old fool,' Smale hissed, grabbing the phone from her. 'He's talking through his hat.'

'Might I sit down, please?' Jim asked, pulling out a chair.

'Of course you may.' Davina sat down too.

'Oh, for heaven's sake,' cried Phillip. 'Do you want me to do tea and biscuits?'

Jim looked up and smiled sweetly. 'What a splendid idea, Phillip. It's just like old times.'

Smale, looking furious, stormed out of the room.

'Old times?' Davina asked.

Jim explained his connection with Phillip at the MCC library and how Smale had come to know about the scorecard. Davina, who had formally introduced herself, got up and made us all a drink while Jim continued his story.

'Jim, perhaps we should go,' I said to him as he gratefully sipped the tea Davina had given him.

Suddenly the house was plunged into darkness. Jim and I reached out at the same time, grabbing hold of each other. I heard Davina shoot up like a cat and dart into the hallway.

'Phillip?' she called.

'Let's go, Jim,' I said, guiding him towards the back door.

'Toby, we need that scorecard. I feel that now is our best chance.' His voice was desperate and he seemed to be breathing heavily.

'Then I'll go. You head outside and wait in Pixie.'

'No!' he said firmly. 'Come on. This is it.'

So we crept back through the kitchen, groping for the doorway leading to the hall. Then the lights came back on. We searched the house, but there was so sign of Smale.

'Toby?' a voice called from outside. It was Georgie.

I ran to the front door and opened it to find Georgie and Ally standing there.

'Is everything okay?' Ally asked. 'We just got this garbled sort of —'

'Oh, yeah,' I said, pulling out my mobile and switching it off. 'Things hotted up in there for a moment so I opened up the line.'

We headed back inside. Davina and Jim were in a small room, obviously Smale's study, staring at a row of *Wisden*s.

'He's gone,' Jim sighed, turning as we entered.

'What the —?' Davina said, her eyes narrowing.

'Oh,' Ally said, giving her a small wave. 'Hi!'

'Jessica! So, you two *do* know each other.' She looked at me coldly.

I ignored her. 'Jim, we have another problem,' I said, turning to him.

'Oh?' He picked up a 1960 *Wisden* from the desk. But as he leafed through it, it dropped onto the desk in front of him, caught the edge and fell to the floor. I couldn't believe that Jim would drop a book, especially a cricket book — and a *Wisden* at that.

One moment he was standing there, the next he'd fallen to his knees and his face had gone deathly white.

'Toby!' Georgie gasped, rushing forwards.

'Jim?' I whispered, panicking, dropping down beside him.

'Stand back,' Davina said, crisply. 'Jessica, call triple zero. You,' she said, nodding at Georgie, 'run out and check the house number. Toby, get some water. Quickly!'

As we all left the room my mind was blank. I knew Jim wasn't well, but his collapse was such a shock.

Georgie was giving Ally the address for the ambulance as I returned with a glass of water.

'Leave it there,' Davina said, not turning round. 'Now off you go.'

'But I can't —'

'I said off you go. I know what I'm doing.'

'But what's happened?' I asked, as I stared at Jim lying on the floor.

'It's hard to say. Perhaps he's had a mild heart attack, or he may just have fainted. His breathing's quite steady and his pulse is rapid and fluttery but not weak. That's a good sign. But I suggest you leave now, before the cavalry arrives.'

'The cavalry?' Georgie asked from the doorway.

'I'm expecting the ambulance *and* the police,' she said. Gently she settled a cushion beneath Jim's head.

'Come on,' said Ally, glancing at her watch. 'We're way over time.'

I walked over to Jim and gave his old hand a squeeze while Davina fussed with something nearby. Suddenly I felt a firm hand grip my wrist; I looked at his face. One eye gleamed and the other winked. I felt another squeeze and then he let go as Davina turned back to him.

I hurried out of the house after Ally and Georgie, telling them that I thought Jim was just fine.

'What?' Georgie said.

'I think he was just making sure we were out of the way when the police came. Smale's onto us big time.'

'I'd rather arrive home on my own feet than in the back of a police car,' Ally said, starting to run.

When Shane Warne claimed the wicket of Marcus Trescothick in the Third Test of the 2005 Ashes series, Warne became the first bowler to take 600 Test wickets. He achieved this remarkable record in his 126th Test match.

19 So Close

Sunday — morning

SUNDAY morning was bright and sunny. I headed back to the Scorpions' ground, this time in the family car. Jim was right — the distractions of the night before had kept me from worrying about the game. I just hoped that Jim really was okay. What if the wink had just been a blink? No, it can't have been.

I felt surprisingly fresh as I stroked Mr Pasquali's practice deliveries neatly back to him.

'It's time to play the innings of your life, Toby,' he said, grinning. 'I'll be out there with you, though there's not much I can do. Good luck and enjoy it.'

Watching Scott Craven warming up was making that very hard to do, but I was determined to stay positive, play my shots and see what happened. Isn't that what the Aussie team did when it was in a corner? Those players didn't shrivel up and die; they stayed calm and confident, believing in their ability to get themselves out of strife.

And after four overs my confidence was sky high. I'd played Scott with the full face of the bat, picking off occasional singles and even a four that whistled past point and down to the fence.

'It'll come, Scotto,' the Scorpions players kept calling out.

'Not if I can help it,' I muttered under my breath. Every ball was a new challenge. I was doing it for Jim; I was doing it for Dad; I was doing it for Riverwall and my team-mates sitting on the boundary. And I was doing it for myself.

We hadn't made many runs and we'd lost Cameron and Rahul (who had been promoted in the order ahead of Jimbo), but when Mr Pasquali called for drinks, I finally looked up at the scoreboard.

Jones, 28 not out. Jimbo was on 7 and the overall score was 3 for 62.

'Job one: make them bat again,' Jimbo said, taking a drink. 'Job two: make them worry. It's you and me, Toby.'

Scott bowled two more overs after the break, but his pace had dropped. We still played him with respect, but the Scorpions sensed we were playing it safe and waiting for the next bowler. They spread the field out more, but Jimbo and I were able to knock up ones and twos with much more ease.

I looked over at Mr Pasquali at one point. He nodded, gently tapping his temple with one finger. I knew what he meant: play smart and don't get sucked in and try to score big fours and sixes.

By lunch we'd taken the score along to 3 for 131. The game had changed.

'Scott will resume after lunch,' Mr Pasquali said to Jimbo and me while munching on a chicken sandwich. 'Put that entire morning out of your head and start again. The job is *not* done, you hear?'

We both nodded.

The rest of the team left us alone — no one wanted to break the spell that had come over the game. Even Jay, usually always on for a chat, kept his distance.

Scott Craven did come back on and he bowled as fast as I'd ever seen him. Jimbo was struck on the helmet when he tried a hook shot, but he stood his ground, hardly flinching. Scott walked up close to him, but Jimbo just turned away to adjust his helmet.

The next ball was in the same spot but this time Jimbo was onto it. He smashed it magnificently over backward square leg. It crashed into a huge gum tree about halfway up the trunk then dropped onto the gravel road beneath, along with a dead branch.

The yelling and cheering from the boundary and the sense of excitement amongst the spectators was in total contrast to the mood on the field. The Scorpions were struggling, and they weren't used to that. It was the most critical time of the game.

Jimbo and I pressed on, scoring another 44 runs before I got out. It was getting too easy and I lost concentration, lazily wafting my bat at a ball pitched well outside off-stump. It caught the bottom edge and cannoned back into the stumps. I'd made 71 — my highest score ever!

Jimbo went on to make 91 but, as in the first innings, our batting performance fell away quickly. We lost our last seven wickets for only about 60 more runs. But we were in with a chance, and when Mr Pasquali told us that the whisper around the ground was that the Scorpions might be 'chasing the outright', I felt our chance of success was even greater.

We'd finished with 234 runs and the Scorpions needed 147 for an outright win.

'They don't *have* to get the runs, do they?' Martian asked, adjusting his hat. The sun was getting higher and the temperature was rising.

'Oh, no,' Mr Pasquali said. 'They just have to survive — then they win the game on the results of the first innings. But somehow I don't think they'll settle for that.'

'How many overs are left, Mr P?'

'We have to bowl 38,' he replied.

'Less if we get them all out,' I said, catching the new ball that Mr Pasquali tossed to me.

He smiled. 'Exactly.'

By the time Scott Craven marched to the crease, the game was evenly poised, with the Scorpions at 4/81. They'd held Scott back, maybe hoping to get well towards the target before bringing him on. Their scoring rate was down a bit: at the start of the innings they'd needed just under four runs an over to win. Now, with 15 overs left, they needed 4.3.

We were able to pick up wickets at fairly regular intervals, but Scott was like a rock. There were no fireworks from him, just careful batting and good placement of the ball.

With two overs to go the Scorpions were 8/134, and Scott was in control. We brought the fielders in, hoping to keep their number 10 batter on strike. He didn't score off any of Rahul's first three balls, but nicked the fourth past gully for a single. Then Scott blocked Rahul's last two deliveries.

I took the ball for the last over of the match — the last over of the season. Jono and I had a long talk about the field before settling on three slips, a gully, point, cover, short mid-off, short mid-wicket and a fine leg. It was a stacked off-side field.

Scott ambled down and said a few words to his partner before returning to the non-striker's end.

I looked at the spot on the pitch I was aiming for, then strode in to the wicket.

The batter pushed across his crease, expecting a ball on or outside his off-stump even before I'd bowled. It was exactly what I was hoping he'd do, and instead I bowled a fast yorker that smacked into the bottom of his leg stump.

Scott swore, tossing his bat to the ground. They were 9/135.

We were one wicket away from winning the championship, but the Scorpions needed to survive five balls.

I pitched the next delivery right on middle stump. Their number 11 batter pushed at it, spooning the ball back towards me. I lunged desperately but it was dropping fast. I flung out my left hand, aware that as he flashed past me Scott was screaming at the other guy to run. I got a fingertip to the ball, nothing more. It trickled harmlessly down the pitch as the batters completed their run.

Had I just dropped the championship trophy?

There were just four balls left and now Scott was on strike. The Scorpions were eight runs away from an outright victory.

I brushed down my pants and told Jono that I wanted a change in the field. Maybe I should tempt Scott — what was there to lose? I beckoned to Jason, who was at fine leg, to come squarer, and moved Jimbo out of third slip to mid-wicket, about 15 metres off the boundary. Scott looked on nonchalantly, resting on his bat.

'Come on, Toby, let's have him!' Georgie yelled.

I banged the third ball in short. Scott seemed to be in two minds, but at the last moment he pulled out of a hook shot and the ball sailed through to Ally.

I did exactly the same with the next ball and this time Scott was onto it, belting it way over Jimbo's head.

The tense silence of the last few minutes was broken by a dozen car horns blaring approval.

Suddenly the Scorpions had jumped to 142. Another four would tie the game but give the Scorpions the championship because of their higher first innings total.

'Do you want to make a change?' Jono asked me from the slips.

I shook my head. What would Scott expect? Another short one? Could he afford to risk a hook shot? I watched him from the top of my run-up before checking the field, and Jimbo out at mid-wicket in particular.

'Jimbo,' I called. 'Move round five?' With my hand, I indicated that he should come closer to mid-on. This might create some doubt in the batter's mind. It was my only chance.

I ran in hard to bowl the second last ball of the game. It was short again, but wider outside the off-stump. Sure enough, Scott went for it, trying to pull it square. It caught the end of the bat and flew away towards third man. All the slips raced after it, Jono eventually hauling it in, only centimetres from the boundary.

The batters had run three, which put Scott up at my end and the Scorpions on 9 for 145.

Our eyes met as I brushed past him. 'It's not over yet,' I said quietly.

'As good as,' he sneered, tearing off his gloves. He knew he'd stuffed up in going for that third run. Scott walked down and spoke to the number 11, who looked nervous and was fidgeting with his pads and helmet.

Meanwhile, Jono and I brought every fielder in closer, to try and stop them getting a single.

An eerie silence settled over the ground as I waited at the top of my mark. There were even some cars that had pulled over — maybe the drivers had noticed the larger than normal crowd for a junior cricket match, or maybe they were just curious. People out walking their dogs had stopped to look, and a bunch of kids over on the playground had crept closer during the last few overs. I noticed an old man standing just to one side of a tree way past fine leg. Somehow he looked familiar — he looked very much like Jim.

I looked down at the ball in my hand, positioned the seam upright, and charged in. As the ball left my hand I watched it sail through the air, on a perfect line outside off-stump. The batter swung at it, cross-batted and connected. I dived full-stretch to my right, knocking the ball down.

Scott had charged out of his crease, thinking the ball had gone past me. 'Run, idiot!' he yelled, before realising that I was gathering up the ball.

'No!' the other guy yelled, holding up a hand. Scott stopped dead and scrambled round desperately. Still kneeling on the ground, I backhanded the ball at the stumps. Scott dived for the line, his bat reaching out, as the ball smacked into the off-stump.

The whole Riverwall team roared in appeal.

Mr Pasquali grimaced, then slowly nodded and raised his right index finger to the sky.

542

Scott swore and smashed his bat into the ground. There was a horrible cracking sound. For a moment the shouts, cheers and car horns all stopped; then they started up again — even louder this time.

I'd run Scott out by about half a metre. I lay back on the grass in sheer relief as my Riverwall teammates rushed towards me.

Glenn McGrath was the last Australian to take a hat trick in a Test match. He achieved this feat in Perth against the West Indies in 2000. In all, eight Australians have taken hat tricks, and Thomas (Jimmy) Matthews and Hugh Trumble have each taken two. Matthews bagged his hat tricks on the same day in 1912, but in different innings!

20 Trouble for Ally

Sunday — afternoon

MR Pasquali interrupted the post-game celebrations to announce that the awards presentation would not be taking place at the Scorpions' clubrooms. Georgie caught my eye.

'No one can find our manager,' one of their players told us.

'Mr Smale?' Ally asked.

'Yeah. He's just vanished. He hasn't been seen all day. He's the only one with the keys.'

'Toby!' Dad called, waving frantically. He was holding a mobile phone to his ear.

'Is it Jim?' I shouted, racing over to him.

Dad nodded.

'Jim?' I said into the phone. 'Are you okay?'

'Hello, my boy. I'm on the mend. Peter has told me all about your exploits today.'

'I think someone's got a video of the game. Maybe we can watch it together?'

'Perhaps I'll get along to see some of the game one day,' he chuckled. The image of the man behind the tree flashed into my mind.

'Jim! I think —'

'Listen, Toby. There's another matter you need to attend to, and without the scorecard only you can do it.'

I knew Jim was talking about the man left behind in Brisbane. 'But Smale's disappeared,' I said, moving away from Dad. 'Maybe he's gone back to get Colin?'

'Absolutely not,' Jim answered quickly. 'He has other problems to deal with.'

'What problems?' I asked. 'And anyway, we've run out of time. Remember, you've only got two hours when you go back into the past.'

'Two hours, yes, then slowly the body starts to fade. All this is true.' Jim's voice had become so soft I could barely hear him. 'But the fading process takes a while.'

'How long?'

'It varies. It depends on your age, your degree of fitness, how far away from your own time you've travelled, whether you're the carrier or being carried ... many things.' Jim was silent a moment. 'Toby. It is time to destroy the scorecard and stop our travels. I have promised Peter that I will come and live with you. But you must promise me that after this final travel, we will both stop our journeys. We will focus on the present and the future.'

'Jim?' I said, after a pause.

545

'Yes, Toby?'

I took a deep breath. 'I agree,' I said firmly.

'Good. You'll have to take young Ally with you, but make sure you hold her hand, all right?'

'Yes, Jim —'

'And don't you let go.'

After I hung up the phone I wondered if Jim could have time-travelled to my game. It didn't seem likely. An international one-dayer was being played in Melbourne today, but it wasn't in any *Wisden* — not yet, anyway.

Perhaps he'd simply gotten out of his sick bed and come to the game in Pixie.

Mum and Dad were determined to make up for the disappointment of the presentation night being cancelled, so they'd invited the whole team, including Mr Pasquali, back to our house for a party. On our way home we'd made a brief detour to the shops for supplies — it was going to be a big night.

Half the team had already arrived, and the rest were on their way. We were watching the last half hour of Australia's innings in the one-dayer when the news came on the telly.

'Peter, quick!' Mum called, standing at the door. A few moments later Dad arrived in time to hear the report.

'And although police are drawing no links yet between the two, local film director and arts administrator Colin Dempsey is also missing.'

The camera showed a woman standing in front of her house, clutching two sobbing children. *'He left last night. He was only going to be away an hour,'* she explained, sounding desperate. *'Colin,'* the woman pleaded, staring into the camera, *'whatever is troubling you, please come back.'*

'Anyone with information . . .'

I didn't wait to hear any more. Ally sprang up and rushed out of the room, so I followed her out the back.

'Are you okay?' I asked.

Mum arrived a moment later. 'Ally, is everything all right, dear?'

She nodded. 'Sorry, Mrs Jones. It's j . . . just that —'

'Ally thought she recognised one of the kids,' I explained. 'We'll be back in a tick.'

Georgie slipped past Mum, who was heading back to the lounge.

'Come on,' I said. 'Let's do it.'

'Go to Brisbane?' Ally said, wiping the tears from her eyes.

I nodded.

'But Ally can't go,' Georgie said. 'And nor can you. You've been —'

'Ally has to go and so do I.' Turning, I bounded up the stairs to get the *Wisden*, the girls following. 'She's the only one who can recognise Colin, and we don't have the scorecard so I have to go. Georgie, you're going to have to cover for us. Hopefully, we won't be long.'

'But, listen,' Georgie said. 'He's already dead. It's been almost a day.'

'It won't be once we get there.' I opened the *Wisden*. 'Ally, we'll do this just like last time.' I held my hand out to her.

Georgie cursed quietly and left.

'Here,' Ally said, guiding my finger to the page.

'It's a two,' I breathed.

'Yes,' she whispered, gripping my hand tighter.

It happened so quickly. It was getting faster and faster each time I travelled. We tumbled gently onto a stretch of grass. We both turned to look at the scoreboard.

'Okay, we've arrived a little bit after our last visit, but not by much. Keep your head down, and don't let go of my hand, okay?' But she wasn't listening. 'Ally!'

'Toby, oh, my God! There he is!'

'Ally, no!' I yelled as she burst away from me, running towards a group of people closer to the fence. 'Ally, stop!'

Then everything went into slow motion. I heard her call Colin's name, and a guy slowly turned towards us. He looked deathly pale. I could almost see through him. He tried to stand up, but stumbled, pitching forwards onto his face. No one around seemed to notice. Were they too interested in the game? Or had he already disappeared from their reality?

But I really began to panic when I noticed Ally falter. As I ran towards Colin I watched in horror as Ally started floating sideways, faster and faster.

548

She turned to look at me, and her face was distorted in bewilderment and pain. I don't think I will ever forget her look of terror as this incredible force took her away.

She had flown 30 metres when suddenly, as if she'd hit some invisible wall, she collapsed.

I grabbed Colin's arm, urging him to get up. 'Please,' I cried, hauling him to his feet. 'C'mon, you're about to die!'

'W ... who are you?' he said, his voice shaky and weak.

'I'll explain later. Please!' I dragged Colin towards Ally, who was lying by a bench. 'If we get away before the last ball, everything will be okay.'

Everyone we passed was glued to the action out in the middle. The final over was unfolding, the last ball about to be delivered.

'Ally?' I said urgently, bending down and shaking her. 'Ally?'

Someone turned to look at us, but quickly looked back to the game as screams and shouts broke out around us. The action on the field had everyone's attention.

I made sure I had a hold of Colin, then took Ally's hand and recited the final lines of the poem, worrying that I hadn't been either calm or clever.

> *Respect this gift. Stay calm, stay clever,*
> *And let the years live on forever.*

We arrived back in my bedroom. It was empty. I opened the door to find Rahul, Jimbo, Jay and Georgie sitting on the stairs. They all jumped up at the sight of me.

'Rahul and Jay, quick! Get this guy home,' I said as Colin staggered to the door. 'Remember the bus in India? He's got the same problem, though way more advanced. Jimbo, you be on the look-out.'

'Where's Ally?' Georgie said, pushing past me as the others snuck down the stairs.

Ally lay on the floor behind me; she hadn't moved. She was breathing evenly, but slowly. Her face was pale and she looked like she was a million miles away.

'Something's happened to her,' I said. 'I need to talk to Jim.'

'Sounds like he's just coming up,' Georgie said, racing out of the room. She came back a moment later with Jim in tow.

I closed my eyes, took a deep breath and explained what had happened. 'Jim?' I said, after pouring out the whole story. 'Say something, Jim. What is it? What's happened? Will she be okay?'

Jim stooped down beside Ally. He looked deeply concerned. 'I ... I'm not sure,' he said.

'But she's just asleep —'

'Food's ready guys!' Mum called from the bottom of the stairs.

Georgie and I looked at each other. I felt sick to the core.

'Coming in a tick, Mrs Jones,' Georgie shouted, trying to sound cheerful, as Jimbo poked his head around the door.

'How did it go?' I asked.

'Fine. That guy was hugely relieved to be back. He knew where he was and he had his keys on him, so he decided to walk to where his car is parked. We told him that he must have blacked out or something.'

'So he was heading to the Scorpions' ground?' Georgie looked over at Jimbo.

He nodded. 'Is Ally okay?'

'Not sure,' I said. 'Jimbo, grab the others and get them downstairs for a feed. Tell Mum we've just ducked out to Georgie's, but we'll be back in 10, okay?' Maybe Ally will have recovered in that time.

'Got it,' Jimbo said and headed out.

'I'll go too, but I'll be back soon,' Jim said quietly. 'I've just checked her pulse; she's in no danger,' he added.

I wondered if that comment was more for our benefit.

Georgie and I moved Ally to the bed, then sat and talked quietly for 15 minutes until Jim returned. We were both teary by the time he gently knocked and pushed the door open.

'They're all watching the video of the game, but you're not starring yet, Toby,' he said smiling. He walked over to the bed and sat down beside Ally, taking her hand and pressing it to his cheek.

'Jim?' Georgie croaked, looking from him to Ally.

'There is going to be one more adventure after all,' he said, slowly shaking his head. 'And I'm afraid this one will be very dangerous.' Very gently he placed Ally's hand on her stomach.

'*Another* adventure? W ... what? I stuttered, catching my breath. 'Where, Jim?'

'To Lord's, Toby. To the home of cricket. To Father Time.'

'Father Time?' Georgie's head shot up and we glanced at each other.

'Ally is not well. She will wake up soon but she will be very tired, very distant and very vague. She needs our help — and soon.'

'How soon?' I whispered, looking at her peaceful face. 'What's happening to her?'

Jim sighed. 'Come along,' he said, standing. 'You did what you had to do. Ally was the only person who could take you to that man, and you have saved his life.' He put an arm on each of our shoulders. 'Let's make her comfortable.'

Georgie gently placed a pillow under Ally's head and I covered her with my doona.

'Most appropriate,' Jim chuckled, eyeing the cricket scene on it.

All I could think of was an Aussie flag being draped over the coffin of a returning soldier.

'Come along, Toby. I promise you that there is no more to be done right now. Ally is resting. Take a break, you've both earned it.'

We walked slowly to the door.

'A part of her was lost after her first visit to Brisbane, wasn't it, Jim?' I thought of some catches she'd dropped, and times when she'd looked tired. It was so unlike Ally. 'And now more of her has gone ...'

'What do you mean more of her?' Georgie asked. 'More of what?'

'Her spirit, Georgie. Her life. Her will to live.' Jim paused. 'Everything that is Ally: her memories, alertness, vigour, motivation and enthusiasm — her will. She is very vulnerable in this state. We must watch over her carefully.'

'But why Ally?' I asked. 'What about me? I'm not suffering like she is, and I've seen myself in the past.'

'You have, Toby, but you're stronger. After all, you have the gift. No, there's something else going on here, something out of Ally's control. But I'm sure we have got her back in time,' Jim added, trying to sound more cheeful.

Downstairs we joined the rest of the group, who were cheering every wicket of the last session. Georgie and I picked at our food, pretending to be cheerful. Rahul, Jimbo and Jay kept on giving us meaningful looks that we politely ignored. When someone asked about Ally, we simply explained that she was resting upstairs, which was accepted as others had commented that she didn't seem herself.

'She's probably caught that nasty bug that's going around,' Mum said, passing out plates of chocolate cake.

553

'Well, well!' Dad said suddenly, 'Speak of the devil.'

There was Ally, standing at the door to the hallway. She smiled tentatively and, after a moment of hesitation, walked over to the couch where Georgie and I were sitting.

'Room for me?' she whispered, snuggling between us.

'Always,' Georgie said with a smile, putting an arm around her.

At that moment, I think I loved Georgie almost as much as cricket.

'Jim?' Dad said, staring at the TV. 'That's not you over there skulking behind that gum tree, is it? Who's got the remote? Jimbo, hit the rewind button.'

Everyone leaned forwards.

'There!' Dad shouted.

Jimbo hit the pause button.

'You have some explaining to do to your grandson, Jim,' Dad laughed. Meanwhile, Mum and Nat had come in from the kitchen.

'Grandson?' Jim said, sounding puzzled.

'Well, any elderly bloke who gets off his sick bed to come and watch a boy play cricket is a grandfather in my book.'

I felt tears brimming, and Ally gently squeezed my hand. Jim's arms opened wide as I sprang up from the couch and rushed over to him, hugging him tight. I buried my face in his shoulder, only partly drowning out the cheers from all around me.

'Howzat!' Dad yelled, pointing at the TV.

I looked at the screen to see I'd just run out Scott Craven and won us the championship.

'Play it again!' I shouted.

Dad rewound then slowed the tape down, taking us through those final moments frame by frame.

'Geez, Toby, you only just hit the stumps,' Georgie laughed.

It was great seeing the action on TV — the video had some terrific shots of the run-out and the celebrations immediately afterwards.

'I'm sure that won't be the last time young Toby here sees himself on television performing miracles on the cricket field,' Jim said, leaning back in his chair.

'Was that the doorbell?' Mum queried, getting up and leaving the room.

'And if Toby had missed the stumps?' Mr Pasquali said, as we watched yet another replay of Scott Craven being run out.

'Scott would have made his ground and the game would have been a tie,' Jimbo said.

'Yes, and the Scorpions would have got the trophy,' Rahul added.

'Did someone mention the trophy?' Mum asked, coming back into the room. 'Look what I found!' she said, revealing a shiny object she'd been hiding behind her back.

'The trophy!' I gasped, bouncing up.

'Was anyone there?' Dad asked.

'No. Just the trophy on the doorstep and a rather flash looking car speeding away,' Mum said, shrugging.

I glanced at Georgie as I took the trophy from Mum. We both knew who had left it there. But thankfully Phillip Smale hadn't hung around. Even though we'd finished with the Scorpions I knew that we weren't done with Smale. Not yet. But Ally's problems and Jim's talk of Lord's and a final dangerous trip made Smale seem much less important.

'How about a few photos, Dad?' I said.

As the whole team, including Mr Pasquali, gathered around me, I couldn't help but grin. I knew there'd be more time-travel adventures to come, but for now I just wanted to enjoy our win.

'Everyone say "Champions",' Dad said.

We all put our hands on the trophy. 'Champions!'

Arthur Mailey has the best innings bowling figures by any Australian in a Test match. He took 9 for 121 at the MCG in the fourth game of the 1920/1921 Ashes series.

See page 603 for more details about Toby's Under-13 competition.

Brett Lee's Cricket Tips

Like Toby and his friends, I know that it takes more than one player to win a cricket match. Each team member plays an important part in helping their team do its best ... as well as having fun along the way!

BL

1 — CAPTAIN

The captain is responsible for all decisions on the field. Great captains always lead by example, and they should motivate the team as well as setting the standards for the batting, bowling and fielding.

A captain should be thinking about the game constantly, as it is important to anticipate problems in the game before they occur and make any necessary adjustments to counter them.

2 — WARM-UP

It is important that before you undertake any sport you have a solid warm-up. Work up a light sweat by completing a few light runs and then having a good stretch. This is also a chance to play a few short ball games such as fielding soccer or touch football. This will loosen your muscles and allow you more freedom during the course of your match or training session. It is a good habit to get into and you should repeat this at the end of a day's play.

3 – SETTING A FIELD

When setting a field you need to take into account the situation of the game and the conditions. If you are defending a low score then it is likely that you will be a little more defensive. On the other hand, if it is overcast and you have runs on the board then you might look to attack a little more. I normally have three slips and a gully as my attacking fieldsman. I am happy for the batsman to drive through the covers because it has them playing away from their eyeline and opening the face of the bat. This way I am more likely to get a nick to the keeper or the slips. A bowler should have a big say in setting his own field!

4 – OPENING BOWLER

Opening bowlers are given the job of getting the fielding side off on the right foot and setting up the innings. They have to bowl the correct line and length straight away without giving the batters a loose ball and, therefore, an opportunity to play a few shots and settle in. It is important to make an opening batter play as many difficult balls as possible in the first 10 overs to force mistakes and possibly get wickets.

When I am opening the bowling I ensure I make the most of the new ball. When the ball is new it is naturally harder and therefore should bounce more. It is shiny so it should swing more and travel through the air quicker. I feel this is the best time for me to take wickets so I want the batsman to have to commit to a shot every time I let one go. I have to be careful that I am not trying too hard or attempting to bowl too quick. I want to land the ball in a small area on or around the line of off-stump as this way he is hopefully in two minds as to whether to play it or let it go to the keeper. Opening bowlers have to have a 'big heart'; we have to bowl at times on flat wickets in really hot conditions, so my advice is never to give up.

5 – THE GRIP

For bowling: The ball needs to be comfortably positioned in your bowling hand. The thumb should rest towards the bottom of the ball and your index and middle fingers slightly split on either side of the seam. The angle of the seam will depend on the type of delivery you are bowling — in-swinger, seam angled towards the batsman's leg side and the opposite for an out-swinger.

For batting: Lay a bat on the ground face down. Straddle it, then bend down and pick it up with the 'v' between your thumb and index fingers running down the handle. Ensure your hands are a comfortable distance apart, grip the bat and stand up. Do not hold the bat too tight — your top hand should have a firm grip but your bottom hand should be the 'rudder' for your stroke play.

6 — THE RUN-UP

Your run-up should be more about balance and being fluent than speed to the crease. I am learning that a shorter run will conserve energy and assist with building a comfortable rhythm. At the moment I run about 30 metres but I am looking at shortening this.

7 — SHINE

Fast bowlers shine one side of the ball so that the ball will swing through the air. You naturally end up with a shiny side and a rough side. As the ball is bowled, the air will travel over the shiny side more quickly whereas it will be slower over the rough side. This will pull the ball towards the rough side, creating swing. If you hold the ball with the rough side on the same side as the batsman's legs, it will swing from off to leg (in-swinger), whereas if you hold it on the other side it will swing from leg to off (out-swinger). This takes a little practice so don't give up!

Try to keep the ball off the ground as much as possible when passing it back to the bowler for the next delivery; you want to keep the shine for as long as possible.

8 – THE SLOW BALL

The slow ball is a delivery that should be used when you think the batsman is well set. It is a 'surprise' ball, in that he has been playing everything at a similar pace and then the slow ball is bowled and he is too early on the shot, hitting it in the air. Bowlers bowl this ball in a variety of ways. Some roll their fingers over the ball. Others, like Ian Harvey, bowl it out of the back of their hand, and some split the two fingers on top of the ball a long way apart. The key is to bowl it at the right pace. Some people say my slow ball is too slow, as I am bowling around 150 km per hour and then slow to around 110 km per hour. The batsman has time to adjust his shot. The slow ball needs to also be of a full length as you are trying to fool the batsman into thinking he can drive it.

9 – THE YORKER

This delivery, sometimes called the 'sandshoe crusher', is a lethal weapon and every fast bowler should use it. Medium-pacers can also use a yorker to good effect.

A yorker is a ball that is pitched up so far that it pitches close to the crease, where the batter is standing.

Its other feature is that it is bowled quicker than the bowler's normal delivery in order to surprise the batter. This combination of speed and fullness can often lead to problems. The batter can be bowled if his or her bat doesn't get down quickly enough or he or she can be trapped lbw. This happens because the batter doesn't have time to move forwards.

It is not an easy ball to bowl. Too much fullness, and you give the batter a full toss to hit. A little too short, and the batter has a half-volley. And these are juicy deliveries for a batter to receive!

10 – No balls

A delivery can be a 'no ball' for many reasons. Front foot over the line, back foot touching the side crease and, the less common, bending the elbow (throwing). The most common is the front foot no ball and to combat this you must make sure your run-up is in order. Grab a friend and put down a mark on a field somewhere where you will start your run-up. Now run and bowl a ball over whatever distance you feel comfortable with. Mark where your front foot lands. Now pace or, with a measuring tape, measure the distance between the two markers. Transfer this distance to the nets and then into matches.

11 – First-change bowler

First-change bowlers work with the openers as well as spinners and even part-time bowlers. They may have to take an attacking role or just apply pressure and tie up an end. As a first-change bowler you need to have a lot of skill to be able to adjust your game to fit whatever your team needs.

A first-change bowler can expect to bowl a lot of overs throughout a Test or four-day game.

12 — Spin bowler

As with all bowlers, a spinner's main aim is to take wickets. However, spin bowlers can be called upon to play certain roles depending on the situation and the condition of the pitch. They may be asked to tie up an end and put pressure on a batter which the next bowler can capitalise on. Or, if the pitch is providing a lot of turn and movement, a spinner might be aggressive and go for wickets.

It is important to keep the batter guessing as to what delivery is coming next. It is not just about spinning the ball; a good spin bowler will use many variations in the flight and pitch of the ball to entice batters to play shots or simply to put doubt in their minds.

13 — The hat trick

During the 1999 World Cup I found myself on a hat trick against Kenya. I hadn't been on one many times before in international cricket but I had in junior cricket. I remember what my coach used to say: 'Give yourself every chance, bowl at the stumps and make sure he has to play the ball.' I remember bowling a yorker and I thought it hit him on the foot so I started to appeal when I realised it had bowled him. I remember sprinting straight down to fine leg for some strange reason and was met by

Glenn McGrath. I was so excited — It was such a great feeling

14 — Taking guard

I take guard whenever I get to the crease. I do it for a couple of reasons: 1. to appreciate exactly where my stumps are and 2. as part of a routine to get me focused. I stand my bat on end and ask the umpire to line up middle stump at my end and middle stump at the bowler's end. I then put a mark on the batting crease to show me exactly where it is. Some of my friends take different marks, such as 'middle to leg'. Take whichever mark you feel most comfortable with.

15 — Opening batter

In a Test match the opening batters aim to be at the crease for the whole first day of play, and therefore they take a major role in setting the foundation for a big team score. If they do the job well, their side should only have to bat once.

It is important that opening batters establish themselves, and see out the new ball and any early movement in the wicket.

16 — First-drop batter

The best batter in the team is usually the 'first-drop batter'. This is the person who goes in to bat when the first wicket falls. It is a challenging position because they need to be padded up, focused and ready to go as soon as their team's innings begins. If the openers get off to a good start, they could be sitting in the stands for hours — or they could be walking out to face the second ball of the innings.

First-drop batters need to be able to adapt their game depending on how the match is going when they take the crease. If they are in early due to a quick wicket, they need to consolidate their team's position and take on the opener's role. However, if the openers get a big score before getting out, the first-drop batter may need to go in and score quick runs late in the day.

17 — NUMBER SIX BATTER

A batter coming in at this stage of an innings is often faced with one of two situations, each requiring different skills. If their team has been playing well and has a lot of runs on the board, the number six's job is to attack the bowlers. This will keep the run rate ticking over and take the score as high as possible within the overs or time remaining in the game.

However, a number six batter may also come to the crease at a point when the fielding team is doing well. In this case the batter must play safely, forming partnerships with all remaining batters to ensure they see out the designated overs or time while scoring as many runs as they can.

18 — WORKING TOGETHER

Batting is a partnership. It's 11 against two. And two is a whole lot better than one. Take the opportunity at the end of overs to talk to your partner. Offer advice and encouragement. Tell your partner how well he or she is playing. Sometimes it can be too easy for the fielding team to gain a psychological edge over the batters because they outnumber them or they get vocally enthusiastic! Always remember: it's 11 against two.

It's your job to try to rebalance the situation by coming across as strong and confident. Appear in control of the situation, even if you don't feel in control.

A few good overs, a couple of fours, can make a huge difference in your outlook. As a batting partnership, you should set yourselves goals.

You might want to work at pushing some quick singles or perhaps bat in 15-minute blocks.

Above all, support and encourage your partner. With any luck, you will be supported and encouraged in turn.

19 — MAKING THE RIGHT CALL

To avoid being run out there are some important rules to remember when you're batting. There are three calls that batters should make when deciding to run or not: Yes, No or Wait. Saying 'Go!' is definitely to be avoided. It sounds too much like 'No!'. Generally, if the ball is played in front of the batter, then that person — the striker — should make the call. If the ball goes behind the batter, the non-striker should make the call. Sometimes you

can't do anything about a freakish piece of fielding.
You just have to run like crazy, reach forwards with
your bat as you near the crease and hope that the
stumps haven't been broken by the time your bat
crosses that line.

20 – RUNNING BETWEEN WICKETS

I love running between wickets, especially when I
have hit the ball! I love putting pressure on the
fielding team by trying to turn twos into threes and
picking up quick singles. Remember to always look at
the ball when you are running between the wickets.
In order to do that you sometimes have to change
the bat from one hand to the other so that you can
see how quickly the ball is travelling or whether a
fieldsman has made a great save. You should practise
your running between the wickets as this will
improve your judgment. It is amazing how long it
takes for someone to throw a ball over 30 metres —
often you can turn that into a run.

21 – FIELDING

There is nothing better than a fielder pulling off a
great catch or save. It gives the bowler a huge lift
and can often change the course of a match.
Players these days have to be versatile in that they
have to excel in one area of the game and be good
at the two others. My bowling is my strength but I
make sure that I am always looking to improve my
batting and fielding. Fielding is a fun part of the

game — make sure you help out the bowler. You can save runs, shine the ball and encourage your team-mates.

22 — READY FOR A CATCH

You can be sure that the one chance you get to take a catch — because they don't come that often — will be the time when you weren't as ready as you should have been. To give yourself the best chance of taking a catch, here are a few tips.

Walk in with the bowler, if you are not fielding in a catching position — in other words, if you're not too close to the batter. This alerts you to the fact that a ball is about to be bowled, has you leaning forwards, anticipating and on the move. Watch the batter. After the delivery, use the few moments you have to relax, but be on the lookout for any weaknesses in the batter that you can pass on to the bowler or captain.

When taking a catch, the most important thing to remember is to keep your eyes on the ball. Try to get your body into position as early as possible so you can focus on actually taking the catch.

For outfield catches, make sure your fingers are pointing either up or down, so the ball will come to rest safely in the palms of your hands.

For close-in catches, the fingers should be pointing down for balls that come below waist height, and up for those that come at you higher.

Stay relaxed, and keep your hands 'soft'.

One last point. You've got to want the ball to come your way. So if you don't like the feel of a cricket ball, buy one and get to like it. Toss it to yourself. Make the throws higher and higher. Catch 10 out of 10. Then get a friend to toss you more.

Then more, at different heights and speeds. Then more.

23 — WICKET KEEPER

A wicket keeper should act as an energy source for their team, encouraging the fielders and bowlers throughout the match. It is also important for the keeper to be confident and skilled behind the stumps — the worst sight for any bowler is a good ball that beats both the batter and the keeper.

The keeper also helps the captain set the field, as they have the best view of the fielders and where the ball is going.

Keepers should start low and rise with the ball as it approaches. A great tip is to go through a routine before bowlers start their run-up. Set your feet and get into a low stance — this will allow you to react and move left, right, up or down in response to the ball's movement once it has reached the batter.

24 — SLIPS

Slips fielding is all about judging the speed at which the ball travels to you. It is not about reflexes. Stand at a distance where you think the ball will come to you about waist height. It is important for the slips fielders, as well as the wicket keeper, to be set in a well-balanced stance before bowlers start their run-up. Bend your knees slightly and cup your hands with your fingers pointing down. At the time the bowler lets the ball go you should have your hands about 30 cm off the ground. Remember, it is way easier to come up to take a catch than to have to go down to take one. The reason you move your feet is to get your eyes over the ball (the same as batting) so try and catch with your head over the ball at all times.

Also, slips fielders often stand too deep, instead of in a place where the ball will carry to them. The keeper's position is a good guide as to where the slips should stand: first slip should be half a metre behind the keeper and slightly to one side (depending on whether the batter is left-handed or right-handed); second slip should be in line with or in front of the keeper. Practice is the only way you will improve! Great slips fielders spend hours and hours practising, and as a result they rarely drop chances.

25 — TWELFTH MAN

The 12th man is an integral part of a side even though he or she is not in the starting line-up. The 12th man motivates and supports team-mates throughout the game as well as running drinks and equipment to players on the field when needed. A 12th man also has to be ready at all times to take the field if necessary, and therefore must always be focused on the game.

26 — Scorer

The role of the scorer is to keep an accurate record of the match. This information allows the players and spectators to determine the way the match is going, as well as individual performances throughout the game.

27 — Make practice like a match

Taking the opportunity to simulate match conditions during your practice sessions is a great way to give players some experience. You can never totally re-create real game situations, but putting batters, bowlers and fielders under stress is a good way to see who can stand up and perform under pressure.

Turning practice into a game situation also adds interest to the practice. It gives the players something to focus on. Most players love a bit of competition, and most players love to win.

Near the end of a long practice session, introducing a game element, like setting a target to chase, creates the chance for someone to be the hero, if only for a few moments before everyone wanders away to pack up and head home.

28 — Practice in the nets

Net sessions can be very helpful, if done correctly. A batter has the opportunity to focus on a particular area of his or her batting. Being surrounded by netting means that there is little time wasted in retrieving balls — either hit or missed. A batter can face many deliveries in a short space of time.

If a particular stroke needs to be practised, balls can be thrown to give the batter the chance to play the stroke again and again. This should develop his or her skill and technique, as well as confidence.

It is important for bowlers to concentrate on their work too. Make sure that you have at least one stump to run past at the bowler's end and that you're using a reasonable cricket ball. Bowling with an old, tattered or soft ball may not inspire you to work hard enough. And be sure not to bowl no-balls. Your run-up is as important in the nets as in a match.

Finally, keep alert. Never turn your back to the batters. You may cop a full-blooded drive from the next net!

29 — MAKING PRACTICE TOUGH

There are many examples of famous cricketers making practice conditions especially hard for themselves so they could improve their skills. Rodney Marsh, the great Australian wicket keeper of the 1970s and early 1980s, used to throw a golf ball at the pole of a clothesline. He worked on improving his reflexes by catching the ball as it came off at all sorts of angles. And there is, of course, the famous film of Donald Bradman tossing a golf ball against the side of a corrugated iron water tank, then hitting the ball with a stump.

It's a good idea to try to hit a ball using a stump, or even a section of broom handle, for a bat. The next time you play with a real bat, it will feel a lot wider than it really is, giving your confidence a boost and perhaps turning a small score into a big one.

Toby's Interview with Andrew Symonds

Hi Andrew
Thanks so much for answering my questions. I reckon you're an awesome
player. You are the perfect all-rounder and kids love watching you bat,
bowl and especially field.

I hope you don't mind answering my questions that will help me
with my assignment.
Toby Jones

How did you feel when you walked out to bat when Australia was 4 for 86 against Pakistan in Australia's first World Cup game in 2003?

Well, there'd been two quick wickets. I was sitting there in my shorts and a singlet and suddenly I was scrambling around getting all my gear on. There wasn't much time to think — a few overs later I was out there in the middle.

Did anyone say anything to you in the dressing room before you left?

There would have been the usual good luck wishes from my team-mates. 'Go well, mate. Good luck, Roy.' (That's my nickname.) I think there were a few nerves in the dressing room, with us four for not too many.

Your first two scoring shots were fours. What's it like when your first two scoring shots are boundaries?

I can't really remember those first few scoring shots. It was a bit of a blur really. But it's good to put a couple of boundaries away early. It does settle you down quicker.

Is this innings [Andrew scored 143 not out] the highest ever by an Aussie at the World Cup?

Now, that's a very good question — I'm not exactly sure. [*I looked it up on the internet later, and it is. Mark Waugh held the previous record when he scored 130 against Kenya.*]

What did the players say when you came in after the knock?

Well, there was plenty of excitement in the dressing room when we came back in, and some slaps on the back too. They were all smiling like split watermelons.

Did you think you had the game won at lunchtime?

We would have had to play very badly from there. Defending 310 runs is much easier than chasing them.

What did you have to eat at lunch?

I would have used up a lot of energy and lost a lot of fluid batting, so I had lots to drink and plenty of fruit. It all depends on the activity you've been doing.

Do you talk tactics between overs when you meet at mid-pitch with the other batter or do you just chat about stuff?

That depends on the match situation. Sometimes, if things are going really well, you do occasionally relax and chat about other things. But mostly we talk about the game and the bowlers. In one-day games we're often thinking about how many overs a particular bowler has left and then we might plan to attack more or something.

Do you remember the sixes you hit off the last two overs? Were they, like, planned shots or were they just massive slogs?

Well, I'm careful to set up my batting stance so that hitting sixes is easier. I move my front leg out of the way so that I can hit pitched-up balls and shorter ones. Near the end of an innings it's good to try and get a few big shots away.

I know you won't want to say so, but some people (including me) reckon that your innings changed the whole course of the World Cup for Australia. What do you reckon about that? Were the Aussies feeling under the pump a bit with everything going on beforehand?

We were under a bit of pressure. I hadn't scored a one-day 100 before, and I knew someone had to make a big score. Ricky Ponting was fantastic at the other end. He gave me a lot of confidence. We got going and I was in a zone. I really don't remember much about the actual innings.

You wear heaps of sunscreen. There's a few kids at my school who are doing the same, and their mums and dads and the coach are rapt. Do you do it for sun protection or good luck, or a bit of both?

Yep, probably a bit of both. It's just something I've always done. It's a habit. But it's also the best protection against sun and wind burn. Not much sun at night, though, is there, Toby?

No way, Andrew. Thanks for letting me interview you and good luck for all your cricket matches in the future. Also, do you reckon I could visit you one day in the dressing room maybe and get your autograph? And I might go and take a look at the game too.

That's a pleasure. We'll see if something can be arranged. So, you've got a tape of the game, have you? Maybe I'll have a look with you.

Well, actually, that could be a bit tricky ...

2003 Australia v Pakistan Scorecard

Australia v Pakistan World Cup Pool A Match
11 February 2003, Johannesburg, South Africa
Toss: Pakistan • Decision: Australia to bat • Result: Australia won by 82 runs

Australia Innings (50 overs maximum)	R	B	4s	6s
Adam Gilchrist c Waqar Younis b Wasim Akram	1	3	0	0
Matthew Hayden b Wasim Akram	27	41	3	0
Ricky Ponting c Taufeeq Umar b S Akhtar	53	67	7	0
Damien Martyn b Wasim Akram	0	1	0	0
Jimmy Maher c Rashid Latif b Waqar Younis	9	19	1	0
Andrew Symonds not out	143	125	18	2
Brad Hogg run out (Younis Khan)	14	22	0	0
Ian Harvey c Waqar Younis b Shoaib Akhtar	24	19	3	0
Brett Lee c Inzamam-ul-Haq b Waqar Younis	2	6	0	0
Jason Gillespie not out	6	4	1	0
Glenn McGrath (did not bat)				
Extras (byes 1 / lb 9 / w 12 / nb 9)	31			
Total (8 wickets / 50 overs / 219 minutes)	**310**			

Pakistan Bowling	O	M	R	W
Wasim Akram	10	0	64	3
Shoaib Akhtar	10	0	45	2
Waqar Younis	8.3	1	50	2
Abdul Razzaq	6	0	42	0

| Shahid Afridi | 9.3 | 0 | 63 | 0 |
| Younis Khan | 6 | 0 | 36 | 0 |

Pakistan Innings	R	B	4s	6s
(target — 311 runs from 49 overs)				
Taufeeq Umar c Brad Hogg b Brett Lee	21	43	4	0
Shahid Afridi c Adam Gilchrist b Gillespie	1	8	0	0
Saleem Elahi c Brett Lee b Ian Harvey	30	40	3	0
Inzamam-ul-Haq c Adam Gilchrist b G McGrath	6	16	1	0
Yousif Youhana c Andrew Symonds b Ian Harvey	27	49	4	0
Younis Khan c Ricky Ponting b Brad Hogg	19	45	0	0
Abdul Razzaq c and b Brad Hogg	25	36	2	0
Rashid Latif b Brad Hogg	33	39	1	3
Wasim Akram c Ricky Ponting b Ian Harvey	33	44	4	1
Waqar Younis c Glenn McGrath b Ian Harvey	6	29	0	0
Shoaib Akhtar not out	0	7	0	0
Extras (byes 3 / lb 9 / w 10 / nb 5)	27			
Total (all out / 44.3 overs / 205 minutes)	228			

Australia Bowling	O	M	R	W
Glenn McGrath	10	2	39	1
Jason Gillespie	8	1	28	1
Brett Lee	7	0	37	1
Ian Harvey	9.3	0	58	4
Brad Hogg	10	0	54	3

The 1999 World Cup That Toby Did His Project On

On 9 June, in the 1999 Cricket World Cup, Australia was playing South Africa. An amazing thing happened. Steve Waugh clipped a ball off his pads into the hands of Herschelle Gibbs, fielding in close on the leg side. For a split second Gibbs saw Australia's dream of winning the World Cup lying in the palm of his hand. But as he went to throw the ball into the air to celebrate taking the catch to remove the Australian captain, it fell from his hand to the ground.

Waugh was on 28. About two hours later he hit a ball through mid-wicket to take Australia not only to a memorable win against South Africa but to a semi-final. Steve Waugh ended up scoring 120 not out.

Same teams, but this time it's a semi-final. The winner goes through to play in the final of the 1999 World Cup. Hansie Cronje wins the toss for South Africa and decides to send Australia in to bat.

And it seems a pretty good decision. But after only five balls Australia have lost Mark Waugh for a duck. Ricky Ponting and Adam Gilchrist soon have the situation looking good again, smashing the ball to all parts of the ground.

When the score reaches 54, Ricky chases a wide delivery from Allan Donald and hits it straight to cover. Out! Caught. Then, five balls later, Australia are under the pump again when Allan Donald has Darren Lehmann caught behind for one.

Only 10 runs later, 'Gilly' goes for a big hit outside his off-stump and carves the ball to backward point where Donald takes the catch. Allan

Donald has had a hand in the last three wickets to fall. Australia have gone from a steady 1 for 54 to a very shaky 4 for 68.

Michael Bevan and Steve Waugh are proceeding slowly. They can only manage 20 runs between over number 20 and over number 30. South Africa are not taking wickets, but Australia's scoring rate has fallen right back. The pressure is intense. Australia have to be careful as they have only one recognised batsman left.

In the 35th over Lance Klusener is bowling to Waugh. The ball is there to be hit and he launches into a beautiful straight drive for four. To the next ball, he plays another straight drive but lofts it over the boundary rope. Ten runs in two balls. This is more like it . . .

Soon the momentum is starting to swing Australia's way. The batting of Steve Waugh and Michael Bevan is productive. But just at the critical moment when they are beginning to get on top, Waugh tries to edge a ball that is too close to his body away through the vacant slips area. All he manages to do is get a thickish edge and present an easy catch for Mark Boucher, the South African keeper.

Michael Bevan and Waugh have taken the score from a worrying 4 for 68 to a more respectable 4 for 158. They have put on 90 runs in just over 23 overs, at a reasonable rate of 3.8 runs per over. But now Australia are 5 for 158. And only three balls later Tom Moody is walking back to the pavilion — out for a duck, lbw to Shaun Pollock. Two wickets have fallen in an over.

Australia still have another 11 overs to face, but the bowlers are going to have to help Michael Bevan, who now needs to bat through the innings if Australia are going to build a reasonable score.

Michael Bevan has played really well. He hardly ever slogs. He knows exactly where there are gaps between fieldsmen and he has the ability to keep the scoreboard ticking along without you really thinking that anything much is happening.

But Australia's bowlers are finding batting difficult against the classy South African bowlers. Warne manages to knock up 18 very handy runs for Australia off only 24 balls. Together, he and Bevan add just under 50 runs in only eight overs. This is a crucial period of the game. Australia only manage to score another six runs after that. Had either lost his wicket earlier, Australia might not have reached 180.

Mark Boucher takes his fourth catch in the 50th and last over of the innings, and Michael Bevan is out for 65. Australia's total is 213 — not a great score. The South Africans feel confident about their chances of winning and going on to the final at Lord's.

But the pitch is wearing, and will suit Shane Warne. Australia have a great bowling attack and a fantastic fielding team. The Aussies will not be giving up until the final ball is bowled, perseverance being a feature of this team.

* * *

The feeling round the ground as the players take lunch is that Australia haven't scored enough runs. The pitch is still a beauty. The clouds of the morning are breaking up and South Africa have bowled Australia out for well inside the 250 runs that many people felt were needed on such a good batting strip. The South Africans will be feeling confident. They have bowled the Australians out inside their 50 overs and have fielded superbly all day. Now it is their turn to bat.

But there is one hope for Australia: the brilliant Shane Warne. The pitch is considered the equivalent of a seventh-day Test wicket. Normally only three or four days are needed to produce a turning Test match pitch, sometimes even fewer.

Shane Warne is about to be let loose on a seven-day-old wicket. Will he be the difference? Or will the accuracy of Glenn McGrath, Damien Fleming and Paul Reiffel do the job for the Aussies?

Time will tell.

The first 12 overs go smoothly for South Africa. The pitch offers nothing for the Aussie 'quicks' and the South African openers are looking comfortable. Gibbs and Kirsten score freely and race the score along to 48. They are not far from taking their side to a quarter of the required total — and, importantly, South Africa have 10 wickets in hand.

Enter Shane Warne. It is the 13th over of the game. His second ball is tossed up, and pitches outside off-stump. Gibbs pushes at it, probably not expecting too much spin. But spin there is. The ball bites back viciously and clips the off-stump.

This delivery, apart from securing a wicket, will almost certainly have sent a few shivers through the South African dressing room. Five

581

runs are added, then Warne is back for his second over. This time he doesn't need a warm-up ball. On his first delivery, again tossed up but this time outside off-stump, Gary Kirsten launches into a big sweep. But the spinning ball finds the edge of his bat and rebounds onto his stumps.

In the space of five balls, Shane Warne has dismissed both openers, and South Africa have stumbled to 2 for 53. Another two balls later it is 3 for 53, with the South African captain, Hansie Cronje, trudging back to the pavilion, caught by Mark Waugh for a duck.

Three wickets have been taken and only five runs added. South Africa need cool heads at the wicket. But Jonty Rhodes and Daryll Cullinan have everyone on edge with their hair-raising running between wickets. No less than three times the Aussies have the chance to run out one of the batsmen. But their throws are off-target.

Shane Warne continues to bowl well and is really troubling Cullinan. Rhodes then attempts another cheeky single — a push straight to Michael Bevan at mid-off. Jonty makes his ground, but he hasn't calculated on Michael Bevan choosing to ping the ball to the batter's end. This time it is a direct hit and Cullinan is run out.

It is 4 for 61 and the Aussies are on top. But now comes South Africa's best partnership of the match. The same partnership for Australia added 90 runs. Jacques Kallis and Jonty Rhodes do almost as well, putting on 84 runs as well as taking the South Africans into the last 10 overs of the game.

But they are still struggling to score quickly. It is going to be a tense finish. South Africa still have six wickets in hand as the 41st over begins.

South Africa have moved to 4 for 144. The game is evenly poised. The South Africans have some big hitters to come, but first, the Rhodes/Kallis partnership needs to be broken. And at last it is, when Michael Bevan takes a catch at deep mid-wicket from a Jonty Rhodes sweep.

Shaun Pollock comes in and knocks up some quick runs. Shane Warne's final over is dramatic. Pollock skies the first ball out to deep mid-off, but Paul Reiffel misjudges the catch. Then Pollock belts Warne for a six and a four. The fourth ball yields a single, and on Warne's fifth delivery, Kallis pushes a catch to captain Steve Waugh.

In the next over, South Africa lose their seventh wicket with the score on 183 when Pollock plays over a yorker from Damien Fleming, losing his middle stump.

South Africa, still 31 runs away from victory, will be confident while Lance Klusener is at the wicket.

The final overs are likely to be dramatic ...

The pressure is building with every ball. In the 49th over (the second last) Glenn McGrath bowls Boucher with his second ball. But Klusener is hitting cleanly, maybe too cleanly. An easy single off McGrath's fourth delivery becomes an attempted two. But McGrath cleverly pads Reiffel's strong throw onto the stumps — 7 for 196 has become 9 for 198. A single off the last ball means that Klusener has the strike for the last over. Damien Fleming is the bowler.

South Africa need nine runs to win.

Klusener smashes the first ball through the covers for a four.

Five balls left, five runs to win.

Another yorker-length ball, angled in at the batsman, is again clubbed by Klusener — an amazing shot — out through mid-off, for another four.

Four balls left, one run to win. The scores are tied. Steve Waugh brings the fielders in. Fleming changes his angle and comes in over the wicket. Again Lance Klusener belts the ball, but this time it goes straight to a fielder.

At the bowler's end, Allan Donald has backed up a long way. Darren Lehmann picks up the ball and hurls it at the stumps. It misses. Had he hit, the video suggests that Donald would have been run out.

Three balls left, one run to win.

Another whack from Klusener, this time to mid-off. He charges down the wicket for a single. Donald has his back turned, watching the ball. The fielder throws the ball to Fleming at the bowler's end; Fleming then underarms it quickly but safely down to the keeper. By now Allan Donald has set off. But not soon enough. Adam Gilchrist takes off the bails and Donald is run out.

An amazing game finishes in a tie. Australia goes on to the final only because it has defeated South Africa in an earlier stage of the tournament.

In the final, Australia defeats Pakistan comfortably.

1999 World Cup Scorecard

World Cup Semi-final

17 June 1999, Edgbaston, England
Toss: South Africa • Decision: Send Australia into bat • Result: Tie

Australia Innings	R	B	4s	6s
Adam Gilchrist c Donald b Kallis	20	39	1	1
Mark Waugh c Boucher b Pollock	0	4	0	0
Ricky Ponting c Kirsten b Donald	37	48	3	1
Darren Lehmann c Boucher b Donald	1	4	0	0
Steve Waugh c Boucher b Pollock	56	76	6	1
Michael Bevan c Boucher b Pollock	65	101	6	0
Tom Moody lbw b Pollock	0	3	0	0
Shane Warne c Cronje b Pollock	18	24	1	0
Paul Reiffel b Donald	0	1	0	0
Damien Fleming b Donald	0	2	0	0
Glenn McGrath not out	0	1	0	0
Extras (byes 1 / lb 6 / w 3 / nb 6)	16			
Total (49.2 overs)	213			

South Africa Bowling	O	M	R	W
Shaun Pollock	9.2	1	36	5
Steven Elworthy	10	0	59	0
Jacques Kallis	10	2	27	1
Allan Donald	10	1	32	4
Lance Klusener	9	1	50	0
Hansie Cronje	1	0	2	0
	49.2	5	203	10

South Africa Innings	R	B	4s	6s
Gary Kirsten b Warne	18	42	1	0
Herschelle Gibbs b Warne	30	36	6	0
Daryll Cullinan run out (Bevan)	6	30	0	0
Hansie Cronje c M Waugh b Warne	0	2	0	0
Jacques Kallis c S Waugh b Warne	53	92	3	0
Jonty Rhodes c Bevan b Reiffel	43	55	2	1
Shaun Pollock b Fleming	20	14	1	1
Lance Klusener not out	31	16	4	1
Mark Boucher b McGrath	5	10	0	0
Steven Elworthy run out (Reiffel)	1	1	0	0
Allan Donald run out (Fleming)	0	1	0	0
Extras (byes 0 / lb 1 / w 5 / nb 0)	6			
Total (49.4 overs)	213			

Australia Bowling	O	M	R	W
Glenn McGrath	10	0	51	1
Damien Fleming	8.4	1	40	1
Paul Reiffel	8	0	28	1
Shane Warne	10	4	29	4
Mark Waugh	8	0	37	0
Tom Moody	5	0	27	0
	49.4	5	212	7

1999 Australia v Pakistan Scorecard

Australia v Pakistan Test Match

18–22 November 1999, Hobart, Australia

Toss: Australia • Decision: Pakistan to bat • Result: Australia won by 4 wickets

Pakistan 1st Innings	R	B	4s	6s
Saeed Anwar c Shane Warne b Glenn McGrath	0	7	0	0
Mohammad Wasim c Adam Gilchrist b S Muller	91	122	12	0
Ijaz Ahmed c Michael Slater b Glenn McGrath	6	23	0	0
Inzamam-ul-Haq b Scott Muller	12	43	0	0
Yousuf Youhana c Mark Waugh b D Fleming	17	38	0	0
Azhar Mahmood b Shane Warne	27	72	2	2
Moin Khan c Glenn McGrath b Scott Muller	1	3	0	0
Wasim Akram c Adam Gilchrist b Shane Warne	29	77	4	0
Saqlain Mushtaq lbw b Shane Warne	3	28	0	0
Waqar Younis not out	12	18	1	0
Shoaib Akhtar c Adam Gilchrist b D Fleming	5	6	1	0
Extras (b 10 / lb 6 / w 3)	19			
Total (72.5 overs)	222			

Australia Bowling	O	M	R	W
Glenn McGrath	18	8	34	2
Damien Fleming	24.5	7	54	2
Scott Muller	12	0	68	3
Shane Warne	16	6	45	3
Greg Blewett	2	1	5	0
	72.5	22	206	10

586

Australia 1st Innings

	R	B	4s	6s
Michael Slater c Ijaz Ahmed b Saqlain Mushtaq	97	195	10	0
Greg Blewett c Moin Khan b Azhar Mahmood	35	84	4	0
Justin Langer c Mohammad Wasim b				
Saqlain Mushtaq	59	106	4	0
Mark Waugh lbw b Waqar Younis	5	12	0	0
Steve Waugh c Ijaz Ahmed b Wasim Akram	24	45	2	0
Ricky Ponting b Waqar Younis	0	3	0	0
Adam Gilchrist st Moin Khan b Saqlain Mushtaq	6	19	0	0
Shane Warne b Saqlain Mushtaq	0	1	0	0
Damien Fleming lbw b Saqlain Mushtaq	0	4	0	0
Glenn McGrath st Moin Khan b Saqlain Mushtaq	7	15	1	0
Scott Muller not out	0	0	0	0
Extras (b 2 / lb 6 / nb 5)	13			
Total (80 overs)	**246**			

Pakistan Bowling

	O	M	R	W
Wasim Akram	20	4	51	1
Shoaib Akhtar	17	2	69	0
Waqar Younis	12	1	42	2
Saqlain Mushtaq	24	8	46	6
Azhar Mahmood	7	1	30	1
	80	**16**	**238**	**10**

Pakistan 2nd Innings

	R	B	4s	6s
Saeed Anwar b Shane Warne	78	156	9	1
Mohammad Wasim c Glenn McGrath				
b Scott Muller	20	59	1	0
Saqlain Mushtaq lbw b Shane Warne	8	52	0	0
Ijaz Ahmed c Steve Waugh b Glenn McGrath	82	124	13	0
Inzamam-ul-Haq c Mark Waugh b				
Shane Warne	118	191	12	0
Yousuf Youhana c Ricky Ponting b				
Damien Fleming	2	10	0	0
Azhar Mahmood lbw Shane Warne	28	60	4	0
Moin Khan c Adam Gilchrist b D Fleming	6	31	0	0
Wasim Akram c Greg Blewett b Shane Warne	31	74	3	0

Waqar Younis run out (Adam Gilchrist)	0	6	0	0
Shoaib Akhtar not out	5	16	0	0
Extras (lb 6 / w 1 / nb 7)	14			
Total (128.5 overs)	**392**			

Australia Bowling	O	M	R	W
Glenn McGrath	27	8	87	1
Damien Fleming	29	5	89	2
Shane Warne	45.5	11	110	5
Scott Muller	17	3	63	1
Steve Waugh	4	1	19	0
Mark Waugh	2	0	6	0
Ricky Ponting	2	1	7	0
Greg Blewett	2	0	5	0
	128.5	**29**	**386**	**10**

Australia 2nd Innings	R	B	4s	6s
Greg Blewett c Moin Khan b Azhar Mahmood	29	106	2	0
Michael Slater c Azhar Mahmood b Shoaib Akhtar	27	48	3	0
Justin Langer c Inzamam-ul-Haq b Saqlain Mushtaq	127	295	12	0
Mark Waugh lbw b Azhar Mahmood	0	1	0	0
Steve Waugh c and b Saqlain Mushtaq	28	69	0	0
Ricky Ponting lbw b Wasim Akram	0	5	0	0
Adam Gilchrist not out	149	163	13	1
Shane Warne not out	0	0	0	0
Extras (b 1 / lb 4 / nb 4)	9			
Total (113.5 overs)	**6 / 369**			

Pakistan Bowling	O	M	R	W
Wasim Akram	18	1	68	1
Waqar Younis	11	2	38	0
Shoaib Akhtar	23	5	85	1
Saqlain Mushtaq	44.5	9	130	2
Azhar Mahmood	17	3	43	2
	113.5	**19**	**364**	**6**

Rahul's Interviews

Part of Rahul's interview with Dean Jones:

RP: Hello, Dean.

DJ: Hello, how are you?

RP: Good thanks. What was it like out there during your 210?

DJ: Well, it was pretty tough, actually. What made it so hard was the high humidity and the fact that I just couldn't keep any fluid in.

RP: Is it true that you wanted to go off before you were out?

DJ: Oh, yes, I was pretty sick during the afternoon. I had got to about 170 and I said to AB [Allan Border] that I'd had enough. He said, 'Righto, we'll get a Queenslander out here. Someone tough who can stand up to it.'

RP: What happened after you were out?

DJ: I don't remember much. I remember being put into a bath filled with iced water and ice. Do you know what? It felt lukewarm! Everything was fine until I decided to get out. My body cramped up completely. Everywhere. I just collapsed in a heap. That's when they decided I needed a visit to the hospital.

RP: Did you get to the hospital?

DJ: Eventually. I'm told it was a pretty hairy ride. We were flying all over the place. The physio with me had to hold me down to stop me from cramping with all the shaking and swerving the ambulance was doing.

RP: What happened when you got to the hospital?

DJ: Well, I'm told that I was taken to casualty. There was a man there who was needing some attention, but when the doctors and other staff realised that a Test cricketer had just arrived, they all left him lying on his bed and raced over to me.

Part of Rahul's interview with Ray Bright:

RP: Ray, some people say you were the hero of the last hour. What happened?

RB: No, there were plenty of heroes out there. I was actually off the field. I was very dehydrated and struggling to stay on my feet.

RP: But you came back onto the field?

RB: Yes. Allan Border, our captain, wanted me to bowl.

RP: What happened?

RB: Well, it was very tense. Lots of shouting and frustration. I managed to get a couple of wickets quickly and that sort of changed the balance of things. India were in a winning position. I think they needed 20-odd runs off the last five overs with four wickets in hand.

RP: And the last over?

RB: The last over. It probably took about 10 minutes. Greg Matthews bowled it. They needed four runs to win. We needed one wicket. Ravi Shastri was batting really well. He was facing. He blocked the first ball and then hit the next for two. He hit the third ball for a single. The scores were tied. The next ball was blocked, but the fifth ball was a wicket!

RP: What was the reaction?

RB: Well, we were jubilant. We were running around very excitedly. Some of us actually thought we'd won. And I suppose, given what the situation was half an hour before, we sort of had.

1986 India v Australia Scorecard

India v Australia Test Match
18–22 September 1986, Madras, India
Toss: Australia • Decision: Australia to bat • Result: Tie

Australia 1st Innings	R	B	4s	6s
David Boon c Kapil Dev b Sharma	122	258	21	0
Geoff Marsh c Kapil Dev b Yadav	22	66	2	0
Dean Jones b Yadav	210	330	27	2
Ray Bright c Shastri b Yadav	30	59	3	1
Allan Border c Gavaskar b Shastri	106	172	14	1
Greg Ritchie run out	13	18	1	1
Greg Matthews c Pandit b Yadav	44	78	5	0
Steve Waugh not out	12	48	0	0
Tim Zoehrer did not bat	0	0	0	0
Craig McDermott did not bat	0	0	0	0
Bruce Reid did not bat	0	0	0	0
Extras (byes 1 / lb 7 / w 1 / nb 6)	15			
Total (170.5 overs) 7 dec	**574**			

India Bowling	O	M	R	W
Kapil Dev	18	5	52	0
Chetan Sharma	16	1	70	1
Maninder Singh	39	8	135	0
Shivlal Yadav	49.5	9	142	4
Ravi Shastri	47	8	161	1
Kris Srikkanth	1	0	6	0
	170.5	31	566	6

India 1st Innings	R	B	4s	6s
Sunil Gavaskar c & b Matthews	8	21	0	0
Kris Srikkanth c Ritchie b Matthews	53	62	9	1
Mohinder Armanath run out	1	7	0	0
Mohammad Azharuddin c & b Bright	50	64	8	0
Ravi Shastri c Zoehrer b Matthews	62	106	8	1
Chandrakant Pandit c Waugh b Matthews	35	57	4	0
Kapil Dev c Border b Matthews	119	138	21	0
Kiran More c Zoehrer b Waugh	4	21	1	0
Chetan Sharma c Zoehrer b Reid	30	55	2	1
Shivlal Yadav c Border b Bright	19	55	3	0
Maninder Singh not out	0	14	0	0
Extras (byes 1 / lb 1 / w 5 / nb 0)	7			
Total (94.2 overs)	**397**			

Australia Bowling	O	M	R	W
Craig McDermott	14	2	59	0
Bruce Reid	18	4	93	1
Greg Matthews	28.2	3	103	5
Ray Bright	23	3	88	2
Steve Waugh	11	2	44	1
	94.2	14	387	9

Australia 2nd Innings	R	B	4s	6s
David Boon lbw b Singh	49	92	4	1
Geoff Marsh b Shastri	11	40	0	0
Dean Jones c Azharuddin b Singh	24	39	3	0
Allan Border b Singh	27	41	4	0
Greg Ritchie c Pandit b Shastri	28	29	2	1
Greg Matthews not out	27	25	2	0
Steve Waugh not out	2	7	0	0

Australia 2nd Innings (cont)	R	B	4s	6s
Ray Bright did not bat	0	0	0	0
Tim Zoehrer did not bat	0	0	0	0
Craig McDermott did not bat	0	0	0	0
Bruce Reid did not bat	0	0	0	0
Extras (byes 0 / lb 1 / w 0 / nb 1)	2			
Total (49 overs) 5 dec	**170**			

India Bowling	O	M	R	W
Kapil Dev	1	0	5	0
Chetan Sharma	6	0	19	0
Maninder Singh	19	2	60	3
Shivlal Yadav	9	0	35	0
Ravi Shastri	14	2	50	2
	49	**4**	**169**	**5**

India 2nd Innings	R	B	4s	6s
Sunil Gavaskar c Jones b Bright	90	168	12	1
Kris Srikkanth c Waugh b Matthews	39	49	6	0
Mohinder Armanath c Boon b Matthews	51	113	8	0
Mohammad Azharuddin c Ritchie b Bright	42	77	3	1
Chandrakant Pandit b Matthews	39	37	5	0
Kapil Dev c Bright b Matthews	1	2	0	0
Ravi Shastri not out	48	40	3	2
Chetan Sharma c McDermott b Bright	23	38	3	0
Kiran More lbw b Bright	0	1	0	0
Shivlal Yadav b Bright	8	6	0	1
Maninder Singh lbw b Matthews	0	4	0	0
Extras (byes 1 / lb 3 / w 0 / nb 2)	6			
Total (86.5 overs)	**347**			

Australia Bowling	O	M	R	W
Craig McDermott	5	0	27	0
Bruce Reid	10	2	48	0
Greg Matthews	39.5	7	146	5
Ray Bright	25	3	94	5
Allan Border	3	0	12	0
Steve Waugh	4	1	16	0
	86.5	**13**	**343**	**10**

1985 Australia v New Zealand Scorecard

Australia v New Zealand Test Match
8–12 November 1985, Brisbane, Australia
Toss: New Zealand • Decision: Australia to bat • Result: New Zealand
won by an innings and 41 runs

Australia 1st Innings	R	B	4s	6s
Kepler Wessels lbw b Richard Hadlee	70	186	6	1
Andrew Hilditch c Ewen Chatfield b Richard Hadlee	0	4	3	0
David Boon c Jeremy Coney b Richard Hadlee	31	78	3	0
Allan Border c Bruce Edgar b Richard Hadlee	1	7	0	0
Greg Ritchie c Martin Crowe b Richard Hadlee	8	16	1	0
Wayne Phillips b Richard Hadlee	34	115	4	0
Greg Matthews b Richard Hadlee	2	4	0	0
Geoff Lawson c Richard Hadlee b Vaughan Brown	8	27	1	0
Craig McDermott c Jeremy Coney b Richard Hadlee	9	21	1	0
David Gilbert not out	0	0	0	0
Robert Holland c Vaughan Brown b Richard Hadlee	0	4	0	0
Extras (b 9 / lb 5 / nb 2)	16			
Total (76.4 overs)	**179**			

New Zealand Bowling	O	M	R	W
Richard Hadlee	23.4	4	52	9

Ewen Chatfield	18	6	29	0
Martin Snedden	11	1	45	0
Martin Crowe	5	0	14	0
Vaughan Brown	12	5	17	1
Jeremy Coney	7	5	8	0
	76.4	**21**	**165**	**10**

New Zealand 1st Innings	R	B	4s	6s
Bruce Edgar c Wayne Phillips b David Gilbert	17	50	1	0
John Wright lbw b Greg Matthews	46	110	5	0
John Reid c Allan Border b David Gilbert	108	255	16	0
Martin Crowe b Greg Matthews	188	328	26	0
Jeremy Coney c Wayne Phillips b Geoff Lawson	22	44	3	0
Jeff Crowe c Robert Holland b Greg Matthews	35	52	5	1
Vaughan Brown not out	36	113	2	0
Richard Hadlee c Wayne Phillips b				
Craig McDermott	54	45	4	3
Ian Smith not out	2	7	0	0
Martin Snedden (dnb)				
Ewen Chatfield (dnb)				
Extras (b 2 / lb 11/ nb 32)	45			
Total (161 overs)	**7 dec / 553**			

Australia Bowling	O	M	R	W
Geoff Lawson	36.5	8	96	1
Craig McDermott	31	3	119	1
David Gilbert	39	9	102	2
Greg Matthews	31	5	110	3
Robert Holland	22	3	106	0
Allan Border	0.1	0	0	0
Kepler Wessels	1	0	7	0

Australia 2nd Innings	R	B	4s	6s
Andrew Hilditch c Ewen Chatfield b				
Richard Hadlee	12	16	1	0
Kepler Wessels c Vaughan Brown b				
Ewen Chatfield	3	10	0	0

David Boon c Ian Smith b Ewen Chatfield	1	11	0	0
Allan Border not out	152	301	20	2
Greg Ritchie c Jeremy Coney b Martin Snedden	20	60	2	0
Wayne Phillips b Richard Hadlee	2	18	0	0
Greg Matthews c Jeremy Coney b Richard Hadlee	115	205	10	1
Craig McDermott c and b Richard Hadlee	5	22	0	0
Geoff Lawson c Vaughan Brown b E Chatfield	7	22	0	0
David Gilbert c Ewen Chatfield b Richard Hadlee	10	37	1	0
Robert Holland b Richard Hadlee	0	2	0	0
Extras (lb 3 / nb 3)	6			
Total (116.5 overs)	**333**			

New Zealand Bowling	O	M	R	W
Richard Hadlee	28.5	9	71	6
Ewen Chatfield	32	9	75	3
Martin Snedden	19	3	66	1
Martin Crowe	9	2	19	0
Vaughan Brown	25	5	96	0
Jeremy Coney	3	1	3	0
	116.5	29	330	10

1960 Australia v West Indies Scorecard

Australia v West Indies Test Match

9–14 December 1960, Brisbane, Australia

Toss: West Indies • Decision: West Indies to bat • Result: a tie

West Indies 1st Innings

Conrad Hunte c Benaud b Davidson	24
Cammie Smith c Grout b Davidson	7
Rohan Kanhai c Grout b Davidson	15
Garry Sobers c Kline b Meckiff	132
Frank Worrell (c) c Grout b Davidson	65
Joe Solomon hit wkt b Simpson	65
Peter Lashley c Grout b Kline	19
Gerry Alexander c Davidson b Kline	60
Sonny Ramadhin c Harvey b Davidson	12
Wes Hall st Grout b Kline	50
Alf Valentine not out	0
Extras (lb 3 / w 1)	4
Total (100.6 overs, run rate 4.5 runs/over)	**453**

Australia Bowling	O	M	R	W
Alan Davidson	30	2	135	5
Ian Meckiff	18	0	129	1
Ken Mackay	3	0	15	0
Richie Benaud	24	3	93	0
Bob Simpson	8	0	25	1
Lindsay Kline	17.6	6	52	3

597

Australia 1st Innings

Colin McDonald c Hunte b Sobers	57
Bob Simpson b Ramadhin	92
Neil Harvey b Valentine	15
Norm O'Neill c Valentine b Hall	181
Les Favell run out	45
Ken Mackay b Sobers	35
Alan Davidson c Alexander b Hall	44
Richie Benaud (c) lbw Hall	10
Wally Grout lbw Hall	4
Ian Meckiff run out	4
Lindsay Kline not out	3
Extras (b 2 / lb 8 / w 1 / nb 4)	15
Total (130.3 overs, run rate 3.9 runs/over)	**505**

West Indies Bowling	O	M	R	W
Wes Hall	29.3	1	140	4
Frank Worrell	30	0	93	0
Garry Sobers	32	0	115	2
Alf Valentine	24	6	82	1
Sonny Ramadhin	15	1	60	1

West Indies 2nd Innings

Conrad Hunte c Simpson b Mackay	39
Cammie Smith c O'Neill b Davidson	6
Rohan Kanhai c Grout b Davidson	54
Garry Sobers b Davidson	14
Frank Worrell (c) c Grout b Davidson	65
Joe Solomon lbw b Simpson	47
Peter Lashley b Davidson	0
Gerry Alexander b Benaud	5
Sonny Ramadhin c Harvey b Simpson	6
Wes Hall b Davidson	18
Alf Valentine not out	7
Extras (b 14 / lb 7 / w 2)	23
Total (92.6 overs, run rate 3.1 runs/over)	**284**

598

Australia Bowling	O	M	R	W
Alan Davidson	24.6	4	87	6
Ian Meckiff	4	1	19	0
Ken Mackay	21	7	52	1
Richie Benaud	31	6	69	1
Bob Simpson	7	2	18	2
Lindsay Kline	4	0	14	0
Norm O'Neill	1	0	2	0

Australia 2nd Innings

Colin McDonald b Worrell	16
Bob Simpson c sub (Lance Gibbs) b Hall	0
Neil Harvey c Sobers b Hall	5
Norm O'Neill c Alexander b Hall	26
Les Favell c Solomon b Hall	7
Ken Mackay b Ramadhin	28
Alan Davidson run out	80
Richie Benaud (c) c Alexander b Hall	52
Wally Grout run out	2
Ian Meckiff run out	2
Lindsay Kline not out	0
Extras (b 2 / lb 9 / nb 3)	14
Total (68.7 overs, run rate 3.4 runs/over)	**232**

West Indies Bowling	O	M	R	W
Wes Hall	17.7	3	63	5
Frank Worrell	16	3	41	1
Garry Sobers	8	0	30	0
Alf Valentine	10	4	27	0
Sonny Ramadhin	17	3	57	1

1930 England v Australia Scorecard

England v Australia Test Match

11–15 July 1930, Headingley, Leeds, England

Toss: Australia • Decision: Australia to bat • Result: Match drawn

Australia 1st Innings

Bill Woodfull b Wally Hammond	50
Archie Jackson c Harold Larwood b Maurice Tate	1
Don Bradman c George Duckworth b Maurice Tate	334
Alan Kippax c Arthur Chapman b Maurice Tate	77
Stan McCabe b Harold Larwood	30
Victor Richardson c Harold Larwood b Maurice Tate	1
Edward a'Beckett c Arthur Chapman b George Geary	29
Bert Oldfield c Jack Hobbs b Maurice Tate	2
Clarence Grimmett c George Duckworth b Richard Tyldesley	24
Thomas Wall b Richard Tyldesley	3
Percival Hornibrook not out	1
Extras (b 5 / lb 8 / w 1)	14
Total (168 overs)	**566**

England Bowling	O	M	R	W
Harold Larwood	33	3	139	1
Maurice Tate	39	9	124	5
George Geary	35	10	95	1
Richard Tyldesley	33	5	104	2
Wally Hammond	17	3	46	1
Morris Leyland	11	0	44	0

England 1st Innings

Jack Hobbs c Edward a'Beckett b Clarence Grimmett	29
Herbert Sutcliffe c Percival Hornibrook b Clarence Grimmett	32
Wally Hammond c Bert Oldfield b Stan McCabe	113
Kumar Duleepsinhji b Percival Hornibrook	35
Morris Leyland c Alan Kippax b Thomas Wall	44
George Geary run out (Thomas Wall)	0
George Duckworth c Bert Oldfield b Edward a'Beckett	33
Arthur Chapman b Clarence Grimmett	45
Maurice Tate c Archie Jackson b Clarence Grimmett	22
Harold Larwood not out	10
Richard Tyldesley c Percival Hornibrook b Clarence Grimmett	6
Extras (b 3 / lb 10 / nb 3)	22
Total (175.2 overs)	**391**

Australia Bowling	O	M	R	W
Thomas Wall	40	12	70	1
Edward a'Beckett	28	8	47	1
Clarence Grimmett	56.2	16	135	5
Percival Hornibrook	41	7	94	1
Stan McCabe	10	4	23	1

England 2nd Innings (following on)

Jack Hobbs run out (Don Bradman)	13
Herbert Sutcliffe not out	28
Wally Hammond c Bert Oldfield b Clarence Grimmett	35
Kumar Duleepsinhji c Clarence Grimmett b Percival Hornibrook	10
Morris Leyland not out	1
George Geary (dnb)	
George Duckworth (dnb)	
Arthur Chapman (dnb)	
Maurice Tate (dnb)	
Harold Larwood (dnb)	
Richard Tyldesley (dnb)	
Extras (lb 8)	8
Total (51.5 overs)	**3 / 95**

Australia Bowling	O	M	R	W
Thomas Wall	10	3	20	0
Edward a'Beckett	11	4	19	0
Clarence Grimmett	17	3	33	1
Percival Hornibrook	11.5	5	14	1
Stan McCabe	2	1	1	0

Under-13 Southwestern Division

COMPETITION RULES AND DRAW

There will be six teams competing for the Under-13 Cricket Cup this year.

- Benchley Park
- Motherwell State
- Riverwall Cricket Club
- The Scorpions
- St Mary's
- TCC

Competition Rules

Points

Five points shall be awarded to the winning team.

A batting point shall be awarded for every 30 runs scored.

A bowling point shall be awarded for every two wickets taken.

One-day games

The side batting second shall face the same number of overs as the side bowling first manages to bowl in 90 minutes.

Batters shall retire on making 30 runs.

Retired batters may return to the crease only if all other batters have been dismissed.

Any bowler cannot bowl more than four overs.

Two-day games

The side batting second shall face the same number of overs as the side bowling first manages to bowl in three and a half hours.

Batters shall retire on making 40 runs.

Retired batters may return to the crease only if all other batters have been dismissed.

Any bowler cannot bowl more than eight overs.

Finals

After the five round robin games have been played the following finals will be scheduled.

Semi-finals (venue — home grounds of first-named teams)

Game A Team 1 v Team 4   Game B Team 2 v Team 3

Grand final (venue — highest placed winner from semi-finals)

Winner of Game A v Winner of Game B

In the grand final there is no limit to the number of overs a bowler may bowl nor to the number of runs a batter may score. If the game is not completed, the team with the higher first innings score will be declared the winner. In the event of a draw, the team placed higher in the division will win the championship.

Draw

Round 1 (one-dayer)

St Mary's v TCC
Riverwall v Motherwell State
The Scorpions v Benchley Park

Round 2 (two-dayer)

Riverwall v St Mary's
Motherwell State v Benchley Park
TCC v The Scorpions

Round 3 (two-dayer)

Motherwell State v St Mary's
The Scorpions v Riverwall
Benchley Park v TCC

Round 4 (one-dayer)

Riverwall v Benchley Park
The Scorpions v St Mary's
TCC v Motherwell State

Round 5 (two-dayer)

Motherwell State v The Scorpions
TCC v Riverwall
Benchley Park v St Mary's

Semi-finals (two-dayer)
1st v 4th 3rd v 2nd

Grand final (two-dayer)
The winners of the semi-finals

SCORES AND LADDERS

Points

Win 5 points
30 runs 1 point
2 wickets 1 point

ROUND 1

TCC 4/135 defeated St Mary's 5/112
Riverwall 7/164 defeated Motherwell State 107
The Scorpions 5/186 defeated Benchley Park 35 and 68

Ladder	P	W	L	Bat P	Bowl P	Win P	Total
The Scorpions	1	1	0	6	10	5	21
Riverwall	1	1	0	5	5	5	15
TCC	1	1	0	4	2	5	11
Motherwell State	1	0	1	3	3	0	6
Benchley Park	1	0	1	3	2	0	5
St Mary's	1	0	1	3	2	0	5

ROUND 2

Riverwall 8/271 defeated St Mary's 160
Motherwell State 8/214 defeated Benchley Park 6/204
The Scorpions 7/283 defeated TCC 147

Ladder	P	W	L	Bat P	Bowl P	Win P	Total
The Scorpions	2	2	0	15	15	10	40
Riverwall	2	2	0	14	10	10	34
Motherwell State	2	1	1	10	6	5	21
TCC	2	1	1	8	5	5	18
Benchley Park	2	0	2	9	6	0	15
St Mary's	2	0	2	8	6	0	14

ROUND 3

The Scorpions 9/175 defeated Riverwall 9/174
St Mary's 8/142 defeated Motherwell State 131
Benchley Park 109 defeated TCC 9/96

Ladder	P	W	L	Bat P	Bowl P	Win P	Total
The Scorpions	3	3	0	20	19	15	54
Riverwall	3	2	1	19	14	10	43
Motherwell State	3	1	2	14	10	5	29
St Mary's	3	1	2	12	11	5	28
Benchley Park	3	1	2	12	10	5	27
TCC	3	1	2	11	10	5	26

ROUND 4

Riverwall 6/191 defeated Benchley Park 170
The Scorpions 5/213 defeated St Mary's 7/106
Motherwell State 4/161 defeated TCC 118

Ladder	P	W	L	Bat P	Bowl P	Win P	Total
The Scorpions	4	4	0	27	22	20	69
Riverwall	4	3	1	25	19	15	59
Motherwell State	4	2	2	19	15	10	44
Benchley Park	4	1	3	17	13	5	35
St Mary's	4	1	3	15	13	5	33
TCC	4	1	3	14	12	5	31

ROUND 5

The Scorpions 5/282 defeated Motherwell State 9/123
Riverwall 9/256 defeated TCC 172
Benchley Park 5/198 defeated St Mary's 86

Ladder	P	W	L	Bat P	Bowl P	Win P	Total
The Scorpions	5	5	0	36	26	25	87
Riverwall	5	4	1	33	24	20	77
Benchley Park	5	2	3	23	18	10	51
Motherwell State	5	2	3	23	17	10	50
TCC	5	1	4	19	16	5	40
St Mary's	5	1	4	17	15	5	37

THE FINALS SERIES — SEMI-FINALS

Riverwall v Benchley Park
Riverwall's home ground
Toss: Riverwall • Decision: Riverwall to bat • Result: Riverwall won by 68 runs

Riverwall Innings

Jono c Taylor b Gruff	20
Cameron retired	42
Rahul retired	41
Jimbo not out	60
Toby c Kovocev b Russell	28
Martian b Kovocev	11
Ally lbw Gruff	2
Jay run out	0
Georgie c Foley b Kovocev	3
Gavin c Rankin B Ulrich	11
Jason not out	2
Extras (b 3 / lb 3 / w 4 / nb 1)	11
Total (38 overs)	**7/231**

Benchley Park Innings   8/163

Riverwall Bowling	O	M	R	W
Toby	11	2	37	4
Rahul	8	1	28	2
Cameron	7	0	31	1
Jono	7	0	31	1
Jason	3	0	9	0
Jay	2	0	13	0

The Scorpions v Motherwell State

The Scorpions 5/161 defeated Motherwell State 53 and 92

THE FINAL SERIES — GRAND FINAL

The Scorpions v Riverwall
The Scorpions' home ground
Toss: The Scorpions • Decision: Riverwall to bat • Riverwall win the
Under-13 Southwestern Division by 1 run

Riverwall 1st Innings

Jono c Taylor b Wyatt	20
Cameron c Craven b Wyatt	3
Jimbo c Blake b Wyatt	4
Rahul b Craven	0
Toby b Craven	21
Martian c Russell b Craven	6
Georgie lbw Mason	0
Minh b Craven	8
Ally lbw Mason	5
Gavin c Craven b Mason	10
Jason not out	4
Extras (b 3 / lb 2 / w 2 / nb 6)	13
Total (25 overs)	**94**

The Scorpions 1st Innings 182

Riverwall Bowling	O	M	R	W
Toby	13.5	4	35	5
Rahul	11	3	45	1
Cameron	7	0	36	1
Jono	6	0	25	1
Jason	4	0	23	0
Georgie	1	0	12	1

Riverwall 2nd Innings

Jono lbw Craven	5
Cameron c Craven b Wyatt	15
Toby b Mason	71
Jimbo c Krsul b Craven	91
Rahul b Wyatt	16

Riverwall 2nd Innings (cont'd)

Martian b Craven	1
Georgie b Mason	0
Minh b Craven	4
Ally not out	10
Gavin c Craven b Mason	0
Jason b Craven	0
Extras (b 1 / lb 8 / w 6 / nb 6)	21
Total (42 overs)	**234**

The Scorpions 2nd Innings	**145**

Riverwall Bowling	O	M	R	W
Toby	17	2	40	6
Rahul	9	2	43	1
Cameron	5	1	25	0
Jono	5	0	19	2
Jason	2	0	9	0

BATTING SCORES

Game	1	2	3	4	5	6	7	8	Total
Toby	25 ret	32 ret	29	23	31 no	28	21	71	260
Scott	31 ret	6	8	35 ret	134 no	dnp	dnp	dnp	214
Jimbo	dnp	dnp	dnp	30 ret	18	60	4	91	203
Jono	33	57 no	0	18	11	20	20	5	164
Cameron	17	27	33 ret	15	4	42 ret	3	15	156
Rahul	5	61 no	0	11	21	41 ret	0	16	155
Gavin	0	19	19	12	dnp	11	10	0	71
Georgie	12	14	20	8	9	3	0	0	66
Jay	17 ret	13	13	4 no	8	0	dnb	dnb	55
Ally	dnp	1	19 no	11 no	2	2	5	10 no	50
Minh	0	18	dnp	1	7	dnp	8	4	38
Jason	dnp	dnp	20	dnp	dnp	2 no	4 no	0	26
Martian	7 no	dnp	dnp	dnp	0	11	6	1	25
Ahmazru	11	3	0	dnp	dnp	dnp	dnp	dnp	14
(extras)	8	20	13	23	13	11	13	21	
Totals	7/164	8/271	9/174	6/191	9/256	7/231	94	234	

BATTING AVERAGES

	Games	Innings	Not Outs	Runs	Highest	Average
Scott	5	5	3	214	134 no	107.00
Toby	7	8	3	260	71	52.00
Jimbo	4	5	1	203	91	50.75
Cameron	7	8	2	156	42 ret	26.00
Rahul	7	8	2	155	61 no	25.83
Jono	7	8	1	164	57 no	23.43
Jay	6	6	2	55	17 ret	13.75
Jason	3	4	2	26	20	13.00
Ally	6	7	3	50	19 no	12.50
Gavin	6	7	0	71	19	10.14
Martian	4	4	1	25	11	8.33
Georgie	7	8	0	66	20	8.25
Minh	5	6	0	38	18	6.33
Ahmazru	3	3	0	14	11	4.67

MATCH HIGHLIGHTS SOUTHWESTERN DIVISION
UNDER-13

Like Jim Oldfield, Rodney Thwaites is a cricket historian. He has been the chief scorer and statistician for the Under-13 Southwestern Cricket Competition since it began 34 years ago. He has spent many hours going through old notes, scorecards, match reports and statistics to present a selection of his favourite match highlights.

Saturday 9 February 1980
TCC v George St

John Simpson (TCC) struck a six with such force that it cracked a windscreen. The driver of the vehicle next door jokingly decided to sit on the bonnet of her car to protect her windscreen. Three overs later John repeated the shot, though a few metres to the left. With a cry of alarm, the lady managed to throw a hand up to protect herself and her windscreen from being smashed. (Oddly enough, it turned out that the two were John's parents, who had arrived in separate cars!)

Sunday 24 February 1980
George St v St Patrick's Saints

Lenny Harrow, bowling for George St, accidentally caught his bowling hand in his trouser pocket as he was bowling the second ball of the game. The ball dropped out of his hand and rolled halfway down the pitch. The batter left his crease and took a huge swing at the ball, missing it completely and falling over in the process. Quick-thinking Lenny kicked the ball onto the batter's stumps before he could regain his crease and the batter was given out (run out) for zero.

Saturday 13 February 1982
St Patrick's Saints v St John's

Cal Whitten (St Patrick's Saints) was so annoyed with himself for getting out in the first over of the day that he managed to convince Timmy Spencer (the team's number 11 batter) that he should replace him. He strode out to the wicket wearing a large jumper and helmet to help with the disguise. While Timmy hid in a nearby toilet block, Cal (batting left-handed) managed to hit two fours before suspicion was aroused, given that Timmy's previous highest score in five games was one.

Timmy was discovered and given a bat, though he didn't score any runs. St John's was awarded the game, and Cal didn't play again for St Patrick's Saints.

Saturday 27 February 1982
George St v Riverwall

George St could only field nine players on this hot day and Riverwall generously allowed Tommy Barnett to play for them in this one-day fixture. The move backfired spectacularly. Not only did Tommy score 23 crucial runs for George St, but he took the final two catches of the Riverwall innings to help 'his' team to a two-run victory. In tears after the game, Tommy was heard to remark, 'I just couldn't help it. It's harder to drop a catch on purpose in a game of cricket. It didn't matter who I was playing for. There was a catch to be taken and I took it.' Both clubs were full of praise for Tommy. George St offered to declare the game a draw, but Riverwall refused. The story made the newspapers and Tommy received many letters of admiration, including one from the Prime Minister.

Saturday 5 February 1983
TCC v Riverwall

Jeremy Pasco (TCC) hit a magpie with a full-blooded hook shot. The ball still went for four. His father took the injured bird to the vet and the family later adopted the magpie and looked after it. It was named Hook, on account of the shot Jeremy played and the new shape one of its legs had taken.

Saturday 19 February 1983
Kobrow College v Riverwall

Playing on the Kobrow College main oval, one of the home team batters struck a ball which rolled into a sprinkler hole out at deep mid-wicket. To the delight of the local supporters, the batters ran an amazing 23 runs. The ball had got stuck. Seven fielders tried to pull it out. The two umpires (both from Kobrow) made no move to intervene. One of the Riverwall fielders came rushing towards the wicket pleading to the umpires to stop the game. Suddenly, he pulled a wet cricket ball from his pocket and tossed it to the bowler who ran out one of the batters. The umpires decided later that because the ball was not in a fit state for play (it was soaked through) that the run-out would not stand, but the 23 runs would, as it couldn't be determined when the ball got wet. (Kobrow won the game by 19 runs.)

Saturday 25 January 1986
St Mary's v Riverwall

The longest over took place on a hot morning at St Mary's home ground. It commenced at 10.46 a.m. and finished 37 minutes later at 11.23. Strangely enough, the first three deliveries were bowled without incident. The fourth ball was hit into the church gardens for six. It took 11 minutes for the ball to be found. The fifth ball struck the batter a nasty blow. When a runner was finally called out, another nine minutes had elapsed. Two no balls followed. Just as the next ball was about to be bowled, a swarm of bees appeared. The players and umpires fell to the ground as the swarm passed overhead. Eight minutes later the players were ready again. The next delivery was edged into the slips. The catch was taken but unfortunately the fielder split the webbing between thumb and first finger. The final delivery was played calmly back to the bowler. It was the seventh ball, but the umpires had apparently lost count!

(Thanks to Reverend Kosta for his extraordinary memory and his meticulous scoring, which included times.)

Saturday 31 January 1987
Kobrow College v St Mary's

This game will be remembered as the shortest completed match in the competition — especially memorable because it involved four innings. Batting first, St Mary's were bundled out for 24 in 43 minutes. Kobrow College declared their first innings at 0/0, without facing a ball. Ten minutes later Kobrow were bowling again. St Mary's second innings was little better than its first. They were bowled out for 31, this time lasting only 34 minutes. After the compulsory 10 minutes between innings, Kobrow came out and knocked up the required runs (56) in just 22 minutes. The whole game had lasted just under two hours. Both teams had a bye the following Saturday!

Saturday 5 March 1988
TCC v St John's

Ty Jacobs, captain of TCC, was to bowl the last over of the game. The opposition needed just six runs from the over to win the match. His first ball was hit for four, and in bowling it Ty fell to the pitch heavily, dislocating his elbow. To the surprise of everyone, and with his arm heavily strapped and covered in ice, Ty chose to complete his over rather than get a replacement. He bowled the remaining deliveries under-arm, with his left hand. The next three deliveries grubbed along the pitch. After heckles and complaints from the batting team, he tossed the next two balls higher. The first was missed by the batter and the second (and final) delivery landed on the top of the stumps, smashing one of the bails. (There were unsubstantiated reports from a variety of sources that Ty was seen that afternoon playing basketball with the TBC Under–14 basketball team.)

Saturday 19 January 1991
St John's v St Mary's

Playing on one of the windiest days ever recorded, and with the temperature hovering around 43° Celsius, Rachel McKinnon took guard for St Mary's. A fierce northerly wind was blowing into her face. As she prepared to play her first ball, the wind gusted, toppling her backwards and onto her stumps. No one appealed and Rachel was able to continue her innings after all three stumps had been put back into the ground.

Saturday 2 February 1991
St John's v George St

A strange event occurred when Peter Robinson, playing for St John's, was given not out by umpire James Findlay. At the exact moment when the stumps were broken and the appeal was made, a pigeon dropped onto the umpire's head. He fell to the ground in shock. The pigeon had apparently struck overhead power lines. Findlay was unable to rule on the appeal and had to give the batter the benefit of the doubt, ruling not out. After a moment's hesitation, Peter Robinson gave himself out, acknowledging that he clearly hadn't made his ground. He was applauded by the entire George St team for his sportsmanship.

Saturday 29 January 1994
St Mary's v Kobrow College

The scorecard from this game was a delight — a statistician's dream! Although there was nothing remarkable about the game itself, a look at the St Mary's batting scores makes for interesting reading.

J. Lander c P Mason b J. Smith	16
B. Neeld c & b J. Smith	0
F. Duncan b G. Sen	14
P. Denna run out	2
W. Formoza b J. Smith	12
G. H. Hartford-Jones c G. Sen b F. Minnoslava	4
B. Barry c V. Phong Liu b J. Smith	10
J. Drum b A. Dexter	6
T. Thomas c P. Mason b F. Minnoslava	8
M. Kosta c & b J. Smith	8
C. Fenwick not out	6
Extras	4
TOTAL	**90**

Saturday 29 January 1994
TCC v Motherwell

Craig Farmer (Motherwell) scored 28 runs off one over. He hit the first two balls each for four, then the third for six. The fourth, a no ball, was hit for two. Craig then struck two sixes off the next two deliveries, the second of these another no ball. He was clean bowled by the last delivery! The scorers hadn't realised he had reached his 30 runs. (He was on two at the start of the over.) If they had, they would have alerted the umpires and Craig would have been forced to retire before the last ball was bowled.

Saturday 3 February 1996
TCC v Benchley Park

The score was 7 for 123 when little Danny Clifford, only eight years old, strode out to bat for Benchley Park, who were three players short in their attempt to chase 132 runs against TCC. He had been playing on a nearby swing. Katie Hong managed to score the last 10 runs herself to get

Benchley Park past their opponents' score. Danny had to face only four deliveries during the 20 minutes he was out there. He missed the ball each time. (TCC later protested that Benchley Park had played an unregistered player. TCC were awarded the game and received all of Benchley Park's points as well.)

Saturday 2 March 1996
Riverwall v Kobrow College
Damian Monk had an extraordinary day in the field for Kobrow College. He took four catches, including a catch that many described as the finest out-field catch they had ever witnessed. Sprinting around the boundary line at deep third man, Damian launched himself into the air and with one hand managed to parry the ball. He fell to the ground, catching the rebound. He was rolling towards the rope though. Immediately he tossed the ball into the air, rolled onto the rope, then recovered his balance and re-caught the ball back in the playing field. Damian also effected two run-outs and took the final two wickets to fall. He had contributed to eight Riverwall wickets.

Saturday 4 December 1999
TCC v St Mary's
Keegan Thomson (TCC) managed to break two bats during his short but entertaining innings. When he was 11, he struck a ball out past mid-on. The bat fell just short of the fielder. A few overs later, when Keegan was 17, he repeated the shot, breaking a second bat. His father, who works in a sports shop, said that he wouldn't be purchasing any more of the bats his son had been using. Keegan never got to use his third bat, being run out from the next delivery.

Saturday 22 January 2000
Scorpions v Motherwell
Moments before the start of the game, the Scorpions club unveiled a superb state-of-the-art portable electronic scoreboard, with remote control — so that it could sit in a location halfway around the ground and be visible to all. It was carefully set up on a trestle table to record the progress of the game against Motherwell, the visiting team. Sadly though, the Scorpions' opening batsman struck the very first ball of the

game for six. The ball smashed into the face of the scoreboard, sending sparks, glass and plastic flying. The force of the shot knocked the scoreboard off the table. The scoreboard never got to record any scores and still sits somewhere in the Scorpions' clubrooms.

Saturday 12 February 2000
Riverwall v Motherwell

A strange catch occurred at the Riverwall ground. It involved three different fielders touching the ball before the catch was finally claimed. The batter clipped the ball to short mid-wicket, where it struck the fielder on the shoulder. It ballooned into the air. The wicket keeper came around from behind the stumps and made a desperate lunge at the ball. He managed to parry the ball straight into the hands of the bowler, who had come across from the bowling crease. Rod Cross was out, caught and bowled Simon Chou, for 11.

Saturday 3 March 2001
Scorpions v TCC

Benny Roberts (Scorpions) managed to take five catches during the TCC innings. The curious thing about this achievement was that each catch was taken in a different position and none of the catches was taken as a wicket keeper. He took a catch at first slip, one at gully, one at mid-off, one at short mid-on and the final catch was caught and bowled. Benny was the captain and organised the fielding positions!

Saturday 15 December 2001
Benchley Park v Scorpions

At the start of the final over, and with only one wicket to take, the Scorpions' captain made a ring of fielders around Katie Farrow, the last batter in. Benchley Park needed an unlikely 15 runs to achieve victory. Katie swiped the first ball into the deep for two runs, then the next into the same area for four. The fielders spread out and the pair scampered two singles over the next two deliveries. Katie missed the fifth delivery, a no ball, but managed two more runs from the next. Three runs would secure a tie, and four would win the game for Benchley Park. Katie struck the ball over mid-on's head. They ran the first quickly. The ball was hurled in, and had it hit the stumps the batter would surely have been run out taking a second. But the ball missed everything and raced out into the covers. The batters turned and completed a third run, tying the game.

Saturday 14 December 2002
Scorpions v Motherwell

Kane Tzaris, batting for Motherwell, struck a full toss firmly back down the wicket. It hit his partner at the non-striker's end on the leg and dropped into his pad. The bowler rushed over and plucked the ball from the runner's pad as he tried to shake it out. The ball, not having touched the ground, was held up by the bowler as he screamed loudly in appeal. Amidst the confusion, with the umpires looking to each other for a ruling, Kane wandered out of his crease. The bowler hurled the ball to the wicket keeper, who 'broke' the stumps. There was another loud series of appeals from the fielders. Kane was finally given out: caught.

(A closer inspection of the scores after the game indicated that the Scorpions had been given an extra leg bye. Motherwell had recorded a spectacular win.)

Saturday 25 January 2003
Benchley Park v St Mary's

Jane Middlemiss (Benchley Park) recorded the highest score by a female player in the one-day competition: 59. Jane retired on 32, then came back to add another 27 runs (including six fours) before she was caught at deep mid-wicket on the third-last delivery of the innings.

How to Play Dice Cricket

- You will need: dice, paper and pencils, and a friend!
- Each player creates their own team of 11 cricketers, maybe including yourself! You can choose a team from a particular country or an era.
- Each cricketer is given a number of chances before they are given out. The batters in the team have more chances — for example, a great batsman like Steve Waugh might get five chances but a specialist bowler like Glenn McGrath might only get one. Both players must agree on how many chances each cricketer gets, and the total number of chances for each team must be the same. Write the number of chances each cricketer has next to his/her name, and set your batting order.
- Roll the dice to work out the order of play. Whoever rolls the highest number gets to choose whether their team will bat or bowl first.
- Open the innings and roll the dice for the first batter. The number on the dice roll is the number of runs scored, and rolling a one or three also means the batters 'change ends' so that the other batter is on strike.
- If a five is rolled, it is a chance or a wicket. There are no runs scored. If the first roll for a batter is a five, then he/she is out for nothing, regardless of the number of chances available.
- The number 11 player only gets one chance and a maximum three rolls of the dice.
- After a batter is out, roll the dice to see how he/she was dismissed:

1. Bowled	4. lbw
2. Caught	5. Run out
3. Caught	6. Caught and bowled, or stumped – you choose!

- You may like to allocate a number (1–6) to your bowlers to see who takes the wickets. Roll the dice again to work out who dismissed the batter.
- At the end of the innings roll the dice twice each to work out the number of wides and no-balls, and once for byes and leg byes.

How to Play Double-wicket Cricket

This game is ideally played with six pairs, and teams should be as even as possible (try to match a batter with a bowler). Each pair may be given a number or they may like to name themselves after a country or famous partnership, for example, 'The Waugh twins'.

Double-wicket cricket follows the normal rules of cricket, yet there are some differences:

• Each batting pair faces six overs. These overs should be bowled by six different players.
• If a batter gets out, he or she doesn't retire, however the batting pair does switch ends.
• Each bowler bowls two overs.
• Fielders should rotate positions so that everyone has an opportunity to field in different parts of the ground.

POINTS

Wicket (bowler): 10 points
Wicket (batter): -15 points
Run-out (fielder): 5 points
Catch (fielder): 5 points
Run (batter): 1 point per run

Mr Pasquali also uses bonus points to reward good bowling and fielding. Your coach might like to do the same!

Mr Pasquali modifies these rules each year, depending on the number of cricketers available to play, and your club or team may choose to do so as well. Also, you might use a different point system — in the Double-wicket World Championship batters only lose 10 points if they are dismissed. Another feature of these championships is that a permanent team of fielders is used for all the games. This means that pairs can play each other directly: for example, Pair A bowls to Pair B, then Pair B bowls to Pair A.

You might like to visit the website of the Double-wicket World Championship to see the official rules: www.doublewicketworldchampionship.com

For more information on double-wicket competitions and to nominate your all-time favourite partner for a double-wicket competition, visit www.michaelpanckridge.com.au and follow the Toby Jones links to the double-wicket cricket page.

RESULTS OF RIVERWALL'S DOUBLE-WICKET COMPETITION

	Batting	Wickets (Batting)	Wickets (Bowling)	Catches	Run-outs	Bonus	TOTAL
Pair 1							
Jono	22	0	20	10	0	6	**58**
Jason	9	-30	0	5	0	4	**-12**
							46
Pair 2							
Rahul	19	0	20	5	5	8	**57**
Gavin	13	-30	10	0	0	2	**-5**
							52
Pair 3							
Ally	8	0	0	0	0	4	**12**
Toby	25	0	30	0	0	8	**63**
							75
Pair 4							
Jimbo	38	0	10	10	0	10	**68**
Jay	6	-30	0	5	0	5	**-14**
							54
Pair 5							
Minh	13	-15	0	5	0	6	**9**
Cameron	24	0	0	5	0	6	**35**
							44
Pair 6							
Ivan	15	-15	0	10	0	5	**15**
Georgie	17	-15	10	5	0	8	**25**
							40

First place: Ally and Toby
Second place: Jimbo and Jay
Third place: Rahul and Gavin

MICHAEL PANCKRIDGE has worked as a teacher for more than 15 years. He has been a lifelong fan of all sports, especially cricket. Michael has both played and coached cricket but, having lost the cricket ball that the family pet Oscar recently buried, has decided to concentrate on his batting — if only he can find his bat!

Visit Michael's website at
www.michaelpanckridge.com.au

BRETT LEE grew up in Wollongong, New South Wales, and is the younger brother of former international cricketing all-rounder Shane Lee. Brett made his first-class cricketing debut in 1995 and his Australian debut against India in 1999/2000. He is one of the country's fastest ever bowlers, regularly clocking speeds of over 150 kilometres per hour.

Acknowledgments to Book 1

Thanks to Robert McVicker Burmeister for his involvement with the cover. To Neil Maxwell and Dominic Thornley at Insite/ITM for their cooperation. To John Wisden & Co. Ltd for their kind assistance. To Jason Doherty, Peter Young and all at Cricket Australia for their support and suggestions. To David Studham at the MCC Library for his outstanding research and interest in the project. To Dean Jones and Ray Bright for their time, good memory and willingness to be 'interviewed' in the book. To the patient, efficient and talented team of editors from HarperCollins. To colleague Mark Torpey for his wonderful enthusiasm and generosity. To Bill and John Panckridge for their encouragement, support, ideas and editing skills. And lastly, to my patient and understanding family: Jo, Eliza and Bronte.

Acknowledgments to Book 2

Thanks to Robert McVicker Burmeister for his involvement with the cover. To Neil Maxwell and Dominic Thornley at Insite/ITM for their cooperation. To John Wisden & Co. Ltd for their kind assistance. To Jason Doherty, Peter Young and all at Cricket Australia for their support and suggestions. To David Studham at the MCC Library for his outstanding research and interest in the project. To Andrew Symonds for his interest and willingness to be involved. Affable, friendly and modest — just as I anticipated him to be. Colleague Mark Torpey for righting the odd cricket wrong. To the talented Melbourne editors Lisa Berryman and Liana Spoke, and Vanessa Radnidge in Sydney. Always friendly — always accurate! To John and Bill Panckridge for their constant interest and enthusiasm. To Bronte, Lizy and Jo — and my new studio!

Acknowledgments to Book 3

Thanks to Robert McVicker Burmeister for his involvement with the cover. To Neil Maxwell, Dominic Thornley and Matt Easy at Insite/ITM for their cooperation. To John Wisden & Co. Ltd for their kind assistance, and for the wealth of information contained in the *Wisden Cricketers' Almanack*s. To Peter Young at Cricket Australia for his support and suggestions. To David Studham at the MCC Library for his outstanding research and interest in the project. To the wonderful and supportive editors at HarperCollins, particularly Lisa Berryman and Liana Spoke in Melbourne, and especially Catherine Day in Sydney whose talent, professionalism and enthusiasm for the editing task has made this book so much better.

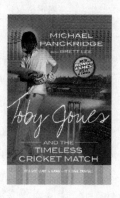

Toby Jones and the Timeless Cricket Match

MICHAEL PANCKRIDGE

WITH BRETT LEE

It isn't Toby Jones' passion for cricket that makes him unusual —
it's his ability to travel through time, back to the great matches of
the past.

Just when Toby thinks his time-travel adventures are over, he
has to make another dangerous journey. He must travel to The
Oval — the famous English cricket ground — to save his friend
Ally, who has been ill since she broke the laws of time travel on
her last trip with him.

Toby will have to face the embittered Cricket Lord, Hugo
Malchev, and the ruthless Phillip Smale, who has his own
agenda as far as time travel is concerned, and doesn't want
anyone getting in the way.

And if that isn't enough, Toby is training at the cricket camp
at the Melbourne Cricket Ground, hoping to be selected for
Australia against England in the junior Ashes. If he doesn't get
stuck in the past during his travels. Or worse . . .

Toby Jones and the Timeless Cricket Match

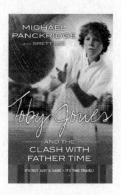

Toby Jones and the Clash with Father Time

MICHAEL PANCKRIDGE

WITH BRETT LEE

Toby Jones is not your average cricket fan. As well as being an ace player, he has the amazing ability to travel through time, back to the great matches of the past.

Toby is playing for Australia in a junior Ashes match at the Melbourne Cricket Ground. It's the most important game of his life so far. But things take a dramatic turn when one of a band of sinister soul-snatchers — known as Grubbers — makes a ghostly appearance in the outfield and takes over the body of one of the England players. To make matters worse, Toby discovers that his friend Georgie has gone missing.

Toby must return to the Timeless Cricket Match and confront the powerful and evil Father Time. Only by doing so can he save all the former and future Test cricketers doomed to be trapped in the past forever . . . and the game of cricket itself.

A thrilling conclusion to the bestselling Toby Jones series.